# THE PEARL OF YORK, TREASON AND PLOT

## Tony Morgan

# Foreword

**Margaret Clitherow** is arguably the most famous woman, and **Guy Fawkes** the most famous man, born in York in the Tudor period. One of the forty martyrs of England and Wales, Margaret is widely known as the Pearl of York. Guy is remembered for his infamous role in the Gunpowder Plot. Both were born into prosperous Protestant families but later converted to the Catholic faith. For a few short weeks in 1586 their lives may have intertwined.

**Tony Morgan** hails from Wales and lives near York in the North of England. *The Pearl of York, Treason and Plot* is his third novel. After researching the history of the Gunpowder Plot, Tony was struck by the parallels with the current day, including government surveillance, terrorism and friction with Europe. He realised he'd found what he'd been looking for - a story he wanted to tell, because he wanted to read it himself. His first novel *Remember, Remember the 6th of November* is a taut thriller, set in the days leading up to the planned attack of Parliament in November 1605. The indirect sequel *7th November 1617* explores what may have happened if the Gunpowder Plotters had succeeded.

The profits from Tony's novels and history talks are donated to good causes. Every book sold in 2020 will raise funds for **St Leonard's Hospice** in York. Details of Tony's books and talks can be found online at **https://tonymorganauthor.wordpress.com/**.

# 1

**Tuesday November 5<sup>th</sup>, 1605**

Is one day like every other? Do you crave an adventure? Reply '*Aye!*' to both questions? You and I were once the same.

I close my eyes. For a few moments I focus my mind and return to simpler times. No longer a boy. Not yet a man.

He... I... lay beneath a sheepskin cover in the bed bequeathed to me by my father's brother. A cock crows. I know I should rise, but I don't. I dither, asking questions, speculating idly, looking forwards toward the future. What will it hold?

Now I know.

My memories meander. The past is certain. I was born in York. I thought I'd die there too. For nigh on sixteen years the city treated me well enough, for most of the time. I was no stranger to tragedy but who is? Losing my father and Uncle Thomas hadn't been easy, but we all die in the end, even the righteous. The good Lord will be their salvation, as He'll be mine.

During much of my youth good fortune watched over me. The Ecclesiastical Court of the Church of England sponsored my education. They wanted me to follow in my father's and grandfather's footsteps. I would leave St Peter's in a year's time, travel to London and study law. What an adventure that would be. Sometimes my head filled with visions of grandeur and buildings such as Parliament in Westminster.

Before then I needed to find a defender for my mother and sisters. Perhaps Mother would re-marry? Maybe not. She was a strong-willed woman. Not many in her position could have forgone a husband for eight long years. There had been no shortage of suitors but she'd refused them all.

My daydream continued.

Once qualified, I'd return to York, and in five years' time I'd claim my inheritance. What would I do with Father's properties? Earn a rental income or sell them off? Perhaps there was another option. I picture the house in Clifton following major renovation. Such a fine home, fit for a proctor, one day an advocate. And his family…

My wife stands in the doorway with a smile on her face which lights up the morning. The little ones and servants wave as I set off to work. I nod in return from atop a sleek stallion, black and glistening like Whitby jet. We canter along Bootham, trot through Petergate and walk the final steps into Minster Yard.

Stable hands jostle for my attention. One of the smaller lads wins the competition. He helps me dismount. I rub my horse's nose and pay a penny to the guy. Shaking my tailcoat, I walk across the cobbles and enter the building.

Inside the office, learned colleagues glance at me with admiration. An underling takes my coat. Lifting my quill, I'm pleased with the inspection. The feather comes from the finest goose; the writing edge has been lovingly sharpened.

Requests are made for me to review a string of judgements. Assistants bring forward my own cases. These are the most complex disputes. I look at my fine oak desk. The wood is sturdy. It gives a polished reflection. I've arrived.

Not for the first time that morning, my mother bawls loudly up the steps at me, 'Guy! Get up!'

One day she'll tell me I love my bed more than my family. It isn't true of course but the time for reverie is over. I stand up and bend down, searching for the pot. It's full. I leave it for Mother to empty, pull on my clothes, climb down the ladder and depart for St Peter's.

Bed, school, bed, school. How I coveted excitement. I knew no better. Be wary of what you wish for. To covet is to sin.

'Wake him!'

I hear the voice in the distance, a strange sound in my dream, but then I'm awake. Once I regain consciousness the pain spreads through my body. I try not to scream, grit my teeth and pray for death to come but I know it won't. My torturers won't allow it.

'What is your name?'

'I've already told you. John Johnson.'

'Speak the truth. What is your real name? Where do you hail from?'

'Netherdale in Yorkshire.'

'I've never heard of such a place. Who do you work for?'

'I work alone.'

'Why did you wish to do such a terrible thing?'

'To blow your Scots king back to his mountains. England for the English.'

The man leans over me, before standing back for a moment. His neck cricks and from the way he rubs the ruff around his shoulders, I can see he knows physical suffering. But not as I do. The fellow strokes a short and well-groomed brown beard on his pointy chin.

'Don't you care about the hundreds of people you would have murdered?' he asks.

'What about all those you and your pursuivants have killed?' I reply defiantly.

It was a mistake, and we both know it.

'So, you're a Papist.'

He considers the news for a moment. It won't have come as any surprise.

'But I'm afraid you're mistaken. We've not murdered anybody. Anything this government does is carried out in the name of the King's majestic law, the law of this land.'

'But it is not God's law,' I say.

'Tell me then, who have we killed? Give me their names. If I can find wrongdoing, I'll investigate.'

'My wife, my son, a woman in York. And for what? Speaking to a priest, not going to church, living in a village with Catholic leanings. You disgust me.'

The man sighs, as if to say this is going nowhere.

'What is your name? Who do you work for?'

I refuse to answer. The man turns away from me, moves across the room and nods to others who I can not see. My ears begin to strain, dreading the terrible noise, but at first all I hear are footsteps as my questioner leaves the chamber. For the next few moments all is silent, but then I hear it. The click. My body tenses, for it knows full well what the simple sound means. The rack will turn another notch.

My body burns. The very joints which hold me together are jolted. Every sinew and nerve tears me apart. I scream.

Hell is a place on Earth. It's located within a tower in London.

A less educated voice speaks out. 'What is your real name, Catholic scum? Where do you come from?'

I need an outlet. I must to return to the past. I must think back to what brought me here. I close my eyes and remember, the girl and the Pearl of York.

# 2

**Wednesday February 2nd, 1586**

Wintry Wednesday mornings in Yorkshire are meant to be cold, February ones particularly so. Father would have called it nithering. After leaving our house in Stonegate, I hurried towards the Minster. It didn't pay to be late. I balled my blue fingers into the palms of my hands and retracted them into the sleeves of my cloak.

The whistling wind pushed me along and made my teeth chatter. Horses pulled carts in the distance, although not down our street. The main sounds here were the tacks of my boots striking the cobbles and the echoes they made rebounding back from the walls of the inn across the way. A few crows cawed from the roof tops. Stars peeped down, sometimes visible and sometimes not. My view of the heavens was often blocked by the overlapping eaves.

I knew the sky would soon brighten and the stars be gone, but for a moment I caught sight of a pair of vibrantly coloured heavenly bodies. They twinkled together. I'd learned their names a dozen time in lessons but could never remember them.

I turned left into High Petergate, the street where I was born. We lived in the house just over there, right up until I was eight years old. When my father died, Uncle Thomas helped Mother move our family to our current property in Stonegate. Not long after that Uncle left us too. I hate the sweating sickness. It took so many.

A few of the affected people's properties still remained vacant, a silent reminder of the previous population. I felt the icy blast of the wind. It pierced the buildings around me, apart from the limestone Minster. Nothing disturbed this. The mighty church dominated the skyline and watched over everything which happened within York's protective walls.

The roadway was wider outside the Peter Prison. Foul animal and human waste paved both sides of the lane. At least it was frozen, although this meant it would stay on the street for longer. The Corporation paid paupers to shovel it up, cart it off and dump it into the river, along with everything else, apart from on days like this. Frozen shit is too hard to shift.

At Bootham Bar I left the main city behind. The gates were manned by men dressed in York Corporation livery. I slipped quietly into Gillygate without acknowledging them. It was late into their shift and they paid little attention to me nor anyone else. I suspected all they could think of was getting out of the cold. As they stamped their feet and waited impatiently to be replaced, I imagined how much they must long for their bed and breakfast.

Beyond the city gates the buildings weren't as grand as before. Most of the houses were smaller. Many were cramped. Some you'd call hovels, although there were inns and workshops too. The day was underway. Men opened shutters. Women emptied buckets. I tried to avoid where the contents landed.

As I passed a narrow snicket, I was approached by a gaggle of immigrant children. It was difficult not to feel something for these scantily clad waifs. They all looked frozen. I wondered if they hailed from Europe or elsewhere in England. Their clothes weren't far off from being rags and there wasn't an ounce of fat on any of them. One held out his hand and I suggested he should go away, none too politely.

Mother would have blushed at my words and our Protestant parson chastised me, but other than sympathy I had nothing to give them. I hoped the foreigners heeded my warning. If the Sheriff's men caught them begging without a licence they'd be in trouble. I crossed the street and quickened my pace.

Moments later I spotted a youth walking a few yards ahead of me near St Giles's Church. Like myself the lad was making haste to get to school. Of course, I recognised him. We all knew each other. He was a local fellow, one of the younger boys. We went home each night and spent Sundays with our families. It wasn't like that for the boarders. Most lived some distance away from the city. For much of the year St Peter's was as much their home as it was their school.

We were almost there now. Rounding the corner, I looked back but was unable to glimpse the city walls behind the buildings of Gillygate. I walked by the horse fair, the highlight of my journey. As always, I attempted to immerse myself in the sights, sounds and smells.

Men, boys and animals moved to and fro. Many of the humans laughed and shouted. Horses neighed. The smell was something else.

There was no other place like it. With many of the residents released for exercise, the stalls and stables were being cleaned out. There was horse shit everywhere, pushed into corners, piled into heaps and loaded onto carts for transporting to vegetable gardens.

The mares and stallions came in all different shapes, sizes, and colours. Some were brown and black, others copper and grey and a few almost white. The larger steeds impressed me the most. These were huge. Despite my dreams I'd never ridden a horse. The stable hands looking after them appeared completely fearless, feeding and brushing their beasts, fixing on harnesses, saddles and other kinds of tack. I couldn't understand why they weren't terrified of being kicked or trampled upon. I would have been.

Within a few moments the horse fair was behind me, although I could still smell and hear it. When the black and white building of St Peter's came into sight, I lengthened my stride in anticipation. Praise be to God! The gates were open. The other boy dashed inside, just a few steps ahead of me, safe at last.

But I refused to run. I was too proud for that. In any case there was something I had to do before I went in. I passed the entrance and carried on a few yards down the lane. As I reached a small indent in the hedging around the school, I stopped. Carefully I checked the street was clear, opened my breeches and emptied my bladder with great relief.

Steam rose up from the icy grassy verge in front of me. I finished the task, leant back and straightened myself out. Looking up, I spied a hooded figure in a grey cloak exiting the school grounds from the side gate normally reserved for tradesmen and deliveries. The fellow was tall but had no cart and didn't look like a worker. His appearance intrigued me.

I wasn't as invisible as I'd hoped. The stranger noticed my observation. He stopped himself dead in his tracks and stared directly back towards me. I felt un-nerved. You hear so many stories. At least my hands were empty. Everything was tucked away. Not that there was much to see on such a cold morning.

The stranger shook his head. He crossed the road and sped off towards Goodramgate on foot, without me being able to see his face. Whether intended or otherwise, his cloak and hood masked his appearance. I recalled I too was in a hurry, turned around and back tracked the last few steps.

The church bells began to toll for seven when I reached the gates. The school gateman stepped forward. He slammed the wood into the hole aggressively behind me. The panels rattled together from the force of the man's actions. I'd made it, but only just. Was it disappointment which crossed the fellow's face? Perhaps he wished to see me beaten. I winked cockily at him and for the first time that morning thought about the school day ahead.

There was nothing Headmaster Pulleyn liked more than to remind us St Peter's was one of the oldest schools in the world. Often, he'd follow this up with how lucky we were to be there. He was probably right. I can remember my father telling me I'd get one of the best educations in the whole of the North of England. English, Latin, Greek, scripture, history; I studied them all.

The school day started early and finished late. For the past decade I'd spent more time here with the boys and masters than my own family. At least I wasn't a boarder. Some of the lads were my best friends but I was never disappointed when it was time to go home.

We said prayers each morning shortly after seven. By this time every boy would be seated in the dining hall. I'd only just slotted myself in between Kit Wright and Robert Middleton when the old man called for silence. As the master spoke, we bowed our heads. My stomach rumbled. After a final 'Amen' a hundred hands reached out for bread and butter, milk, honey and oats. During the last part of his prayer Headmaster Pulleyn had thanked God for providing such nourishing food. He said the meal we were about to receive would strengthen our bodies, cleanse our minds and help us to achieve great deeds in the future.

'Think what we could do if they gave us some meat,' sniggered Kit.

I grinned.

'You're late again,' said Rob, admonishing me slightly. 'You almost didn't make it.'

He was a good lad but always a tad more serious than Kit and me.

'My timely attendance was never in doubt,' I replied.

'Far from it. You must have only just squeezed through the gates. I've been here for ages.'

'More the fool you. Don't you like your own bed?'

'Not as much as you, that's for sure,' he replied. 'I just don't want to see you beaten again.'

Like me, Rob was a day boy. His family were from York. But Kit was a boarder. The Wrights were country folk. They lived near Hull, far away in the East Riding. There were rumours they supported the Catholic religion. Even if this was true, I couldn't hold it against Kit.

He never talked of spiritual matters other than in lessons, and not once had he tried to convert me. Perhaps he wasn't a Catholic. Perhaps he didn't care about religion. Perhaps he was as bored as I was every week when we had to go to church.

One thing was certain. Kit was my friend. And he no longer had to live in the shadow of his brother. Jack Wright had left St Peter's the year before, unbeaten in every sporting discipline, from rowing to wrestling, throwing and sword-fighting.

Us older boys were positioned in the top half of the dining room. We sat in long rows alongside wooden tables close to the fire. Although the frost outside was visible, I could no longer feel it. The orange flames roasted my back. Porridge warmed my insides. Beads of sweat trickled down my shirt. The hard wood of the bench made by bottom squirm.

'The weals on your arse aren't mended yet, then,' noted Kit with a smile.

'Not quite,' I said truthfully. Although the scars were mostly healed, I still felt soreness where the birch strokes had struck me the last time I was late.

There was a steady background hum in the hall. Conversations like ours took place at every table, as boarders and day boys caught up with each other. If the noise became too loud, we'd be instructed to quieten down but the level that morning must have been deemed acceptable.

Following breakfast, the older boys were scheduled to receive one of the headmaster's newer lessons. We filed silently out of the hall. After walking down the corridor we entered the smaller of the two classrooms and sat at our allocated places. The subject today was a second session on the administration of the city of York. Although this wasn't something the school was expected to teach us, Headmaster Pulleyn believed as potential leaders we should know how the city was run and understand the problems of the past to prevent their future reoccurrence.

For the last month we'd been studying York's recent history, in particular the problems behind the city's decline. The dissolution of the monasteries and religious houses had been touched upon briefly, but we didn't really scratch beneath the surface. Digging any deeper would have placed the headmaster at risk of being questioned by the Council of the North. His predecessor was already languishing in prison for suspected Catholic leanings. No-one though worried about Headmaster Pulleyn. The man was as Protestant as Archbishop Sandys.

When identifying the problems behind York's downturn, the headmaster primarily pointed towards disease and illness. The plague, sweating sickness and new ague had all left their scars. For a time the population plummeted. Many died. Others fled. York risked becoming a ghost town, with too few men left to enter the trades, learn apprenticeships and undertake the manual tasks needed to make a city function.

Gaps had to be filled. Immigration from across England and mainland Europe was encouraged. The strict rules barring all but local men from entering the guilds were eased, although recently they'd been tightened up again. The city's plight was recognised. Even in London. Taxes were cut. Queen Elizabeth announced York would become the permanent home for the Council of the North. She gave the city's Merchant Adventurers their first royal charter.

The tide was turning. Trade with many countries in Europe was rapidly expanding. It was no coincidence, the headmaster said, the upturn in the city's fortunes was taking place during the reign of good Queen Bess. We finished the previous session with a rousing cheer of 'God save the Queen!'.

A week ago Headmaster Pulleyn's lecture had focused on the city's administrative body, York Corporation. As always, he began the current lesson by judging how much we'd learned during the last.

'Who runs the major affairs of the city? Middleton?'

'York Corporation, sir.'

'Correct. Who leads the Corporation council? Cheke?'

'The Lord Mayor, sir.'

'Correct. Who elects the Lord Mayor? Craven?'

'The aldermen of the city, sir.'

'Correct. How many aldermen are there? Wright?'

'Thirteen, sir, including the Lord Mayor.'

'Correct. What is the name of the council's central body? Fawkes?'

I hesitated for a moment. There were two possible answers.

'The Twenty-Four, sir.'

'Correct. Who has the casting vote on the Corporation council? Gayle?'

'The Lord Mayor, sir.'

'Correct. How does a man become Lord Mayor? Metcalfe?'

'Um…'

'Come on, boy. Too slow! Middleton?'

'First a citizen must become a freeman of the city. Then he must then take up a minor office…'

'Such as?'

'Bridge-master or chamberlain.'

'Correct, go on.'

'After this, he may be elected to sit on the wider common council. From there, he can be selected to be Sheriff. When his term ends, he'll be invited to join the Twenty-Four, which in turn makes him eligible once a vacancy becomes available to become an alderman. After that, he may be elected to serve as Lord Mayor.'

'Good, well done, Master Middleton. I'm glad someone was paying attention last week. Metcalfe, we'll discuss your ignorance later. Today we're going to discuss taxes, laws and education in this good city.'

I glanced around the room. Each year the class grew fuller. One impact of York's growing prosperity was the pressing need to educate more boys. Pupil numbers were increasing. A healthy competition was underway between St Peter's and the second grammar school in the city, Archbishop Holgate's. They were the Troy to our Sparta. Or was it the other way around?

By law, schools had to support the Queen's religion. Boys attended scripture, religious instruction and many church services. In the bad old days York had been a centre for the old faith. Now it was a beacon of the new. I had no problem with this. The Protestant Church was my father's faith and his employer, as it would be mine. Although I didn't despise the Catholics, I couldn't fathom why anybody would wish to be one.

I was aware I wasn't one of the brightest boys in school like Robert Middleton, but I got by. With my sixteenth and seventeenth birthdays drawing nearer, I knew how important a good education would be for my future. I studied conscientiously. I'd only be accepted to train in one of the Inns of Court in London if they received a suitably positive recommendation letter from St Peter's, so I forced my eyes to remain open. I listened and I learned.

Once the morning's academic lessons were over it was my favourite time of the week. After noon each Wednesday we took part in physical games. In the summer we'd row up and down the Ouse or throw the javelin. Sometimes we'd even play ball games.

In the past Kit and I had secretly spoken about trying out archery, but we knew we couldn't. The pastime was beneath us. Bows could only be used by the lower classes and certainly not by grammar schoolboys. At least we were encouraged to learn the skills of the blade. It was a sign of who we were, carrying a sword remained forbidden for any man of lesser status than gentleman.

Although not as skilful as his brother, Kit was still one of the finest swordsmen the school had ever seen. The only boy who could currently challenge him for the title was Thomas Cheke. His father Henry was the Member of Parliament for Boroughbridge and an official of the Council of the North. A fierce rivalry had risen up between the two boys. For my own part, although I was a fine rower and good at most physical games, I found mastering the blade challenging and was outside the top group.

Our swordsmanship lessons were strictly controlled. Many of the boys' fathers were important men. The school had no wish to inform them of serious injuries to their sons. More often than not, we'd duel with boys of similar ability to ourselves. That day I was paired with Rob Middleton. After twenty minutes of blocking and parrying, we tired. With some relief, I placed my sword into the scabbard and returned it to the rack.

Despite the cold day, the vigorous exercise had made me perspire. Believing a walk would do me some good, I asked for permission to visit the shed with a deep trench which served as our privy. The pig ugly building was positioned well away from the main complex. It stood on its own, beyond the walled garden which provided most of our fruit and vegetables.

On the way back I saw what appeared to be a young woman enter the garden. She carried a basket under her arm and was dressed for the season in long smock and scarf. As with the stranger earlier, her face was masked from me and I was surprised. I struggled to recall seeing a female in the school's grounds before.

I'm not sure why but I followed her into the garden. I stood behind a grizzled old apple tree and watched what she did and where she went. After snipping a few herbs, she picked up a garden fork and attempted to dig leeks from the frozen ground. I could see she was struggling and thought of my mother. If this woman was anything like her, she'd keep on trying until her back gave in.

Looking around, I saw there was nobody else about and walked over to her. I was just a few paces away when she turned around. She almost jumped out of her skin. Her startled face stared into mine. She was about my own age. Some may have claimed her looks were plain and she wouldn't have been missed in a crowd, but they were wrong. Although her hair was covered, her eyes were alive. I was captivated.

'What are you doing here?' she asked.

'The ground is frozen. I thought I'd help you dig out the leeks,' I replied.

'Oh, but you can't,' she said. 'I'm not allowed to speak to the boys.'

My face reddened. She noticed.

'I'm sorry,' she added. 'It's kind of you to offer but I don't want to lose this employment. It's my very first day.'

I looked down at the ground, crestfallen. Confused emotions began to run around my mind and body. I peered into her basket. Besides the sage and rosemary there was a line of beads. I averted my eyes quickly and pretended not to notice them. Dear God, I prayed, don't let her be a Catholic.

'I'm sorry,' I said. 'I should leave you now.'

I walked away swiftly. I fancied the girl may have continued to watch me but I didn't turn around.

# 3

Despite the luxury of my bed, I struggled to get to sleep that evening. My thoughts were full of the girl I'd seen at school. She was enchanting and mysterious in equal measure. Were they really rosary beads? If so, she wouldn't last long. Headmaster Pulleyn would surely discover she supported the old faith and report her to the authorities. It was his duty after all. He had no choice.

The train of thought was disturbed by a metallic noise from downstairs. I strained my ears. There was a second sound and then silence. I listened again. There was nothing more. It was as if someone had opened and closed the latch on the front door. I feared robbers but surely Mother had locked up. If so, no-one would be able to get in, but damn them for trying. Ours was a Godly house, and there was little worth stealing. But if she'd forgotten, anybody could be down there.

I sat up and pulled on my day clothes. The room was filled with darkness. Although it was as black as pitch, every inch was familiar to me. I knew exactly where I'd placed the pot under my bed when I blew out the candle.

Carefully I edged towards the doorframe. There was no lock or catching mechanism. It was simply a case of shifting the large piece of wood from the door shaped hole. I pulled it open gently, careful to avoid scraping noises. I didn't wish to disturb my mother or sisters from their slumber, nor inform any intruders of my plan to intercept them.

As I descended the ladder all was quiet. Here and there I redistributed my weight to prevent the rungs from creaking. When I was low enough, I turned my head and scanned for movement. There was none.

I took a deep breath, and tentatively stepped onto the cold stone floor. A shadow flickered. Something shifted. I turned. It was nothing, a noise from the grate. There was nobody there.

The embers in the fire offered a little illumination. I crossed the kitchen and walked to the front door. The bolt was open. I tried the latch. The door wouldn't budge. It was locked. The key was gone.

The only explanation I could think of was that Mother had gone outside but it was so late. She'd been preoccupied lately. Perhaps there was a problem. As the man of the house it was my duty to find out what the issue was and protect her.

I took my coat off its peg and strapped on my boots. With the front door locked I retreated to the back. The second door had no key. There was simply a pair of sliding bolts, one at the bottom and one at the top. I considered pulling them back but decided against it. It would be too dangerous to leave the place unlocked with Anne and Elizabeth sleeping alone inside.

I climbed back up the stairs. Pushing softly, I managed to open the catch on one of the shutters at the back of the house without much disturbance. I squeezed myself onto the sill and shimmied down the small drop. Eventually I let myself fall the last few feet into the yard. It had been frosty earlier but the moon was now gone, disappeared behind a bank of cloud.

Once through the side gate I emerged onto the street. It had started to snow. I loved the almost imperceptible sound the flakes made as they floated down to earth from the sky. It was already sticking in the narrow gaps between the cobbles and I could feel the flakes in my hair. A pair of small footprints led away from the door at the front of the house. Believing the translucent marks to be Mother's, I followed them.

The tracks led me along Stonegate, past the houses and inns. Everything was quiet. It must have been late. At the junction with Petergate the footprints turned right towards the central part of the city. There wasn't a soul to be seen on the street that night, although I knew men were awake in the larger buildings. Candles burned brightly in the Minster's windows but even these were being extinguished one by one, increasing the darkness outside.

The footmarks ignored the side turnings. They continued on into Low Petergate. For the first time I thought I witnessed a shape moving in the shadows some way ahead of me. I focused my eyes. It looked like a woman. Was that a shawl around her shoulders and a tightly bound coif scarf on her head? The shape and size of the figure seemed about right, if it was my mother.

The snowflakes swirled a little heavier. The street became narrow, and the movements in front of me slowed. I almost slipped over. I had to steady myself so I wouldn't fall and saw a patch of ice glistening through the snow. The figure stopped and glanced towards me. I hid in a doorway. I'm not quite sure why.

We started again. I passed the grubby entrance to Grope Lane. Some of the boys at school said they'd spent money here. I didn't believe them. I certainly hadn't. Ladies of the night. Sins of the flesh. Temptation. Apprehension. Trepidation. This was no place for a respectable woman. Not my mother. Not at this time of night.

I looked up the lane. Darkness. I strained my ears. Silence. Or was it? Could I hear bodies grinding together, writhing and moaning? Could I see a middle-aged woman with no teeth? Did she reach out her hand towards me? Was she beckoning for me to follow her into the shadows?

'How much do you want to pay?' she asked.

I stepped back in revulsion. My body shuddered. I looked again. The voice was imagined. There was nobody there. My quarry hadn't gone that way.

In the almost darkness I spied a small mark on the ground. I crouched down and studied it. The snow had been disturbed. Perhaps this was where the figure had turned around to stare back at me. Was she now headed along Goodramgate towards the Monk Bar? No. Once again, I spotted a slight movement from further up the road. I set off in pursuit, moving more quickly now, closing the gap of my prey.

The woman entered the King's Square. For a moment we both looked towards Christ's Church of the Holy Trinity. I said a prayer. I can no longer recall the words. Some details are harder to remember than others. My mother, if indeed it was she, rounded the church. I lost sight of her, she walked so quickly.

I gazed into Colliergate. The street was empty. For the first time I doubted my assumption of the woman's identity. There was nowhere for Mother to go around here. The shops were closed. The merchants and their wives all slept in their beds. I saw risk and danger in every corner. I was nearly sixteen, young and strong but in the icy darkness even I felt a little scared. How would a woman feel?

The figure must have proceeded towards Newgate or perhaps crept up The Shambles. I investigated. There was no movement in either street. I stopped for a moment. Often, I knew something was about to happen before it did. I felt it then. The nerves and sinews in my body began to strain. Something stirred.

There was a movement in an alcove, just a few feet away from me. My back shivered, but not from the cold. Something stepped out. My heart jumped. I caught my breath. A voice spoke.

'Guy! Thank the Lord, it is you. You frightened me witless. Why on earth are you creeping around at this time of night?'

I wanted to ask my mother the very same question.

I was about to speak out when we both heard something. Within a few moments I recognised the sound of hobnailed boots moving towards us from The Shambles. Whoever was wearing them wasn't afraid to be spotted stomping around in the dead of night. This made them dangerous.

I whispered to Mother to push herself further back into the shadows of the alcove and squeezed into the darkness beside her. A moment later three noisy figures marched past our position. The men were talking and cursing as they went. I couldn't pick up what was said, above the sound of the blood pulsing through my body. We stood stock still. The men must have come within inches of our faces, close enough at least for me to detect onions and ale on their breath.

The sounds moved away. Eventually I was sure I could no longer hear them. Perhaps they were night drinkers, or robbers, or Sheriff's men on midnight patrol. It didn't seem to matter. They were gone. But if they had been the Sheriff's men, I wondered why I felt so frightened. There was no overnight curfew, and we'd done nothing wrong.

But where was Mother going? I asked her quietly.

'Just to visit some friends,' she whispered a little evasively. 'We're close to their house now. You can go back to Stonegate.'

'No,' I said firmly. 'I'm not leaving you to wander past places like Grope Lane at this time of night. It's not safe and it's not proper behaviour. I demand to know where you're going.'

'Don't you try and demand anything from me, my boy,' she replied angrily. 'But you can come with me, if you must.'

We couldn't see each other's faces, but I was sure we glowered at each other.

'If you do,' she continued. 'You're not to pass judgement on me, nor otherwise comment until we get home and I've had a proper opportunity to explain the situation. You may see things which you don't understand. When we get to my friend's house, we'll find a room for you to sit in and wait. But you'll question nothing until we return home. Do you agree?'

I nodded. She remained silent.

'Aye,' I said sharply after a moment, realising she hadn't been able to see the movement of my head.

I followed Mother's lead and stepped into The Shambles. It was a narrow little street, lined on either side with butchers' premises. In the daytime it was hard to move for traders and shoppers, carts and hanging birds but in the evening these went away and the place was empty. The shutters and doors were closed. No light came from inside.

The men we'd encountered must have come this way. If they had, we wouldn't have been able to see their tracks, even in the daytime, for the floor was dry. Snow didn't often touch the ground in The Shambles. The over-hanging eaves reached out to each other. In some places they overlapped. There was too little room left for the flakes to pass through.

Mother stopped about halfway along the street. She tapped quietly at a door on our right snuggled between two butcher's shops. At first there was no answer. She knocked again, with a little more insistency. After the third time the voice of a male child with a strange accent spoke from within. He asked what we wanted so late in the night. Mother didn't respond directly. Instead she leaned forward and whispered.

'Credo in Spiritum Sanctum, sanctam Ecclesiam catholicam, sanctorum communionem, remissionem peccatorum, carnis resurrectionem, vitam aeternam.'

The voice answered, 'Amen.'

Three bolts were slid back, and the door opened. Mother pulled me inside into a darkened corridor and closed the door. Something passed by me and the bolts were closed. A cover was pulled from a wall. The light of a single candle was now glowing around us. A young lad of about twelve picked it up.

'Hello, Johann,' said Mother. 'Where is your mistress?'

'Hello visitor,' whispered the boy. He looked at me, holding the candle to my face. 'You bring a stranger.'

'He's safe. He's my son.'

'Even so, I can not let you in and in any case there is no m… meeting this evening. It has been cancelled.'

There was a sound from the end of the corridor beyond us. Another candle. A woman's voice in the half-darkness spoke with calm authority. The words were simple but I felt there was something good and holy about the woman behind them. Her face was halo-ed by the light of her candle.

'Edith. And Young Guy! You are both welcome in my house, anytime. There has been a slight disturbance this evening but please do come inside for a few minutes. Johann, let them pass but keep a watch on the street until all our guests have left us.'

'Very well, mistress.'

I recognised the boy. He worked for John Clitherow, the butcher. His face was a familiar sight in the area, pushing carts, carrying bags, delivering joints of meat to local families. I remember Mother telling me he was an orphan from the Low Countries, whose family had fled from religious persecution. They'd ended up in York at a time when there'd been plenty of work for newcomers.

His mistress, Margaret Clitherow, and Mother embraced each other warmly. They whispered together for a few moments out of my earshot. After that Mistress Clitherow told me I was a good boy for looking out for my mother.

'How's Henry?' I asked.

Mother shot me a warning glance across the shadows but it came too late.

'I'm afraid he's no longer with us,' responded Mistress Clitherow. 'Last week Henry embarked on the most wonderful voyage of discovery. He's travelling to France. Once there, he'll study at a fine college which specialises in educating English boys.'

'Oh, I see,' I said.

I think I expected to see a little sadness or upset cross the lady's features but, if anything, the opposite was true. She beamed at me, as if her son leaving his family behind was good news. Closer to home, I thought of my sister Anne. She'd always had feelings for Henry and believed one day they'd be married.

'Of course, I tell you this in confidence,' added Mistress Clitherow, now shaking her head. 'There are people in this city who'd make false claim I've sent him away against the Queen's law.'

'Didn't he have time to say goodbye to his friends?' I asked.

Mistress Clitherow knew which friend I was referring to. She smiled sympathetically.

'I appreciate Henry's sudden departure will not go down well with your sister. Even my husband, God bless him, has his doubts. But when the Lord comes a-calling we must respond. And this really is the best thing which could ever happen to Henry. From now on he'll live in the sunshine, not in the shadows as he has had to in England. I'm sure he'll find his vocation there. I'm very happy for him.'

Poor Henry, I thought. And poor Anne. Would Mother tell her the type of college Henry had been sent to? Even if he did return, he'd not be seeking a wife.

'Now, please come through,' said Mistress Clitherow warmly to the pair of us, 'to the rooms at the back. You can keep your boots on.'

I looked at the stone floor. We weren't the first ones who'd left wet footprints that evening. At the other end of the corridor there was a small ante chamber. When we reached this place the butcher's wife placed a delicate hand onto my shoulder.

'Guy, please tarry here a moment. I need to speak to your mother in private.'

They left me alone in the little chamber with a candle. I held this up and surveyed my surroundings. The room contained two obvious entry points. One we'd just used. This led to the corridor and the street beyond. Mother and Mistress Clitherow had departed through the opposite door. I assumed this gave access to one of the butcher's shops and a house behind.

When I looked at the floor my eyes were drawn to the left-hand side. A single pair of footprints appeared to finish directly facing into the wall. Perhaps this person had backtracked on themselves. For a closer look I lowered my candle. The heat immediately began to evaporate the tracks. Within a few seconds they were gone. Hearing somebody approaching I stood up. Mistress Clitherow and Mother returned to the room.

'There's been a change of plan, Guy,' my mother said. 'I've recently started spending some time with Mistress Clitherow and a few of her friends. We talk of matters which are… difficult to discuss in front of those we can not trust. I'll explain more later but tonight there's been a problem.'

I studied the two women earnestly. What had Mother got herself into?

My mother appeared worried but Mistress Clitherow smiled benignly. I found it disconcerting. I wasn't used to standing so close to a woman outside our immediate family. You don't like to think of your friends' mothers in such a way but she was an attractive lady. In the enclosed space I looked into her eyes. They were lovely but ancient. I guessed she must have been over thirty years old. I couldn't see her hair. The scarf on her head reminded me of the girl at school. My eyes widened. I wondered what colour the girl's hair was.

'Guy, listen to me,' said Mother. 'Sheriff Fawcett has decided he doesn't want people having meetings like ours. His men followed one of our friends here tonight, although thank goodness they lost sight of him before he arrived. Mistress Clitherow feels it's best we go straight home now and leave through the back door. Will you help me get home safely?'

'Of course, Mother,' I replied obediently.

We left quietly through a hatch at the rear of the building. Apart from the odd flake it had largely stopped snowing. We glided past the Butchers' Guild Hall. There were dozens of empty stalls here and a myriad of pens holding farm animals. Our footsteps were muffled by the sounds of sleeping sheep, pigs and poultry. At the corner we took a last look and left the waiting room for the butchers' shops behind. Together we headed for Stonegate.

We sat down and looked into the final throes of the fire. Our faces warmed slowly. At first, we uttered no words. I didn't know which questions to ask and suspected Mother wished to tell me no lies. The room wasn't quite dark. A single orange flame rose from the fireplace. The last log shifted awkwardly. When it fell into the ashes and moved across the grate, the tut-tutting noise broke the silence.

'I want to explain about this evening, Guy,' whispered Mother. 'If I do, will you let me talk in my own time and listen without interrupting?'

'I'll try,' I said.

She moved her head from the fire and looked towards me with something akin to sadness and determination.

'I need to go back to the time of your father's parents. As you know, your grandfather Will was a legal man, and an early convert to the new religion. It was a prosperous time to be a lawyer in the Church of England. The religious laws were changing, the monasteries were being dissolved and many estates broken up. There were disputes aplenty. Someone had to resolve them and there was a lot of money to be made.

'Will was an ambitious man. And in your grandmother Ellen he found a good match. She wanted their sons to become successful lawyers and marry well, as she had. But your Uncle Tom, God bless his soul, disappointed her. As soon as he was old enough, Tom turned his back on the law and entered the wool trade. Ellen was none too pleased but there was nothing she could do about it, other than place even more pressure on her second son, your father, to do her bidding.'

I was intrigued. Mother had never spoken of these things before.

'Edward was a good son. He studied law and delighted his parents by becoming a proctor in the Ecclesiastical Court in York. But all those land disputes and boundary changes needed legal men to visit the grounds in question. During one case he spent several weeks in the area around Scotton. That's when we met. I fell in love, and he felt the same. All he had to do was arrange our wedding.'

She smiled a smile which said *if only things were that easy.*

'Your father was a man of due process. He spoke to my Pa. My family was delighted. Even Will warmed to me but one obstacle remained, your grandmother Ellen. She didn't believe her son should marry someone as lowly as a country merchant's daughter. She was already in correspondence with a legal man in London. He had connections in the royal court and an eligible daughter of his own almost old enough to be married. When I came along, Ellen was sorely disappointed.

'Your father had no wish to upset his mother, but he was adamant. You Fawkes's are a stubborn bunch. Edward told Ellen, his heart was set on me, and asked if she wished to break it. She relented, and we were quickly wed.'

Mother took a breath. I wished to delve deeper but deferred. For once I held my tongue, heeding her advice.

'I don't think Ellen ever forgave me. If we found ourselves alone in the kitchen, or mending or sewing, she'd remind me of her family's success, and the fact her father had been Sheriff and Lord Mayor. She'd ask me what my family had ever done, knowing I had no reply.

'Eventually your father was promoted. Edward's office was moved to the Minster Yard. He became an advocate for the Archbishop himself. But still she resented me. If anything, Ellen's animosity grew over time. It was then I realised, this wasn't just about my social standing. There was something else. First she dropped hints. She ranted on about recusants who refused to go to the Sunday service. Finally, when Anne was almost due, during my confinement she accused me of being a Papist, although I'm sure I never betrayed any signs to her.'

I laughed in disbelief. The thought of Mother having any preference for the old faith amused me. Father had been a devout supporter of the Church of England and one of the greatest believers in the new Prayer Book. I can still remember him constantly championing the fact services were held in English, so all people could understand the word of the Lord rather than just a few Catholic priests. And Mother was the same. I couldn't remember a single Sunday when we hadn't been to Church. And then I checked myself. I thought about the strange events of the evening. Mistress Clitherow had a certain reputation.

'But...,' I said.

'Hush, Guy.' She pulled me gently towards her breast and kissed the red hair on the top of my head, before releasing me.

'We live in a world where choices have to be made. Your Uncle Tom chose the wool trade. Your father chose law, and he chose me. It would have been easier for him if he'd agreed with his mother's match making but he didn't. In return I chose him. I loved your father more than anything, until you little ones came along, and then we both loved you too.'

She looked into the fire, as if it conjured up old memories.

'But as a child, it was true. I was taught the old ways in religion. We heard the Mass in Latin. Our whole village cried when Queen Mary died. The villagers mourned even more when the laws began to change in favour of those who practiced the new religion. My family, like many around us, remained true to the old ways but stayed out of trouble by doing so quietly.

'When I moved to York and married your father, I had a difficult choice to make. I could continue to be a church Catholic, attend the service every Sunday and sneak off to Catholic Mass later. Or, I could put my old life behind me. I opted for the latter. I knew if I was caught, your father's career would be threatened, and I couldn't do that to him.'

Mother wiped a tear from her eye and continued on quietly.

'Many in York have faced such a dilemma. Take my friend, Margaret Clitherow. Over the years she's been sent to prison more times than I can remember for refusing to go to church. Her husband Thomas the butcher isn't a Catholic but he's a good man. Each time he's paid her fines and comforted their children, but the strain on his face is plain for all to see. And from tomorrow they'll need to be doubly careful.'

'What do you mean?'

'Margaret's stepfather, the *adulterer* Henry Maye, is being made Lord Mayor of York.'

'Yes, I know. The whole school is going to his inauguration ceremony,' I said.

'As a Catholic, Margaret must be an embarrassment to him. Once he's in in office I wouldn't be surprised if Henry Maye seeks to get Margaret arrested. It would be awful for Thomas and the children. I couldn't risk that sort of thing happening to your own father, so I made my choice and put the old religion behind me.'

'Then why did you go to The Shambles tonight?' I couldn't help but ask. 'From what everyone says, Mistress Clitherow could be a Catholic still.'

'It's a fair question, and for once you've been patient.' Mother inhaled. She took a breath before speaking again. 'For many years I've mourned your father. Despite offers, I've refused to re-marry.'

It was clear she was finding the words difficult. I wanted to tell her it was fine. I understood and had no wish to stand in the way of her happiness. If she had found somebody else, so be it. But in the end I remained silent.

'I don't quite know how to tell you this. Recently I've found myself tempted by another and I've seen the opportunity for a better life for us all.'

'Is he a good man?' I asked.

'I think so,' she replied. 'But there's good and bad in all of us. A few years ago he asked me to marry him but at that time I wasn't ready. He said he would go home and wait until I was. Now I am ready but I fear it's too late, although he has told me he wishes to be with me now more than ever. I'm in a quandary. And in this time of need the Good Lord has forsaken me. I've prayed for His guidance but my prayers remain unanswered. I think God is punishing me for abandoning His true faith all those years ago.

'But Margaret is a good woman. She recognises my pain and has spent time comforting me. She's persuaded me to go back to the old faith. She says if I do, she's certain the Lord God will forgive my sins and give me the strength I need to go on. Tonight, she planned for me to attend a Catholic Mass and afterwards seek guidance from a priest.'

My mother a Catholic? I looked away from her. Although I couldn't see them, I knew there were tears on the way.

'You should have spoken to me,' I whispered. 'I could have advised you.'

She shook her head. We both knew these were topics neither of us were comfortable with.

'If it means anything, you have my blessing to re-marry,' I said. 'I want you to be happy.'

'But I can't, Guy,' she replied. Her tears fell more quickly now.

'Why ever not?' I asked.

'Because the man already has a wife.'

I was dumbfounded. I found it hard to believe the words I'd just heard. Was my mother saying she wished to commit adultery? Without speaking another word, I stood up, left the room and climbed up the steps in anger. Mother remained downstairs, sobbing quietly. She wouldn't wish to disturb my sisters.

# 4

**Thursday February 3rd·, 1586**

As we entered Coney Street six or seven beggars filed slowly past us in the opposite direction. Each carried a blanket and a few worldly possessions. One or two hung onto dog leashes as their hounds avoided the boots of the men behind them, dressed in best Corporation livery. This was no day for eyesores.

Headmaster Pulleyn shook his head, I assumed in disgust at the homeless vagabonds. We followed him through the Common Hall Gates and down the slight incline into the square in front of the civic hall building. On the opposite side, in the one area which caught the sunshine at this time of year, were the masters and boys of Archbishop Holgate's.

'Smug little tykes,' whispered Kit.

'Silence!' commanded Teacher Robinson.

The wind was still cold, even if the weather was fairer. As we stood in the shadows cast by the walls of the Common Hall, Headmaster Pulleyn caught his breath and complained about something to Teacher Robinson. With their cloaks billowing in the breeze, they shook their heads before nodding in unison.

It wasn't yet the eleventh hour but a large crowd had already assembled. Whether peasants or gentry, the people about us stamped their feet and moved around to keep warm.

It's funny how easily schoolboys get bored. When their teachers weren't looking, the Holgate lads made rude hand gestures towards us. The St Peter's boys responded in kind, none more gleefully than Thomas Cheke. Perhaps his father had passed on a few tricks he'd learned in Parliament.

Every now and then the crowd glanced up expectantly towards

Coney Street, hoping to see the arrival of the new Lord Mayor. He'd have the power to steer the city's spending towards his own agenda. In certain circumstances he could even have people arrested but equally the Lord Mayor risked being held to account. The Twenty Four in York, the Council of the North, Parliament and even the Queen would be quick to apportion blame if anything went wrong. There was a fine line between profiting from corruption and getting caught. At least that's what my mother said.

When I got up that morning, Mother was already busy in the kitchen, scrubbing something clean in a bucket. We didn't discuss the events of the evening before. It was almost as if the late-night adventure and conversation hadn't happened. Instead she told me all she knew of the new Lord Mayor, although much of the story seemed to centre around her friend Margaret Clitherow.

Mistress Clitherow's parents were called Thomas and Jane Middleton. Thomas had been both Sheriff and an alderman in York. He was warmly remembered for being a prosperous and generous family man, if not a well one. Few were surprised, Mother said, when he died leaving behind, amongst other things, a wealthy widow and a fourteen-year-old daughter.

It was only a few months later when Jane remarried. Eyebrows were raised and tongues wagged for her new husband, Henry Maye, was much younger than she. More importantly, he'd been born into a lower social class. Although their motives were questioned, over time the couple confounded the gossips. Despite his lowly origins, Henry was a hard worker. With Jane's financial backing, he slowly ascended York's social ladder. Their business interests prospered. His wealth grew, until eventually Henry was invited to become an alderman, himself.

'How did he treat his stepdaughter, your friend Mistress Clitherow?' I asked.

'By all accounts well,' replied Mother. 'She once told me she couldn't have wished for a better stepfather. But of course, we should treat all this with a pinch of salt. Margaret never has a bad word to say about anyone. And lately, his attitude towards her has changed.'

'Why so?'

'For being a Catholic,' Mother replied.

'Is he deeply religious?' I asked.

'No, no more than most laymen,' Mother laughed scornfully. 'But he's a man who craves power and wants to be seen doing the right thing. Having a prominent recusant in the family, one who has been sent to prison, can't be good for his reputation. I'm sure he'll have demanded Margaret repent her religion, but I'm equally certain she'll have refused. This wouldn't have mattered so much in the past when Jane was there to protect her, but now with her mother gone the *adulterer* has a free hand to do what he likes.'

'Why do you keep calling him that?' I asked.

'It's common knowledge,' she said. 'When Jane fell ill last year, he started carrying on with a younger woman. Knowing his wife was likely to die, he installed a new one in waiting.'

'You shouldn't always believe what you hear,' I said.

'Well, it didn't take him long to remarry, did it?' said Mother. 'And like Jane before him, his second spouse was much younger than the first. You'll see the hussy today. She won't be hard to spot. Just look out for mutton dressed as lamb.'

Such was the backdrop to the day's events. If the accusation of adultery against Henry Maye was true, I couldn't condone his actions. But for the rest of the tale, it seemed one all Englishmen should be proud of. Here was a man born holding a bow, who'd married well and worked hard. I, for one, was pleased he'd earned the right to carry a sword.

Mistress Clitherow had always struck me as a good woman, whether Catholic or not. She was closer to the people and events than the gossips Mother listened to. If she remained true to Henry Maye, surely it was because he was a good man. His election as Lord Mayor appeared to confirm this. In any case, I found it difficult to illicit much sympathy for Mother's views that morning.

A cheer rose up from around the corner. We began to hear the sound of horses' hooves and cartwheels on the cobbles of Coney Street. Riders emerged. People stood back as a group of horsemen in Corporation livery entered the square. They were soon followed by a fine ceremonial carriage drawn by a pair of beautiful chestnut horses, with a driver at the front and sufficient room for four dignitaries to sit in cushioned comfort in the compartment behind.

The largest of the occupants was the current Lord Mayor. Seated on one side of the carriage with his back to the driver, he gesticulated and waved his pudgy hands to all and sundry. As the coach turned tightly in a full circle, for the briefest of moments his gold chains glinted in the sunshine, illuminating a pair of chins so immense even a double-sized ruff couldn't hide.

As always on these occasions, the Lady Mayoress sat alongside her husband, as rotund as him but on a smaller scale. Her heavily powdered face made it difficult to see if she was smiling or not, but I got the impression the couple were enjoying their final engagement. Or were they simply anticipating the feast which would follow?

On the opposite side of the carriage sat the new Lord Mayor, Henry Maye. He was a good-looking man. The lines across his brow hinted at worldly experience. His temples were greying. He too signalled fairly regally to the crowd, as if born to the occasion. After a brief glance around the multitude, the soon-to-be mayor's mouth adopted a politician's smile, whilst his gaze returned to the gold on the other man's chest. Soon enough, soon enough, his eyes seemed to be saying.

If the features on Mistress Clitherow's stepfather's face were pleasant enough, the youthful countenance of the woman beside him was almost breath-taking. Mother had made a mistake. I saw no mutton, just the most succulent cut of lamb.

A small number of additional horsemen completed the procession. Most of the guests with formal invitations to the inauguration ceremony would already be inside. Everyone would be waiting for Henry Maye, for this was his day.

When the wagon pulled up alongside the Common Hall doors, four footmen stepped forward and assisted the mayoral party down from their carriage. There were a few more waves to the crowd and a second huge cheer. Within moments the group was gone, although the throng's applause continued.

'And now we've got to stand here like wassocks for an hour and a half in this sharding cold,' whispered Kit, with his usual grin.

He clapped his hands enthusiastically like the rest of the crowd. I suspected he was doing so just to keep his hands warm. Maybe we all were.

We listened to the bells chime through a series of quarter and half hours, until at last they rang out continuously to announce the ceremony inside the hall was ending. Everyone strained their eyes towards the double doors in front of us. And when finally they opened a few minutes later, the new Lord Mayor was proudly wearing the golden chains his eyes had coveted.

Soon he was joined by his good lady wife, the aldermen of the city of York and a host of other dignitaries, as one by one they exited the building and entered the space cleared for them in front of the Common Hall. The throng around Coney Street was even busier now. Many more people had arrived to see the new Lord Mayor and hear his speech.

I'd been to these events before. They were usually much the same.

The city's leader would speak out on the importance of the rule of law, keeping the streets clean and the need to increase or decrease taxes. I wondered which way the new Mayor would go.

There was a roll of drums and a blast of horns to signal the speeches were about to begin. The city's crier called for silence. Once his request had largely been observed, Edwin Sandys, the Archbishop of York, said a short prayer, which ended with a blessing for the new Lord Mayor and Lady Mayoress. Many male eyes were already upon her. She was an attractive woman, there was no doubting that. We cheered for the Lord Mayor, our city and the Queen, before clapping our hands wildly to bring some life back into them.

Once all this was complete, Lord Mayor Maye stepped forward and opened a scroll. 'I would like to start by thanking the Archbishop for his blessing and the good aldermen of York for electing me to this lofty position. This role is a great honour and I intend to fulfil my duties with the upmost honesty and integrity.'

'First time for everything,' whispered Kit, beneath the applause.

The mayor continued. 'Who was it who said, "*Day by day, what you choose, what you think and what you do, is who you shall become*"?'

'Well, Master Fawkes, who was it?'

Neither Kit nor I had noticed Headmaster Pulleyn stealthily move himself through the crowd until he was stood directly behind us.

'Heraclitus of Ephesus, sir,' I said quickly. The lessons on Ancient Greece had been useful after all.

'Good lad,' said the headmaster. 'But remember "*Abundance of knowledge does not teach men to be wise*".' He moved on.

'What's that supposed to mean?' asked Rob Middleton.

'I don't know.' I shrugged my shoulders.

'Don't worry about it,' said Kit. 'It's just Old Man Pulleyn. He loves quoting the Greeks.'

We received a dirty look from one of the craftsmen standing behind us. Another said. 'Stop chattering, or we'll miss the speech.'

After that we gave the Lord Mayor our full attention. As he paused for effect, he glanced down at the thick chain of gold across his shoulders and smiled. I wondered if he'd been tutored in public oration. He looked back up and read from the scroll.

'Whoever it was,' he said, 'they were correct.' Henry Maye scanned the crowd. 'Good people of York, this city has reached a crossroads. We can continue along the way we've been going and face further decline or move the right way towards a more prosperous future. If we do that, what we think and what we do, shall be what we become.'

Another pause. 'Which way do you want to go, prosperity or decline?'

A plethora of peopled called out for 'Prosperity'. There were loud cheers and shouts of 'Aye!' from around the square.

The Lord Mayor continued, 'There are two blights on this great city. These have been holding us back. For York and its people to prosper they must be defeated. Are you with me?'

'Aye!' Roared the crowd.

For my own part, I wondered how York Corporation could contemplate defeating the sweating sickness and plague.

'We all know what they are,' he said. 'The first is the scourge of mass immigration.'

The noise in the crowd abated a little.

'We men and women of York are hospitable people. I, myself, give alms to many good causes, as I'm sure you all do but… we must learn to help ourselves before we try to help others. For the past twenty years this city has often been too welcoming. These days York is home to far too many foreigners. A few have settled down here and work hard. We welcome them, but too many others do nothing other than beg and scrounge for our charity.'

I scanned the crowd. Whilst there wasn't any loud cheering yet, I noticed nods and a general feeling of agreement with Henry Maye's sentiment. Only a few remained stony faced. One I spotted across the way was my mother. She held my sisters tightly to her skirts. Looking back, I think she suspected what would come next.

'The second issue we must address is religion. God bless the Queen!'

'God bless the Queen!' answered the crowd, including myself, in unison.

'Queen Bess has been clear on this point. We live in a Protestant country. The darkness of the old religion is a danger to us all. It forbids people from swearing allegiance to her crown and to England. It doesn't even encourage our citizens to worship God. English Catholics are traitors who bow down only to their anti-Christ, the Pope in Rome.'

The crowd booed and hissed at the Papal reference.

'But there are Catholics amongst us, some here even today.'

People began to look around nervously and, in some cases angrily, at each other.

Henry Maye continued with his speech. 'Yes, these are the recusants who refuse to attend Sunday service. Make no mistake, during my time in office the punishments against these people will be pressed furiously, whether fines, imprisonment or worse.'

The crowd cheered.

'But our biggest problem is not these recusants. We know all about them. We have a list.'

He held up and shook the scroll of parchment he'd been reading from, as if it included the names of all the city's openly Catholic residents upon it. Another cheer went up.

'But there are others too.' A further pause.

The crowd hushed. Henry Maye's head moved from left to right, as if searching for specific faces in the square.

'As we all know, practicing as a Catholic priest in England is punishable by death, yet still some live amongst us. They come over here on their evil missions on the orders of their Pontiff in Rome. One or two may even dare to visit this city, although when they do, we always catch them and send them to the Knavesmire. It's the others I want to talk about.'

What others, I thought.

'They live amongst us, even here in York. Have no doubt, there are traitors in our midst, even today. Often they purport to be our friends. They smile at us and pretend to pray to our God but every night they crawl through the gutters like rats spreading disease and heresy in the name of the Pope. They hide his priests in their houses and let them hold their secret Masses, where the only words spoken are in foreign tongues. They seek to undermine us. And, yes, it is true. Many of the foreigners who've come to this great city are in league with them. Fear not though, for we shall defeat them all. Sheriff Fawcett and I will pursue every Catholic-loving one of them. What do you say, good people of York? Are you with us?'

Stirred up by the mayor's rising rhetoric, the majority of the crowd cheered enthusiastically. I felt myself in a dilemma. Although a good Protestant, my parents had always encouraged me to be tolerant of others. At St Peter's I'd been taught the benefit of political debate and argument over persecution, but the law banned Catholic priests and knowingly harbouring one was now a capital crime. If Lord Mayor Maye advocated these policies, the law was on his side. And Father had brought me up to believe in the rule of law.

By now most of the boys from both schools were shouting raucously, none more so I noticed than Thomas Cheke. As the speech continued, he and his friends waved their fists angrily and cheered and jeered in all the right places. In contrast Kit and Rob alongside me appeared angry and worried in turn. I speculated whether the rumours regarding Kit's family were true. Perhaps he feared for their safety, but I was sure he and the other boys in the school would be fine. Unlike his predecessor, Headmaster Pulleyn ran a strictly Protestant institution. There were no Catholics to root out of St Peter's.

At the end of the speech, I clapped my hands along with everyone else. With only a year left of my schooldays I had no wish to get into trouble. There was little point in being singled out by Headmaster Pulleyn for not toeing the line. By the time the boys had been counted, and we were ready to depart from the Common Hall, I'd lost sight of my family. As we left the square, Thomas Cheke shared a joke with one of the dignitaries. I knew who he was. They were the spitting image of each other.

Due to the sheer number of people pushing through Coney Street, we made slow progress. I was thankful we weren't walking the other way, like the Archbishop Holgate boys. There'd be a huge squeeze past the prison and toll booth on Ouse Bridge as the mass of people marched along the one route available to reach the other side of the river.

One section of the crowd left us at St Helen's Square but Teacher Robinson directed our own party through Lendal. There was still quite a throng, even here. I couldn't see Headmaster Pulleyn. Perhaps he'd gone ahead or stopped to speak to one of the aldermen.

'Once a filthy Catholic, always a filthy Catholic. Just like the rest of your family.'

The comment came from behind us and was clearly aimed at Kit. When we turned around Thomas Cheke had a snide grin on his face. The crowd kept pressing us forward and we had to move on. Two of Cheke's friends, William Craven and Francis Gayle, walked alongside him, one on either flank. All three pushed us hard in the back with balled fists.

'They'll be rounding you up soon Wrighty, along with Middleton here and all the others.'

Kit's face reddened but he knew he was being goaded. He attempted to ignore it.

'Shut up, Cheke,' I said. 'Leave him alone.'

'Shard off, copper top. Keep out of it, unless you're one of them too. Well, are you?'

As we passed the piece of road that separated the ruins of the old Augustinian friary and St Wilfrid's Church the crowd stuttered to a halt for some reason. The people at the rear were forced to push themselves into the backs of those in front of them. Cheke used this as cover to punch Kit hard in the kidneys.

It was a struggle to move my shoulders but I turned around to face him. I wanted to hit Cheke but before I could even take a swing at the boy, two pairs of hands grabbed at my arms and pulled them up behind me. I tried to twist away from them but Gayle and Craven held me tightly and the throng hemmed us in. I couldn't wrench myself free.

'Come on, Wrighty, have a go if you want to,' sneered Cheke. 'Nobody'll notice in this crowd. It's just you and me. Are you scared we haven't got a teacher here to ensure you don't get hurt like in the swordsmanship lessons at school?'

I couldn't understand why Kit didn't just strike him. I would have.

'Ah, never mind,' sneered Cheke. 'I understand you haven't got the bollocks for it anyway. Talking of bollocks, I understand your sister Ursula copulates with horses. They say she likes the size and feel of them.'

This was too much for Kit. He threw a good punch. Blood spurted from Cheke's nose. He would have fallen back too but the crowd held him up. Seeing his friend stunned, Gayle released his grip on me and pushed towards Kit. I struck Craven with the back of my free hand and yanked the other away from him.

Most of the men around us were craftsmen or apprentices making their way back to work at the King's Manor. Our altercation was an unexpected delight for them. They quickly cleared a space in the crowd for us to struggle in and began chanting, 'Fight! Fight!'

By now Cheke had recovered. He thrust his own fist into Kit's face, and Gayle came at Kit from the other side. When I tried to intervene, Craven grabbed at me. I looked at Rob, but he stood watching with the other boys and did nothing. Kit was knocked backwards. A dozen arms in the throng held him up and shoved his body back into the ring. By now his own fists were pumping, reminding me of his brother Jack in his prime. Kit struck Gayle with an uppercut, and the other boy staggered backwards.

Craven slipped to his left but somehow he managed to wrestle me to the ground. As we rolled around from side to side on the cobbles, I saw Gayle and Cheke double up on Kit again. Things didn't look good but just at that moment Headmaster Pulleyn appeared, as if out of thin air. He blew his whistle loudly, whilst Teacher Robinson pushed his way towards us to intervene. Loud words were spoken and the scuffle was halted, much to the disappointment of the baying crowd.

Their sport for the day over, the heaving masses began to move forward again. Teacher Robinson led the majority of the boys, including Rob, along Lendal but the five of us involved in the fight were taken to one side by Headmaster Pulleyn. He lectured us loudly beneath the windowless walls of the ancient friary, apoplectic with rage.

'You're supposed to be young gentlemen, but instead you bring shame to my school. Brawling in the street like common ruffians, what did you think you were doing? It's the birch for the lot of you when we get back. I'll not have this. Do you understand me?'

Not once did he ask what the fight was about, or who had started it. This didn't seem to matter to him. The school's reputation was all he cared about.

One by one we were taken to the headmaster's office and the birch applied to our bottoms. I found the strokes doubly painful due to the weals left by my previous punishment. Once we were all done, Headteacher Pulleyn dismissed Cheke and his cronies but held Kit and I back. Cheke grinned at us, as if knowing we'd face additional punishment.

When the others were gone, the headmaster instructed us both to sit down. Kit acquiesced, carefully positioning himself onto the wooden bench, but I asked for permission to remain standing. This was granted. The old man sat behind his desk. He shook his head as he looked at us.

'So, what did Master Cheke have to say to you?' he asked me.

'Nothing, sir.' I said truthfully.

'And what about you, Wright?'

'He made a personal insult about a female member of my family, sir. I apologise, but in all honesty I'd do the same thing again tomorrow if he repeated what he said.'

'But you're letting him win, lad, by reacting like this. That's what he wants. Don't you see?'

'I had no choice, sir. It's a matter of honour.'

'Did he say anything else? Insult your family in another way? About religion perhaps?'

The headmaster looked at Kit sternly in the eye. When he didn't reply I held my breath. The silence was over-bearing. If I was aware of the Wrights' recusant ways, Headmaster Pulleyn would surely know of them. The inference in Kit's lack of response was clear, and the old man was as sharp as a needle. He wouldn't have missed it.

'Boys, I'm disappointed in you both.' The headmaster shook his head wearily. 'When the sons of men like Henry Cheke run amok there's little I can do to stop them. Hopefully his father will understand I had no choice but to birch his son's buttocks, as I'd already applied the cane to four other boys. Perhaps he'll consider it a rite of passage. I'm sure he'll have been punished, himself, many times when he was a youth.'

The afternoon was taking a strange turn. I couldn't fathom why Headmaster Pulleyn was speaking so candidly to us. The next moment he turned back towards me.

'I know of Master Wright's religion, of course, but I'm surprised at you, Fawkes. Your father was in the Ecclesiastical Court.'

'I'm no Catholic, sir,' I said firmly.

'Are you not?' He laughed. 'Then why were you seen sloping around the alleys behind the back of The Shambles last night? It's a well-known haunt for people returning from secret Catholic Masses.'

I almost gasped. How did he know?

'Don't worry boy,' he said. 'You can speak freely to me. We're all friends here.'

What was happening? Was he trying to trick me? I had to compose myself.

'Come on! Out with it boy. What do you have to say for yourself?'

'Nothing, sir. I wasn't there. Your source must be mistaken.'

I looked at the old man, as he sat at his desk beneath the leaded window and studied my face.

'Good. Well done. Your cheeks are a little pink but you handled my questions well. If anybody else makes enquiries such as these, you deny them quickly, bluntly and out of hand. No boy from my school will be found guilty of being a Catholic. Do you understand?'

Kit looked at me and nodded slightly. What did he mean?

'Yes, sir,' I said quickly. I didn't know what else to say.

The headmaster stood up and instructed us to wait in his office. We were left alone for a short time. When I was certain there was no-one else in earshot, I looked at Kit.

'Do you think he really suspects me of being a Catholic?' I whispered.

'If you are, it's a surprise to me,' Kit replied. 'Although then at least there would be three of us.'

'What do you mean?'

'Surely you'll have heard the talk? My family have always remained true to the old faith. But we're not alone. There may be less openly recusant people these days but there are still many secret church Catholics. The Lord Mayor was right about that.'

Kit beckoned me towards his seat. I leaned towards him and he whispered in my ear.

'I think Old Man Pulleyn's one of us.'

I shook my head. I wasn't a Catholic and there was no way Headmaster Pulleyn was either but before I could respond, the door opened. When the headmaster entered the room, he wasn't alone. The girl from the walled garden was with him, a basket on her arm.

'Give them to them,' nodded the old man.

She reached into the basket. With delicate hands she gave Kit and I each a small bundle of fragrant green leaves. I issued a sigh of relief. There was no sign of the rosary beads. When her fingers touched mine, I felt a shiver of excitement run up and down my body like I'd never felt before. Her brown eyes were dark and wonderful. I struggled to take my gaze away from them. I whispered my thanks, and from the corner of my eye I saw Kit smile at me.

'Sage,' said the headmaster. 'Crush the leaves and rub them into your skin when you get home where the birch took its toll. You'll find it alleviates the stinging, and it will prevent your wounds from going bad.'

He looked at Kit. 'Oh, Wright. You're not going home, are you? Well, just try and find a little privacy somewhere. And both of you, stay well clear of Thomas Cheke. There must be no second occurrence of what happened this afternoon. He and his friends will get the same warning as you but perhaps not the salvia. Now, return to your lessons.'

And with this, we left him. And her too. I could hardly breathe.

# 5

**Sunday February 6th, 1586**

Mother, my sisters and I sat down at the small table, ready to break our fast. The Sabbath was the one day of the week when I was allowed to stay at home with my family, although there was never much time for sleeping. We had to prepare and dress in our Sunday best clothes, for soon we'd be on our way to the Sunday service. When Mother said the prayers at the table that morning, she spoke slowly with her eyelids closed. We were all supposed to, but I kept mine open and peeped at the faces around me.

Mother and I still hadn't spoken about matters of a personal nature since I'd left her crying on Tuesday evening. Her words had disturbed me. Could she really harbour feelings for a married man? Even worse to my mind, I feared for her future if she risked reverting to the Catholic faith of her youth. I knew I should confront her on these issues but I hadn't yet plucked up the courage.

For eight years I'd been the man of the house but in my sisters' eyes I'd always be second best to Mother. On a day to day basis she did all the things which allowed our family to function. Since Father's death, with many of his assets unavailable until I came of age, we no longer employed servants. She did all the work herself. When issues arose, she always knew what to do for the best. Challenging her, though I knew I must, wouldn't be easy.

Although Anne was a little younger than me, half a decade separated Lizzie and myself. Sometimes the age gulf between us seemed too large to cross. It could have been fifty years. I loved my little sister but often I didn't know what to say to her and assume she felt the same.

Anne and I were much closer. Sometimes we'd confide in one another, confident our secrets would never be betrayed. I was sad to see her eyes red and puffed up. Mother had done her best to break the news about Henry Clitherow as gently as she could, but there was no easy way of telling your daughter the boy she felt for had been exiled to another country.

The one blessing I could think of was Anne hadn't yet realised why Henry had gone to France. The only reason colleges abroad would welcome English boys from non-noble families would be to train them for the Catholic priesthood. She'd find out in time, but I hoped by then the candle she held for him would have burned lower.

After breakfast, the girls climbed upstairs to get into their dresses. They shared the second bedchamber of the house with Mother. She remained downstairs and placed her hand on my wrist.

'I see you're moving less comfortably again,' she said softly. 'What happened?'

I couldn't remember lying to my mother, so I told her the truth. I described the fight and my subsequent punishment. The only details I omitted were about the girl, the sage and Headmaster Pulleyn's allegation I'd been seen behind The Shambles.

'That young Master Cheke is dangerous,' she said. 'You should stay away from him and his friends. And you must remember, it's reckless for you to be seen openly defending Catholics.'

'But Kit is my best friend,' I protested. Somehow, I managed to stop myself from telling Mother she was a hypocrite.

'I know, Guy, but his family are well-known recusants,' she said. 'You must be careful. Your father worked so hard to get you into St Peter's and the Ecclesiastical Court has been good to us since he passed away, providing the money to keep you there. You have a great opportunity to become a lawyer for the Church, like your Pa. There isn't long to go. Please, keep your nose clean.'

'I'll try,' I said.

Her voice choked a little. 'Oh Guy,' she said. 'What must you think of me? I'm lecturing you when my own actions have placed us in danger. I haven't been thinking straight. I shall go to one last Mass, give Confession and ask for guidance. After that, I'll stay away from every Catholic in York. Do you believe me?'

'Of course,' I replied. 'But the streets are dangerous at night. If you go again, I must accompany you, although I'll take no part in the religious activities. Like Father, I only support the new ways. I believe the prayer book should be in English.'

I hoped I sounded suitably earnest, but later when I thought about it, I regretted mentioning Father. Or did I? I was confused. I wanted to make a point but Mother was in such a fragile state. Hopefully this would be the final time she'd attend Mass. And surely, if she did confess and seek guidance from a priest, he'd have to tell her to put aside any thoughts she had for this married man, whoever he was.

## Thursday February 10th, 1586

A week had gone by since my latest birching, and I could now walk without too much discomfort. The sage had worked well. Every time I applied the green leaves, I saw the girl's face and felt her fingers touch mine. But we hadn't seen each other since the previous Thursday. Although I constantly looked out for her, we'd only met again in my thoughts and dreams.

My mind remained unsettled as I walked home from St Peter's. I wandered past the horse fair and ventured into Gillygate. It was evening time and the ale houses were already making a steady trade. Loud sounds of laughter and the clinking of tankards could be heard through the shutters.

A man staggered into the street from one of the inns across the way, clearly inebriated. The fellow zig-zagged into a gutter and began peeing onto the external wall. When he finished his business, he missed his step, slipped in the mud and fell over. The streets had no cobbles to grip onto outside the city walls. What was it my father would say? There were two certainties in life, drunkards and taxes.

As I neared the ginnel where the immigrant child beggars had approached me the week before, I heard a cry of alarm. It could have been an animal, or perhaps a child. I looked inside. There was only darkness. But I heard a whisper. I took a step back. I had no wish to be dragged in there.

'What's going on?' I called.

'None of your sharding business,' came the reply.

'Help!' a voice shouted out.

It was promptly silenced. Well almost, but what was left was a muffle.

'Should I call for aid from the Corporation men at Bootham Bar?' I asked. 'If they catch you, you'll be in trouble.'

'Not as much as you will be, freckle boy.'

Thomas Cheke emerged from the shadows. 'Let the little shit go,' he instructed, looking back.

His friends Craven and Gayle appeared. An immigrant boy with a bloody nose ran past them into Gillygate. Once he reached the next snicket he darted into it and was gone but before he disappeared, he looked back. I recognised him. It was Johann, the young boy from behind the door at Mistress Clitherow's house in The Shambles.

'What were you doing to him?' I demanded.

'Teaching the little Flemish shit a lesson,' replied Cheke. 'We were about to ask him if he was a good Protestant or a sharding Papist. Now, maybe we should ask you instead.'

'Not that it would make much difference,' said Craven coldly.

'I don't know,' disagreed Gayle. 'We give them all a good beating but we save the best stuff for the Cathos.'

'So, Fawkes,' said Cheke, as he edged closer towards me. 'What about you? Are you a God-fearing Protestant or a pink-livered Papist like your pal Wright?'

'I don't answer to you, Cheke,' I replied. 'But if you must know I've always been true to the new religion.'

'That's a pity,' said Craven. 'But I still think we should give him a beating.'

'I have to say I agree,' grinned Cheke. 'If the two of you grab him, I'll give his arse a good kicking. That should open up his birch wounds, and it won't leave any new marks on him.'

Gayle and Craven took a step towards me. One of them laughed. 'When did we care about leaving marks?'

'I don't want him telling tales to Old Man Pulleyn, and risking my father finding out.'

'Finding out what?'

Cheke didn't answer. In the darkness and tension none of us had heard the three horses approach. Perhaps this was the difference between muddy tracks and cobbles. In the city we'd have heard them coming a hundred yards off. The riders were now looming over us. Even in the gloom I recognised the first one as Henry Cheke.

'Well, Tom, what are you and your friends doing here, out of school at this hour?'

'Good evening to you, father,' replied Cheke, thinking on his feet. 'Headmaster Pulleyn has sent us on errand...'

I never learned what the supposed errand was. I slipped off down Gillygate. When I reached Bootham Bar I felt safe. The streets around here were my territory. Arriving at the front door in Stonegate, I knocked and called out. When the door opened, I stepped inside.

## Sunday February 13th, 1586

The morning service at St Michael-le-Belfry had finished a few minutes earlier. After leaving the little parish church the congregation stood beneath the grey sky in the shadow of the Minster. Small talk was the order of the day. For once the men and women were in no hurry to rush off to work or to clean their homes, prepare meals or look after their children. It was the one time of the week when the good people of York could relax and catch up with their friends.

Mother stood in the centre of a lively discussion. It was nice to see her face become animated again. Those around her included John Clitherow, Mistress Margaret's husband. I knew Mother regarded the man highly. He was about the same age as Father would have been, if he'd lived.

The butcher was certainly an amiable enough fellow. He smiled and laughed and told stories. Whilst Lizzie ran around with her friends, Anne stood quietly, invisible, on the fringe of the adults' conversation. I knew what she was doing. She was listening out for snippets of news about Henry. It was unfortunate. There'd be no mention of him amongst the churchgoers. To them Henry no longer existed. His mission to France was illegal. I was sure it had been engineered by his mother and her Catholic contacts, not the smiling man before us. I wondered how he felt inside. Did he miss his son, but think it best to hide this from us?

I wasn't sure why Henry's father was with us that day. His usual place of worship was Christ's Church of the Holy Trinity. When challenged, he said it was always good to visit a neighbouring parish. A woman asked where the rest of his family was. He responded by saying his wife was *'under the weather again'* and the children were looking after her. It was more likely, I thought, Mistress Clitherow had returned to her recusant ways. I hoped she wouldn't push the patience of the authorities too far, for all their sakes. Or perhaps she thought she could do this more comfortably these days, under the protection of her stepfather, the new Lord Mayor.

A moment later I lost all interest in the Clitherows and almost everything else in the world. I saw her. She was walking along Petergate in the company of Headmaster Pulleyn. I just had to speak to her. I broke away from Mother and the others and made for the cobbles.

'Sir! Sir!' I called.

When the old man heard me, he stopped. I had no idea what I was going to say to him.

'Ah, young Master Fawkes. At Sunday service with your family.

Excellent!' he said.

I hadn't realised but Anne had followed me across the road. She suspected my motives and thought she could learn something about my secret. I realised Mother wasn't the only one in our family who'd been acting strangely. And for once I hadn't confided in Anne. She must have been wondering what was going on.

'And who is this charming young lady?' asked the Headmaster.

'My sister, sir. Please let me introduce you to Miss Anne Fawkes.'

'Charmed, I'm sure,' smiled Headmaster Pulleyn.

Anne curtseyed slightly but mostly she placed her attention firmly on the old man's companion. By this time Mother and Lizzie had joined us too.

'Headmaster Pulleyn, what a delight to see you again, and so soon,' said Mother.

Pulleyn smiled. I wondered what Mother meant by this, for she couldn't have seen him for several weeks.

'And you must introduce us to your companion,' she said.

'Ah, yes,' said the old man. 'Mistress Fawkes, this is my distant kinswoman, Maria Pulleyn. The girl's joined me from Scotton to work at St Peter's for a few weeks, whilst we recruit two new kitchen assistants. The old ones have left us to work at Archbishop Holgate's, of all places. Can you believe it? Of course, we don't normally employ females. It's unfair on the boys. But it's only temporary. I'm doing my best to keep Maria out of harm's way until we can find more permanent replacements.'

Maria, I thought. What a wonderful name.

'Scotton?' said Mother quizzically. 'I hail from those parts myself. I had no idea your family had ties to the Pulleyns of Scotton Hall.'

'No, no,' the headmaster said blustering a little. 'At least not those Pulleyns anyway. As you know, it's a common enough name around there. Most of my family live in the East Riding.'

The old man's apprehension was understandable. Even I knew some of the residents of Scotton had a reputation for recusant tendencies.

'Your secret's safe with us,' said Mother. I do believe she was teasing him, but he took it well enough.

'We've been to the Sunday service at St Giles,' he said smiling. 'And we're now off for a walk around York. Maria hasn't yet had the opportunity to see the major sights of the city.'

'The Minster is beautiful,' said Maria, looking up. 'Although I do find it a little bit foreboding. How on Earth can men build something which reaches so high into the sky?'

We all followed her gaze. She had a point. The light tan coloured stone walls rose steeply before us. A raindrop and then another fell into my face. I lowered my head. Maria was looking at me. I held my breath.

'Come along then, Maria,' said Pulleyn, grasping her wrist. 'It appears we must make haste if we are to avoid the worst of the inclement weather.'

I watched their backs as they departed along Petergate. More accurately I watched her back. And her head, and her legs and her body. How elegantly she moved. I wished so much to be able to remove her coif scarf and see the colour of her hair. Every movement she made was quite exquisite.

When they finally stepped out of sight, I saw Anne grinning at me. We walked back towards Stonegate and she whispered into my ear. 'I may have lost my first love but I'm gladdened to see you've found yours.'

I squeezed her hand. I loved my family.

# 6

**Sunday February 20th, 1586**

The next week passed by quickly and quietly. When the teachers weren't looking Thomas Cheke and his cronies taunted and sneered at us but by and large we were kept apart. I think Headmaster Pulleyn believed the fight would soon be forgotten and life at school would return to normal. He was wrong.

Back at home Mother appeared more settled and much more like her old confident self, the concern and indecision of the past few weeks appeared almost to have gone. Almost, for every now and then from a slight variation in her voice, a momentary look in her eye, or a movement, I suspected the troubles remained.

We attended the next Sunday service as usual. After church the parishioners met up as they always did. They wore their best clothes and discussed the same old topics, the price of food, the weather and local gossip.

But there was something else too. During a few conversations I noticed certain people's words begin to reflect Lord Mayor Maye's speech. Concerns were raised regarding immigration. One or two men, it was usually men, offered up angry opinions on what should be done about the Catholics.

When these words were uttered Mother's face took on a gloomy pallor but she said nothing to dissuade the speakers. I wondered if she was thinking, like I was, how quickly they'd forgotten. In the middling past most of the older people in this congregation must have been Catholics themselves, before the state had forced their conversion.

The growing danger for the underground Catholic population was writ large on my mind. Mother had told me she intended to attend a secret Mass that evening. As usual, Mistress Clitherow had organised everything, including speaking to a priest about my mother. The Father was scheduled to spend some time with her afterwards. I'd confirmed I'd come along to ensure safe passage but equally I continued to insist I would take no part in the service. Only when I was assured I could wait in a room alongside did I agree to go.

That evening we walked together in silence through the streets of York. We imagined the Sheriff's men hidden in every corner but we saw none before our arrival outside the butchers' shops of The Shambles. Mother knocked lightly on the door and repeated the pass phrase. The Flemish boy Johann welcomed us in. He showed no signs of recognising me from the incident in Gillygate. I'd not been expecting thanks. Holding his candle, he led us nervously down the passageway to the place where I'd waited during our previous visit. A smiling Mistress Clitherow met us there. She told Johann we were the last of the visitors she was expecting that evening and he returned to his post.

I looked about me. There was one difference in the chamber from last time. There were now three doors in the room, rather than two. The third doorway was half the height of the others. Whilst they were wooden, this one appeared to be made from the same stone and mortar as the walls around it. Effectively this section could be detached and pushed back and fore to allow entry and exit. When fully closed it would simply resemble another section of the wall.

Following our hostess, we crouched and squeezed through the small door. On the far side was a narrow corridor illuminated by infrequently positioned candles placed in recesses in the wall. The path led us to the top of a series of sharply sloping downward steps. Thankfully a rope had been fitted, tied to occasional hooks. Where it was dark, or wet and slippery, we used this to guide us. After a little while the steps led up again. At times I had to crouch not to bump my head.

Once on the level we passed through several twists and turns. It appeared the Clitherow's butcher's shop and house couldn't be the only buildings in The Shambles through which the passageway must pass. Although by then I'd lost all sense of direction.

Eventually we came to a solid wooden door, firmly locked from the far side. There was a spy hole, and on our approach, bolts were slid across and the door was opened from within. The room beyond had no shutters and was fairly cramped. I wasn't sure if it was above or below ground. I felt a little fearful about entering such a small space.

At the far end of the room was a makeshift altar with crucifix and candles. Alongside these stood a golden chalice and the paten used by the priest to distribute the Eucharist. On the floor beneath I could see a small silver container with a lid on top. I didn't know what it was then but, in the years to come, I came to learn the pot was called a pyx, and used to carry the Eucharist to people too ill to travel to Mass. With Catholic priests outlawed and unable to hold their services inside an English church, many carried their own pyx. This allowed the priest to hold a Mass anywhere, even in a dark windowless room above or beneath a butcher's shop in York.

As my eyes became more accustomed to the low level of light, I could see the walls were adorned with finery and icons, typical of the Catholic Church. Over the years St-Michael-le-Belfrey had been stripped of such trinkets, in favour of becoming a simpler and more austere place of worship. I wasn't sure which I preferred.

There were a number of other people in the room filling the space, but our body odours were masked by the sweetly sick smell of burning incense. The chamber contained not one but two Catholic priests. The first knelt at the altar. The other, a taller man, had permitted our entry. I felt like I'd met him before but his face was unfamiliar.

The congregation included Margaret Clitherow and her twelve-year old daughter. Like my sister she was also called Anne. Next to them was a local woman I knew to be Mistress Dorothy Vavasour. Apart from Mother there were two others, John and Maria Pulleyn. The headmaster gave me a tight-lipped frown. It couldn't have been a pleasant feeling knowing one of his boys was aware of his darkest secret.

I wondered if he realised how shocked I was to see him there. I'd discounted Kit's claims against him immediately. Not for a moment had I believed Headmaster Pulleyn could be a Catholic. Maria's face maintained a neutral look but I felt warmth in her eyes. These at least smiled at me. Or did I imagine it?

As the others prepared for the service, Mother knelt down and made a silent prayer. I hoped she was thinking of my father. I began to feel awkward. Noting this, Mistress Clitherow came over to me. She smiled and explained I had two options.

I studied her face in the candlelight as she talked. I'd never noticed it before but she had the most extraordinary complexion. Her skin was pale and smooth. There wasn't a scar, pockmark or blemish, and her countenance emanated a kind of platonic love for all those around her. I sensed there was a strange kind of goodness about this woman.

Perhaps the incense was having some sort of effect on me but for a moment I felt as if time and place weren't important. I know it sounds strange. It's difficult to describe in words. Something spiritual was happening, the like of which I'd never experienced before. For a little while I felt quite light-headed.

I forced myself to focus on the words and look at the face in front of me. Mistress Clitherow said I could wait outside in the corridor or, if I wished it, I could remain in the chamber. With a glint in her eye, she urged me to stay. For an instant she had the zeal of conversion about her but she needn't have worried, I'd already decided.

To my shame my initial reaction was physical rather than spiritual. If I left, I couldn't look at Maria but now there was something else too, less earthly, pulling at me to remain. Mistresses Clitherow and Vavasour were delighted by my decision. They introduced me to the pair of priests, Father Ingleby, who would be leading the service and the older taller man, Father Mush, who'd be watching the door.

The Mass commenced. It was made up of two parts, the Liturgy of the Word and the Liturgy of the Eucharist. Although Father Ingleby's cantations and the replies received from the tiny congregation were in Latin, I understood most of what was said from my lessons at school. The Father faced away from the others. Everyone, including he, looked towards the altar. There was a genuine passion in his voice.

Despite my long-held conviction against Catholicism I found myself being drawn into the moment. Perhaps the strange language, the tiny space, the shadow of the candles and most of all the smell of the burning incense created a theatre and spectacle. The Mass felt more heartfelt than any service I'd attended at our own parish church. I closed my eyes and bathed in the Godliness of it all.

As we reached the part where the priest would bless those present with the body and blood of our Lord Jesus Christ there was an urgent knock on the door. Father Mush hadn't been paying attention to the spy hole but now he jumped up and looked through it. We all held our breath. He unbolted the door.

'What is it, Johann? You shouldn't be here,' he said.

The boy looked frightened.

'The Sheriff's men are outside, Father. They're knocking on every door along The Shambles.'

A look of panic ran across all the faces in the room, apart from one. Mistress Clitherow remained a picture of serenity and calm.

'You must all leave now through the escape route,' she said, addressing the room. 'Johann, please go downstairs. Speak to my husband. Tell him if the Sheriff's men are planning a search, he must keep them talking. Just for a few minutes, until I come down. I'll be along shortly.'

She turned back to the rest of us. 'Now we must all depart this room and close the door quickly, so no incense escapes. Father Mush, what will you do?'

'I'll remain here and pray for everyone's safe passage, my good lady.'

He began blowing out the candles. Mistress Clitherow ushered the rest of us through the door. Johann had already left. We proceeded along the passageway with Father Ingleby at the rear, extinguishing the remaining candles as he passed them.

When we reached the room with the three doors, Mistress Clitherow addressed us again. 'Father Ingleby will take you from here. Headmaster Pulleyn, please keep a count of everybody and make sure nobody gets left behind. Once beyond the buildings of the Butchers' Guild, I recommend you split into groups and move away in opposite directions. God speed and the Lord bless you all.'

As she spoke, Father Ingleby manoeuvred the secret door back into place. I knew it was there but otherwise, particularly in the gloom, it would have been almost impossible to see where the doorway began and the wall ended. However, I'd heard about the pursuivants. The most professional of them would find it in no time, and the darkened corridor would lead them directly to the place where Father Mush was hiding.

Mistress Clitherow left us then. She stepped through the doorway towards the front passage. The good lady went off to see her husband, ready for a potential confrontation with the Sheriff's men. Her daughter Anne followed. Headmaster Pulleyn wedged the door shut. The rest of the party exited via the third door at the back. We closed this, leaving the chamber in darkness. There was still fear but no longer panic. Mistress Clitherow had seen to that.

After a while Father Ingleby stopped. He began carefully running his fingers along the base of the wall, until he found something and opened a second secret passageway. We descended another flight of narrow stone steps. At the bottom we had to crouch down to move forward. Following Father Ingleby's candle we proceeded in single file. At times we were almost crawling, and I was worried about the state of the women's clothing but before long we reached a gentle slope upwards. Nobody said a word.

At the end there was a ladder. Once we'd gathered together, the father pointed skywards. He blew out the candle and began to climb. Next went Maria and then Mother. There were only eight rungs. I counted them as I ascended. After that I felt a rush of fresh air on my face.

This was clever. We emerged into the open through a grating which appeared to be an entrance to a drain. Our exit point was positioned directly beneath a tarpaulin covering a stall where links of sausages and faggots would be sold in the daytime. The surface of the grating was slightly raised so rainfall couldn't naturally run down it. I wondered how many of the street's butchers realised where the shaft and passage led. Perhaps none of the others knew. Perhaps they all did.

Once we'd climbed out, we crouched low to the ground and listened. If the Sheriff's men were searching the area at the back of The Shambles, they couldn't have failed to hear the noise we'd made when we scrambled out. However, everything appeared to be quiet. After a few minutes of waiting and listening it was agreed we should leave. Father Ingleby and Mistress Vavasour whispered their goodbyes. They went one way. The rest of us went the other.

Beyond the first lines of meat market stalls I made out the dark shape of the Butchers' Guild Hall. After this would be Parliament Street. We had no wish to go there. In the wide open spaces we'd be too easily seen. To get home to Stonegate, and for the Pulleyns to safely return to St Peter's, we needed to head north and then make our way eastward. Thankfully the hours of hide and seek of my childhood stood me in good stead. After a few whispered words with Headmaster Pulleyn, it was agreed I would lead the way.

Our first challenge was to cross the narrow streets of The Little Shambles and Newgate without being spotted. We weaved our way through the animal stalls by feel more than anything, until we reached the point where we could cross the first street. We stopped and stood in a soundless row of people with me at the front.

I felt my heart beating. I took a risk and peeped out. A man was standing guard, barely a few yards away from me, where The Little Shambles met its longer namesake. The fellow held aloft a lamp but thank the Lord the light didn't carry. I retracted my head quickly and took a silent breath.

For a moment I was bewildered, but then I pushed the others back a few yards, and whispered my plan. Thankfully we all wore shoes or boots with soft leather soles, to minimise the noise of our footfall on the cobbles. I tip-toed to the turning, stepped out into the road and kept walking. The others were ready to run. I expected to be challenged, but after three or four steps I'd already crossed to the other side.

I couldn't signal to the others. The night was as black as pitch and we couldn't see each other. Thankfully the guard hadn't spotted me. Mother finished counting to twenty and followed my lead. After her Maria did the same. Once again, I felt a thrill run through my body as she approached and held onto my hand. Finally, the headmaster joined us, and we continued.

If I remembered rightly there was a good hiding place near a backyard around the corner, and after that an alleyway which would lead on into Newgate. We edged forward in a chain, each gripping another. There was myself, disappointingly Mother next to me and then came Maria. Old Man Pulleyn lurked in the final position.

A dog barked, waking a few hens which clucked loudly at us. To my mind the noise sounded like a host of buglers trumpeting for attention. I imagined the pursuivants appearing all around us and worried what might happen to Maria. A terrible rage rushed through my body, but the animals soon quietened down and appeared to go back to sleep. When we reached Newgate, there was nobody there. We crossed the street using the same method as before.

There were two ways we could get past St Sampson's Church. We halted for a moment. I pondered which would be better. The small snicket behind the building had some advantages but it came out onto the corner of St Sampson's Square, near to where the Thursday market was held. If the Sheriff had men stationed there, we'd be trapped. The other way led past the orchard along Patrick Pool. This was the route I decided to take.

We carried on, treading carefully. Most of the city was asleep. Only rats, pursuivants and those who sought to avoid them would be about at this time of night. Loud shouting rose up behind us, penetrating the silence. All four of our party stopped at once. The urgent calls weren't far way. Something was happening. Either the Sheriff's men were onto us, or they were after someone else. I thought of poor Mistress Vavasour. We'd left her alone with a Catholic priest. My heart sank.

As I listened, more dogs began to bark. What if they had mastiffs? What if they unleashed them? What if they found us? They'd be onto us in no time. For a moment dread ripped through my stomach, until I realised I had a job to do. Although we'd make more noise, we had no choice. I whispered 'Run!' and we all ran, as if it our lives depended on it. I think they did.

The chain fractured almost immediately in the darkness. When I gripped onto a hand again, I knew it was Maria's. Her fingers clasped mine. I vowed to keep her safe. She was my responsibility now, like

Mother and the girls. I hadn't forgotten about my family. We slowed for a moment, until Mother caught up with us. I gripped her hand with my own and led them both on. The headmaster can look after himself, I thought, but almost immediately I relented and waited until we heard his footsteps behind us. When he reached our position, I urged everyone on.

As we flew across Church Street, I was surprised to see candlelight shining from inside St Sampson's. Who would be there at this time of night? The parish parson or the Sheriff's men? I didn't care. I wouldn't let them catch us. We passed through the orange glow and dipped into the shadows of the night. When we reached the start of Swinegate the bells had begun to strike loudly for midnight. Maria's fingers caressed mine. Disaster loomed but I'd never felt so alive.

I wondered what was happening behind us. When we reached a small ginnel, I pulled the group to a halt. Maria held my hand. I listened to Mother's breathing. It was only a little heavier than usual but Headmaster Pulleyn was struggling, panting for breath. It would be good to give the old man a rest. We stood in the darkness and listened. There was clearly a commotion going on, but it was now further off. We heard loud calls and shouts of joy and triumph. It appeared the seekers weren't after us after all but we couldn't take any chances, we had to get home. I led the others forward again, a little slower and quieter this time.

The most obvious route would be to work our way around Little Stonegate, but I shook my head in the darkness. If I led the pursuivants, I'd position a man at the far end to prevent any access into the larger street. With two of the most important people in my world behind me, I had no wish to take unnecessary risks. It would be safer if we continued on through the back ways, even if this led us past places I'd rather avoid.

Once the headmaster's breathing recovered, we recreated the chain and set off. Ignoring the turning into Little Stonegate, I led the way as we entered one of the smaller alleys. We'd only gone a few yards when I thought I heard a noise in the darkness beyond. I signalled for the others to stop, disengaged my hand from Maria's and crept forward. The shouting behind us was quieter now. I could hear the wind and my own breath. If I led the pursuivants I wouldn't use men with lamps. I'd hide them in the blackness, in a spot like this. I wouldn't shout. I'd strike with decisive force. And face questions later, if anyone was left to ask them.

I heard the sound again. And a half-footstep, which I thought must be human. Someone was out there. Heavy breathing. A movement of clothing. A sword unsheathing, or a hitching of skirts? I sensed danger. I thought of Maria, and worried I'd failed her.

The wind blew again. The moon shone, and I saw their faces. There were two of them, crouched low in a covered porch. One looked aggressively happy, the other despondent and accepting of its fate. When they saw me, the first face changed to anger. The second remained the same, acquiescing and consenting to what was happening to the body beneath. I hoped she was drunk.

'Shard off, sonny, unless you've got money and you're prepared to wait.'

Seeing no threat, the man twisted his neck away from me and carried on rutting the blank-eyed woman. I knew he wasn't a customer. I'd seen the man before. Grope Lane wasn't far from our house. He was one of the men who "protected" the women who worked there and took money from them. It appeared that wasn't all they took. I was disgusted.

The cloud cover moved, until thankfully our mutual invisibility reappeared. I returned to my companions and said it was safe. We passed by the porch quickly. I heard the noise the man and the whore were making and hoped the others didn't understand. Making our way around two more corners we entered a straight alley. I was on my home turf now. The next turning would take us directly into Stonegate, barely a few yards from our house.

For some reason, these days I know it to be fate, I've always had a fear of failing at the last moment. More than once Robert Catesby has called it my terror of turning victory into defeat. I felt it then, as we entered Stonegate. I was confident the Sheriff's men would be out there waiting for us but there was nowhere else to go. We'd be arrested, beaten and tortured. I'd never see Maria, Mother or my sisters again.

Sure enough, as Mother turned the key to unlock our front door, a hand fell onto my shoulder. I felt numb. Closing my eyes, I said, 'Please God, no!' but no sound came out.

Headmaster Pulleyn spoke to me. 'I must thank you, Master Fawkes, for without you I'm not sure we would have made it this far.' He was stood right in front of me.

'Shhh!' Mother whispered. 'Headmaster, you must come in. Your kinswoman and yourself can stay the night and leave first thing in the morning.'

'I thank you good lady, but no,' he replied softly. 'We must return to the school. I have an arrangement with one of the men on the gate at

Bootham Bar. We will travel through unhindered. I bid you both a good night and a safe one hence forth.'

Stood there in the total darkness we couldn't see each other's faces but I realised I was still holding Maria's hand. I turned slowly towards her. Silently in the blackness she kissed me softly on the lips. It was over in an instant. I wanted to kiss her back and hold her body against mine but it was not to be. Mother pulled me inside and Maria's cousin dragged her away. I was safe but I didn't sleep a wink that night. I lay awake, worrying and thinking youthful thoughts about Maria.

# 7

**Monday February 21st, 1586**

I walked to school the next morning, troubled but somehow exhilarated by the events of the evening before. With an effort I shook off the sense of foreboding from not being certain Maria was safe. When I arrived in the dining hall, Kit and Rob were talking happily to the other boys at our table. I slotted myself in between them and took my usual place.

Headmaster Pulleyn appeared in the doorway. I breathed a sigh of relief. If he was unscathed, surely Maria was too. The morning prayers were shorter than normal. Not once did he mention the ancientness of the school, or how fortunate we were to be there. I wondered if any of the others noticed how tired and haggard the old man looked.

Without saying so, he hinted, as he often did, about the wrongdoing of Catholics. For the first time I began to realise how clever he was. Headmaster Pulleyn never outwardly accused the Catholics of anything. He simply mouthed a few sentences which could easily be misconstrued. We boys and any visitors would be left to read between the lines and jump to our own vicious conclusions.

After the early meal we retired to our classrooms for scripture hour. This was one of the times when we didn't need any teaching. A number of passages of the Bible would be listed on the wall, and the boys left to their own devices to quietly read them. We'd be tested on the contents later.

A few minutes into the session I was called into Headmaster Pulleyn's office. As I stood up and walked through the classroom, Thomas Cheke smiled at me. He went through the motions of giving a birching with his hands. Kit raised his fingers at him. Rob looked morose, clearly believing I was in for another beating.

Old Man Pulleyn ushered me into his office. We sat down on wooden seats on the opposite sides of his desk. I felt quite alone. He looked at me, as if assessing the depth of my character. There was little doubt now I'd been wrong about him. Instead of being hellbent on rooting out Catholics he was one himself, just like his predecessor, only better at hiding it.

'Good morning, Master Fawkes,' he said in a quiet tone.

The headmaster looked greater than his years, which I thought must be about fifty. I had to admit though I could have been wrong. I wasn't proficient at judging men's ages.

'Good morning, sir,' I replied.

'I must thank you again for your actions yesterday,' he whispered. 'My kinswoman and I may have not returned safely to St Peter's were it not for your assistance. We're both grateful.'

God be praised! Maria was safe. I thought of Mistress Clitherow and Father Mush. Perhaps their prayers for our safe passage had been answered.

'You know my secret now. And I know yours. But it would be better for us both if we never speak of these events again. However, I have news.'

The lines on his face appeared even more grey.

'Father Ingleby was arrested last night, not too far from where we split up. This must have been the excitement we heard behind us. I know about this thanks to Mistress Vavasour. She tells me the Sheriff's men spotted them both, but when their capture seemed inevitable, Father Ingleby ran noisily and quickly away from her. The pursuivants gave chase and she, thank the Lord, managed to slip away to her own house.'

'What about the others?' I asked.

'I've heard nothing more. I assume Mistress Clitherow and Father Mush are safe. At least for now…'

I understood the inference. Father Ingleby would be tortured, leaving the rest of us in a precarious position. A few stray words from the priest and we'd be transported to York Castle, Mother and Maria included. What a mess we'd got ourselves into.

'When you go home tonight, you must tell your mother about this but never speak of it again. If Father Ingleby does talk, there's nothing we can do, but knowing the man as long as I have, I think he'll hold out.'

The headmaster looked at the door, as if wishing he could escape through it.

'I also wanted to let you know I'll be visiting The Shambles this afternoon to place an order for beef. When I get there, I hope to speak to Mistress Clitherow alone. If I can, I'll recommend she holds no further Masses and harbours no priests, at least until things have quietened down. With her record of recusancy she's certain to be one of the Sheriff's main suspects. I imagine the only thing keeping her out of jail at the moment is her family relationship with the new Lord Mayor. In the same vein, my guidance to the Widow Fawkes and yourself is to stick to the Sunday service at St Michael le Belfrey for the foreseeable future.'

That would suit me, I thought.

'Now, Fawkes, get back to your lessons,' he instructed in something more akin to his usual voice.

When I left Headteacher Pulleyn's office the place was strangely quiet. I glanced along the corridor but there was nobody else about. The older boys and younger ones would be studying scripture for another hour at least. Teacher Robinson was with them, and before I'd even taken my leave, the headmaster had buried his head inside a ledger. The teacher would think I was with the headmaster and vice versa, whilst the rest of the school would be largely unoccupied apart from the servants, including Maria, and me.

I'd already decided I must see Maria that day, if only to behold her from a distance. Most likely she'd be in the kitchen, washing up our breakfast bowls or beginning preparations for the midday meal. As I walked along the passageway, a door opened. I held my breath but was disappointed to see the servant who manned the gates. Despite his lack of social standing the fellow sneered at me. He clearly didn't like associating with the boys, apart from seeing us beaten.

'Shouldn't you be in lessons?' he snapped.

'Shouldn't you stop stealing from the school?' I retorted.

His reddening face told me my instincts had been correct. Now I had a hold over him.

'I won't tell anyone,' I said. 'But you'd better ensure the gates don't close so quickly in the mornings from now on, at least while I'm about.'

With this, I left the man behind, his mouth gaping open. He watched my back as I walked away. I smiled, and decided it was going be a good day after all. With the threat of arrest still looming over me, I no longer worried about more mundane matters. At that moment I was pleased to find some adventure, and the awful feeling of dread was gone.

I pushed open the kitchen door, and saw Maria at one side of the room, adjacent to two middle aged men. Each held a bucket for cleaning pots. She was the only one who noticed me. I stepped back outside and heard her say she needed to change her water. Without hesitation, I headed off towards the pump, and slipped into the shadows behind a thick holly bush.

'Master Fawkes?' she said, although I didn't think she could see me.

'My name is Guy,' I replied. It was the first time we'd really talked.

'Why are you out of class?'

'Because I wish to be. There are many things I can do, if I put my mind to it.'

'Yes, I noticed that last night,' she said.

We both smiled. She began emptying the bucket into the spoil heap.

'I have feelings for you,' I said.

It wasn't a great thing to say but at least it was the truth. We might not have much time.

'You speak to the point.'

'You kissed me.'

'You may have saved my life. I thought it was the right thing to do.'

'As did I,' I said.

'The kiss or saving me?'

Talking to girls was trickier than I'd imagined.

'Both,' I replied.

Maria laughed, then looked at me with those dark brown eyes. I was still hiding behind the holly bush but, from where she stood now, she could clearly see me. She bent forward, ready to prime the pump.

A few wisps of light brown hair fell from the front of her coif. For a second I closed my eyes. I wanted to remember how she looked at that moment. Despite everything that's happened down the years, that's how I sometimes remember Maria.

'My distant cousin tells me I mustn't talk about what happened last night. He says I must stay away from the boys, especially you and your friends, Wright and Middleton.'

'I understand staying away from me but why them?' I asked in surprise.

'Don't you know how dangerous it is to be caught in the company of a Roman Catholic in York?'

So, Rob Middleton was one too. I wondered if Headmaster Pulleyn and the boys had ever spoken about this or met to discuss their religious beliefs. Perhaps they'd even accompanied him to Mass, as

Maria had.

'Do you think I should do what the headmaster tells me?' she asked. Her bucket was half full.

'Yes, about the others,' I said. 'But not about me. I'm special.'

'How so? Will your name be remembered down the years?'

'I doubt it.' I laughed. 'I'm special, but only for you. I don't care if anybody else in the world knows my name, as long as you do.'

'Then, I'll give you a special name,' she said. 'One that only I will know about. It will be our secret.'

'Can I use it if I get into trouble?'

'Certainly,' she smiled. 'From now on, your name is John Johnson and you hail from Netherdale. What do you think of that?'

'Splendid,' I said. 'Perhaps one day I'll call you Mrs Johnson.'

Maria laughed. 'You're incorrigible. Let's not rush into things. We've only just met.' But then she hesitated for a moment. 'Perhaps in time,' she whispered, as if to herself.

I'd blurted out the question without even thinking, but Maria's answer was better that anything I could ever have imagined or wished for. She stood up, until her back was straight once more. The bucket was full. I stared into her lovely face. Maria's eyes fixed onto mine.

'Things are difficult now,' she said, 'but one day, perhaps, we could to get to know each other properly. Would this please you?'

'More than anything,' I said.

'Then we must be patient, John Johnson. I have to return to the kitchen now and you to your lessons. But first…'

She glanced around, but we both knew we were alone. The garden was empty. She carefully placed the pail on the grass and took a step towards me. Her body seemed to float past the bush and when her lips brushed mine, I was in heaven. I closed my eyes. She pulled me towards her, and our bodies touched. She was warm to hold, firm and lovely. I kissed her with a passion I'd never known before. Every nerve tingled.

After a few moments, which seemed to last like hours, Maria gently pushed my aching body away from her. I reopened my eyes. The love of my life smiled, and for a moment I was permitted to caress her hands. She kissed me gently on the lips once more, skipped past the holly, raised the bucket and was gone. Who would have thought paradise could be found in the grounds of St Peter's?

I felt like I'd died and gone to heaven. Soon enough, Soon enough.

The pain sears through my body. At first, I hear, and then I feel the turn of the screw. The torturers demand I must tell them my name, where I hail from, and my motives.

I say the same words I told their Scots king.

'My name is John Johnson. I hail from Netherdale in Yorkshire. I wanted to blow those Scotch beggars back to their native mountains.'

They don't believe me. I scream and pass out.

## Tuesday March 1st, 1586

During the next week I constantly thought of Maria. At home I was distracted, but not too distracted to notice Mother had become subdued again. We didn't discuss anything of any worth. I put her melancholy down to the fact she'd missed her priestly advice. Like me, Mother focused mostly on menial things, the day to day tasks which had to be done. Anne noticed the tension rising up between us but she didn't press. In fact, she too said little about anything. Looking back, I wished I'd spent more time helping them both. Luckily little Lizzie acted like younger children do. She was oblivious to everything but the moment. Domestic life in the Fawkes household went on.

During the long hours at St Peter's I tried to study but found concentration increasingly difficult. Teacher Robinson would say something, and I'd realise I'd lost all track of time, and had no idea of what was going on. More than once he admonished me for staring blankly through the gaps in the shuttered windows. I lost all interest in my schoolwork. They say falling in love does this to boys. Perhaps it will have the same effect on girls, if ever they're educated.

I glimpsed Maria once or twice in the distance as she went about her business in the school grounds. I constantly watched out for her, hoping for any chance to see her walk towards the walled garden to pick herbs, or carry a pail to fill or empty, but we hadn't spoken since our second kiss. I didn't care. My heart filled with hope, and I was ready to wait for the right time, as she suggested.

Whilst academic learning was a challenge for me, I gained a new-found confidence in sporting endeavours. I threw the javelin further than ever before. I even looked forward to practicing swordsmanship and was pleased when our physical exercise lesson was brought forward a day.

Teacher Robinson was instructing the younger lads. He left the older boys unsupervised for a few minutes as we prepared for our training and practice bouts. As we stood in the corner of our dressing area, Kit confided in me. 'My parents came to visit me on Sunday,' he said softly. 'They instructed me to keep a low profile, and not to go anywhere near Thomas Cheke. Ma says it's no time for lads like me to be challenging boys with powerful fathers. And they told me another thing,' he added conspiratorially. 'Pa believes Lord Mayor Maye's policies are not of his own making.'

'How so?' I asked.

'Pa thinks he's doing the bidding of the Council of the North. They're seeking to make life difficult for immigrants, so some will go home, and they plan to persecute Catholics in the vain hope we'll repent and convert to their own religion.'

'But why?'

'Because York Corporation and the Council both wish to gain favour and finance from the Queen. My brother Jack says picking on foreigners and Catholics is a good way to do this, for she fears the threat they place on her throne.'

I mused for a moment, not quite comprehending what it all meant. I didn't understand politics.

I'd only just ceased being concerned I'd be arrested. Surely if Father Ingleby was going to talk, he would have done so by now. My only obsession was Maria.

At that moment Thomas Cheke began loudly boasting to his friends that his father was having relations with a serving girl at the King's Manor. The father had promised his son he could 'take a turn on her' after Lent. I knew Thomas's mother had died when he was young. His father had remarried but neither father nor son appeared to respect the new bride. I felt sympathy for the woman, though I'd never met her.

Headmaster Pulleyn returned to the fencing area. Teacher Robinson stood across the way, waving his arms to demonstrate a new move to the younger lads. The old man tasked our group to work on parrying and defensive exercises, something which many of the boys didn't like. Most wanted to get on with the fighting. After half an hour we were given time to rest and apple juice was shared around from a cask. The headmaster left us and went off to watch the younger boys for a while.

'Have you seen that new serving wench in the kitchen?'

I turned my head sharply to see Francis Gayle speaking to Will Craven.

Before Craven could answer, Thomas Cheke interjected. 'Aye, I've seen her. She's a bit of alright.'

'Out of bounds, though,' said Gayle. 'I hear she's related to Old Man Pulleyn.'

'That's a pity,' said Craven.

'Nonsense!' Cheke laughed. 'No woman's out of bounds for me. I'll have her before Easter - you wait and see.'

Instinctively my hands gripped into fists. Knowing my feelings for Maria, Kit placed a restraining hand on my arm but it was too late. Cheke had seen my reaction and turned tauntingly towards me.

'What's wrong, copper top, you fancy a go on her too, do you? That's a pity,' he sneered. 'I don't think she'd want it from someone with a permanently sore arse.'

Gayle laughed. Craven snorted. I took a deep breath and tried to ignore them, but all I could think of was knocking Cheke's head off his shoulders. Completing my schooling meant a great deal to my family, and would open doors for my future, a future which I'd started to believe could include Maria. So much so, these days when I dreamed of leaving the house in Clifton to work at Minster Yard, she was the wife in the doorway waving me goodbye. I said nothing. I had to control myself.

'Never mind,' said Cheke. 'I didn't think you had the bollocks to stand up to me. And without those you'll be no good to her anyway. Don't worry though, she's going to want what I'm going to give her. When I'm finished, she'll probably beg me to do it all over again.'

He stood up and started making thrusting actions with his body. I took a step towards him but before I could do anything, we were interrupted by Headmaster Pulleyn, the old man oblivious to what was going on.

'It appears Master Cheke is ready for action,' he said. 'That's good but he'll need to keep his body straighter than that. Today's session is all about improvement. I want the more accomplished boys to practice defence and those with more work to do to focus on their attacking skills. We'll start with Masters Wright and Middleton. Robert, you must attack Christopher. And Christopher, you must defend. Offensive actions are not allowed from you. Do you understand?'

Both boys nodded.

For some minutes, Rob threw everything he had at Kit but got nowhere. Kit was an accomplished swordsman and Rob lacked aggression and the will to win. It was a hopeless mismatch. Kit looked bored but stuck manfully to his instructions, until eventually Headmaster Pulleyn called a halt to their proceedings.

'Perhaps, Master Middleton, your calling is elsewhere. What do you think boys?'

There was general laughter. Even Rob grinned. He was under no illusions about his fighting prowess. He and Kit placed their swords onto the wooden rack, shook hands and pulled their cloaks around their shoulders to prevent them from catching a chill.

'Right, who's next?'

When Cheke raised his arm, I did so too. Craven and Gayle rubbed their hands in anticipation. Rob closed his eyes. Even Kit looked worried. Out of the corner of my eye, I looked at Thomas Cheke. He was licking his lips with glee.

A thoughtful expression crossed Headmaster Pulleyn's face, as if he was considering whether this was a good idea. Clearly it wasn't, but then he hadn't heard what had been said about his young female cousin. And hopefully he had no idea how strongly I felt about her. The headmaster's only concern was whether any residual bad feeling remained from the scuffle in the street, because this time we had swords. Blunted or not, we had the ability to do real harm to each other.

'Do you understand the rules, boys?' he asked.

Cheke nodded. I did the same.

'Vey well, but there'll be no nonsense. Do you understand? Swordsmanship is an honourable vocation and there'll be no silliness from either of you when you hold your blades. Do you give your word as gentlemen?'

We nodded again.

'Good, then please prepare.'

Cheke retreated to choose his weapon, surrounded by Gayle, Craven and one or two others. I did the same on the opposite corner of the grass, accompanied by Kit and Rob. Kit, the master swordsman, offered me instructions. Do this. Don't do that. Watch out for the other thing. I didn't hear any of it. Rob seemed to be praying.

With our weapons selected, we stepped into the middle of the square. By this time the younger boys had finished their exercises and came over to observe us. We were now surrounded by almost every lad in the school. My heart pounded, and the iron sword felt heavy in my hand. Thomas Cheke lifted his.

'So, boys, it's the same instructions I gave to Masters Wright and Middleton. Master Cheke, you are to parry only. Master Fawkes, you will be allowed to attack but no blood is to be shed. One, two, three! You may begin.'

I lifted my sword and charged forward, madly swinging my blade at Thomas Cheke's body. He grinned, and shifted his weight, creating a good angle to block me. My attack was easily deflected. It all seemed so simple. Although I gripped the hilt of my sword with both hands, with one clink the weapon was thrown sideways and my wrists sprained as they turned over.

The blade hit the turf and my body was placed at Thomas Cheke's mercy. But to my surprise, he obediently followed the rules. He nodded courteously towards me and stepped back into his own starting position. I was confused, but when Old Man Pulleyn looked away, Cheke winked and goaded me to try again.

I knew I had to do it but the result was much the same. A few of the younger boys began laughing at me. I picked up my weapon, took a deep breath and thought they were right to do so. Thomas Cheke hadn't made a fool of me. I was doing that myself.

The next time we stepped apart, I nodded politely and remembered what Jack Wright had once told me - skill overcomes rage, a gentleman should always use his blade in a controlled manner. I'd made things too easy for Cheke by venting my fury at him, but we weren't finished yet.

From that moment on my assaults became more measured. I challenged his defences again and again. The boys stopped laughing. The sneery grin departed from my opponent's face, replaced by perspiration and sometimes apprehension. My attacks became relentless and brutal, but always controlled.

But still he held me off, until one last time I got through to him. Damn Old Man Pulleyn, I thought, if I have this opportunity to hurt Cheke, I will. I surged forward, but at the last moment Cheke pushed me off, and I sank to my knees. As we stepped apart for the umpteenth time, I had to admit to myself Thomas Cheke was too good a swordsman. The boy battled with his head and his body, but not with his emotions. Even when I'd calmed down and attempted to do the same, I couldn't beat him. Headmaster Pulleyn finally called a halt to our bout. As I lifted the sword, my arms were as heavy as lead, and I was mentally and physically exhausted.

We slotted our swords into the racks. Everybody clapped. The bout had been ferocious but skilled. We each stepped back to the middle to shake each other's hands. We bowed. I'd not beaten him, but I felt I'd earned the Parliamentarian's son's respect.

We lowered our heads. He spoke softly into my ear, 'Now I know you can't stop me; I'll shag your mother and sisters too. From on top and behind. What do you think of that?'

Some nights in my dreams and in my nightmares, I still see that ratty sneer on his face, and remember my voice roar with anger. My fatigue was forgotten. I threw myself at him. When my shoulder hit his, he had no sword in his hand to block or parry me. His body fell to the ground with a thud. I followed and forced his chin up and began punching him.

I didn't stop. He tried to defend himself, but he couldn't. I wouldn't let him.

Kit told me later the headmaster and teacher were screaming at me, but I didn't hear them. I was focused only on one thing, hurting Thomas Cheke. If I achieved nothing else that Tuesday in March, I achieved that.

I'm not sure if he was conscious or not when they finally pulled me off him. I've killed many men since but this was the first time I had a glimpse of what a man's really capable of, a man like me. I'd have killed Cheke with my bare hands if they'd let me, but of course they didn't. Eventually they dragged me away.

Still swinging wildly, one of my fists struck out and hit Teacher Robinson in the ear, bloodying his neck. He responded by punching me hard in the face several times. Although his blows were brutal, I couldn't blame him. It was he who gave me the black eye, not Thomas Cheke. He didn't lay a finger on me. I was the master of that fight.

Removed to the headmaster's study, I was birched and lectured. Old Man Pulleyn's eyes bulged from his face as he raged at me. Every word he said was as you'd expect. What else could he do? He'd have to explain to a Member of Parliament and the Council of North how his son had been beaten to a pulp in front of the school. There was a serious risk he'd be investigated. And what would they find if they dug too deeply?

With a closing eye and a stinging arse, I staggered home. I knew my school days were probably behind me. Despite the life-changing consequences, I felt blissfully happy. I'd taken on St Peter's biggest bully and won. Every boy in the school had witnessed his comeuppance. Many who watched those events would have been only too pleased at Thomas's Cheke's defeat. But then it struck me. Maria! After seeing what I'd done to Cheke, Headmaster Pulleyn would never let me go anywhere near her again. I was devastated.

# 8

The first person I met in our house in Stonegate was my sister Anne, sewing in the parlour. She looked at me quizzically. I wasn't usually home in the afternoon. When she saw the bruising forming around my eye, she set down her needlework, got up and rushed towards me, concern writ large across her face.

'What happened?'

'I got into a fight with one of the boys at school,' I replied. 'I've been sent home in disgrace.'

She was already dampening a cloth in water to douse my face. Although two years younger than me, Anne was always more practical. She pushed me down onto the seat where she'd been sitting only a few moments before and began to clean the grass, blood and tears from my cheeks and eyes. I'd not cried during the fight, or when I was punished, but the tears had come quickly enough when I realised I might never see Maria again.

'And he did this to you, this boy?' she asked.

'No, that was Teacher Robinson. The boy didn't lay a finger on me,' I replied defiantly, still proud of the achievement of beating up Cheke.

'The teacher did this?'

I nodded.

'And afterwards Headmaster Pulleyn birched me, so be careful how you move me around in this chair.'

'I'll fetch a soft cushion,' she said.

Anne put the rag down and climbed up the stairs. When she returned, she was holding a small piece of sacking filled with duck down. She'd sewed it together herself. I placed it under my buttocks and said it felt better, although in truth the cushion didn't really help. The front door opened and Mother came in, with Lizzie in tow. Thank goodness they were alone.

'Guy!' exclaimed Mother. My eye was now closed. 'Did they catch and beat you?'

'Who are *they*?' asked Anne.

Lizzie stared open-mouthed.

'Nobody,' I replied to my older sister. To our mother I added, 'I'm sorry but there's been another fight in school. The other boy goaded me but I know I'm to blame. I lost my temper and I shouldn't have. I should have turned away, as Kit did, but... I could not. I'm sorry. I don't know what Headmaster Pulleyn will do now.'

'Never mind that,' she said.

When I stood up, she pulled me towards her and hugged me, as if her whole world depended on it. She held me in a way she did with the girls sometimes but hadn't done with me for years. I placed my arms around her and hugged her back for all my worth. My sisters came to us and clasped their arms around us too.

When the tears were over and my face cleaned up, my mother asked the girls to go upstairs and sew for a while in the bed chamber. After they dutifully left us, she sat me down to talk and I explained what had happened. I included the allegation that Cheke had made lewd remarks, although I refused to reveal the exact words he'd used and left Maria out of the story altogether. It was easier that way.

'Oh Guy,' said Mother. 'I worry this is down to the excitement of visiting Mass and our escape afterwards. I've placed the family in danger.'

'No,' I retorted. 'This isn't about that.'

'Isn't it?' she said. 'Isn't it really?'

I thought she'd weep but she forced the tears away and tried to be strong.

'What do you think the Ecclesiastical Court will do?' I asked her. 'Do you think they'll stop funding my education?'

'It depends,' she replied. 'I'll speak to Headmaster Pulleyn. He's a good man, and he owes you for getting him and his cousin away from harm. Even if the Court does have a problem, friends of your father still work there. I'll speak to them. There's one in particular who I'm sure will help.'

Was that a look of concern on Mother's face? If it was, I ignored it. I still felt the shame but Mother's words were beginning to make me feel a little better, and that was what mattered. As always, she put the needs of her family before her own. I understand that now but back then I was a callow youth and still angry about the events of recent weeks.

I think Mother was about to say something but even if she was, she was interrupted by a knock on the door. She didn't wish for anyone to see my face, nor for people to know I wasn't at school, so she scurried me around the corner to hide. She didn't ask the visitor to come in. Peeping through a shutter I saw the grinning face of the school-gate servant. He handed Mother a message and left.

She brought the letter inside. Unlike many women my mother had always been able to read and write. The note was addressed to her and written by Headmaster Pulleyn. Having taken part in a violent incident, I'd been suspended from school, pending investigation until further notice. Mother and I were now requested to attend the headmaster's office in St Peter's at ten bells on Thursday morning to discuss the matter further.

## Thursday March 3<sup>rd</sup>, 1586

Gillygate was bustling with activity that morning. It was some time later than my usual passage and consequently there were many more people around. The yards in front of the tradesmen's workshops were particularly busy. My left eye was now partially reopened but the cheek beneath it was puffed up and the bruising a bright shade of purple.

At the snicket where I'd prevented Cheke and the others from beating up Johann, I saw the most wonderful sight in the world. Maria was standing there, clearly waiting for us. The coif on her head was tightly wrapped and she wore a shawl and scarf but I could see she'd been crying.

'Maria,' said Mother. 'Whatever do you want?'

'I must talk to you both,' she said.

She beckoned for us to follow her further into the ginnel. When we'd rounded the first bend and were out of sight of the road, she halted and began to speak. She informed us that Thomas Cheke's father Henry had been to St Peter's that morning demanding I be arrested and flogged.

Mother gasped. 'How do you know this?' she asked.

'I've never done so before but this morning I listened at the door of my kinsman's office,' admitted Maria.

I thought how pale and beautiful she looked.

'But the headmaster defended you,' she continued, looking at me. 'He said it takes two to start a fight and no boy from the school has ever been arrested. If one was to be, he said, it would bring shame on all the families who had boys there. Henry Cheke changed his tone a little after that but he's obviously been checking up on you. He said he was aware you were sponsored by the Ecclesiastical Court and if the headmaster didn't expel you, he'd do two things.'

'What were they?' I said.

'First, he would go to the office of the Court and tell them everything, so they would stop funding you and push for your expulsion.'

'I'm afraid the headmaster will have to tell them anyway.' I said. 'What was the second thing?'

'Member of Parliament Cheke said he'd make as much trouble for my cousin as he could. He said he'd heard the previous head teacher was arrested for being a Catholic and wondered whether he might be able to find proof Headmaster Pulleyn was the same.'

At the talk of Catholics, Mother faltered for a moment. I stood beside her and took her weight until she recovered herself.

'So, your schooling and future are all but lost, Guy,' Mother said to me. I thought she'd cry but once again she didn't. 'Well, we'll see about that,' she said more firmly.

'No, Mother,' I said. 'There's nothing we can do. Headmaster Pulleyn has no choice but to expel me. Even if he doesn't, the Court will stop funding me. The effect on my schooling will be the same but the repercussions of a wider investigation could be much greater and quite serious for the headmaster and lots of others, including ourselves.'

'Please don't blame him,' pleaded Maria. 'It's not his fault. He wishes to help but there's nothing he can do. Please believe me. I know you're off to see him and I'm worried if Widow Fawkes challenges him strongly his heart will react badly. He's been in a nervous state ever since... well, you know when. And this matter has only made things worse. Be kind to him.'

'We will,' I said. 'Nobody is at fault here, apart from Thomas Cheke and myself. He goaded me into hitting him and I let him do it. The error is mine, not the headmaster's, and I must take responsibility for it. We thank you for giving us forewarning for what is to come. You'd better make haste now and get back to the school.'

'I shall,' she said. 'But I have one more thing to tell you. I'm being sent home to Scotton some time in the next few weeks. My cousin insists it's too dangerous for me to remain in York any longer. I'm to move back to the village to live with my father, until he can find suitable work or a husband for me.'

With these last words my heart sank. I wondered how Maria felt. From the look she shared with me, I believed we felt the same desolation. I assumed Mother was oblivious to our plight.

Maria left us then. I'd expected she'd hurry past us and journey along Gillygate but no, she headed down the ginnel and away from the road. Once she'd turned the corner and was lost from our sight, I realised how badly I wanted to be with her. But the situation was ridiculous. I was a fifteen-year-old schoolboy, and the potential future and security I could have offered her were being taken away. It felt I was losing everything. Damn Thomas Cheke!

After that, the conference with Headmaster Pulleyn was a formality. He did his best to ignore me. For the main part the old man simply took it in turns to inform Mother about his plans and apologise for them.

The headmaster's final words were a warning for us both. The weeks ahead would be dangerous, he explained, lowering his voice. Everyone, particularly those with links to the Catholic faith, should be careful. Such individuals and families would do well to leave York, for the time being at least. More importantly, they should do nothing to antagonise men with influence, men such as Henry Cheke. And by extension his son Thomas. We left the school, for what surely must be the last time, worried and dejected.

To shake off the dark clouds hanging over me I began a long and rambling walk through the streets of York. It was an attempt to clear my head of what had happened over the past few days. I tried to focus on the options for moving forward. If I could identify what these were and consider their strengths and weaknesses, perhaps I could make positive progress. But it was useless. I could only think of Maria and how much I wanted to be with her.

As the late afternoon transitioned into evening, I found myself gazing up at the high prison walls of York Castle. I couldn't recall which way I'd walked to get there but there I was. My mind had been preoccupied. As I looked up at the pale Tadcaster stone, I wondered if Father Ingleby remained imprisoned inside.

There'd been no word from the priest since his arrest almost two weeks before. I took this to mean he hadn't betrayed any details of those who'd protected and prayed with him. But surely by now he must have been tortured. Nobody else connected with the night had been arrested, so he must have held out. I speculated whether I'd be able to do the same in a similar situation. The brave man's fortitude was inspirational.

It was beginning to get dark. I turned and sauntered back towards the central part of the city, and eventually my home. The most direct route passed through The Shambles, and for a moment I remembered the shouts at the time of Father Ingleby's arrest. I considered avoiding the place altogether but kept on walking. Why shouldn't I go that way?

Most of the butchers' shops were shut by this time as I passed through the narrow passageway. One or two helpers were finishing off following the day's trading. They took down the hanging poultry and game birds from outside the doors and swept the straw away from beneath them.

About halfway down the street I saw the boy Johann emerging from one of the side yards. Behind him he dragged an empty trolley. The lad looked tired and frightened. I hoped this was his last job of the day and he'd be able to get some rest inside, away from the evil looks and persecution being whipped up in the city.

When I reached Stonegate, I needed the privy, so I entered via the backyard. All was quiet around us. After washing my hands in a bucket of cleaner cold water, I entered the house via the back door. The bolts weren't yet across. I did so quietly in case Lizzie was in bed. From the other side of the wall I heard a man's voice, talking to my mother.

'You know I'm fond of you, Edith. Always have been. Poor old Bess has been gone a good six months now. A man starts to get lonely when he's left to his own devices. We don't have to get married or anything. I just want to spend a little special time with you. I think you know what I mean. It's nature's way of bringing a man and woman closer together but I won't make you do owt you don't want to.'

Mother said nothing. At this stage I almost burst into the room but I'd been studying the voice as I thought I recognised it. I hesitated for a moment. Before I could move, the voice spoke again.

'And if you and me get together... say at seven tomorrow evening at my place... it'll be nice and quiet... I'll see what I can do in return. You scratch my back and I'll scratch yours, if you know what I mean.'

He paused. I prayed to God Mother hadn't instigated this.

The man continued. 'Next week I'll use my influence at Minster Yard to see if we can get Guy reinstated at St Peter's. How about that? I'll tell the others in the office it's well-known Cheke had it in for him. You say your boy has got a black eye? I'll tell everyone it's a clear sign young Cheke started it. Aye, and if we get any complaints from Cheke's father, I'll speak to him myself. I'll do this for you, Edith, as long as I get what I need in return. And don't worry, you'll enjoy it. I know you will. Why don't we start with a little kiss and a cuddle now?'

I made a loud rustling sound and noisily opened and closed the back door behind me.

'Mother, I'm home,' I called.

I stepped into the main room and recognised the middle aged, balding, pot-bellied man in front of me as Advocate Thomson. He'd risen through the Church's legal ranks alongside my father and was now a senior officer in the Ecclesiastical Court, one of Archbishop Sandys's most trusted advisors. Each year Thomson attended my annual progress review at Minster Yard. Although he'd never uttered a word against me, I'd never liked the man. He stepped somewhat guiltily away from Mother's side as I entered.

'Young Guy,' he said, peering towards me through the fire and candlelight. 'You do have a proper shiner on you. Your mother has been telling me the details of your troubles at school.'

'Good evening to you, sir,' I said rather curtly. 'I do hope I haven't interrupted any important business but… and I trust you don't mind me saying this… isn't it a little improper for you to be alone in this house in the company of a widow? I apologise in advance if I appear to be impertinent but with my father gone, it's my duty to…'

'No need to apologise, lad,' he said. 'I've only just arrived and I believed you'd be here doing your duty as you say, protecting your mother and sisters, who I believe must be in bed upstairs, rather than leaving them all in the house alone to the mercy of strangers. It's a nice house too and Stonegate's a friendly little street but all the same it's none too far from Grope Lane, it it? And we know what goes on there. I beg your pardon for mentioning it, Widow Fawkes.'

I'd entered the conversation a little too aggressively. The legal man was now pushing me back and I struggled to find a suitable retort to what he'd said.

'Never mind all that, though,' added Thomson. 'It's you I've come about. This afternoon the good Widow Fawkes brought your unfortunate situation at St Peter's to the attention of the Ecclesiastical Court. I've been tasked with verifying if there's anything I can do to be of assistance in the matter.'

'Thank you, sir,' I said, pausing for a moment. 'Can you?'

'Can I what?' A little more annoyance began to sneak into his voice. The advocate appeared uncomfortable.

'Assist with my situation at school.'

'Well now, I've got all the details, so I can look into the options,' he replied tersely. 'I can't promise you anything mind. It does appear your headmaster has excellent grounds for expulsion but as I said to your mother, I'll see what I can do. Anyway, I must be off, for it is supper time and my stomach's all a-rumbling. Good day to you, young Master Fawkes, and to you, Edith. Please do consider my proposition, and I hope to see you again very soon.'

Not liking the leer he gave her, I stepped forward and thrusted Advocate Thomson's coat into his hand. Mother said nothing, but I felt there was a look of shame on her face as she glanced at me. I suspected she knew I'd overheard parts of their conversation. The advocate pulled on his coat and donned his hat. Mother opened the door and he left us. When the wind caught and blew it shut, she walked over and slumped into her chair.

'Whatever you heard, it wasn't my idea,' she said wearily. 'Oh Guy, what are we going to do?'

'For one thing, I'm not going to go back to school,' I replied. 'So, if any more weaselly toads like Advocate Thomson slip out from beneath their rocks and creep up to you, you must tell them to shard off.'

'Guy!'

'I'm sorry for my language, Mother, but the man makes my skin crawl.'

'Mine too,' she said sadly. 'But what if he can persuade Headmaster Pulleyn to change his mind? I'll do anything to get you back into St Peter's.'

'No, you won't,' I replied firmly. 'Have you no shame?'

Immediately I regretted the question. It was hurtful and unfair.

'In any case,' I continued, 'the headmaster won't change his mind and, even if he did, Member of Parliament Cheke would only force him to change it back again. No, we must accept things as the way they are. I'm not going to return to school and I won't be studying law. I'll be sixteen next month. I'm old enough to work. I'll find a job.'

'Doing what?'

'I don't know, Mother,' I said, 'but tomorrow I'll begin to look.'

# 9

**Sunday March 6<sup>th</sup>, 1586**

Once again, I accompanied my mother through the dark streets of York towards the Shambles. We knew we were taking a risk but Mother was adamant she must go one last time. It was difficult not to imagine pursuivants hiding in every corner but we saw no sign of the Sheriff or his men. Upon reaching the Clitherows' residence, Mother gave the passcode and Johann showed us in. After slipping through the passageway, I entered the hidden room with little expectation. I had no idea how my life would change that evening.

The congregation was much the same as previously, although there were a few differences. Mistress Clitherow, Mistress Vavasour and another of their circle, Mistress Anne Tesh, knelt and prayed nervously in a line close to the makeshift altar. Behind them kneeled Anne Clitherow, my mother and Maria. Headmaster Pulleyn was nowhere to be seen. I wondered for a moment how Maria had travelled to the house in The Shambles but I didn't really care. She was there, in front of me, and that was all that mattered. The only reason I'd agreed to escort Mother to Mass was the possibility she might be.

I sat alone at the back, slightly away from the others, still wishing to keep myself apart from their service. They had their religion, I thought, and I still had mine. It was the one my father had brought me up to believe in, and despite the effects of the previous Mass, to date I'd seen no compelling reason to deviate from it.

When the Mass began, I rested my eyes. The pinky-white hue of the candles remained in my vision. My nose filled with the aromatic incense. I thought I could even taste it. At first, I didn't realise their impact but Father Mush's words began to move me. After a while I stopped translating the Liturgies in my mind from Latin into English.

The righteous sounds simply flowed through me. It was the calmest and most content I'd felt for a very long time, as long as I could remember. My troubles still existed but I felt cleansed and better able to face them.

By the time the Eucharist began there were tears in my eyes. I didn't hear God's voice in my head, as some people claim, but I believe the Lord reached out to me. I'd never felt so emotional during any Protestant service. Was it possible everyone else was wrong? Queen Elizabeth, her Parliament, the Council, the Corporation and all the bishops? Had my father been deceived? What if this Catholic religion wasn't heresy after all but the true word of our Lord spoken in the language of His choosing?

For the briefest of moments, I thought of Father and all that he'd taught me. I'd always agreed with his views that every man should be able to understand the word of our Lord, and the prayer book should be in English. But wasn't there something mystical and perhaps even wonderful about spoken Latin? Like Thomas, I doubted. I wasn't yet a true Catholic believer but my journey had started.

I can't say much more than that, other than I felt a sort of euphoria. It just happened. There were no blinding lights, no momentary epiphany. I still had questions and concerns, but I felt my life had more purpose. I didn't know what it was then but I was confident in time I would. And so it has turned out.

When the Mass was over, Father Mush smiled at me. He took Mother away to his private room and heard her Confession. I hoped he'd give her wise guidance. Mistress Clitherow and her female friends appeared to be at least partially aware of the effect the service had had on me. One by one, she and the others hugged me. Each gave me a blessing. After this, all three women and the girl Anne left the room, leaving Maria and I alone.

Whether this was a deliberate act or not, I wasn't sure. Maria had prayed continuously since my arrival and her head was bent to the ground throughout the Mass. When she turned to face me, I glimpsed rosary beads in her hand. She stood up and took a few steps towards me.

My mind was a confused tangle of feelings, both physical and spiritual. I didn't think this was the time or place to kiss Maria, although I wanted to. We simply held each other's hands. Maria told me she'd left the school. Headmaster Pulleyn had placed her in the temporary care of Mistress Vavasour until secure passage could be found to transport her back to her family's cottage in Scotton, some twenty miles to the west. It felt more like a thousand.

She placed a note in my hand and made me promise not to read it until I returned home to Stonegate. It was addressed to John Johnson.

'You can write?' I whispered, with surprise in my voice.

'Aye, I can read and write in English, and in Latin, and I'll wager despite all your expensive schooling, I can do so just as well as you. Does this concern you?'

For a moment there was fire in her eyes. I'd not seen this before.

'No,' I replied honestly. 'I'm simply intrigued.'

'I received my education at home in Scotton when the men were out at work. I was taught in the parlour by a local woman, just as your mother was.'

'What do you know of my mother?' Again she surprised me.

'Plenty. Edith Jackson was a Scotton girl, wasn't she?'

I'd never thought about this before. I'd assumed Father had taught Mother about words and numbers. The education of women folk was beyond my sphere of knowledge. I was glad all the same. When Maria was my wife, I wanted her to feel as if she was almost my equal.

I smiled and nodded at her. The candlelight from the altar created a lovely glow around the scarf which covered her hair. How I longed to take it off. But I said nothing. I just stood there, holding her hands, and looking into her eyes. Where the fire had shone a few moments ago, I now only saw love. Very gently we kissed.

Mother reappeared. She seemed less tense. Maria and I quickly stepped apart as Father Mush returned to the altar and began to pray silently. Mistress Clitherow came to the door and beckoned with her hand for us to accompany her back through the passage.

It was a nervous time for all of us but the streets outside appeared empty and Johann gave the all-clear to leave. We whispered our goodbyes in the darkened corridor, and Maria released my hand. Once again, we exited in small groups, this time through the front door, and walked out into the pitch-black night beneath the overhanging eves of The Shambles.

Maria departed in the company of the two older ladies. A few moments later, Mother and I set off in the opposite direction. The short journey to Stonegate went by quickly. All was quiet and we remained uninterrupted. We didn't speak but our minds were busy.

### Thursday March 10th, 1586

Looking for work proved to be more difficult than I imagined. My opportunities were limited due to my lack of skills and social standing. Henry Maye may have risen from humble origins but some professions were beyond me and equally I was much too high born for others. My knowledge of commerce and business was minimal. I knew no trade. Apprenticeships began at a younger age and entry was planned for years in advance.

In her letter, Maria informed me she was leaving for Scotton the very next day. I suspected she hadn't wished to tell me this in person at the Mass for fear of upsetting us both. She added she hadn't known John Johnson for long but she loved him dearly. She'd attempt to persuade her father from forcing her into an arranged marriage, for as long as she could. If John Johnson visited Scotton and asked for her hand, she saw no reason why her father wouldn't agree.

Although we were already some distance apart, Maria's words warmed me inside. She loved John Johnson. And he loved her. I'd been equally surprised the previous evening, when Mother announced she'd written to an old friend in Scotton, to ask if it was possible to find temporary accommodation there. Who knows, she said, I might even be able to find work in the area.

The timing of this news excited me greatly. I wondered how much Mother suspected about my feelings for Maria. I hoped it wasn't obvious. My anxieties were eased a little when Mother admitted her correspondence was prompted by the advice she'd received from Father Mush. Echoing the words of Headmaster Pulleyn, the priest had warned York was a dangerous place for all those with ties to the Catholic faith.

Whilst Mother waited for a reply to her letter, we attempted to go about our business as normal, although it wasn't quite normal, as I wasn't in school. She decided to buy a little meat from one of the butcher's shops in The Shambles. With little else to do, I accompanied her on the errand, whilst Anne and Lizzie remained at home by the window mending the bedsheets.

Not long after we'd left the house, we were interrupted by a gossiping neighbour. The old woman asked where we were headed. When Mother told her we were off to The Shambles, the goodwife was delighted. 'Have you heard about the butcher, John Clitherow?' she asked. 'I think I've seen you conversing with him outside the church on a Sunday morning.'

'What about him?' asked Mother, looking worried.

'I heard this morning he's been called to appear in front of the Council of the North. It must be about his wife. You know, the recusant. I've been sworn to secrecy but between you and me I've heard she's sent her lad abroad to join a foreign church. Whatever will these Catholics do next?'

Mother looked at me with alarm on her face. If the Council knew about Henry's illegal journey to France, Margaret and John Clitherow would both be in trouble. Margaret's recusancy was common knowledge. A few citizens felt sympathy for the time she'd spent in prison but most couldn't understand why a woman would devote more time to a church than the needs of her husband and children.

The old lady glanced a sly look up and down the street, before whispering conspiratorially into Mother's ear, although the words were loud enough for me to hear what was said. 'There's more. I've heard rumours. Mistress Clitherow's Catholic ways have progressed far beyond skipping the Sunday service. My friend Maggs tells me she's heard tell the woman keeps a Jesuit priest in her house, and invites her friends to hear him give Mass. What do you think about that then, Widow Fawkes? I'll wager you'll be buying your offal from another butcher from now on?'

The woman took a step back, looking pleased with herself. Mother suppressed a shudder. What this woman described was illegal and punishable by death, and worse, we both knew Mistress Clitherow was guilty.

'You hear so many things these days,' said Mother flatly. 'I don't believe the half of it. Both John and Margaret Clitherow have always priced their meat fairly. I see no reason not to continue giving them my business.'

'No, no, you're right of course,' said the woman. 'Although you can't be too careful these days, can you?' There was still an edge to her voice. 'You don't want to be upsetting the new Lord Mayor by being too pally with any of those immigrant types either. Maggs says the Clitherows keep a whole host of them and pay them seed money to run their house and deliver the meat. Cheap labour, my husband calls it. Anyway, I need to be off now. It's been nice chatting with you. Have a good day, won't you?'

With both a sneer and a smile on her face, the old hag turned to leave us. Mother said nothing. I'd never once heard her curse, although I hoped she was thinking the same words as I was about the gossip.

We left Stonegate and walked along in silent contemplation until we reached the King's Square. The route appeared much less intimidating in the daytime, and I enjoyed watching a solitary robin bob along the edge of the road, moving his head carefully, surveying the street for food. As we passed the Church of the Holy Trinity, the alcove where we'd hidden in the shadows filled with sunshine. The stone and mortar in the church walls took upon a healthy glow and for a moment I thought happy thoughts.

Visions of a new life in Scotton were interrupted by a shout and a wider commotion from further along the street. In fact, the disturbance seemed to originate from around the corner, near our destination in The Shambles. A moment later we both stepped into the narrow road.

A look of horror crossed Mother's face, and probably my own. She gripped my hand tightly, as we joined a small group of butchers, shoppers and passers-by gathered under the overlapping eaves. Ten yards further on, in the cramped lane beyond John Clitherow's house and shop, behind the hanging hens and geese, stood a second group. The Shambles was a tiny street. The two crowds easily blocked it at both ends.

The space between was filled by a group of relatively well-dressed men. A butcher's dog had been barking at them but was now dragged away. The men were commanded by the Sheriff of York, Roland Fawcett. Virtually everyone in York knew him or had done business with the man, for he owned everything from inns to tailors and drapery shops.

Sheriff Fawcett was speaking forcibly to Margaret Clitherow. He was loudly demanding she permit entry into her husband's house and shop, so the pursuivants could search the premises. Mistress Clitherow talked of this and that. She appeared to be stalling him. Only when her daughter Anne came outside, nodded and stood alongside her did she relent. Anne was accompanied by the boy Johann and a few other children who I didn't recognise.

The Sheriff instructed two of his men to venture inside. They walked through the passageway I'd exited only a few days before. Despite Fawcett's raised voice, Mistress Clitherow remained calm. She continued to smile at him. The constancy of her good humour amazed me. It would do even more so in the days to come.

My mother remained transfixed to the spot, fearing for her friends and their family. More passers-by were arriving by the minute, and we no longer stood at the back. A few people complained about the Sheriff's actions but some were supportive. One or two hurled insults at Mistress Clitherow and egged him on.

I whispered to Mother, recommending she go home in case things turned sour. I promised to stay and find out what would happen. Once the situation was clear, I'd return and report back to her. After that we could decide what to do. She appeared to be caught in two minds, until a group of guild apprentices began aggressively shoving their way past us to get to the front of the crowd. After this, she reluctantly relented. As she began to weave her way back through the throng, she mouthed for me to be careful.

A few minutes later the searchers re-emerged from the unbolted doorway. They shook their heads as they returned to the street empty handed. The Sheriff looked at his men with disbelief, as if certain there was something, or someone, inside the building. Anger and frustration showed on his face.

The reaction of the crowd remained mixed. I think the apprentices wished to witness an arrest before they returned to work. One man shouted '*Shame!*' and '*Go home!*', although it was difficult to ascertain if his calls were aimed at the Sheriff, Mistress Clitherow or the immigrant children.

The Sheriff was insistent. He clearly wanted to make an arrest, although I wondered why he had such confidence in his mission. His men approached the children. Fawcett demanded they each tell him their name and abode. One by one they walked through their details. Following this, he allowed most of the children to leave, until there was only Mistress Clitherow, her daughter Anne and Johann left.

After Anne gave her name, she stepped back to hide behind her mother's blood-stained apron. It was Johann's turn next. He looked frightened. I didn't hear what he said but his answer was well received. No doubt the Sheriff realised the boy was Flemish. A gleeful look of spite spread quickly across Fawcett's face. I pushed myself a little closer to hear what was being said. As I moved forward, I received angry looks and elbows from the people around me but most let me through. I kept on moving until I reached the second rank with only the apprentices in front of me.

'So, little Johann, you're a foreigner, are you?' Fawcett taunted.

'Leave the boy alone,' shouted a voice from the other side of the street. 'He's only a child.'

'Who said that?' replied Fawcett turning towards the opposite side of The Shambles. 'Some sort of Catholic sympathiser, are you? Show yourself and I'll question you too.'

Nobody stepped forward and, to their credit, no-one on that side of the crowd implicated the source of the interruption. There was a growing sense of unease in the air. A number of people began to leave. With only a single row of shoulders now to look over, I had a clear view of Mistress Clitherow, the open door to the passageway and

Johann before me.

For the first time I could properly see the features of Fawcett's face. His nose was large and red, as if he'd spent too much time on the wrong side of the bar in one of his inns. Mistress Clitherow attempted to step in front of Johann to protect the boy from the Sheriff, but the searchers blocked her way.

'Keep out of the road, mistress,' instructed Fawcett. 'I'd like a word with this boy without your treacherous influence. Two of my men will accompany you to the far end of the street. You'll wait there, while we complete our inquiries.'

'I won't leave my daughter alone with you,' said Mistress Clitherow adamantly.

'Very well, the girl may accompany you,' replied Fawcett. 'But the boy stays here.'

For the first time Mistress Clitherow was no longer smiling. The Sheriff's men dragged her down the street by her wrists to the opposite end of The Shambles towards the Bull Ring. Anne Clitherow followed dutifully behind, with a look of thunder on her face at her mother's treatment. When they were gone, Fawcett turned his attention back on Johann.

'I'm going to ask you some questions now, Johnny Dutchman, and you're going to answer them truthfully. Do you understand me?'

Johann looked quickly towards the Bull Ring but Mistress Clitherow was already out of sight. He turned his head slowly towards Fawcett. The boy looked at the Sheriff with wide open eyes and nodded. In the years which followed, I witnessed many men die in pain, some on the battlefield, and others who knew their time was up, but to this day I've never seen anyone look as terrified as Johann did at that very moment.

'Have you seen any Catholic goings on in this house?' asked Fawcett.

The boy looked down at his wooden shoes.

'No, sir,' he said, shaking his head, avoiding eye contact. 'I just deliver the meat.'

Fawcett grabbed Johann by the chin and forced the boy to look up at him.

'We'll see about that, you lying little shit,' he said. Turning to one of his men, Fawcett added, 'Strip him and get me my whip. It's time we gave this little foreigner a flogging.'

There was an audible gasp from the crowd. No-one had expected this. On the far side of the street one or two men rubbed their hands with anticipation. One winked at his mate. The apprentices were equally appreciative. Not only had they managed to get a few minutes off work, they'd now be able to witness a flogging. It was an unexpected bonus.

Fawcett's men pulled the clothes harshly from the boy's back. Ripping sounds could be heard. By the time the garments were torn off him, his flimsy coat and shirt were ripped into shreds. One of the men tugged down his breaches. They forced him out of his shoes. The boy stood forlornly alone in greyish undergarments. After that, he was forced to remove these too. His puny white body shivered before us, as naked and exposed as the day he was born.

Mothers with children began dragging their little ones away and heading home. Others followed. The throng became smaller. Many of those committed to stay wished to witness a public beating. The crowd was now completely adult, with the exception of Johann.

The boy held his hands over his private parts, and I feared for him. I felt a rage inside me but what realistically could I do to prevent his punishment? I could fight, but they'd easily overpower me. I'd be arrested. What would happen to Mother and my sisters? Worst of all, would I ever see Maria again?

I bent myself low, as if to fix something in my boot. When I rose, I had a cobble hidden in my hand. I wasn't sure what to do with it but its presence was reassuring.

In front of me, Sheriff Fawcett began to speak again. 'I'm asking you for the last time, boy. Have there been Catholic goings on in this house? Answer me truthfully, or I swear I'll use this whip and flail your flesh until it's bare, in front of all these people right here in the street.'

'I'll tell you. I'll tell you,' cried Johann in terror. He raised one hand and pointed down the passageway. 'Let me show you. Let me show you.'

As he did so, he caught my eye before looking away again. His shame was complete.

A firm hand fixed itself upon my shoulder.

Johann disappeared down the passageway with the Sheriff and his men. I turned around. The man gripping my shoulder was none other than Father Mush. The tall priest gently placed an index finger to his lips and motioned for me to follow him. He wore a gentleman's grey cloak and hood, which I realised I'd seen before. We walked off past the Church of the Holy Trinity.

'Don't blame the boy,' he said in St Saviourgate, out of earshot of any passers-by. 'Only cruel men like Sheriff Fawcett are to blame for this.'

'But Father…' I said.

He shushed me. 'Please don't call me that. It will be safer for both of us.'

We continued to walk in the direction of the wool market. Father Mush explained how he'd abandoned his hiding place in The Shambles only a few minutes before, following a hurried warning from Anne Clitherow. Earlier in the week her father had been summoned before the Council of the North but the butcher had somehow managed to avoid his appointment. This morning he'd been called to the Council again.

Butcher Clitherow hadn't been seen since he'd left for the King's Manor that morning. Father Mush believed he'd been moved out of the way to make the raid on the house easier, and to raise less sympathy with his neighbours.

Although he forgave the boy, the priest was in no doubt Johann would be telling all he knew to the Sheriff's men. He'd lead them straight to the secret rooms where Mistress Clitherow allowed fugitive priests like Father Ingleby and himself to hide and hold Mass. He was certain the good lady would be arrested and taken to jail.

What of her husband, I asked? He didn't sympathise with his wife's Catholic actions, although he turned a blind eye to them. The Father said it was most likely John Clitherow would be arrested but perhaps he'd later be released. After all, he was a freeman of York and a Protestant businessman.

I wondered what might happen to Anne and the Clitherows' other children in the meantime. Little did I know how badly Anne, in particular, would be treated by the Protestant foster parents assigned to take her in. They didn't take kindly to Catholic offspring.

'Why did you come to me?' I asked. 'You must know it's not safe.'

There was a grave look in his eyes. 'Forgive me, my son, if I've placed you in danger.'

'It's not that,' I said. 'I fear for your arrest.' He could see I spoke the truth.

When the Father replied, there was a mixture of fury and compassion in his voice. 'I come only for the benefit of Mistress Clitherow,' he said. 'She's a pearl inside this monstrous oyster.' He pointed at the high walls of the city as he spoke. 'Mistress Clitherow is the finest woman in the north, perhaps the whole of England. After all, the Pope has designated Queen Elizabeth a heretic who should be replaced by one of our own. Yes, to my mind, Margaret Clitherow should be known by all as the Pearl of York.'

There were footsteps behind us. The Father stopped talking. If such words were overheard, they'd send us to the gallows. But we needn't have worried. Two bare-footed immigrant boys scampered past us. One gripped a loaf of bread in his hands, the other an apple, both probably stolen from the food market. Luckily there were no pursuers. They dived into an alleyway and within moments they were gone.

The Father shook his head sadly. 'Stealing is a sin but at least they have something to eat.'

We turned slowly towards the wool market. The trading spaces were empty that day. Although we were alone, this time Father Mush spoke in a quiet whisper. 'The timing of the arrest of Margaret Clitherow is no coincidence,' he said almost silently. 'York Corporation and the Council of the North are vying with each other to demonstrate their loyalty to the Queen. The Privy Council in London is fearful. They worry the great northern cities like York and Hull are full of Catholics. To gain the Queen's trust, the Council and Corporation need to demonstrate what they plan to do about this.'

'What can they do?' I suspected I knew the answer.

He paused before replying. We stopped walking. As I stood still, a chill ran right through me.

'They can enforce the Act which outlaws seminary and Jesuit priests like me from being in this country, and now makes harbouring them punishable by death. I believe the authorities are planning a show trial, a public demonstration to display their loyalty to the Queen. What better time and place to do this than York Lent Assizes? The travelling court comes to the city next week.'

'It opens on Monday,' I said quietly.

'Yes,' Father Mush nodded. 'Have no doubt, Mistress Clitherow will be brought in front of the judges on the very first day and placed on trial, charged with high treason.'

'Surely, they wouldn't dare to execute a woman, Fa…' I stopped myself before completing his title.

'I'm sure they would,' he replied. 'Can you think of a better way of striking fear into the Catholic population and encouraging their Protestant neighbours to inform on them?'

As his words sank in, he looked me up and down, as if meeting me for the first time. 'Despite your expulsion, your headmaster says good things about you. John Pulleyn says you are honourable lad and can be trusted. Will you help me?'

'What can I do?'

'You can drop that for a start,' he said, glancing at my closed fist. 'We are men of peace. God has no wish for us to bear arms.'

The cobble slipped from my hand and bounced away along the road.

'But you are correct,' he said. 'Even with my disguise, I'm taking a risk appearing in the street like this. I could be arrested and if I was, I would be of no further help to the Pearl and her husband. It would be madness for me to attempt to attend the Assizes in the Common Hall next week. But you could go there. You could be my eyes and ears. The court will be held in an open public session. You could attend and report back to me. Will you do this, Master Fawkes? For Mistress Clitherow's sake, if not for mine?'

'Aye, I will,' I said quickly.

'Good. We must now take time to consider how best to support and give guidance to Mistress Clitherow in her hour of need. I must hold conference with one or two others. I'll find temporary lodgings near here. It's best you don't know where they are. We can meet in the yard behind the Black Swan Inn. Let's say at eight bells on Saturday morning. By then I should have devised a clear plan of action.'

# 10

When I arrived back at home, my mother's face betrayed relief and worry. The girls were upstairs sewing but we weren't alone. One of Mistress Clitherow's friends, Anne Tesh, had paid us a call. The woman was a renowned recusant and despite my growing enthusiasm for the old faith, I didn't think it wise for us to be welcoming a well-known Catholic into our abode at such a dangerous time. But when I saw Mistress Tesh's face, I relented a little.

There were tears in her eyes. It would have been uncharitable for Mother to have turned her away. The two women held drinking vessels filled with small beer. I sat down alongside them and felt the warmth of the fire but didn't partake.

'You can speak freely in each other's company,' Mother said.

Hearing this and remembering Mistress Tesh had attended the Mass last Sunday, I recounted what I'd seen at the Clitherows' house, and my subsequent discussions with Father Mush. Both Mother and Mistress Tesh thanked the Lord when they heard the priest hadn't been arrested.

'Anne, please tell Guy what you told me,' Mother said when I finished.

'It was awful, young man,' the woman said. 'I must have arrived just after you left, for the Sheriff's men were carrying out vestments, candles and the Father's altar through the passageway. I'm sure it all will be used as evidence against dear Margaret. Sheriff Fawcett separated Margaret from Anne and the little ones and arrested her. She was led off to York Castle but unfortunately I have no idea what happened to the children after that.'

'How do you know she was sent to the Castle?' I asked. There were several prisons in York.

'Because I followed them,' she said. This clearly brought back bad memories for more tears came, and she had to wipe them away from her eyes.

'Go on,' I said.

'It's what they did to her on the way. I thought they must be taking her to the prison on Ouse Bridge but they diverted their route and went to the riverbank by the King's Staith. Once they got there, Sheriff Fawcett ordered his men to douse Margaret into the river. She was clearly shocked. It wasn't deep but she was soaked to the skin. She stood there up to her waist in the dirty water, coughing and spluttering. They didn't see me, so I called out. I pretended I thought someone was drowning. A number of men and women came down from the street to see what was going on.

'When he saw them, Sheriff Fawcett shouted at his men to pull Margaret from the water. They pretended to be saving her. He scolded Margaret for jumping in, told her not to do it again and marched her off. This time they went directly to the Castle. I left as soon as I saw them enter the gates. It was awful. Poor Margaret was shivering with cold. How could a respectable citizen like Sheriff Fawcett do such a thing?'

'What happened to Johann?' asked Mother.

'The Flemish boy? I think they took him off somewhere for more questioning but I don't know. I could only follow one of them. Oh, Lord, what will happen next?'

'The Assizes Court on Monday,' I said.

Both women looked at me with shock on their faces.

## Friday March 11th, 1586

We promised to visit Mistress Tesh the next morning to discuss what could be done for the Clitherows. She lived in a house on The Aldwark, not far from the city walls near Peasholme Green. Given the woman's recusant reputation and current climate in the city, we decided it would be better to approach the premises from the rear. We left the main street some way from her house and ventured through the adjoining ginnels before knocking on her back door.

Mistress Tesh welcomed us into her cottage. The house was larger than ours. I assumed the good lady had a husband but saw no sign of manly things. Certainly, no children lived there. Maybe they'd reached maturity and left home or died during infancy. Or perhaps for some reason there'd never been any.

As Mistress Tesh embraced my mother, I glanced around. There was a low fire burning in the hearth. The main parlour was clean and tidy and the place appeared to be well looked after. I wondered if Father Mush might be staying there. If so, he'd regularly bump his head on the low doorways. The presence of the priest would also make the house an even more dangerous place to visit.

'Now, Anne,' said Mother, 'have you heard anything from the Castle?'

'Only a little,' replied the other woman. 'From what I hear Margaret and John have been arrested but are being held separately. They're not even allowed to speak to each other.'

'What of the children? Has the Lord Mayor taken them under his protection?'

'If only he would do such a thing,' replied Mistress Tesh with exasperation. 'I was certain Master Maye would intervene on his stepdaughter's behalf but no. From what I can tell the man has offered no assistance at all. The little ones have been split up and placed in households of Protestant families of the strictest persuasion. Poor Anne, if they attempt to convert her, I'm sure she'll run away. The streets are no place for such a vulnerable girl.'

'How do you know this has happened?' Mother asked.

'I visited the Common Hall after I left you yesterday and offered to take care of Anne and the others, but the Corporation men scolded me. They said if I was a friend of the Clitherows, I was probably a Catholic myself. And as such I wasn't fit to offer pastoral care. When I demanded to see the Lord Mayor, they just laughed at me. One of them pushed me back towards the door, but not before taking my name and address. I fear I've done myself no good.'

The silence at the end of the conversation was interrupted by a double rap on the door. Each one of us jumped. A man in the street shouted out Mistress Tesh's name and demanded entry so he could search the premises. The good lady pointed towards the back of the house. I took Mother by her hand and led her quickly until we were out of sight.

As I glanced back, I saw Mistress Tesh touch her head with her hands. She checked her coif was straight and none of her grey hair was showing. As she walked to the front door to open it, Mother and I left through the back.

I prayed nobody would be watching the rear garden. The Good Lord acknowledged my request. We rushed past an apple tree and a few rows of winter greens. A cage full of hens bred for eggs and their meat clucked at us. We closed the back gate gently and sneaked through the same snickets and ginnels by which we'd arrived.

Some way along Aldgate I pushed my head over a wall to gain a better view of the street. Two men in Corporation livery were striding down the road towards us. Ducking down, I whispered for Mother to stay back. The men passed the snicket without looking our way. Between them they dragged a clearly distressed Mistress Tesh. I signalled for Mother to retreat. We walked away and hid behind a corner for several minutes before proceeding.

This was the last time I saw Anne Tesh, although I heard a tale of her about a decade later. We were preparing to siege a town in Flanders. During the previous battle we'd lost many men, and our ranks were being bolstered with new recruits. Some, like me, were Catholics over from England, ready to fight for the Spanish cause. When one learned I was from York, he asked if I knew Mistress Tesh.

'I may have once,' I replied, 'what of it?'

The fellow said the old woman had been found guilty of converting a Protestant minister to Catholicism. I took a sharp breath, for I knew the sentence for the crime was burning at the stake. It was a horrible thing. The prisoner would scream with pain until nothing could be done. When the fellow said mercy had been shown, and her sentence commuted to life imprisonment, I was mightily relieved.

I remember looking to the heavens and thanking the Lord for looking out for Mistress Tesh. Beneath my breath, I said a prayer for her friend, Margaret Clitherow. We all knew her by then as the Pearl of York. The good lady had become my inspiration. I'd left England partly because of her, and I'd return home from my exile one day to fight for her too. We served the same cause.

## Saturday March 12th, 1586

I slipped out early the next morning, whilst the two girls were in bed. Mother held me tightly before allowing me to leave. She gripped me closely and kissed my cheek. When I unlocked the door, she looked haggardly towards me and beseeched me to be careful. I promised I would.

It was a misty morning outside. A cold fog had risen up in the night from the Ouse and the Foss. The river mist blanketed every church, street and garden in the city. The atmosphere was eerie in the pre-dawn light of a place no longer fully asleep but not yet quite awake. The walk would take me about fifteen minutes.

Along the way I twice encountered Corporation men in uniforms carrying halberds. I didn't like the look of the axe-heads and the spikes at the end of their poles. The men guarding the gates and the walls wielded these too, and we'd see them at official events but to witness men patrolling the streets at random with such deadly weapons was concerning.

The talk of the town yesterday had been of Mistress Clitherow's arrest and coming trial. Everyone said it was common knowledge her case would be the first heard at the Assizes. The circuit judges would be arriving in the city shortly to meet with the leaders of the Corporation who would be hosting the trials.

An alderman who knew Mother complained events were controlled by the Council of the North. The gossips in the street, depending on their point of view, blamed or credited the Corporation. For my own part I wondered if they were working in cahoots. Mother doubted this. She said she didn't know who or what to believe but the Corporation and Council had always schemed against each other, and she saw no reason for them to collaborate now.

The neighbours' opinions of the Clitherows were split down the middle. The more Puritanical Protestants denounced them. Others claimed they'd been treated harshly, particularly Margaret's husband. Many believed the butcher should be released immediately, even the ones who complained he hadn't sufficiently disciplined his wife.

Mister Clitherow, they said, was an honest man. He served his customers well, paid his taxes and gave alms to the poor. And in the past when Mistress Clitherow had behaved badly, he'd paid her fines and scolded her, if perhaps not sharply enough.

Even Mistress Clitherow's plight garnered sympathy in some quarters. Her supporters would have included church Catholics, but these kept a low profile. Only a few people spoke up for her. They said she'd always been a pleasant woman, a good mother and gave education and work to the poor. If she strayed in religion, at least she kept this out of sight and didn't force her beliefs onto others. And if the authorities were to round up every Catholic in the north there'd be no room left in the jails. No-one seemed to know or care about Anne Tesh or Father Ingleby.

With factions and arguments on all sides and risks of protests breaking out, the city was placed on high alert. Perhaps this wasn't the most sensible time to be venturing outdoors to meet a Catholic priest. I smiled. Nothing I'd done in the past few weeks made much sense, apart from meeting Maria.

Whilst we awaited a reply to Mother's letter, I'd pinned all my hopes on it. Legal trials didn't usually take longer than a day, and most much less than that. I'd attend the Assizes on Monday, report back to Father Mush and work out how we could to travel to Scotton as soon as we could.

When I reached the wool market, a number of stalls were being set up. It was the wrong season for a full wool fair, but men and women had come into town from their farms and cottages to sell their wares to the city dwellers. I saw one table being loaded with thick warm shirts and wondered how they'd been assembled.

One or two of the smaller hand carts were being pushed or pulled along Peasholme Green. There was a secondary gate in the city walls called Layerthorpe Postern. This short cut allowed some entry to the city across a narrow bridge over the Foss but most traffic, including anything led by a horse or donkey, had to pay the larger toll and come through the main gates, such as Monk Bar.

Peasholme Green was a pleasant enough little street. One half was dominated by the greenery surrounding the Church of St Cuthbert but I didn't go that far. The inn of the Black Swan was nearer to the wool market. It wasn't as grand as the Bowes house further along, although it looked prosperous enough. I remember Father telling me it was where the Queen's officials sometimes stayed when there wasn't enough room in the King's Manor to accommodate them all.

Like most of the buildings in the city, the inn was timber framed. The black and white panels looked newly painted. The tiles on the roof appeared well cared for. To the left of the building was an entrance to the stables and a back yard, so I went that way, not knowing what I'd find.

There were splashes and a pile of vomit next to a wall where one of last night's revellers had spilled his guts. I stepped over this carefully and walked onwards. The entrance to the stables was on the opposite side, so it was easy to avoid being seen by the stable lads. From inside the building I heard the clinking of plates on pewter. I assumed the servants were clearing up after the last meal or preparing the next one.

The yard at the back was empty. In the distance I heard different sets of bells ring out for eight o'clock just a few moments apart. It appeared I was on time. I found a darkened corner covered by an overhanging yew tree planted in the garden next door. I stood beneath the evergreen foliage in the shadows, hoping to see but not be seen. Grey mist filled the air but at least the day was getting lighter.

Nobody came. Eventually I crept over to the back door and pushed it open. Avoiding the rooms where the noises came from, I explored a long passageway. Before I'd got very far, I heard the creaking of steps. A grumpy looking gentleman appeared at the bottom of the stairs and pushed his way past me as if I wasn't there. I waited for a moment but he didn't return.

Nobody else came by. I continued. At the end of the corridor there was a plain wall, covered in fine oak panelling. I touched the wood. I didn't know what to expect. I continued to caress it. At one point I moved my hand to the right. I felt a projecting piece of wood. It looked like a lever. I pulled on it. Nothing happened.

'Are you looking for a priest hole or something?' said a voice from behind me.

I froze. I'd been found out and would be arrested. I didn't have a dagger. There was no way I could escape.

'Come on, lad,' said the voice. 'I know who you're looking for. Let me take you to him.'

I turned around. It wasn't Sheriff Fawcett, nor one of his men but I had a shock all the same. The man standing behind me wore the robes of a Protestant parson.

# 11

The pastor studied my face with a playful look in his blue-green eyes. 'Come on then,' he said.

We marched along the corridor and out through the rear of the building. Although he wasn't a tall man like Father Mush, the parson had a long gait and a most peculiar stride. At times I struggled to keep up with him. We soon left the grounds of the inn behind and crossed an open field. My boots weren't waterproofed and the damp dew from the wet grass soaked into them.

We departed the field at a spot I didn't know. The houses of the poor were all around us. It wasn't a place I'd ever visited before. After this, we entered a foul-smelling alley. In some spots the roofs on either side scratched out at each other. My nose twitched at the smells of unfamiliar food from the fires and kitchens in the hovels around us. This must be where the other half of the population lived, in a place the Corporation didn't wish the rest of us to see.

I felt a strong intuition not to follow the man any further. Sensing my hesitation, he stopped. 'Don't you fancy spending some time around the Black Horse Passage then?' he asked, with the look of mischief on his face.

I tried not to react. Frankly I didn't know what was going on. I felt I'd gone somewhere I shouldn't have and was out of my depth. At first, I'd believed the man was about to expose me as a Catholic supporter, but I no longer felt this. My over-riding emotion now was one of uncertainty. Anything could happen here and, if it did, nobody would know anything about it. I saw my mother's lips telling me to be careful.

'Don't worry,' said the man in priestly robes. 'The place where we're going is quite safe. The majority of people around here are decent enough God-fearing folk, as they are all across England. They may be hard-pressed but most of them won't rob you. You may think the Lord has deserted them but He hasn't. He's here, even now, watching us. Everywhere.'

Had I mistaken the look of mischief? Was it really zeal? Was this man one of the new breed of preachers who believed in taking from the rich to give to the poor? People said these were dangerous men with crazy ideas. What might he, or they, do to me?

'I see you've found him then?'

I tuned around in surprise. The voice belonged to Father Mush. He poked his head through a door which appeared too little for his body to pass through. The priest beckoned for us to go inside. There wasn't a fire in the house. I counted two women and five children. The only man, apart from us, sat in a corner sleeping. He was covered in a makeshift blanket and looked ill.

The room was clean and tidy. Each of the other occupants, apart from the sleeping man, left through a back door. Where they were headed, I didn't know, but it gave us space to talk. There wasn't silence though. The man in the chair snored fitfully the whole time I was there.

'I doubt the Sheriff will look for me here,' Father Mush offered cheerfully. 'What say you, young Guy?'

He shook the hand of the other man warmly, as if they were friends. Once again, I didn't understand. Such men were meant to be enemies. Perhaps they wouldn't fight but surely, they'd denounce each other, and turn the other one in given half a chance?

'Who is this man, Father?' I asked.

'Didn't he introduce himself to you? No, I expect he didn't. This is an old acquaintance of mine, Parson Giles Wigginton. He hails from Northamptonshire.'

'And sometimes Cambridge and sometimes Lambeth,' added the parson. 'I'm pleased to meet you, Master Guy.'

'How did you recognise me inside the inn?' I asked.

'It wasn't difficult. Father Mush asked me to hunt down a ginger lad, who might be looking for a Catholic priest. I caught you red handed, didn't I? Well, red headed really. What were you looking for in that wall? Did you think something would spring open? Were you searching for a secret compartment? I don't fancy you'll find many priest holes or fugitives in there. The place is riddled with the Queen's men.'

'Enough, Giles,' said the Father. 'Don't ridicule the boy. He's offered to help.'

'Aye, he has,' replied the parson. He turned towards me. 'Forgive me for my humour, lad, but you're such an easy target.'

There was a sharp snort. The man in the corner moved restlessly, before becoming quieter again.

'The poor fellow hasn't got long now,' whispered Father Mush softly.

Both priests looked at each other.

Father Mush nodded. 'Aye, he's one of mine. I'll administer the last rites after you leave.'

The conversation paused.

'Thank you for coming, Guy,' said the Father. 'I should explain. Parson Wigginton and I sit on opposite sides of the religious divide but we hold some things in common. We both believe the people of this land, and all others, should be governed by God's laws.'

'And not those of the Queen, nor the Corporation, nor the Council of the North,' added Pastor Wigginton. 'Have you heard the phrase my enemy's enemy is my friend?'

'Have no doubt though, we both believe in our own faith,' continued Father Mush. 'Unfortunately for Pastor Wigginton, this means in the future I'm certain he'll face eternal damnation.'

'Or quite possibly, Father Mush will rot in hell,' replied the pastor smiling. 'You get the picture. Neither of us believe in religious persecution in this world, only the next.' He turned to Father Mush. 'Did you know, John, the Archbishop of York, Edwin Sandys himself, once put me into prison in London for my political views?'

'You may have mentioned it once or twice, Giles. Our job now though is to make sure nobody else goes to jail, or if they do get sent there, we get them out quickly. God forbid anything should happen to Mistress Clitherow.'

'Like Marmaduke Bowes?' I asked.

'You know of him?' said Wigginton softly.

'Of course. Last November the school went on a trip to the Knavesmire to witness his execution.'

'Yes, like Marmaduke Bowes,' replied Father Mush sadly. 'The first man in Yorkshire to be executed for showing a simple kindness to a Catholic priest. And now they want to do the same to a woman…'

With this the conversation stalled for a longer time.

'Well, we're not going to let them,' said Parson Wigginton eventually. 'Try as they might, we have plans enough to foil them.'

The look on his face said Father Mush disagreed. At the very least, he appeared less confident in the success of their mission than his colleague. The two men then told me what they were planning and what my own role would be.

Afterwards Pastor Wigginton led me back across the wet grass to Peasholme Green. When we reached the street and approached the wool market, we bade each other farewell. It was agreed we'd both attend the public gallery in the courtroom on Monday but sit separately and make no contact with each other. After the session, we'd return separately to the Black Horse Passage and meet once again with Father Mush.

Suddenly I found myself staring into the face of Thomas Cheke. The boy was stood just a few feet away from me. Whereas my black eye was largely recovered, his face remained a mottled mess of purple. A strange mixture of revulsion and pride welled up inside me. For the first time I realised the damage I'd done to him. I dreaded to think what would have happened if the teachers hadn't pulled me away.

When Cheke noticed me, he stopped in his tracks. His first instinct was to get away, but he didn't make a run for it. He halted and steadied himself. I had to admit he showed some presence of mind, and within a few seconds his frightened face took on a more familiar sneer.

'Hello, copper top,' he said. 'Shouldn't you be back at St Peter's now? Oh no,' he laughed. 'I forgot. You've been expelled. You poor thing! What are you doing here? Cleaning out latrines or selling your arse to middle aged men? You won't earn much doing either, I'll wager.'

I knew I had to curb my temper and wanted to ignore him, but his taunting persisted.

'What a shame! Little Mister Fawkes won't be going to law school after all, so he can't follow in his father's footsteps. I bet the gnarled old man must be turning in his lawyer's grave. I think I'll go and dance on it.'

'Shard off, Cheke,' I replied. 'Unless you want another beating.'

I took an aggressive step towards him. But by now he'd regained his composure. 'Hit me! Go on, hit me!' he said, thrusting his chin towards me.

It was tempting, and I almost followed his instructions. But I stopped myself. 'You want me to, don't you?'

His eyes filled with conflicting emotions. I saw aggression and cockiness but fear too. 'Yes, go on. We're not in St Peter's now, after all.'

So that was it. He'd have me arrested. I was no longer subject to the school's jurisdiction.

'No, I won't,' I said. 'I bid you good day.'

I tried to turn away from him but he grabbed at my arm.

'Go on, do it! My father will get the Sheriff's men to put you in the paupers' prison. He'll have a word with the judge. He can do that. He knows all of them, even the ones at the Assizes. The whole school will come to see you swing from the gallows. You'll become St Peter's most infamous pupil.'

He talked so quickly and desperately I could hardly understand his words but I'm pretty sure that was the gist of it. Enough, I thought, enough. I had more important things to do. I shrugged off his hold and made to leave.

'I must say I was surprised to see you with Pastor Wigginton,' said Cheke, as he attempted to keep me talking whilst he thought of something nastier to say. 'What interesting company you keep. I'd had you down as a Papist like your friends Middleton and Wright. Certainly not a Calvinist. My father says Wigginton is a trouble-making arse who should be locked up and the key thrown away. I suppose at least you have that much in common.'

I took a deep breath. Sticks and stones, as long as it wasn't about my family or Maria.

'What are you doing out of school anyway?' I asked him.

'I've been given time to recover from your assault. I must say I'm enjoying it. I thought I might spend some time boning that Pulleyn girl but she seems to have disappeared. Don't worry I'll keep on looking for her.'

I clenched my fist and Cheke saw this, of course. He was loving it. He moved closer towards me to press home his advantage, so near I could see the spittle frothing up on his lips. My enemy would do anything to rile me further and instil a reaction.

'Shall I tell you what I'm going do when I find her?'

He made an "O" shape with the thumb and forefinger of his left hand and began pushing the fingers of his right hand in and out of it. My face flushed with rage. Once again, I wanted to hit him and keep on hitting him until he dropped to the ground. I felt the anger burning up inside me. It was a fury which would kill many men in the future.

I left him. How often had Mother told me I must control the rage which rises up inside me? The difference this time was I listened. If I didn't, I was doomed.

There was a growing crowd of people around the wool stalls. I dived in between them and kept on moving. I pushed my way through the crush, past the people and the smells of sheepskin and sweat until my head spun and I felt sick. I could hardly believe I was running away from the little bastard but I had to do it. The crowd thinned and I looked around. He was gone. One day, I thought. One day soon, Thomas Cheke, your time will come.

## Monday March 14th, 1586

The area around Coney Street was crowded. Another event was being held inside the Common Hall. My mother and I had arrived early to get a good spot outside. We left the girls at home. I'd wanted Mother to stay behind too but she insisted on coming. It was important, she said, that her friend should see supportive people who believed in her when she arrived.

Over the weekend wicked rumours had circulated around York about Mistress Clitherow's character. Scurrilous stories abounded of her offering sanctuary to Catholic priests in turn for sexual favours. I saw an unspeakable sketch of the good woman on all fours with a priest behind her. The claims went on and on. Mother cried when she heard the talk in Stonegate of Mistress Clitherow encouraging her children to watch.

Of course, nobody who'd met the good woman believed the lies but an orchestrated attempt was obviously being made to sway the jury ahead of the trial. The atmosphere in the streets was raucous. Small groups were arguing for and against the accused all over the place. By mid morning the mood had become menacing with a real possibility of civil disorder. So began one of the most incredible days of my life, and I say this as a man who later attempted to blow up Parliament.

After a while we heard the sound of horns approaching from the direction of Lendal, signifying the procession was on it way from the King's Manor. Although York Corporation hosted the Assizes in its offices at the Common Hall, the judges and their entourage had decided to lodge in the more luxurious accommodation in the headquarters of the Council of the North.

The crowd pressed out from the main square on three sides. Guardsmen pushed us off the street to make way for the series of carriages arriving at the front of the Common Hall. An Assizes Court is a large operation. Many of the legal fellows, recorders and the like would already be inside. The people arriving in the covered wagons were the more senior officers, the ones who wallowed in the limelight and enjoyed the pomp and ceremony of it all.

The first to step out of his carriage was Lord Mayor Henry Maye, without his wife today but resplendent in his scarlet city robes. The man looked like he was loving every minute of it, despite the fact his own stepdaughter was being placed on trial. The Lord Mayor was flanked by two well-dressed officials. One held his sword. The other bore his mace.

After this came two senior judges. Unsurprisingly I recognised neither. I'd never been to an Assizes court before. They were followed by the Lord Mayor's esquires, six or eight of them in total. Immediately behind them came Sheriff Fawcett, a more junior sheriff and a number of sergeants. Lastly at the back they were pursued by a range of ceremonial officers. I had no idea who or what their roles were.

Once each carriage was emptied, it departed and was replaced by another. It must have been a busy morning at the stables and horse fair. The whole parade was flanked by uniformed halberdiers, who held out their pikes and observed the populace as if scanning for troublemakers. I hated to think what damage the spikes and axe-heads would do if used in anger against the crowd.

With the officials now moving inside, I thought about going into the courtroom to get a good seat but Mother told me there was no need to hurry. The dignitaries would be on their way to the banqueting hall for their dinner. She assured me nothing would happen inside for a few hours at least.

For a while there was nothing to do but wait. Some in the crowd departed. Monday was the beginning of the working week and each day was long enough already. Many couldn't afford to spend time waiting around here. I took a look about the square and saw there were no school visits that day. Perhaps they were waiting for the executions afterwards.

As the church bells struck noon a sudden hush came down from further along Coney Street, off towards Spurriergate. Everyone in the square in front of the Common Hall craned their necks in an attempt to see who or what was coming. The anticipation was palpable.

Two minutes later the prisoner became visible. Mistress Clitherow was dressed in her finest clothes, as if going to a Sunday service. The irony wasn't lost on me. Most strikingly she wore a fine hat on her head. The good woman was surrounded by an officer and a patrol of seven halberdiers, as if that many would be needed to prevent her escape.

After the silence there was shouting. I realised it was time to go inside and squeezed Mother's hand. As I left, I heard cheers of support battle it out with cries of 'harlot' and 'traitor' from the local population.

Agreeing with Mother, I hoped Mistress Clitherow's friends would catch her eye before she was taken inside.

When I approached the courtroom, I wasn't alone. A whole crush of people was attempting to get inside the building. Officials waved their arms in an effort to direct us. People shouted and there was general confusion. Three or four officers manned the courtroom door. One challenged a boy ahead of me. He must have been about my own age. When he was turned away, I worried they might bar my entry but they didn't stop me. I walked inside.

It was a big room, full of open space with high ceilings. There was a stage at the front, with grand seats for the judges, a dock cage for the accused and set places where the witnesses would stand. A man held a quill in his hand, seated at a desk to the left of the benches. I assumed this must be the primary recorder. There was a general hubbub and murmur of anticipation. Over the next few minutes the noise grew louder.

The public gallery was populated by row after row of rickety wooden benches. As I pushed my way down the central aisle towards one of them, I gazed around the room. What a place this would be to earn a living, I thought. Trials for coining, horse theft, murder and more mundane matters. Good legal men would always be needed to make preparations, build prosecutions case and prime the defendants to make their arguments. I wondered if Mistress Clitherow had received legal advice. The defence wasn't allowed a counsel. She'd have to make her own case.

Despite my ambitions, I'd never been inside a courtroom before. The experience gained would be far better for me than any lesson. Even though the atmosphere beguiled me, I remembered my fate. I was no longer going to be a lawyer. Not for the Church. Nor for anybody else. I wasn't even sure if I believed in their Church anymore, not as my father had anyway. And I was no longer a pupil at the school where he'd sent me.

My life was in turmoil, but it could be resolved. I could find a suitable job and marry Maria. In the meantime, I was here for a purpose. For the rest of the day nothing else could matter. I was attending the courtroom to watch and to listen. I had to take in every detail and report it back faithfully to Father Mush. Perhaps if I did, I could play my own small part in helping save a good woman from the gallows.

# 12

I seated myself halfway along one of the central rows on the left-hand side of the gallery. The hall was packed full but despite the size of the crowd it didn't take me long to spot Pastor Wigginton's robes. He must have arrived early in order to secure such a prominent position on the second row from the front.

Most of the men staring back at us from the raised stage were adorned in expensive looking clothing. There were lawyers in their black robes and others in brighter colours. Listening to the people around me, I discovered the two men in the most prominent seats were the Judges, Clench and Rodes.

'Look at that Rodes, lad, 'e's an 'anging judge for sure, you can tell from 'is face,' asserted one of the fellows sitting in front of me. From the look of his clothes, he was a working man, perhaps a tanner.

'That's as may be,' replied his younger but similarly dressed companion, 'but what's 'e doing 'ere? The man works for the Council of the North. I thought Assizes judges weren't allowed to 'ave links to their circuit?'

'Then 'e can't work for 'em,' said the first fellow.

'But 'e does,' the other man insisted. 'My brother-in-law George said so last week.'

The comment was met with a dismissive shake of the head. 'That explains it then, you daft apeth. You can't believe a word that rogue tells you. You've said that yourself.'

'Aye, mebbe you're right. George does talk through his arse. What do we know about the other one then, Clench, 'im with the grey hair?'

'From down south, I reckon. You can always tell a Londoner...'

'But you can't tell 'em much,' said his friend, completing the joke. 'Nay, not in my experience. You can't tell 'em nowt. But the blacksmith tells me that Judge Clench has some family in Leeds, so mebbe 'e's not so bad after all.'

'Bloody Leeds! Worse than London if you ask me. Always 'as been.'

The conversation might have carried on in a similar vein for several hours but for a sudden shout from the front of the courtroom.

'Call Margaret Clitherow.'

Everyone stood and stared as the good lady, escorted by two minor sergeants, entered the hall. The crowd jostled to get a better view of the prisoner. There was an almost collective intake of breath as the folk in the gallery witnessed the accused's clothes and her demeanour. She wore a fine long dress, matching her status as a prosperous businessman's wife. And the tears I'd feared simply weren't there. Mistress Clitherow was smiling. She gave the impression of attending a celebration rather than arriving at a courtroom to be tried by the jury.

I tried to fathom what she must be thinking but failed. As she passed close to me, for a moment I studied her face. The first flush of youth was gone but she wasn't old. I was sure many men would find her attractive. She was what my father would have called a handsome woman.

Eventually Mistress Clitherow was led to her allotted position. Once her bonds were released, she carefully positioned herself into the dock cage. To underline her place in York's society, she hadn't worn a simple scarf or coif to cover her hair but a large and elaborately embroidered hat, coloured in various shades of green. It was extraordinary, as was the beaming and confident face beneath. Once her eyes had finished scanning the officials, she turned and looked at the public gallery. Like many others, as she did so, I avoided her eyes and began to sit down.

With everyone else seated, I could just about make out Mistress Clitherow's self-assured face. The woman was calmness personified. The courtroom appeared to be her usual place of business, rather than a habitat reserved for judges and felons. I suspected the officials felt this too. Some appeared to be on edge. Whilst the Lord Mayor's face expressed surprise, Judge Clench looked uncomfortable. Even the man who'd arrested the prisoner, Sheriff Fawcett, shook his head. Of all the officers, only Justice Rodes returned the accused's gaze with fearsome ferocity. He scowled at Mistress Clitherow and the gallery in equal measure. If his face was a verdict, we'd all be condemned.

There was a shuffling of papers. As people began to settle, hundreds of whispers filled the room, until the officials called for silence. Judge Clench regained his composure and slowly and deliberately began to read out the indictment against the prisoner.

'Mistress Clitherow, it is alleged in your husband's house in The Shambles in York in the year of our Lord 1586 you have harboured and maintained Jesuits and seminary priests, traitors one and all to the Queen's majestic laws, and you have encouraged them to hold their Catholic Mass in Latin in secret within said premises.'

He paused and looked gravely at her. We all did, but the good lady simply smiled back, before beaming at the benches in the gallery with the unblemished face of an angel.

'Well, Margaret Clitherow, how say you? Are you guilty of this indictment or no?'

If a pin had dropped in the courtroom at that instant it would have exploded with the sound and fury of thirty-six barrels of gunpowder. Nobody breathed. We all stared, transfixed by the woman. Everyone waited for the good lady's response, but just as she was about to speak, Judge Rhodes leaned forward and interrupted her.

'Take that confounded hat off your head, woman,' he commanded. 'To wear it in this court is an insult.'

The accused gently reached up with a steady hand and withdrew two long pins from her hair, taking care not to drop them. She untied a piece of ribbon and worked with her fingers. Once the hat was undone, she passed it, the ribbon and the pins to an official. After this, with every eye in the courtroom still upon her, she took a moment to bunch up her brown hair and fix a simple coif scarf over her head.

To me at least, these actions spoke of a gentle defiance against brutality which all manner of men might struggle to defeat. The good lady's deeds were deliberate and mesmerising. And when she spoke, it was with the type of mild voice my mother might have used to calm a child or tease a kitten from a tree. The words were clearly enunciated, and there was an aura of goodness and innocence about them.

'I know of no offence whereof I should confess myself guilty,' she uttered softly.

From the look on his face, Justice Rodes was ready to rail up against this but the more senior judge held up his hand. It appeared Judge Clench wanted to demonstrate it was he who primarily controlled proceedings.

He caught Mistress Clitherow's gaze and held onto it. 'You have offended Her Majesty the Queen's laws,' he said firmly to her. 'For you have harboured and maintained Jesuits and Catholic priests. You must know these people are Her Majesty's enemies?'

Your enemies' enemies are my friends, I remembered.

'I neither know, nor have harboured any such persons,' replied Mistress Clitherow. 'God defend I should harbour or maintain those who are not the Queen's friends.'

'Nonsense,' said the judge, 'How will you be tried?'

'Hear me, my Lord,' the good lady responded quickly, looking directly into Judge Clench's eyes. She shook her head gently as she spoke. 'Having made no offence, I need no trial.'

'But the courtroom has informed you of what you are accused of, Mistress Clitherow,' stated Judge Clench. 'It is alleged you have offended the statute, and therefore you must be tried. I ask you again, how will you be tried? Are you guilty of these indictments read against you? Yes or no?'

A furious Justice Rodes tried to intervene once more, only for Judge Clench again to hold him back. Instead the older man Clench allowed Mistress Clitherow a minute or two to collect her thoughts. Once she appeared ready to answer him, the judge beckoned with his hand for her to speak to the court. As before, she smiled and scanned the room. I think she tried to catch the eye of her stepfather but deliberately or not, he avoided this, until she fixed her vision back onto the judges' bench.

'If you say I have offended, and that I must be tried, I will be tried by none other than God, and by your own consciences,' she said.

Judge Clench hunched his shoulders and sighed. He'd put up with this to-ing and fro-ing to date but I could see he was losing patience and wanted to move on.

'No, you cannot do so,' he insisted, shaking his head. For the first time he raised his voice, if only slightly, to the lady. 'We are sitting here to see justice and law, and therefore you must be tried by the country.'

From my father's time I knew '*country*' was a legal term for the jury. Justice Rodes leaned over and whispered something into his senior colleague's ear, but Clench shook his head for a second or two. It wasn't clear whether they'd reached any agreement.

Once more, Judge Clench addressed the dock, but the conversation between justice and prisoner simply carried on in the same vein. Like the stories I'd heard of King Henry playing tennis, the arguments went back and fore until it appeared the grey-haired judge had had enough.

Reluctantly he turned to Justice Rodes and mouthed, 'Very well.'

The younger judge made a signal to a man stood in the corner of the room. The fellow disappeared through a door, and everyone in the gallery and most of the officials wondered what would happen next.

It was something none of us could have expected. Two men were led into the courtroom, each carrying a sack of items. Justice Rodes instructed one of the sergeants to attend him before the bench. The sergeant reached down into one of the sacks and pulled out a collection of chalices, icons and pictures, similar to the ones removed from all Protestant churches in recent years.

Another officer brought out vestments and articles of church gear in the style worn by Catholic priests when they held secret Masses. I knew what these looked like, of course, having so recently been to one. The trinkets appeared familiar and one gown in particular looked suspiciously like the robe Father Mush had been wearing when he'd said Mass a week last Sunday.

Next, two other men were called forward. At first, I suspected they were witnesses but I quickly realised this wasn't the case. In the end I wasn't sure whether they were jesters or drunks, or perhaps both. The priestly clothes were placed upon their backs, and the pair played out a macabre and mocking Catholic service with the utensils before them.

Eventually they swung rosary beads, like Maria's, high above their heads. The two men began pushing and pulling at each other. I'd never witnessed such a bizarre carry on in all my life. The mayhem continued until one of the buffoons turned to Mistress Clitherow.

'Behold thy gods in whom thou believest,' he said in a high-pitched voice.

Both men continued to walk around in circles until they looked rather dizzy. The smile hadn't fully vanished from the good lady's lips but what was left looked a lot like pity. One of the two men stumbled, and the other had to help him back to his feet. At this point Judge Clench clapped his hands and bade both men be taken from his courtroom. Whilst a few people in the gallery had sniggered at the show, most seemed as shocked or bewildered as I was.

Considering the moment an opportunity to pounce, Justice Rodes took over the questioning. 'How do you like these vestments now?' he taunted Mistress Clitherow, with disdain on his face.

'I like them well enough, but only when they are on the backs of those who know how to use them in God's honour, as they were made,' she replied. 'You put me on trial, yet you are the ones who dare to make a mockery of His worship.'

Judge Clench issued a silent oath through his teeth. He looked like he'd woken up and found himself inside Bedlam. He pushed his body forward and placed himself in front of the more junior justice. When Rodes responded by trying to do the same, Clench stood up and moved in front of him.

'Enough of these games,' he commanded. 'Mistress Clitherow, who do you believe in?'

'I believe in God,' she replied.

'But in what God?' asked the judge.

For a moment she closed her eyes. When she opened them, she smiled at both justices, as she had before, and addressed Judge Clench and everyone else in the room.

'I believe in God the Father, God the Son, and God the Holy Ghost,' she said clearly. 'In these Three Persons and in One God I fully believe, and by the death, passion and mercy of our Lord Jesus Christ, I must be saved.'

Judge Clench returned the look Mistress Clitherow gave him and appeared to be somehow resigned to the events unfolding around him in the York Lent Assizes.

'You speak well,' he said.

Returning to his chair, he sat down for a few moments in silence. After this, Rodes moved towards him and whispered softly into the older man's ear. Clench responded in kind. At last it appeared the two men had agreed a plan of action.

'Margaret Clitherow, how say you yet? Are you content to be tried by God and the country?' asked the senior of the two judges.

The prisoner replied, 'No.'

When Judge Clench spoke next, he appeared to address every person in the room, although his words were directed solely at the prisoner. Just as Father Mush had instructed, I continued to look around. I studied the officers and the mood in the chamber. It was difficult but I attempted to commit every last detail to memory. The priest had instructed me to make a mental note of everything, saying a minor point I might consider inconsequential could prove later to be of the utmost importance.

These were the words spoken by the judge. 'Good woman, consider well what you do; if you refuse to be tried by the country, you make yourself guilty and an accessory to your own death, for we cannot try you but by order of the law. Having said that, you need not fear this kind of trial, for I think the country cannot find you guilty upon the slender evidence of one child alone.'

I found the first sentence confusing. I couldn't comprehend what it meant. Hopefully Pastor Wigginton or Father Mush would understand, but the later words greatly surprised me. Judge Clench appeared to be admitting the only evidence against the good lady was the word of one boy, and this wouldn't be sufficient to convict her. The evidence would be weaker still if the jury knew Johann was a foreigner, I thought.

When the final words from Judge Clench failed to illicit any additional response from the accused, Justice Rodes decided to have another go. 'Now, let's talk about your husband,' he said.

Mistress Clitherow's lips straightened slightly, a reaction which told the officials this was an angle worth pursuing. Judge Clench appeared to make a note with his quill.

'Is it not true your husband, the butcher and meat trader, John Clitherow,' continued the junior judge, 'has been privy to your keeping of priests in his house and supports all that you do?'

'No, God knoweth I could never get my husband to join me in my good cause, no matter how many times I have tried.'

'Perhaps though, you would happily force him to suffer from your fate? We must proceed by law against you, which will condemn you to a sharp death if there's no trial. Who will look after your husband and children then?'

'God's will will be done. If I have to suffer death for His good cause, I'll look up to heaven and thank Him for it,' she replied.

I pulled a face and wondered again what they were talking about, and then I heard one of the tanners in front of me whisper to his mate, 'If she refuses to make a plea, by law she'll be crushed to death,'

'Bloody nasty way to go,' replied his friend.

At last I understood. I'd never heard of such a statute but refusing to make a plea must be a crime in itself. If Mistress Clitherow didn't plead one way or the other, she couldn't be found guilty of the crimes she was accused of, but she would be executed anyway. Whispers began spreading rapidly around the courtroom, as ignorant folk like myself were educated by our neighbours.

More thoughts began to spin around inside my head. Judge Clench appeared to be offering an olive branch by explaining how flimsy the court's evidence was. Like so many that day, at that moment I couldn't understand why Mistress Clitherow didn't grasp it.

Observing the dock cage, I was further confused. Mistress Clitherow's smile seemed to be even brighter now. My mother's friend's face was almost serene, and I wasn't the only person in the gallery who spotted this.

A man behind me remarked, 'The woman must be stark raving mad.'

'Taken over by evil spirits, I'd say,' said another.

A goodwife attempted to put them both in their place. 'Be quiet,' she said. 'The truth is obvious. Mistress Clitherow seems happy, but only because she's moved a step nearer to God. '

'A bloody lot nearer than one step, my love,' replied an anonymous wag.

With the hubbub in the courtroom increasing, Justice Rodes called for silence. Clearly, he was ready to continue his attack. He whispered and nodded to one of the courtroom officers. Later that evening, I told Father Mush this was when things got really nasty. During the coming period the crowd became agitated, both those for the good lady and even those against her.

Judge Clench looked unhappy, as if this wasn't how things were meant to be done. Have no doubt though, the man was responsible for what happened next. He could have a put a stop to this outrage, there and then, before it started, but he didn't.

The other judge was equally culpable, as of course it was Justice Rodes who orchestrated the sneering attack on Margaret Clitherow's good honour. And then there were the other man, the junior official, he bade join in.

Rodes started by motioning to an ugly fellow with a sour looking mouth to approach the prisoner. The man began glaring and shouting at the good lady. If this wasn't enough, he took a sudden and aggressive step towards her. The Mistress flinched and the gallery became silent. I prayed for God to strike him down dead, but before he could touch Mistress Clitherow he stopped himself, less than a yard from her face. For the first time Mother's friend looked frightened and vulnerable.

From then on, he struck out at her again and again with verbal and moral blows. The pain they caused was plain to see in her face, as every rumour, gossip and vulgarity spoken about in York over the weekend invaded the Common Hall.

The leech stared and jabbed his finger at Mistress Clitherow. 'All in this courtroom, indeed everyone in York, knows it's not for religion that thou harbourest priests,' he claimed.

What did he mean?

'But for whoredom!' he shouted. The gallery gasped.

'What do you say of this, Margaret Clitherow?' the man demanded.

'Such allegations merit no response,' the good lady replied, with a shake of the head.

The words gained many a nod from the crowd around me. I turned and looked to see the reactions of others. All were transfixed, and many saddened, by the entertainment now being laid out in front of them.

'So, you don't deny it then,' pressed the officer. 'The whole of the city knows of your harlotry. An artist has even drawn some pretty pictures of it. Would you like to see them? Would you like to share details of what you did?'

For a moment Mistress Clitherow faltered. I thought she'd look away, but she stopped herself and held her head up high.

The sneer on the man's down-turned mouth grew even wider. 'And as for the priests you bed down and squirm with, we all know why they choose to reside with comely and beautiful young women such as yourself. They do so only to satisfy their carnal lusts.'

A few found this too much. For the first time there were shouts and boos in the courtroom. Others looked bewildered. One comedian shouted, 'She's not that young!' Only a few men laughed.

'Silence!' shouted Rodes. 'Order, order, order in this court.' He turned to Mistress Clitherow and said. 'Do you not deny these allegations against you?'

The good lady ignored him. Instead she turned towards Judge Clench with an imploring look on her face.

'Please answer the question, Mistress Clitherow,' Clench said firmly but quietly, and I wished him dead too.

The noise in the galley hushed as people strained to hear the prisoner's response.

'Of course, I deny it,' she said, as calmly as she could. 'This court, and everyone else in York, knows it not to be true. I share my bed chamber with my husband and obey his instructions in there. But everywhere else I follow the commands of the Lord.'

Believing in her righteousness, a number of people began to applaud. Not all joined in but it was enough to make Judge Clench realise he'd made a mistake by allowing Rodes and the unnamed man to make their seedy intervention. Due to their foolish actions the officials risked losing control of events and the people in front of them.

Without uttering another word Judge Clench raised his body up into a standing position. At first the people ignored him. Many continued to shout, gossip and laugh, but after a while the men and women in the front rows of the gallery noticed what he'd done. They became quieter and seated themselves back down onto the benches. This movement was repeated in waves across the hall until almost the whole of the courtroom was seated in silence. The atmosphere became tense, as the gallery waited impatiently to see would come next.

'This Assizes court is now in recess for the rest of the day,' said the senior judge. 'We shall reconvene in the morning. Tomorrow, those in the public gallery will display an improved respect for this court and its officers, or members of it will be removed, fined and imprisoned.'

He then turned to the accused. 'I beseech you Mistress Clitherow to reflect overnight on the responses you have made so far to this court. Perhaps the long hours of darkness will persuade you of your folly. The evidence against you is flimsy at best. You will place your husband and children in danger if you persist with this reckless approach. Worst of all, you will suffer a horrible death if you refuse to make a plea, far beyond any punishment this court could give you for the crimes you come here accused of. Each of these arguments should be enough for any sane man or woman to change their mind and allow themselves to be tried by God and the country.'

Judge Clench turned next to the officers of the court. 'The prisoner is to be bound and escorted back to jail but note this, Mistress Clitherow is not to be returned to the relative comfort of York Castle. Instead she will be incarcerated within the commoners' prison on Ouse Bridge. Do I make myself clear?'

Ayes and nods came from around the front benches. Two junior officers approached Mistress Clitherow. The men tied ropes tightly around her wrists. All about me, citizens were getting up and leaving their seats but I continued to watch the prisoner's face. Although Mistress Clitherow was clearly in discomfort, she began to smile once more, as if somehow happy with the day's events.

# 13

Parson Wigginton was barely a few steps ahead of me when I joined the crowd leaving the courtroom. We'd agreed not to acknowledge each other's existence, and I watched his back as he made his way through the gossips in the crowd. After he left the square in front of the Common Hall, he ambled along Coney Street in the direction of Spurriergate. I followed behind, keeping a distance between us but being careful not to let him get too far ahead.

I recalled the stories Kit had once told me of government watchers and spies. In London, he claimed, there were hundreds, maybe thousands, of informants who tracked the movements of important men suspected of treason and much lesser crimes. Where was the problem with that, I asked? If you do nothing wrong, there's nothing to worry about.

Like my father, I'd been raised to believe in the rule of law, but, somehow, these days I wasn't so sure. Certain crimes didn't appear to match their punishment. What would happen if I was found guilty of meeting a Catholic priest, of not informing the authorities of his whereabouts? Was this treason?

I glanced over my shoulder, but the faces around me looked like ordinary citizens going about their business. Most chatted about the events of the afternoon, but what did they do when I wasn't looking? Did any of them follow me? Were they gathering information? Walking down the street in York didn't feel like it used to.

When we reached Peasholme Green, Pastor Wigginton delayed. He let me pass by, without saying a word. Once I arrived at the inn, I thought it best to go to the meeting house directly and decided to go first. I walked through the back yard and across the grass. Once outside the door of the secret house, I knocked twice but the door was already opening.

Father Mush ushered me quickly within. There was no sign of the sleeping man in the corner. We were alone but I had no time to ask what had happened to him. The Father urged me to quickly recall a summary of what I'd observed during the day. Before doing so, I asked a question which had been troubling me.

'Father,' I said, 'as Pastor Wigginton is also attending the Assizes, why do you need me?'

He glanced through the spy hole, checking the area outside the door was clear before making his reply. 'I trust Giles,' he said. 'But only to a point. We agree with each other that the government should prosecute only those who transgress God's laws and not those of the Queen, but our views about what His laws are are somewhat different. Much of what Giles stands for, I stand against. Whilst I wish to change the state religion, Giles wants to upend the natural order of things and men's very place in the world. If he, and those like him, get their way, there will be chaos. God has no wish for that.'

He paused for a moment, to peep through the shutter. 'We're allies now but this won't last forever. I need you to give me an independent view on what's going on. In any case, one of you may miss something which the other one sees. It's too late now though, Giles is here.'

The Father opened the door and the pastor stepped inside. In the darkened room, lit by a single candle, we recounted two overlapping versions of the day's events. Most of what each of us said was in line with the other's description. The parson didn't appear to embellish his account or omit any key facts.

But Father Mush had been right in one respect. Pastor Wigginton spotted things I hadn't picked up on, including the frequent passing of notes to and from Judge Rodes, one of which came from the Lord Mayor, Henry Maye. The others entered the courtroom from outside, written by unknown hands.

When we were finished, Wigginton asked Father Mush to describe the priestly vestments and trinkets he'd left behind, hidden in the Clitherow household. The Father's descriptions matched the clothing and items used by the fools during the bizarre scene played out in the courtroom.

'But there's one thing you should know,' added the Father. 'The hidden chamber where these things were left and the Catholic services were carried out wasn't within John Clitherow's house. It was located next door, in the home of one of his relatives.'

''Tis strange,' the parson said. 'But no mention was made of these items being found in a neighbour's house.'

'Indeed,' said Father Mush. 'But this is hardly surprising. Such news would muddy the waters regarding the good lady's guilt or innocence, and the Corporation and Council mean to find her guilty, do they not?'

We thought upon this for a moment, before Father Mush spoke again.

'Your account of the day proves the court will do anything to confirm Mistress Clitherow's guilt.'

'What do you mean?' I asked.

'Well, you say Judge Clench told the prisoner the only evidence held against her was based upon the words of a child?'

We both nodded.

'Then this is clearly a lie,' he replied. 'For they have already highlighted the vestments and vessels used for Mass. Is this evidence not even more damning?'

'Unless they already have a priest,' interjected Pastor Wigginton. 'Don't forget no word has been heard from Father Ingleby since his arrest.'

'No!' For the first time Father Mush raised his voice. 'Father Ingleby would martyr himself before he'd betray one of his parishioners.'

'Even under torture?'

'Even under torture. I know the man.'

'Perhaps the judges realise they can't use the other evidence because it was found in somebody else's house?' I suggested.

'Alas, no, Guy,' replied Father Mush sadly. He placed a hand onto my shoulder. 'These judges will bend the rules as they see fit. The room in the other house will belong to Mistress Clitherow's abode, if they wish it to be so. The good lady has no defence counsel. When the trial begins, they'll find plenty of evidence against her and the jury will lap it all up.'

'Aye, the jury,' sighed Pastor Wigginton. 'And we all know who selects the men who sit on that.'

'York's senior Sheriff,' confirmed Father Mush.

'Who this year happens to be Roland Fawcett, the man who arrested Mistress Clitherow in the first place,' I said slowly, realising the point the men were making.

They nodded and smiled at me sympathetically, as if to say I was learning. The whole day had come as quite a shock to me. The proceedings in court appeared to be so heavily loaded in favour of the prosecution. Was this always the case? If so, where was the justice? Perhaps it was a good thing I wasn't going to be a lawyer.

The two men began to discuss next steps. They came up with something I hadn't thought of, although their conclusions were quite different. They both realised there was still one course of action which could save Mistress Clitherow from the executioner. She simply needed to denounce her Catholicism, repent her previous behaviour and announce her conversion to the state religion. If she did this, there'd be no execution. There may not even be a prison sentence.

'I feel this is the outcome Henry Maye has been planning for all along,' concluded Pastor Wigginton.

'I agree,' said Father Mush. 'The man's a snake. He's only got where he is today by marrying Mistress Clitherow's dear mother, God bless her soul, and using her money and connections, but I don't think he wishes to see his stepdaughter dead.'

'No,' agreed the pastor. 'But having a well-known recusant in the family isn't good for a man with political ambition. What a coup it would be for him, if he could claim responsibility for converting her. He'd turn his embarrassment into a triumph.'

'And gain great credit from Archbishop Sandys and the Church.' Father Mush nodded slowly as he spoke. 'The Corporation and the Council would reward him. He may even be asked to kneel down before the Queen. Sir Henry Maye of York. What do you think of that?'

'We can save Mistress Clitherow then?' I said, with sudden excitement in my voice. For the first time during the day I felt hope for the good lady.

'Yes,' replied Pastor Wigginton. For a second the zeal in his eyes shone through even in the darkness. But it was soon extinguished. I think he guessed the response we were about to receive from the other man, his religious opponent.

'No!' said Father Mush firmly.

'What do you mean, Father?' I asked.

'Mistress Clitherow has no wish to convert, and we're not going to ask her to.'

A dark look came over all of our faces. I couldn't understand what was wrong.

'But she doesn't need to convert,' I argued. 'She just has to say she has, and she'll be safe.'

'But that's not how the world works, laddie,' said the priest. 'The Pearl of York can't tell lies about her religion.'

'If she converts, she won't have to,' interjected Wigginton. 'In doing so, she'll save her soul, both here on earth and in heaven. For all eternity.'

'No. I forbid it.' Father Mush's voice was harsh. He spoke in a way I hadn't heard before.

'You would rather see the good lady die?' I asked in dismay. 'And die so horribly?'

'If the Lord wishes it to be so,' replied the priest tersely.

I couldn't believe his words.

'I'll say nothing more on the subject,' he added firmly. 'You should both go now. Observe what happens in the court tomorrow, and report back to me here afterwards. We can then discuss what to do next.'

I wanted to shout and scream at him but I couldn't bring myself to challenge the Catholic priest. What was happening? Every day the world seemed to be turning upside down. And I lacked the ability to do anything about it. One day, I thought angrily, one day, I'll take back control.

Pastor Wigginton left the house first, whilst I had to wait a few minutes. Neither Father Mush nor I spoke another word to each other in the darkness. We didn't even look at each other. I was so upset, and he had no wish to console me. I didn't consider his feelings. Or think about why he'd taken the stance he had. In hindsight, perhaps I now even agree with his view but at that very moment I hated him for it. I counted silently in Latin until it was time to leave. No farewells were said.

When I reached the street, the late afternoon had almost completed its daily transformation into evening. Like the atmosphere in the city, the weather had been gloomy before but as night neared the clouds were departing. Low in the sky, the sun cast a long shadow from the spire of St Cuthbert's. Pastor Wigginton waited for me beneath it. He gave me a shrill whistle to attract my attention. I turned and walked over towards him.

'Don't worry, Master Fawkes,' he said cheerfully. 'The good lady can still be saved. I plan to visit her this very evening. It'll only take a few coins to bribe the warders. I'm sure they'll show me to her cell. In my line of business, I spend a lot of time in and out of prisons.'

'As a visitor or an inmate?' I asked sharply.

'Both,' came the reply.

Not knowing much of the history of the man, I wasn't sure if it was a joke or not.

'I'll ensure Mistress Clitherow fully understands the situation she finds herself in. We'll discuss scripture and the value of hearing the Gospels in English so everyone can understand them. I'm certain she'll take comfort in the Lord's words.' The burning light was back in his eyes.

'In some ways Father Mush is a good man but he remains blinkered in others,' continued the parson. 'It's much the same with all his kind. If Mistress Clitherow sees the light, her sentence will be lifted.'

'But what if she won't convert?' I asked.

'I won't ask her to lie,' he replied, shaking his head. 'Neither she, nor God, would wish that.'

He saw the fear for her fate in my eyes and attempted to reassure me.

'But neither would He wish Mistress Clitherow, or any other woman, be crushed to death in such a barbaric way. If she won't repent, I'll convince her to make a plea and face the country. It's possible the jury will see how flimsy the evidence is and acquit her on the spot.'

'But if she's found guilty, what then?'

'Then they'll hang her. But at least she'll die quickly on the gallows.'

When I arrived home, I shared a late meal at the table with Mother and the girls. We ate our vegetable pottage in silence. I didn't think I'd be able to eat anything after the day I'd had, but I soon realised I was famished. Mother was a fine cook. The food went down well and I scraped the bowl clean.

When we'd finished eating, the girls were asked to go upstairs. Lizzie went straight up but Anne protested. She said she wasn't much younger than me and it wasn't fair I was allowed to stay up and go off on adventures when she had to remain at home, doing her chores and looking after her sister.

Mother admonished her sharply for this. She told Anne she should be grateful for what she had. Many girls suffered much less comfortable lives. Anne apologised but I could see she was still angry. Mother despatched her to bed with the message that there were some things it was better girls didn't hear about. Reluctantly Anne followed her sister and climbed up the steps, catching my eye as she went.

Afterwards Mother and I sat down again. For a second time I recounted events in the courtroom. I also outlined the meeting with Father Mush and Pastor Wigginton, although I omitted to mention the final passages of what was said. I had no wish to burden Mother with more anxiety. Instead I asked her if there had been news from Scotton. She shook her head. There was none.

I retired upstairs. My plan was to collapse and go straight to sleep in my uncle's bed. I began to remove my clothing. A rustling noise emerged from beneath the sheets. I stood still for a moment. There was silence. I thought I heard it again. I lifted my candle. Something was moving slowly beneath the covers of my bed.

For a moment I thought it must be an attacker. But the shape was too small. It seemed more like a girl. My heart leapt. A shiver ran through my body. With great excitement I whipped back the bedding and received my surprise. But I was disappointed. It wasn't who I'd hoped to see.

'Anne,' I said, struggling to mask the disappointment in my voice. 'What are you doing in here?'

'I need to talk to you,' said my sister. 'I want to know what's going on. You and Mother only speak in whispers these days. What is happening? And why are you looking at me like you've never seen me before. Who were you expecting to find?'

I kicked off my breeches, kept on the long woollen shirt and climbed into bed. Anne moved to the centre and we sat close to each other, our backs against the headboard with the bolster supporting us. We'd never kept things from each other before. Anne told me virtually everything about her life and I'd mostly done the same. With all the activity of the last few weeks, I realised I'd lost sight of her feelings.

I blew out the candle, and in the darkness of the room I updated her on all I knew about Mother's Catholic conversion. I began with the night I'd followed her to The Shambles through the snow. To my surprise I even talked about Maria and the feelings I felt for her. Lastly, I gave Anne an edited version of the day's events in line with what I'd told Mother.

'What do you think will happen to Mistress Clitherow, the butcher and their children?' she asked.

'I don't know,' I admitted. 'It all depends on what happens at the Assizes tomorrow.'

'How can that woman behave with such disregard for her family? Do you think she'll ever change her mind?'

'I hope so,' I said.

'If she's taken away, or even worse, and Mister Clitherow is imprisoned too, what will happen to poor Henry if he returns to York? Where would he live?'

I had no good answer for this.

'Why did she send him away? Perhaps he'll hear about all this and never return.'

I realised how foolish I'd been. I'd wrapped myself up in the goings-on around me and thought no further. It was as black as night in the room but I knew there were tears in Anne's eyes. I'd fallen in love with Maria, struggled with my faith and spent the whole day on edge, worrying about Mistress Clitherow. In doing so, I'd forgotten about what had always been important to me, my family.

I put my arms around my sister's shoulders and without a word encouraged her to cry. I understood. She needed to let her feelings out. Anne couldn't talk to Mother. Lizzie was too young. We'd always been there for each other but for a while she must have felt like I'd abandoned her.

Anne was fourteen. She was a young woman now. The boy she cared for most in the world had been sent away to France by his mother. She'd not even been given time to say goodbye to him. It was no wonder Anne questioned Mistress Clitherow's motives. She'd placed Henry's whole family in danger. There was a real possibility he'd never return home and Anne would never see him again. How would I feel, if it had been Maria?

And what of Mother and her crises of heart and religion? Who was this man who had a wife? What anguish must Mother be feeling inside? What, if anything, did Lizzie fret about? I regretted I'd not been there for all three of them. Instead I'd spent time rushing around risking my neck for people I hardly knew. Once the Assizes court case was over, I was determined to put my efforts into supporting my family, getting a job and marrying Maria. I hoped word would arrive from Scotton soon.

# 14

**Tuesday March 15th, 1586**

After the first day of the Assizes subsequent sessions usually began around ten each morning. Erring on the side of caution, I decided to leave the house at least an hour earlier in order to gain a good seat in the gallery. However, it must have been before eight bells when we heard the rap on the door. I unlocked it with the iron key, pulled the bolt back and pushed the heavy wooden panel aside to find a street urchin standing before me. Keen eyes stared up into mine.

'Is your name Fawkes?' he asked.

I nodded.

'Then I got a message for you,' he said with a heavy accent. Another immigrant boy.

'What is it?' I asked.

'The Assizes is opening early.'

He opened the palm of his right hand towards me.

'What? Who sent you?'

'Don't know. Just do what I'm told.'

His hand stayed out. Searching the kitchen, I found a coin of the smallest denomination and passed it on to him. It wasn't much and I expected the boy to complain but he didn't. As I closed the door, he walked off merrily. I surmised he'd already been paid. There was little doubt in my mind who'd sent him.

After passing the message onto my mother, I ate a chunk of bread and pulled on my boots and coat. Anne was clearly jealous. I knew she wanted to come along but she didn't say anything. She'd have been good company in the courtroom too but Mother was correct as usual. This was no business for girls.

'Be wary, Guy,' Mother instructed.

When I arrived in the gallery, I didn't have a problem finding a seat. Although a few people were already there, the place was largely empty. I sat on the right side of the central aisle in the third row, deliberately taking the opposite end to Pastor Wigginton, who'd already positioned himself at the very front.

I wondered what, if anything, he'd been able to achieve with Mistress Clitherow during the previous evening. A miraculous conversion? A plea of not guilty? Either outcome could save her life. Perhaps the good lady had relented and would speak a few contrite words to the courtroom. How happy this would make me.

Apostasy was what they called it. The act of renouncing your religion. Since King Henry's time there'd been a lot of it about. Perhaps if his children had all been raised in the same faith, things would have been different. But no. When Edward, Mary and Elizabeth replaced each other they each put their own stamp onto the state religion. And, of course, the people were forced to change along with them. But not everyone embraced such a change.

When we'd discussed this in school following the first fight with Thomas Cheke, Kit had been confident. It would soon happen all over again, he predicted, arguing Mary, the dethroned Queen of Scots, was the obvious heir to the English crown. She already lived in the country, albeit as an unwelcome guest of her cousin Elizabeth. Those of the old faith just had to sit down quietly and wait for the Queen to die. Or for someone to kill her. I'd shushed him then. This was treacherous talk.

Somehow, I doubted such a turn of events could ever happen. I certainly didn't consider the possibility Mary's son, the Scots viper James, would ever take the throne. The very thought of his name fills me with pain, as his henchmen do their worst to me. With an effort, I force my mind back to my own history.

There was a shuffling of papers and a movement of men and seats, as the court officers confirmed their attendance. It seemed the objective of the early start was clear. They hoped to have Mistress Clitherow's case done and dusted before the public gallery filled with people who might wish to voice their concerns. The Assizes could then continue. No doubt there was a long list of felonies and punishments ahead. After the raucous close to proceedings on the previous day, I suspected Judges Clench and Rodes would be keen to see the back of this case.

The shout went up. 'Call Margaret Clitherow.'

For a second time, the good lady was marched through the courtroom to stand before us. This time though she wore a plain dress and her head was hatless, a coif scarf covered her hair and her hands were bound in front of her. Her apparel and walk may have had the look of a common prisoner but her face remained serene. When she reached her allotted position in front of the dock cage a junior officer untied her hands. She used her slender fingers to rub some life back into her wrists where the bonds had cut into them.

When this was done, Mistress Clitherow looked around. The good lady smiled at the officers and the gallery as benignly as she had yesterday. I wondered whether this meant she intended to take a similar approach, or was she relieved, perhaps even confident she no longer faced death? I hoped so.

Mother believed a declaration confirming abandonment of the old religion would be enough to see her pardoned, perhaps even acquitted. How great it would be to see the good lady walk away from the court a free woman, ready to run into the arms of her loving husband.

For a moment Mistress Clitherow's gaze settled onto her stepfather. The smile she gave the man was even warmer than the one she blessed the rest of us with. And this time the Lord Mayor didn't avert his eyes but latched onto her gaze. The two relatives through marriage continued to look at each other for several seconds, until Henry Maye nodded and smiled. He must know something, I thought. The look the pair shared was enough to convince me Pastor Wigginton had been successful. I issued a long and satisfying sigh of relief.

The officials of the York Lent Assizes in the year of our Lord 1586 were now seated or stood in their standard positions, with one addition. In the midst of a small group of anonymous officers I spied the more familiar face of Henry Cheke, father of Thomas, Member of Parliament and non-legal Secretary to the Council of the North. I wondered what he was doing here. Perhaps he was interested in a later case.

Judge Clench leaned forward. His manner appeared more confident than his previous day's demeanour. It looked as if he too believed the session was going to end with a more positive outcome.

'Margaret Clitherow, how say you?' he asked. 'Yesternight we passed you over without judgment, when we might have pronounced against you. But we did not. We gave you the opportunity to do something more comfortable, and put yourself to the country, for otherwise we would have been forced to take alternative action against you. It is the law. We see no reason why you should refuse us. As explained yesterday, there is but small witness held against you, and the country will consider your case most carefully.'

'Indeed,' said Mistress Clitherow.

The sparsely populated public gallery became quiet. This was clearly the most conciliatory word she'd uttered during the proceedings to date. Or had it been merely ironic? As the good lady continued to smile, I waited for her declaration. Everyone else in the courtroom waited too.

I attempted to read what I could from her features. Behind that smile I saw steely determination, or was it simply manufactured by my imagination? I asked myself what I knew of Mistress Clitherow. She was a good woman, with an unshakeable belief in the Bible. She'd faced trials and tribulations before but never once had she lost her resolve, even when she'd been banished from her family and sent to prison for refusing to attend the Sunday service.

After a long pause, she spoke again, and I was glad I wasn't paying for my seat, for I only used the edge of it.

'I think you have no witness against me but the words of children. With an apple and a rod, you may get them to say what you will.'

My eyes closed, and tears almost welled up. In my heart I think I always knew the good lady would never compromise, even when her life was in jeopardy. I felt regret and pity but mainly admiration. There would be no apostasy but I still had hope. She could yet make a plea.

'Obviously we have more evidence against you than that,' intervened Justice Rodes. 'It is plain for all to see you've taken priests into your husband's house, by the things which were found there. Did you not see the ornaments and vestments we placed on display in the courtroom yesterday? It will be hard for the country to consider you anything but guilty.'

Judge Clench's face turned from understanding to thunder, as he glared at his colleague. Clearly his preference was to downplay the likelihood of the good lady's conviction. Equally we all knew the approach was a sham. Everyone, including the accused, could see the weight of evidence the court held against her. A not guilty verdict seemed as unlikely as a fresh plum at Easter.

 But there was something else. The so-called evidence was flawed. I almost stood up. I wanted to shout out, 'The clothing and vessels weren't found in her husband's house. They were secreted in a hidden room in a neighbour's dwelling.' But to my lasting shame I remained silent.

The prisoner responded instead. 'As for good Catholic priests, I know of no cause why I should refuse them as long as I live. They come to our houses only to do myself and others good.'

There was unease in the room at this, for with these words the prisoner appeared to be openly admitting her guilt. For a moment I closed my eyes in despair. After less than a second I forced them open again. I'd been tasked with remembering everything which happened inside the courtroom, and I was determined to do so, even though I'd begun to detest all that went on there.

'Shame on you, Mistress,' roared Justice Rodes, pointing his finger angrily at her. 'Every Catholic priest is a traitor, a rascal and a deceiver of the Queen's subjects.'

'No,' she replied softly. 'God forgive you. You would not speak of them in such a way if you really knew them.'

With this, the good lady gave the judge a special type of smile, one filled with compassion. It was if she was saying to the courtroom, '*It's not this man's fault, for he is a simpleton who lacks the wit to understand what's going on. He warrants our sympathy, rather than our contempt.*'

Rodes reared up. When he replied there was hatred in his voice. *She* was the one who didn't understand. 'You would detest them yourself if you knew their treasons, and all their wickedness, as we on these benches know them,' he shouted.

She shook her head softly and smiled. 'I know them only as virtuous men, sent by God to save our souls.'

Additional people had entered the public gallery by this time, and more were arriving every minute. There was a general hubbub now in the courtroom as people caught up and reacted to what was being said.

Every time she spoke, Mistress Clitherow did so clearly, boldly and it appeared to me somehow modestly. I realised I had nothing but respect for this woman's courage and steadfastness in the face of such adversity. But equally I feared for her life.

'Order,' demanded Judge Clench.

Yet again, he was determined to take control of the proceedings. The judge turned to the prisoner. 'What say you? Will you put yourself to the country? Yes or no?'

The accused took a sharp breath. For a moment it appeared she was listening to a tiny voice inside her head.

'I see no good cause why I should do so in this matter,' replied my mother's friend, her voice as soft as lambswool. 'I refer my case only to God and your consciences. Do what you think is good.'

No, please no, I thought. Someone must intervene. With each word Mistress Clitherow was lifting another weight and placing it down upon her heavily pressed body.

Conversations began to start up all around me. A man and his wife complained about her obstinacy. Many people couldn't understand why the good lady didn't renounce her Catholic faith in order to save her life. At the very least she should place herself at the mercy of the country. Surely the jury couldn't find her guilty with so little evidence. The hearsay of one or two children wouldn't be enough. And as for the vestments and ornaments, the scene played out by the court jesters yesterday hadn't been well received by the public, and the people in the gallery considered the jury would feel the same.

Judge Clench shouted again, 'Order! Order!'

Once he was confident he could be heard, he spoke afresh to the prisoner, but his voice seemed resigned. 'Well, then, you give this court no choice. We must pronounce sentence against you. Mercy lieth in our hands, and in the country's, but only if you will allow us to place you on trial. Otherwise, you must face the law.'

This was awful. I feared what was coming, Death by pressing. I shuddered to imagine the good lady laid out beneath a door with heavy stones crushing the very life out of her. How loudly would she scream? How much agony would she feel? I pushed the pictures away and refused to listen to the terrible noises inside my head. As an alternative, I looked at the smiling countenance in front of me. I listened to her softly spoken words and wondered how she could do this to herself.

After that, there was even more noise in the courtroom. Some men and women appeared to be urging her sentencing. Others railed against the prospect. I heard one fellow shout loudly in particular but I couldn't hear what he said due to the melee around him. After a few moments I realised the man calling out was Parson Wigginton.

At first the judges and officials ignored him. For a while I think they couldn't hear his voice above the clamour, but as his words grew increasingly louder and more frantic, eventually Judge Clench spotted him. When he finally brought the court to order he beckoned for the Protestant preacher to speak.

Wigginton stood. He called out to the judges and officials. 'My lords, I thank you for giving me leave to talk.'

'What is it, man?' asked Clench. 'Get on with it.'

I think the judge must have suspected someone like Justice Rodes had encouraged the pastor's intervention. A Protestant parson would surely denounce the prisoner. In a rare moment of clarity, I suddenly thought the same. Had Giles Wigginton been spying on us all along? What had he learned from Father Mush? In despair I worried he was about to denounce Mistress Clitherow.

'My lord, take heed what you do here today. You sit to deliver justice but this woman's case is touching life and death. You ought not, either by God's law nor by man's, judge her to die solely upon the slender witness of one foreign boy. No, this can not be, unless more substantial evidence is provided to the courtroom by at least two or three Englishmen of good reputation. Therefore, look to it and consider your position, my lord, for I fear otherwise your case will go sour.'

The judge answered, 'I may do so by the law.'

I couldn't see Pastor Wigginton's face but I could imagine the fervour in his eyes. I'd misjudged him again. He was still on the good lady's side. He always had been. I knew now he always would be.

'By what law?' he demanded.

'By the Queen's law,' responded Judge Clench.

'That may well be,' said Wigginton, raising his voice at the judge, 'but you cannot do so by God's law,' he shouted.

The words seemed to leave a powerful impression on the senior judge. But before he could give a considered reply, his colleague Rodes intervened. 'Sit down, man!' he demanded.

Supported by the junior officials in the court, Rodes waved his papers angrily at the parson. Giles Wigginton tried to speak out again but they wouldn't let him, and eventually he slumped back down onto his bench at the front of the gallery, dejected and defeated. But at least he'd tried. He was a Puritan, a Calvinist, a Protestant, a preacher of the sort I'd grow to hate as my enemy. But despite all that, he was a decent man.

No doubts lingered any longer in my mind. I knew now he'd spent much of the night attempting to convert the good lady towards his own views on religion. And when, inevitably, this had failed, he'd implored her to plead not guilty. He'd have highlighted the flimsy evidence from Johann and the fact the trinkets were found in somebody else's house. Equally I pictured Mistress Clitherow sat in her dark cell, her face frightened but unbowed. She'd have shaken her head steadfastly and refused to implicate any of her neighbours.

After this, I thought of Father Mush and his own part in the proceedings. I inhaled sharply as a dreadful thought flashed through my mind. The fellow next to me asked if I was alright. I nodded but I wasn't. For the first time I thought I fully understood the Father's motives in this nasty business. For the first time I lost all hope. For the first time I was fully convinced Mistress Clitherow's life was doomed.

Had Father Mush planned such an outcome all along?

'Good woman,' urged Judge Clench yet again. 'I pray, please put yourself unto the country. There is no evidence but a boy against you, and whatever the country decides, we, the judges, can show mercy afterwards.'

'No, I bow only to God's laws,' she replied.

After Mistress Clitherow's refusal to change tack, there was a movement on the benches behind. Lord Mayor Maye made a noise, shaking his head, almost weeping. Perhaps there was goodness in the man after all. Although if there was, he hid it well later.

Clearly the Mayor hadn't expected the day's events to turn out like this. He was visibly upset. At one stage I thought he might stand up and leave the courtroom but he remained. Henry Maye was a pragmatist, who changed his mind with the political wind. Only too late had he grasped his dead wife's daughter was different. Margaret Clitherow was a woman of principle and conviction. Once she made up her mind on something, she'd stick to it, whatever the consequences.

I scanned the officers. Henry Cheke was surveying the scene impatiently. He moved from his place and began exchanging angry whispers with Justice Rodes. I got the impression he was advising the man what to do next. Perhaps he was. When Rodes turned and spoke publicly to his senior colleague, for the first time the junior judge seemed to use guile rather than bluster.

'Brother Clench, you are too merciful in these matters. Let us not waste any more time on this wicked and wilful woman. We need to dispatch her now, so we can get on with the other cases. We must remember Mistress Clitherow isn't the only defendant at these Assizes. Many others wait downstairs, ready to hear our wisdom. Unless we can make progress, this court won't be finished until well after Easter. I'm sure the recorder will have noted your repeated and valiant attempts to make the mistress see sense. The courtroom and the people thank you, but surely enough is enough?'

Justice Clench nodded, appearing to agree with his colleague's summation. He stood up, an ashen look on his face. Not for the first time a hush of anticipation came over the courtroom. People stopped talking and moving about. The latest entrants to the hall stood still in the aisles, waiting for the proclamation.

'Mistress Clitherow,' said the judge sternly. 'If you will not allow us to put your case to the country, this must be our judgment.'

I held my breath.

'You will be returned from whence you came. Once there, in the lowest part of the prison or another suitable building, you will be stripped naked and laid upon the ground. Your hands and feet will be tied to posts and a sharp stone placed beneath your back. As much weight will be laid upon your body as it can bear. And you will be pressed to death, slowly. This punishment will continue for up to three days, with no food except bread and a little puddle water. And on the third day, if breath be left in your body, additional weights will be placed upon you, and your life brought to an end. What do you say to this?'

The good woman stood, with no change or fear in her countenance. The gallery gaped open mouthed.

'If this judgment be according to your conscience, I pray God sends you a better judgment when it's your own time to come before Him,' she said firmly.

'You should not speak such words,' admonished Judge Clench, clearly affected by the rebuke. 'I do this according to the law. And I tell you, this must be our judgment, unless you allow yourself to be tried by the country.'

'I shall not,' she replied. 'I thank God most heartily for this punishment.'

'Then consider this,' continued the judge, looking down at his notes. 'Who will look after your husband and your children when you are gone, Mistress Clitherow? I warn you, do not cast yourself away from them.'

'Ha!' replied the good lady, with a wilder look in her eyes. 'If it is God's will, I will be content to see my husband and children suffer the same fate as me for such a worthy cause.'

The judge was taken aback. The people in the gallery were shocked. They didn't like this, and for the first time during the Assizes the majority of the room turned against her. I could see the men in the seats around me question themselves. They queried if this woman in the dock was genuinely saying she'd be happy to watch her family die in the same agonising manner as she was so intent on bringing on herself. The crowd became restless and noisy.

Judge Clench demanded silence, and I looked again at Henry Maye. The Lord Mayor had seemed brow-beaten earlier but a change had now came over his face. His best laid plans to convert his stepdaughter had come to nothing. For his political survival, he'd have to do something else. He shifted forward in his seat and spoke to his friend Sheriff Fawcett.

Maybe it was because I was near to the front, or I was able to lip-read his words, or perhaps I imagined them. In any case this is what I thought he said. 'The stupid bitch is committing suicide. I wash my hands of her.'

Judge Clench spoke to the prisoner. Despite everything which had happened, even now he persisted in attempting to dissuade the good lady from her course of action. I wondered why. If I was him, I would have lost all patience. Pastor Wigginton told me later it was because Judge Clench found himself between a rock in the Council's intention to see Mistress Clitherow executed, and a hard place, should the Queen ever discover he was the man who ordered it.

'How yet, Margaret Clitherow? Are you content to put yourself upon the trial of the country? Although we have given sentence against you according to the Queen's law, we will show mercy if you will help yourself.'

Mistress Clitherow lifted her eyes and her hands towards heaven. She spoke in a cheerful voice, like the one she used in the butcher's shop to greet old friends and customers. 'God be praised,' she said 'All that He sends me shall be welcome, for I am hardly worthy of such a good death as this. I may deserve death, I must confess, for any offence I may have made against God. But certainly not for anything I am accused of in this court.' For the first time I felt Mistress Clitherow was ranting a little

Justice Rodes turned to his colleague. 'You've tried to help this woman too many times already, my lord. You must let her go.'

Clench nodded. He beckoned for Roland Fawcett to come towards the judge's bench and spoke to him. The Sheriff instructed two of his own men. They walked to the dock and secured the prisoner's arms together with a strong piece of rope. Mistress Clitherow stepped out of the cage, looked towards the heavens, whispered a prayer and smiled at us all.

This was too much for the gallery. Catcalling began.

'See that smile? The Devil's inside her!'

'Shame!'

'Don't you know suicide's a sin?'

'Think of the butcher and the little ones!'

'Shame on you!'

And so it went on. As the sheriffs and sergeants led her from the room, the throng surged forward. People had to be pushed back and controlled. Somehow one woman prostrated herself at the good lady's feet. 'I believe you get your comfort directly from the Holy Ghost,' she said. 'I feel such a pain inside me. I beseech you, good lady. Share your comfort and heal me. I don't want to die.'

Sheriff Fawcett shoved the woman aside. Her husband tried to drag the distraught figure away. I thought he'd strike her down too, but

Mistress Clitherow shook her head and he stopped himself. Some time later people claimed the man had seen the holy features of the Lord Jesus Christ in the good lady's eyes. Whether this was true or not, the old woman made the symbol of the Catholic Church and the couple hurried away.

'Call Andrew Turner.'

A man with a limp in his left leg was led to the dock. After all the excitement of the previous hour, there was little interest in this case about coining. Most of the people in the courtroom now stood up to leave, myself amongst them. I glanced over at the far side of the gallery. Parson Wigginton remained in his seat.

His eyes were closed but his lips were moving. He appeared to be making a silent prayer. I focused my mind and urged him to follow me. We had a plan to devise. Even if we couldn't prevent the good lady's sentencing, there was perhaps one course of action we could still take to save her. I wanted to tell him what it was.

# 15

When I emerged into the open air, the streets were brimming with conversation. Very few citizens had been aware of the early start. Some were still arriving and clearly disappointed to discover they'd missed the excitement. Friends filled each other in across all four corners of the square. The talk combined accurate reflections with exaggeration, and soon second and third hand accounts were being passed around by people who hadn't even attended the hearing.

If the mood of the city had been mixed the day before, on that Tuesday morning the people's feelings had taken a sharp turn against Mistress Clitherow. There were claims the good lady had been hell-bent on sacrificing her own life all along. Almost everyone decried the words she'd said in court about wishing her husband and children could die in agony alongside her.

The salacious allegations of sexual improprieties between the butcher's wife and any number of unnamed Catholic priests returned. Most decent citizens dismissed these immediately, saying they were fabricated. Those who spread the stories claimed it wasn't only Mistress Clitherow who was involved, but a whole host of women from York. Many were accused of taking in Jesuits to satisfy their carnal lusts, when they should have been cavorting with local men.

At last I saw Pastor Wigginton leave the Common Hall. His face had taken on a grey pallor which made him look like death on legs. He walked close by to me. I don't think he pretended when he didn't know who I was. His face was a blank scroll. The man seemed to recognise nobody. Utterly defeated, the parson gave the appearance of being trapped in a world of his own.

I allowed him a twenty-yard start and followed. His route made no sense at all. We walked along Coney Street, past the latest extension of

Henry Maye's inn on the corner of Davygate, crossed the empty Thursday market and traversed Parliament Street. When he reached The Pavement, Parson Wigginton turned into it but before I could follow, he turned around.

Still not seeing me, he walked through Coppergate in the direction of the river. I thought we must be heading back towards the prison on Ouse Bridge, but at the very last moment he turned right again and before I knew it we were back in Coney Street. It wasn't long before we'd fully returned from whence we came.

The pastor sat down on the cold stone floor, next to one of the oldest inns on the street. It was only a few yards away from the entrance slope to the Common Hall. He slid his back down to the ground and moved his cloak so he could sit more comfortably. The place wasn't open yet. Once again, we were surrounded by talk of what had occurred in the Assizes and what might happen next.

The majority of people considered it wouldn't be long before the pressing would begin. A group of fellows next to me speculated the likeliest day for the mistress's execution would be on the morrow. They wondered if it would be possible to watch or whether it would be held behind closed doors to prevent trouble on the streets.

I looked at Parson Wigginton. Surely, he was able to hear what was being said. The door of the inn opened. A voice shouted. 'For anyone thirsty, we're now open and serving.'

A few men began to walk over. Giles Wigginton hauled himself up. I could see the good man planned to seek solace in strong drink.

'No, parson!' I shouted.

We needed him. I needed him. Mistress Clitherow needed him. A few people looked at me but most carried on about their business. The pastor turned towards me. He looked at the alehouse. Which option would he choose?

'That's the parson who was shouting out in court,' said a woman.

'Sharding idiot!' said another.

'Leave him alone, he was only trying to help her.'

'Probably wants to give her one himself, like all those Catholic priests.'

'Where's the harm in that? Protestant parsons can marry now, can't they.'

'But she's already married to the butcher, in't she?'

'Oh aye, fair point.'

By now the parson had made up his mind. He strode quickly along Coney Street, with me in tow. Despite his long stride and uneasy gait, I managed to keep up with him. As if noticing me for the first time, he turned angrily and faced me.

'Come on then, lad,' he said. 'We'd better report back to your friend. Do you think he's got what he wanted? Another Catholic victim of injustice to add to his list?'

Hearing his words, one or two heads turned towards us, and I hoped the parson would shut up. This was dangerous talk, even for a Protestant priest. But after this he said no more and I was relieved when we began walking towards Peasholme Green in silence, apart from the sound of the cobbles beneath our boots.

Parson Wigginton had clearly experienced the same revelation as I had in court. Unlike the pair of us, Father Mush hadn't sought to save the life of Mistress Clitherow. On the contrary, I now believed he'd been petitioning for her execution all along. What a martyr she'd make in the quest to influence the Queen against the immorality of her government's actions.

For this, a member of the Jesuit order such as Father Ingleby or himself would do no good. Many priests had been killed before and few people cared. Even executing laymen no longer caused a stir. The sad fate of Marmaduke Bowes had proved that. But a woman, particularly one in the prime of her life with children hanging from her skirts, perhaps that would be different. I'd been told in school the Queen abhorred all violence against women. Was this true? We were about to find out.

When we arrived at the house, Pastor Wigginton was angry. 'Was this your idea, John? Did you put her up to it? A few subtle words here and there, so she'd believe God wanted her to make the ultimate sacrifice? You're wrong, you know. There's so much more people can do in the name of the Lord when they're alive than dead.'

'No,' replied Father Mush firmly. 'I would never do such a thing to harm the Pearl of York.'

'Argh!' exclaimed the parson, holding his head in his hands. 'How do you expect me to believe you when you've already bestowed such a saintly title upon her head? God or the Devil, they'll take us all in the end. What's your hurry? Margaret Clitherow has children, man. How can you do this to her?'

'I'm not guilty of what you claim, Giles. But neither is this good woman guilty of treason. I don't care what you think.'

I sensed danger could come from the rising animosity between the two men. The words in the pokey room could easily be carried out into the street. There were large rewards for turning in Catholic priests, and the folk around here needed the money more than most. Father Mush would be arrested, and Parson Wigginton and I accused of harbouring him.

'Calm down,' I demanded. 'I'm happy for the two of you to continue arguing, but not like this. On all you consider holy please speak more quietly.'

For a moment there was a hush in the room. Father Mush stooped slightly; his face still angry at the accusations made against him but he nodded his head. The parson did the same.

'The boy is right. We should finish this discussion another time, but before we talk about the events in the courtroom,' whispered Pastor Wigginton. 'I'd like to inform you of what happened last night.'

'So, you did go to see her?' hissed Father Mush through his teeth. 'Is this the real reason for your anger against me? Because you failed in your mission to turn the Pearl into a hypocrite?'

If I was Pastor Wigginton, I think I would have hit him then, priest or no priest. Unlike his Catholic counterpart the parson had done all he could to save the prisoner, including placing himself in real jeopardy by intervening so loudly in court. But the man's constitution was sterner and his temper cooler than mine.

He let the priest's comments pass, took a deep breath and told us what happened. 'Aye, I went to Ouse Bridge. I paid the toll but not to the road men. I gave my money to the warders. It didn't take many coins to get into Mistress Clitherow's cell. She sat there in the gloom, all alone, without even a candle. The place was dank and stank to high heaven, but she's been to prison before. She didn't seem too fearful.'

'What did she say to you?' I asked.

'If I'm honest, she didn't want to see me but I'd paid off the guards, so she had no choice. Mostly I talked and she listened, though sometimes she tried not to. Before I forget, she asks for messages to be sent regarding Mistress Anne Tesh. She met her the night before when they shared a cell together in York Castle. Now Mistress Clitherow is in Ouse Prison she fears she'll never see her friend again. Mistress Tesh is well but needs money for food and candles. Will you pass this information onto your contacts?'

Father Mush nodded.

'At first I attempted to convince Mistress Clitherow of the folly of her religion and convert to mine. But of course, this was no good. I made no progress at all. After that I did my best to persuade her to renounce her faith. As young Guy suggested yesterday, I even hinted she could retain this in private if she wished to, but again she refused. I felt there was only one avenue left. I strongly recommended she pleaded not guilty. As the judge said, there's little evidence against her. Additionally, I said we would ensure everyone in the court would be made aware the boy was a foreigner.'

'But they have Father Ingleby's chalice and my vestments,' protested Father Mush.

'Yes, but these were found in somebody else's house. I said she should tell this to the court.'

'But she wouldn't?'

'No, she refused,' he agreed. 'She feared if she did it would only implicate her husband's kin who live next door. And she won't even speak out against the boy Johann for fear people will turn against him, despite the fact none of this is his fault.'

'Treacherous little runt,' I uttered.

'Or poor damaged child. That's the way Mistress Clitherow sees him. After speaking to her, I agree. They would have done terrible things to the lad to gain a confession. It was better he talked straight away.'

Poor Johann, I thought, remembering the horror on his face as Sheriff Fawcett stripped and interrogated him in front of the throng in The Shambles.

'I said she could ignore the boy and the location of the room but still make a plea. But in her view even this placed others at risk. Most of all, Mistress Clitherow was concerned about the butcher, their children and the servants. She was worried some of them might be tortured for information and forced to testify against her.'

'Especially as they have so little evidence,' I said, understanding the dilemma my mother's friend had found herself in.

'Yes,' agreed the pastor. 'Mistress Clitherow is trapped on all sides. Even if she pleads guilty, she's worried they'll chase down more evidence to prove the case against her. She thinks there's only one way out which won't do harm unto others.'

With this, he stole another hateful glance at Father Mush. I think he still believed the Father had played a major part in the good woman's downfall despite his protestations. On balance, I agreed with him.

'What's more, Mistress Clitherow is convinced the verdict of her trial is already written. The Sheriff selects the jury, and the Sheriff and Lord Mayor are in cahoots in their attempt to boost the reputation of the Corporation. And behind them, the Council of the North continues to press for her prosecution, as proven today by Henry Cheke's presence in court.'

'But surely she must believe her stepfather will try to save her?' I asked. But even as I said this, I remembered the words the Lord Mayor uttered in the Common Hall about washing his hands of her.

'The good lady knows this won't be the case, even though for some reason she still retains charitable views towards him. She knows he was expecting and hoped for a different outcome. Her apostasy would have been his triumph, but now she's refused this, there can only be one verdict from the trial.'

'Guilty,' said Father Mush. 'No matter how flimsy the evidence against her, she would be sent to the gallows. The way she thinks so much of others is inspiring.'

'There is one more thing we can do,' I said. 'We can break Mistress Clitherow out of jail.'

Both men looked at me aghast and shook their heads.

'No,' said Father Mush. 'I'll not condone one act of violence to prevent another. It's out of the question.'

'Forgive me, Father,' I said. 'But I doubt your motives. Perhaps you don't wish to see the good lady saved?'

'Watch your tongue, lad,' the Father responded angrily. 'I've heard you had a temper on you. Both your headmaster and mother say so. You should think before you speak out.'

He was right. I did feel the anger welling up inside me, but couldn't he comprehend? All I wanted to do was rescue Mistress Clitherow. I turned to Parson Wigginton for his support. Surely, he'd understand.

'In this case I'm afraid I have to agree with Father Mush,' he said, much to my surprise. 'Even if I truly believed we had the means and wherewithal to see this through, I'd not allow it.'

'But why, pastor?' I asked.

'Above all, from now on we we must consider the wishes of Mistress Clitherow. She'll thank none of us for setting her free. And even if we could, what then? Would you have her flee around the country as a fugitive? Every night moving to a different house, in constant fear for her life, whilst she awaits news of her family, never knowing who amongst the people helping her might turn her in, or be caught and punished?'

I closed my eyes. I was tired. There was merit in the man's words but something had to be done. A plan began to formulate inside my head. There was a knock on the door, and a jolt in my heart. We all stopped. Wigginton reacted first. He pointed for Father Mush to head to the back. There were shutters on the holes in the walls, you wouldn't have called them windows, and thankfully they were all nailed closed. Nobody could see inside. The pastor directed me to sit in the chair where the sleeping man had been. I wasn't keen and looked towards the back room.

'They'll have heard us talking,' he whispered. 'There needs to be at least two of us in here. Pull the blanket up over your eyes.'

He picked up the single candle which lit the room and moved it away from the chair, so my face would be deeper in the gloom. There was a tap again. I slunk into the seat as the parson went to the door.

When he opened it, we were safe. Mistress Vavasour, another of Mistress Clitherow's friends, rushed in. She'd attended the Masses held at Mistress Clitherow's house, including the one when Father Ingleby had been arrested. I wondered again what had become of him. Mistress Vavasour looked quite surprised to see Pastor Wigginton. She closed the door tightly. It was obvious she was looking for Father Mush. When he heard her voice, he stepped back inside.

'Father,' she said. 'I have a plan to save Margaret.'

Until recently Mistress Vavasour was the sort of person Mother would have tried to avoid. A renowned recusant, like her younger friend Mistress Clitherow, she'd served several prison sentences. There was also a rumour she harboured Catholic priests. Knowing where to find Father Mush appeared to back up this notion.

'It was I who persuaded Margaret Clitherow to support the true faith,' she boasted. 'And now I can't simply stand aside and let her life be ended like this.'

Despite her age, there was a surprising level of vim and vigour about the woman. Wisps of grey hair peeped out from beneath her coif, and her face was lined with wrinkles.

'We've just discussed the matter at length, good lady,' said Parson Wigginton quietly. 'Sadly, there's nothing we can do.'

Mistress Vavasour shook her head in disdain at the pastor. She looked towards Father Mush for reassurance. Should she speak further in front of this man? Only when she'd received his nod did she continue.

'There's always a way, young man,' she said. 'Have you heard of Queen Elizabeth?'

'The Pope calls the Queen a heretic,' interrupted Father Mush. 'It's her laws which have placed the Pe... Mistress Clitherow in so much peril. The current Queen of England is no friend of ours.'

'Come, Father,' said the woman. 'How many times have I told you we must seek to understand our enemies?'

She gave Pastor Wigginton a withering look as she said the word *"enemies"*. I couldn't help but smile. She'd only been with us for a few minutes but I was beginning to like her. The world needed more women of action.

'Queen Elizabeth is an educated woman with beliefs. Although she's clearly mistaken in religion, some of her other thoughts have merit.'

I wondered what Mistress Vavasour meant by this. 'Which thoughts in particular?' I asked.

'Good question, my lad,' she said. 'For a while, my husband Thomas lived in London. He tells me it was common knowledge the Queen loathed any violence meted out towards women.'

'I heard the same thing said at St Peter's,' I remarked. 'But what of it?'

'Most weeks the Queen attends a few days at the royal court, where entreaties are made, pardons are given and so on. In Thomas's experience she's never once rejected a personal request to take a more merciful stance for someone of the female sex, no matter what they were accused of.'

'What are you proposing?' asked Father Mush. He looked concerned.

'We send word to London to ask for clemency.'

'But that would take days, maybe even weeks,' resisted Parson Wigginton. 'Even if we were successful, I'm afraid Mistress Clitherow would have been executed long before any official reply from the Queen could be returned.'

Upon hearing this Farther Mush's face relaxed a little.

'Then we must delay the execution,' I said.

'Yes, indeed, young Master Fawkes. Edith told me you were a fast learner.'

I wondered if Mother had spent more time with the tightly knit group of York's Catholics than she'd let on. They all seemed to know something about me.

'But how?' asked the parson.

Before I could intervene and outline my own rescue plan, Mistress Vavasour answered. I had to admit her strategy had a much better chance of succeeding than my own scheme. Everything depended on us getting a message to the Assizes judges before the end of the afternoon.

# 16

When we arrived at the Common Hall the Assizes had adjourned for a break between cases. Groups of people loitered around the square chatting, but the crowd was sparser than before. I assumed most of the people still present must have had some connection to the accused or victims or were witnesses in proceedings still to be heard. Most looked glad of the opportunity to escape the hard benches of the gallery for a while.

As soon as we ventured inside, we realised our timing was good. Many of the officials had temporarily left the chamber in search of refreshment or the privy. All we had to do was find our man.

We went back outside in search of our prey. I followed Parson Wigginton down a small path which ran alongside one side of the building. The track ended in a narrow strip of land positioned above the riverbank. Ten or twelve men had gathered there, talking or peeing into the river. A little further along there was a low hedge, behind which a couple of women squatted to protect their modesty.

As our eyes scanned the menfolk it was apparent there were no officials present. We looked at the backside of the Common Hall. At this exact moment an anonymous turd exited the building, at the point where it jutted out over the embankment, and plopped into the river below. This must be where the officials had their privy. Perhaps our man was there.

Once back inside the hall, Parson Wigginton approached the records keeper. At first the man shook his head but after a few coins were exchanged, he gave us a quill, ink and some materials for the pastor to write down a note. A junior official took this through a door into the body of the Corporation building, where ordinary citizens weren't allowed without appointment or summons.

A few minutes later one of the Lord Mayor's lackeys came out looking for the parson. The two men walked back through into the offices. I was instructed to remain behind at the edge of the public gallery. Standing there, I felt alone and exposed. The court would soon be back in session, and I was desperate to hear what was being said within.

I approached the doorway, but the man guarding the entrance challenged me. I had to think. I told him I came with a verbal message which I'd been instructed to deliver personally to the ears of Henry Cheke. To give the message some importance, I said I came from St Peter's with news of his son. Once I'd claimed this, I panicked a little. Perhaps they'd march me directly to Thomas's father. What would I do then?

Thankfully things turned out alright. The guard was lax. He told me he thought Henry Cheke had returned to the King's Manor after the first case of the morning, but I was welcome to look inside to double check. I nodded my thanks and wandered in.

The place was a confusion of open and closed doors and a warren of corridors. I asked a man in a uniform where I could find the Lord Mayor. He pointed upstairs and advised me to go left. I progressed up the stone steps two at a time. As soon as I reached the top, I almost bumped into the two circuit judges, as they made their way back to the courtroom. Quickly I stepped aside to let them pass.

As they ignored me, I studied their faces. Justice Rodes looked in good spirits but Judge Clench appeared to have the whole world on his shoulders. After passing me they descended the stairs. No words passed between them.

At the first corner I heard Parson Wigginton's voice beyond. I remained where I stood and listened to the conversation. 'Are you sure about this, parson?' I recognised the voice as the one I'd heard outside the Common Hall in February speaking of a crackdown on Catholics and immigrants.

'Whether she is, or whether she isn't, is not for me to say,' replied the pastor. 'But executing a woman with an unborn child in her belly is against the law. It is a heinous crime and anyone allowing it would be punished by the Queen herself.'

'Good God!' exclaimed the mayor. 'This day is going from bad to worse. Roland, what should we do?'

'There's only one thing for it,' said a voice I assumed to be Sheriff Fawcett's. 'We must have her examined. If she isn't pregnant, we'll go ahead as planned. If she is, we'll have to defer the pressing until the child comes out. The Council and the judges won't like it but they'll have to lump it. The parson is right. I won't take any responsibility for her execution and risk the Queen's wrath. It'll only go ahead now if she's declared without child, or someone else very senior orders it. We need to speak to Judge Clench.'

There was a quick tread of footprints, and I sat myself down onto a bench outside one of the offices. The Lord Mayor and the red-nosed Sheriff of York stepped past me. The lackey followed behind, accompanied by Parson Wigginton. His look of surprise lasted only a moment. After that he did his best to avoid my eyes and walked on. Within a few seconds they were gone.

Now inside the Corporation offices I wondered where I could go next and what I could find, but I shrugged. I wouldn't know where to start, so I made my way back down the stairs. When I got to the bottom an argument was going on in the corridor. Clearly Judges Clench and Rodes had been informed of Mistress Clitherow's alleged pregnancy.

As part of Mistress Vavasour's charity to others, she provided birthing support for local women. In Father Mush's hideout, she'd said her friend had confided in her last week she'd missed something. Due to this occurrence both women suspected Mistress Clitherow was in the early stages of being with child.

Parson Wigginton had treated the news like gold dust. Pregnant women couldn't be executed. We all knew this was the law. Even Father Mush had urged us to hurry and inform the good lady's stepfather to gain agreement for a stay of execution due to the unborn child. And here we were. In parallel, Mistress Vavasour was using her husband's resources to get a message to London. My mood lifted. The good lady could yet be saved.

'There's no way in hell I'll authorise the execution of a pregnant woman,' stated Judge Clench firmly, with relief writ large across his face. I wondered if he considered his career reprieved as well as the prisoner.

'This is nonsense based upon hearsay,' argued Justice Rodes. 'Brother, you are too merciful in these cases.'

'No,' said Judge Clench. 'It is the law.'

There wasn't much the younger justice could say to that but still he tried. 'Well, in that case we must at least ensure the woman is examined, so the court can agree whether this is true or not. I'll wager it's just some sort of speculative rumour.'

'Of course,' said Judge Clench. He turned to Sheriff Fawcett. 'You will assemble a jury of matrons to examine Mistress Clitherow. Select four honest women and have them visit her in her cell on the morrow. Once this is done report the findings back to Judge Rodes and myself and nobody else.'

Henry Maye coughed.

'And the Lord Mayor of course,' added Clench, knowing full well Fawcett would have done this anyway.

'In the meantime, consider the execution stayed. Ensure Mistress Clitherow's cell is made more comfortable. But see she shares it with staunch Protestant prisoners. Tell them if they manage to change her mind on religion, they'll get a pardon for their crimes. I'll pay their outstanding fines myself if I have to.'

He turned to his fellow judge. 'Let us put this delay to good use, Brother Rodes. In the meantime, we should get back to the Assizes, How I love making judgements about coining and horse theft.'

## Thursday March 17<sup>th</sup>, 1586

When the family sat down for our dinner on Thursday afternoon, I was a happy man. Mother smiled at me. Anne squeezed my hand. Even Lizzie wanted to sit next to me. Never give up, I thought, never give up. Light can shine through even in the darkest hour.

We'd received word from Pastor Wigginton. The four honest women had updated the judges. Whilst they found it difficult to be certain at this stage, they believed there was a fair chance Mistress Clitherow was in the early stages of pregnancy. This could be confirmed one way or another in about a month's time.

How the parson came by this news we didn't know. Neither did we care. All that mattered was the good lady couldn't be executed for the next four weeks or so. The time we needed to buy was ours. The Assizes would soon close and move on. The judges would have no choice but to issue a formal stay of execution until the pregnancy could be validated.

In the meantime, Mistress Vavasour's plea for clemency would reach Queen Elizabeth, and some time during the following weeks a message would arrive in York ordering Mistress Clitherow's reprieve. The good lady would likely have to serve a long spell in prison but she'd be alive.

Life felt good. Soon it got even better. A man came to the door. He carried a reply to Mother's letter. The whole family had been invited to spend some time at Scotton Hall.

'That sounds grand,' said Anne, with genuine excitement in her voice. 'Who do you know there?'

'It's a long story,' replied Mother. 'Are you sure you wish to hear it?'

'Yes, please,' replied my sister enthusiastically. The good tidings received from the pastor had already brought about a rapid change in her disposition.

'We'll be the guests of the widow Frances Pulleyn.'

Mother noticed my eyes widen.

'I'm afraid Frances is no relation to your old headmaster, Guy. Nor to any of his kin,' she added with a piercing look. 'I know from my own childhood it's a popular enough name in the district. There are many Pulleyns in the area who share it. Perhaps we can visit some of them.'

Again, she looked at me knowingly. My eyes widened.

'Tell us about Frances,' said Anne. 'How do you know her?'

'She's a lovely woman,' replied Mother. 'We've been friendly since I was a child. I've had links with her for a number of reasons over the years but she's not always been a Pulleyn. In fact, Frances has had four different family names in her lifetime.'

'How so?' I asked.

'Frances was born a Vavasour. She's related by birth to the Vavsour families of York and Hazlewood.'

I speculated a possible link to Mistress Clitherow's friend and confidante Dorothy Vavasour but remained silent.

'Why did she change her name?' asked Lizzie.

'For the same reason all women do,' answered her sister. 'She got married, of course. Who did she marry first, Ma? Will we recognise the man's name?'

'I think so,' replied Mother smiling, clearly enjoying telling the story. 'Frances's first husband was called Anthony Fawkes, to whom we may or may not be related. Frances thinks he could well have been a distant cousin of your father's father but they didn't know each other. The newlywed couple settled down in a small village near Otley. But around this time there were many outbreaks of plague and sweating sickness. Good men and women were taken away from us. Unfortunately, poor Anthony died whilst he was young. He left Frances behind, a grieving widow in an area she didn't know. It must have been difficult for her.'

'Who did she marry next?' asked Lizzie. 'Was it Mister Pulleyn?'

'No, darling,' replied Mother. She ruffled Lizzie's hair. 'I said Frances had four names. Mister Pulleyn was her third husband. We haven't got to him yet.'

'Who was it then?' I asked abruptly. 'I'm sorry, Mother, I didn't mean to be impatient. Please do carry on.' I was simply keen for her to get to the Pulleyns, even if they weren't directly related to Maria.

'Frances's second husband was a man named Philip Bainbridge. He was from further north, a place called Wheatley Hill. Philip didn't last long either but long enough for them to have a child together, a little boy called Dionysus.'

Mother hesitated for a moment.

'That's a funny name.'

'Lizzie, don't be rude,' said Mother with mock sternness in her voice. 'Anyway, when Philip died, Frances moved to Scotton and married the owner of Scotton Hall, a man called Walter Pulleyn. That's when I first met Frances. She was a lovely woman, very pretty and always happy. Before he met her, I remember Mister Pulleyn was a frightful man but their marriage brought about an amazing change in him. Afterwards, everyone in the village said he was a new man, no longer sullen and money-grabbing but friendly and approachable. I suppose that's what love does to some people. They were very happy together.'

'But she's a widow again now?' asked Anne.

'Aye,' replied Mother sadly. 'I don't think she'll marry again but I've met her a few times in recent years. She sometimes visits York with her son. She's always been such a kind woman, so I wrote and asked her if there were any opportunities in Scotton for a family like ours. In her letter she says the best way to discover this would be to visit and find out for ourselves.'

I looked around the table and counted three happy faces. If we'd had a looking glass it would have been four.

'Scotton Hall is owned by Walter's grandson Jack now. In her letter Frances says there's plenty of room in the Hall and Jack has given his blessing for our visit. I met him once. He seemed like a nice boy. I'm sure we'll all like him. What's more, he's offered to help Guy find suitable work.'

Beneath the table Anne squeezed my hand. She'd been counting on her fingers.

Mother smiled. 'Go on,' she said.

'Very well. I can't remember all the husbands' Christian names but I can tell you Frances's history of surnames,' replied Anne. 'She was born a Vavasour and married a Fawkes. Next she became a Bainbridge and finally now she's a Pulleyn.'

'Very good,' Mother said. 'It wasn't that difficult, was it? We travel tomorrow, so I want everyone to start packing all you need. Assume we'll be there for about a week. Take as little as possible. Remember, there may be some carrying involved. And I want you to go to sleep early. No chattering or whispering in your beds tonight.'

Anne looked at me with that face, the one which said how did Mother know everything?

'Will we get there in one day?' I asked.

'Aye,' said Mother, 'but only if we make an early start.'

# 17

**Friday March 18<sup>th</sup>, 1586**

The morning was still dark when the fellow who'd delivered Widow Pulleyn's letter came to our door. He informed us he worked on her grandson's estate. To avoid the tolls, he hadn't brought his wagon into the city, so we walked the first mile. The man took a bag from Mother's shoulder but we hauled the rest of the luggage ourselves.

On the Ouse Bridge Mother silently crossed herself as we squeezed past the prison. I thought of Mistress Clitherow within and wondered if she'd heard the good news. If she had, it must have come as a huge relief. With one less problem to worry about, I was relieved too. A smile came over Anne's face as she spied the jail. In my heart I knew she was thinking of Henry. Lizzie hummed a playful tune; unaware her words masked a story of misery and death.

The way became steeper as we climbed the cobbles of Micklegate. When we reached the churchyard of St Martin and St Gregory, Mother stopped the man and asked if we could rest for a few moments. The second part of the church's name had been added only recently when two parishes were merged into one. St Gregory's, like many other places of worship, had been closed to reduce the Church's costs. Some people complained, but to me it made good sense. If there were two things York wasn't short of, it was churches and inns.

When we started again, I took Lizzie's bag. We continued on past the workshops, homes and what were said to be some of the liveliest ale houses in the city, but they were all quiet now. For a few moments the moon became visible ahead of us before being reclaimed by the clouds. At the top of the hill the slope evened out and we were faced with the imposing sight of Micklegate Bar, or Traitor's Gate as it was sometimes known. In times of rebellion this was where the authorities placed the heads and other parts of executed men. They were stuck onto spikes, to warn the good citizens of York what would happen to them, if they turned bad.

The bar was one of York's four main gates. Like the other three it was guarded by York Corporation men. They allowed some people to leave and others to enter. When I'd attended St Peter's I'd left the city walls on most days of the week but I'd never travelled far, no further than a few hundred yards. This would be the longest journey Anne, Lizzie and myself had ever made. Scotton was more than twenty miles away! I wondered what life would be like outside the city. I was about to find out.

Beyond the gates there was an area of orchards. Some of the apple and pear trees were almost budding. Within a few weeks the whole place would come alive with blossom. When Anne and I were little, Mother and Father used to bring us here on windy Sunday afternoons after the weekly service. We'd run around, as the white petals rained down upon us. Happy memories indeed.

Many carts and wagons were parked on the open stretch of land called the Knavesmire. When asked, the Scotton man admitted he'd slept here with his horses to ensure nothing was stolen. Farmers and tradespeople moved around us, rousing and readying themselves for a day of selling or travelling onwards. Bedding down on the Knavesmire allowed them to keep an eye on their wares and, best of all, avoid the costs of an inn.

Mother and Anne clambered up onto the back of the carriage. I lifted Lizzie into the air and joined them. There was a small seat at the front, with sufficient room for one man to control the horses. At the back, where we were, the main space consisted of a flat boarded area. Wooden planks had been nailed together and connected above a wooden frame, set above two pairs of axles. On three sides the contents were bound in by oak rails, the fourth across the back was designed to be removed and replaced when needed. The floor of the trailer was carpeted with straw but there was no cover above us, so we hoped for fair weather. The driver checked the horses, released the brake and set off.

'What an adventure!' said Anne excitedly.

'Yes,' agreed Lizzie. 'But what is that?'

My younger sister pointed towards a wooden structure. We could just about make it out in the pre-dawn light. The construction was set aside from the field and stood on its own. I knew what it was, of course. I'd been to school trips there. This was York's Tyburn, the execution place. Criminals guilty of murder, rape and horse theft would be sent here to meet their maker. Those who transgressed more political crimes would be hung for a shorter time, before having their insides ripped out whilst they were still alive. It wasn't a pretty sight. I remembered Marmaduke Bowes.

Mother glanced at me and I looked at her. How soon should the horrors of the world be shared with innocent children? Was ten years too young, or was it too old? Neither of us knew what to say. Telling a lie seemed inappropriate but the truth too terrible to be told.

Thankfully, Anne intervened and saved us both. 'It's where the bad men are sent, Lizzie,' she said. 'But we don't want to talk about them today. What do you think our bed chamber in Scotton Hall will be like?'

At that very moment we went over the first of many bumps we'd encounter on the road during the day. The four of us were jerked high into the air. We landed quickly and noisily back down with a bump. The driver had tied our bags to the frame of the wagon but not us. After the incident we pressed our bodies against the side rails and held onto them tightly. Mother placed Lizzie between the two of us for safety, and from then on, we did all we could to ensure she was secure.

'Quite grand, big and airy,' Lizzie said eventually. 'With the smell of sunshine.'

We all smiled but I watched Mother's eyes. They didn't leave the gallows for a moment until the Knavesmire and Tyburn were out of sight. I thought about that haunted look again today.

The wagon crossed the road towards Tadcaster just as the sky began to brighten. I looked at the main route, remembering my father saying it went all the way to London. But the big city wasn't for us. As we set off through the warren of lanes which traversed the northern Ainsty, my mother reached past Lizzie and squeezed my hand. She was going home.

After climbing a hill out of the city, the first place we reached of any size beyond York's walls was called Acomb. The place was a tiny hamlet consisting of a higgledy-piggledy collection of cottages, set to either side of the Church of St Stephen. Apart from God's house, the most prominent building nearby was a coaching inn with some stables behind it, although a few moments later we spied a fine-looking manor house in the distance beyond.

The ground here was separated into long strips, and I asked Mother why this was.

'Most of the land in these villages will be owned by the gentleman of the manor, whoever that may be,' she said. 'His own men will farm the strips, or he'll rent them out. A few though, maybe like the ones behind those cottages, will be owned by the smallholders themselves. And do you see that?'

She pointed to an area some distance from the church. 'That's clearly common land. Animals can graze freely there, no matter who they belong to. Your grandpa used to say God would strike down any man who tried to enclose them.'

Mother looked a little sad for a moment. She rarely mentioned her own side of the family. If truth be told, I think few had survived the rampant diseases which had swept across Yorkshire in the decades gone by, and certainly none closely related or rich enough to invite us to spend any time with them.

'Will you know anyone in Scotton, apart from the widow?' I asked.

'I'm sure there'll be a few people from my day, Guy,' she said, 'and then there's Frances's family, her step-grandson, Jack, and her own son, Dionysus. I know him quite well.'

The conversation tailed off for a while. We endured the bumpy ride in silence, trapped in our own thoughts. It was definitely not a good cure for a birched bottom, even if my last beating had been some weeks ago. Despite my discomfort, I did my best to take in the wonders of the journey. In many places the lanes were narrow and hedged. A few times when we met a wagon coming the other way the driver had to pull back on his reins and urge the horses to one side. Whenever this happened, he swore quietly at the animals and everything else besides. If he imagined his words were beneath his breath, he was mistaken. Hearing his curses, Mother suppressed a giggle, and so did we.

After a word or two of oaths, followed by pleasantries and a few minutes of manoeuvring, somehow the vehicles would pass each other by. I studied the other carts with interest. Most were smaller vehicles carrying winter crops such as turnips. I assumed these were destined to be sold at the market in York or transported down-river to Hull.

A little while later we passed through the village of Rufforth. It looked a lot like Acomb. I wondered how many places such as this there must be in the whole of Yorkshire and beyond, right across England. Men and boys worked in the fields. Their ploughing season had just begun. It looked like hard work, even when they were supported by a horse or an ox.

'Where are the women folk?' asked Anne.

'Indoors,' said Mother, 'weaving cloth or brewing ale, for sure.'

All my years struggling in school seemed an easy life, when compared to the way men laboured here. I wondered what the future had in store for me, now I'd be no longer be working at Minster Yard. And I thought of Maria and felt a little happier. I'd only known her for a few weeks, but what weeks they had been. I remained confident we'd be together again soon.

Between the villages we often didn't see a soul for miles on end. Much of the land was uncultivated, with some areas heavily wooded by oak, beech, horse chestnut and the like. At a place called Long Marston we reached a crossroads.

The driver headed right and told us we'd be travelling up the old road to the top of Marston Moor. It wasn't a steep incline, but I felt it was almost a welcome change to the flatness of the Vale of York, at least until we had to grab onto the rails to prevent our bottoms from sliding back along the straw and out through the stern of the wagon. Sitting down for a long time could be more painful and tiring than I'd realised.

At the top of the moor we reached another hamlet called Tockwith. Master Pulleyn's man said we could get out here and stretch our legs here for a while, as he needed to rest the horses. He spoke to a fellow in a coaching inn, and between them they brought over some hay and water for the mares. After this the driver took his own break and had a bite to eat.

By now it surely must be late afternoon, I thought, convinced we'd travelled an extremely long way. When I strolled past a row of cottages to the edge of the village, the truth put paid to my lie. In the distance I could see the stone and shape of York Minster. One of the smudges beneath must be Stonegate, I speculated.

After this I walked past a cow byre to get back to the others, and Mother shared out some bread and honey she'd brought for the journey. I took a hunk of the sweetly smeared crust and ate it gladly. Anne offered a piece to the driver, but he shook his head and said he preferred his own cheese.

'This area's called the Ainsty,' said Mother. 'It was once a wapentake of the West Riding of Yorkshire.'

'What's a wapentake?' asked Anne, taking the words from my mouth.

'It's just an old word for an area of a county,' said Mother. 'It comes from the Norse language. Five hundred years ago the Vikings controlled much of Yorkshire. It's why some of the people around have such blonde hair.'

'Then why is my hair so red?' I asked. Everyone else in the family was a mousey brown.

'Who knows, Guy,' replied Mother, 'other than it is God's will.'

We sat and ate peacefully, munching away quietly until the driver said it was time to get off. Finding a patch of thick bushes, we each went behind a different one, and relieved ourselves.

The horses were reattached to the wagon and we set off again. Once our bodies settled back into the rhythm of the road, Lizzie and Anne fell quickly to sleep. I attempted to re-engage Mother in conversation.

'I'm curious,' I said. 'I know little about your childhood in Scotton.'

'There's not much to tell,' Mother replied softly. 'My parents were good people, although the countryside was a little backward compared to York. It seems such a long time ago. You must remember, I was quite young when I had to... when I married your father. And it's a very long distance from York. I haven't been back since.'

'Tell me about your parents,' I said, wondering why it felt such an awkward topic.

'Well, my father was a merchant trader, and my mother kept house. We lived in a decent enough little cottage, along with my two sisters. One was older and one was younger than me. It was even colder than our house in Stonegate in winter, but I remember being happy there. What else is there to say?'

'But what happened to your family?' I asked. 'You never talk of them, like Father used to talk of his.'

She swallowed and took a moment before beginning to reply. 'Some time after I moved to York, I received a letter from my older sister, Grace. All three of us could write.' Mother stopped and looked into the distance.

'She told me there'd be an outbreak of plague in Skipton,' she whispered eventually. 'The villagers suspected Father had caught it when he'd travelled there to sell some leather goods. All four of them were struck down and locked into the cottage. Only Grace came out. Ma, Pa and my lovely little sister, Maggie, all died.'

'I'm sorry,' I said. After a few moments of silence, I asked, 'What became of Grace?'

'She asked me to come home to spend some time with her, but I couldn't. I was with child.'

'Could she not come to York?'

'That's what I wanted her to do. I wrote immediately, inviting her to our house in Petergate.' Mother sighed deeply. 'But in her next letter, she said she couldn't come to York, as it was an ungodly place. And on the reverse side she wrote some hurtful words, saying I'd abandoned my family and faith and one day I'd be cursed for it.'

I didn't know what to say. It was little wonder Mother never talked of these things.

'Lastly, Grace wrote, with Maggie dead, she no longer considered she had a sister. I was upset and angry but your Pa persuaded me not to reply. And time is a great healer. I think I understand Grace more now. She must have gone through such a terrible experience; the whole thing was awful. I no longer hold the letter against her, and perhaps in some ways, she was right.'

'But where is she now?'

'I don't know. I had one further letter from her about a year later, saying she was getting married to a man of proper religious conviction and was moving to his house, some way away from Scotton. She didn't say where she was going. And at the time I was too angry and proud to ask. In any case I had my hands full with my new family and your father. But now, you, Anne and Lizzie are all I have left.'

I thought she'd weep then, but she didn't. She simply said, 'Stay true to what you believe in, Guy.'

We went back to watching the road after that, until eventually Anne woke and looked around. 'Where are we?' she asked.

'Close to the river, I think,' replied Mother. She called to the man in front of us. 'Where will we cross the Nidd?'

'At Cattal, Mistress,' he said. 'Just like the Romans did.'

'The Vikings and the Romans,' said Anne. 'I wonder if any of us will be remembered by history like them?'

I didn't reply.

When we got to Cattal, the crossing wasn't a solid affair like I'd been expecting. I'd not seen many bridges, but clearly men couldn't build houses and prisons on this one like they did on the bridge over the Ouse in York. There were a few stone arches but above these only a rickety looking wooden structure, which rattled loudly as the horses trotted across it. I, for one, was glad our wagon wasn't loaded with anything heavier than ourselves.

Once on the western side of the river, the driver counted out a few coins. When we reached the toll booth, he handed these over to a gnarled old man, with staggered lines on his face. I couldn't help but think he looked a little like his bridge. The two men obviously knew each other, and for a few moments they exchanged words and sentences about one another's families and the weather. I looked up at the light clouds. We'd been lucky. There was still no sign of rain.

After crossing the water, we carried onwards, as the afternoon passed in a similar fashion to the morning before it. The wagon shuffled past cottages, marked-out strips of land, farmsteads, forestry and a large fenced-in estate used for hunting. As well as deer, rabbits and hares we saw many herds of sheep but much of the common land was only sparsely populated by a few cattle or pigs.

Mother saw the confused look on my face. 'Were you expecting to see more stock, Guy?' she asked. 'In the country many of the animals are slaughtered when the grass stops growing in the autumn. The meat is eaten or salted or smoked for preserving. As few beasts as possible are kept through the winter, and only then the best ones for milking and breeding. Otherwise it costs too much, apart from the sheep. They provide wool, they're hardy and will graze on the poorest land, which makes them a lot cheaper and easier to look out for than cows or swine.'

After passing the prosperous village of Goldsborough, we headed on into the valley of the River Nidd. The township of Knaresborough was the largest settlement we'd encountered since leaving York. The place was grand and important enough to warrant its own castle, set in a dominating position overlooking the river. We saw tradesmen and workshops in the streets but most of the townspeople looked more like the villagers we'd seen during the day than citizens of a grand place like York.

The town has been constructed on a steep incline in places, and several times the driver was forced to use his handbrake to slow down the wagon or pull back the horses in case they reared up in front of us. Beyond Knaresborough, we followed the winding path of the river through the bottom of the valley, before beginning to climb steeply back up again towards the far slope, passing through a wooded hillside.

The horses did well, and when we reached the higher ground, the driver stopped to look back. We followed his gaze and admired the view to the rear across the woodland and beyond towards the Vale of York and in the very far distance the Wolds. It was only Mother who didn't glance that way. Instead she stared intently in the opposite direction.

'Netherdale,' she said. 'We'll reach Scotton shortly.'

She was coming home at last. And so was John Johnson.

# 18

Journeying along the track towards the village of Scotton, a large and imposing manor house soon became visible ahead of us. Unlike the dwellings I was accustomed to seeing in York, Walter Pulleyn's house was situated away from its neighbours in substantial grounds of its own. Scotton Hall wasn't the King's Manor but I was impressed.

The thick walls were constructed with a hard-grey stone which seemed unaffected by the weather, and there was something of a timeless quality about the place. The building could have been built twenty to two hundred years ago. Constructed over two large floors, a narrow line of mullioned windows peeped out from each. When we were closer, I could see the glazier's work on the individual panes. Each piece of glass was connected to the others through an intricate latticework of leaded beading. The local carpenters were no fools either, if the frames, shutters and oak doors were anything to go by.

Looking above, I saw three chimneys. The largest reached out from the centre of the building. A swirling funnel of wood smoke rose up from it. The roof below was steeply pitched, as if it had once been thatched, but these days it was topped with row after row of neatly placed over-lapping pantiles. They spanned down as far as the gable ends, which jutted out abruptly from the eaves of the building.

The driver applied the brake and called the horses to a halt. I undid our bags, climbed down and helped the others off the wagon. My body stiffened and began to ache from the journey. There was an obvious spy hole near the doorway but this wasn't needed, for three women were already standing outside waiting to greet us. The oldest of these was a smartly dressed woman of well beyond middle age. She stepped forward and embraced my mother.

'Edith,' she said, 'it's so good to see you. And the little ones too, although the boy's too old and tall now to describe in such a manner.'

Mother smiled. 'This is my friend, Frances Pulleyn,' she said to us.

I bowed. Anne attempted to curtsey, and Lizzie gave a wide-eyed smile at the three women and the large house behind them. Although her clothing was dark and her features austere, Widow Pulleyn had a positive presence about her. Later that evening in a quiet moment, Mother told us more about her friend and her husband's story.

Decades before he'd met Frances, Walter Pulleyn was happily married. Supported by his wife Margery, he'd established himself as a leading member of the local community. For twenty or more years Walter's wealth and family expanded. He was a canny man. Over time he extended Scotton Hall, purchased land and built cottages to house the growing sections of his family in. But the Pulleyns, like so many, were struck down by illness and accidents. One by one, Walter's wife Margery and their three sons were taken from him. The master of the manor turned to drink and raged at the world around him.

The most difficult period of Walter's life came to an end when he met Frances. She took the bottle from his mouth and following a few turbulent weeks they married. Finally, he was happy again. Although she bore him no children, her husband apparently doted on his stepson Dionysius. Of course, blood speaks more loudly than words, and when Walter passed away the majority of his fortune was inherited by his closest remaining heir, his grandson Jack. Thankfully Jack was a man of charity, and the ancestral home was large and rambling. Multiple generations of Pulleyns now lived there, often in harmony. In time I came to know many of them. By and large they were good people.

Frances said, 'This is Margaret.'

We said hello to a woman of middling age. She smiled at us demurely, as wisps of untidy grey hair tried to peep out from under her head scarf. I soon discovered Margaret had been married to one of Walter's deceased sons. With no family other than a daughter, now herself married, first Walter and then Jack had permitted Margaret to stay on at the hall. She was grateful and worked hard for her keep in the kitchen and garden. Although most of the time you'd hardly know she was there, in my experience Margaret was ever present, responding quickly whenever help was needed.

'And Katherine.'

Katherine was younger and prettier than Margaret. Her layers of clothing were cut from more expensive cloth, less austere but of similar quality to those worn by Frances. With a smile on her face, she said hello and ruffled Lizzie's hair. I'd soon discover Katherine Pulleyn was the feistiest woman in the household. And as Jack's wife, she was the lady of the hall, but to her credit she treated Frances with respect. To everyone else she'd speak her mind but I came to admire Katherine also, for she and Frances were the heartbeat of the hall. They kept this large family together through thick and thin, handling every crisis, even as the men around them struggled.

We were welcomed into the hall, and our bags taken by two female servants. At times, the house seemed packed full of women. As at home, Mother shared her bedchamber with Anne and Lizzie, whilst I was given a smaller chamber of my own. Until recently someone had obviously been sleeping in there but I didn't complain. I wasn't sure which Pulleyn had been forced to make way for me but I was grateful, even if I did miss the comfort of Uncle Thomas's bed.

Over the next twenty-four hours we were introduced to a wide variety of members of the Pulleyn family, their workers and servants. Sometimes it was difficult to distinguish between them, but at other times, particularly when Katherine was around, the distinction became clear.

It was almost dark when Jack Pulleyn arrived home. He invited us to sit at his table. I'd not eaten hare stew before. The taste was finer and richer than rabbit. Jack was pleasant and jolly that evening. His welcome towards us was genuine.

We sat at his big oak table inside the great room, with the fire blazing. Frances quizzed Mother about the latest fashions in York arriving from London. They talked of ruffs and laced collars and the Pulleyns laughed raucously at Mother's description of the codpieces worn by visiting dignitaries.

After a good deal of merriment, it was finally decided the majority, including the younger ones, should go to bed. I was given a candle.

Jack turned to me, as I was about to leave the room. 'Young Guy,' he said. 'Will you accompany me on my way around tomorrow morning? I'd be interested to see what a city lad thinks of the country.'

I nodded eagerly in response. 'Gladly, sir.'

'Good, but before you go, let me ask you a question Grandfa' Walter used to ask me.'

There was a collective groan from the Pulleyns in the room, as if they'd heard this all before.

'The question is - how many horses' tails does it take to reach the moon?'

Everyone looked at me, wondering whether I'd even attempt to make an answer. If I did, what might it be?

I looked at the ceiling, as if deep in thought for a moment. 'One, of course,' I replied respectfully, stretching out my arms, 'but only if the horse's tail is long enough.'

Jack smiled, and the whole room erupted with cheering, laughter and applause. Walter's riddle had been solved at the first attempt. Jack beat the table with his fist and took a swig of ale from his grandfather's tankard. I could see how pleased he was with me. They all were. And I was relieved to have passed this test. I thought it might be the first of many. My time at St Peter's would stand me in good stead. I knew a lot of bad jokes and riddles.

I only woke once in the night. The small beer must have been stronger than the ale we drank at home. My head ached a little. I was thirsty and needed to use the pot. After addressing the second task, aided by a little moonlight from the window, I decided to venture downstairs to the kitchen to see how I could satisfy the first.

I'd extinguished my candle when I went to bed and had no means of relighting it. The first-floor landing was as dark as the blackest night, but I had a good memory and was confident I'd find my way down. After navigating the stairs, I reached the entranceway to the great hall. Shadows played across the gap between the floor and the door indicating the fire wasn't totally out. I considered going in there for a moment to enjoy the warmth. My bare feet were freezing, But I stopped myself when I heard two voices speaking. One was Mother's.

The other came from Widow Pulleyn. 'What do you think of Mistress Clitherow's chances?'

'Once they fully confirm she's pregnant, they'll surely have to place a stay on her execution until the child is born,' said Mother. 'And well before then messages should have reached and returned from London forbidding her death. The worst I think is she'll face a long term of imprisonment.'

'I'd hate that,' said Frances.

'As would I,' replied Mother. 'But Margaret's used to spending time in jail. And it has to be better than the alternative. I couldn't face that.'

'Who could?' asked the older woman. 'From everything you've told me it's not safe for good Catholics to be in York at this time. You did the right thing by bringing your family here. I know you have reservations but I'm sure it will work out.'

'How is he?' I recognised trepidation in Mother's voice as she spoke.

'Well enough,' came the reply. 'She's still with us but each day she slips a little further away. It's just taking so long. I hope it ends soon, for all our sakes. This illness isn't sudden like a fever or plague. It creeps around at night and slowly takes breath from her body. And he suffers too, watching her.'

There was silence for a few moments, before Widow Pulleyn spoke again. 'You know I've never liked the woman but I wouldn't wish this on anyone. He simply shouldn't be in this situation. After all, he promised you he'd wait until you were ready. And then he went back on his word and married her. Every argument I made against their match fell onto deaf ears.'

The room became quiet again. Vague orange shapes played around on the cold floor in front of me. I waited, ready to leave, as I didn't wish to be caught eavesdropping. But if there was more to be said, I wanted to hear it.

'You mustn't blame him,' whispered Mother eventually. 'It wasn't his fault. In a way it was mine. He asked me to marry him but I wasn't ready. I still missed Edward. I thought he'd live forever. I had no wish to be with another. I still miss him.'

A tear escaped and ran slowly down my cheek.

'You can't live alone in this way for much longer, Edith,' said the widow. 'I should know. I've been married three times, once for love, once for security and once for comfort in my later years. I was a good wife to all three husbands, but like you I married a Fawkes and loved the man with all my heart.

'Even though I can sometimes barely remember his face, I still think of Anthony and dream how we could have grown old together. But he's gone and it's not going to happen. When Guy reaches maturity Edward's properties and income will be his. Despite his problems at school, he seems a good lad but who knows how he may wish to spend his money. You have to think about yourself and the girls.'

'But,' said Mother.

'No ifs and no buts,' interrupted Widow Pulleyn firmly. 'You're still a young woman, don't become a spinster. After he met you at Michaelmas in York, he told me he'd realised what a terrible mistake he'd made, as soon as he came home. He said he knows he should have waited for you. She's made a fool of him. But will you wait for him now? It won't be long, and you can all stay here in the meantime.'

'I don't know,' replied Mother. 'I feel terrible even talking about it. The poor woman isn't even cold.'

'You've never met the *poor* woman. Trust me, she's a money grabbing hussy who's used her charms and lies to trap him into marrying her. In the process she's turned him from being a steadfast man to one who's broken the most solemn promise. That woman was no more with child when she said they had to marry than I am now. But God rest her soul, she can't last much longer. We just have to wait patiently for a few more weeks.'

Mother didn't answer.

Frances continued, 'Remember, he's a man. He's not as strong as us. He needs someone to look after him. He loves you, Edith, and if you don't love him already, I'm sure you will in time. He's no Anthony or Edward but he's not a bad man either.'

Hardly a glowing recommendation for a future husband, I thought. The two women stopped talking and I heard gentle footsteps cross the room. There was a clink of drinking vessels being tidied up, ready for the servants to collect and wash in the morning. I decided to skip quenching my thirst and crept back upstairs to bed.

# 19

**Saturday March 19<sup>th</sup>, 1586**

Jack Pulleyn's cheerful mood extended into Saturday. When he asked if I'd ever ridden a horse before, I thought it better to be honest. I admitted I hadn't but was eager to learn. Jack smiled and said this wasn't an issue. After this, he called over one of his men, and for the next hour or so I was put through my paces. My allotted steed didn't seem as big as some, although once I was astride her, the ground seemed a long way down.

I learned how to fix a saddle onto the mare's back and climb on and off her, albeit with a little help for the first time. Over the next few minutes I was shown the basics of moving forward, stopping and turning to either side. For a few moments I felt born to ride, right up until the time my mount accelerated from a trot into a gallop, although I was later told it was a canter.

Whatever it was, I struggled to hold on, and just when I thought I'd be thrown off and die for sure, my instructor rode up confidently alongside me and gave me a toothless grin. He reached over, took hold of my reins and slowed both our horses down. Before long I was back in control, and we trotted around the paddock together for twenty minutes more, whilst I regained my confidence. Finally, we reached the stables behind the hall and came to a halt.

'That's enough for today, lad,' said the workman.

I took a foot from the stirrup. Noticing this, the mare turned her head towards me, reared up and shook herself, turfing me off. I landed in a heap at Jack Pulleyn's feet.

'She always does that to first timers,' he laughed.

The other man chuckled and led the horses away. I climbed up and patted myself down. Nothing seemed to be broken.

Jack smiled. 'You did alright, Guy. You're a fast learner, indeed. Now it's time for a trip around the area.' He must have seen the look on my face because quickly he added. 'Don't worry. We're taking a carriage.'

Two of his men had already set up the best wagon, a two-seater with a sleek design, quite unlike the agricultural dray we'd travelled on the back of the day before. The seating was more comfortable too.

Scotton appeared to be a decent enough place to farm. Jack outlined the parish was bordered to the south by a steeply wooded gorge, which rose up from the River Nidd, and in the north by a low-lying line of moorland hills. Both created a natural barrier but in between there were good fields, some set to pasture and others used for crops. Jack explained how these roles would be reversed in the coming years. I learned more about rotation, leaving fields to lie fallow, and other farming methods than I ever thought possible.

Making our way around the area, Jack pointed to cottages and areas of non-common land, saying they were owned now, or had been in the past, by himself, Walter, or other members of the Pulleyn family. His face often cracked into a smile when he talked of his grandfather. The two men had obviously been fond of each other.

It appeared Walter had been a man with an eye for a profit. Over the years he'd become the most prolific buyer and seller of property in the area. Whilst this had made him and his family wealthy, he hadn't always been popular with the neighbours.

'Take the Percy family,' said Jack. 'They're probably the most well to do folk around here but back in the day they twice accused my grandfather of swindling them. In reality, all he did was buy parcels of land they considered to be of little value and eventually sell them off at higher price. The Percys should have calculated their real worth, just like Grandfa Walter did.'

'What else did he get up to?' I asked.

'All sorts,' grinned Jack. 'He would say he'd lived through the reign of three kings and two queens. Although I think it troubled him at times, he made an awful lot of money from the religious changes they brought with them. He was involved in some sort of skulduggery up at Fountains Abbey, although he never did share the details. There was another story from back in King Edward's time, when he was accused of stealing bells and all sorts of vestments and jewels from some of the Protestant churches.'

'Was he guilty?'

'Oh aye, but they never proved it and he was happy with that. We've still got some of the stuff buried at the back of the hall.'

'Can we have a look at it later?'

'Not today, lad, but maybe one day.' Jack smiled a wry smile. 'He was a grand old boy, and more like a father to me when my old man died. I'm glad he found Frances though. For a while he turned into a cantankerous old bugger.'

'What did he do?'

'He drank too much, and when he did, he became a bit of a bastard to the common folk around here. But all that nastiness soon got knocked out of him when he married Frances. Things went back to the way they'd been before. A lot of the people you'll meet today work for me now or rent their houses or land from us. Walter knew how to treat 'em, even if he did lose his way for a while. Do you know the most important thing he ever told me? Happy workers are harder workers. They pay their rent more quickly too.'

We visited many people and places that day. The majority of locals appeared pleased to see us. The men would stop what they were doing and chat for a few minutes. Perhaps they were relieved we weren't there to talk about bills or payments, or they realised Jack's steward wasn't with us.

'My steward has a tough old job, alright,' said Jack, as he turned the carriage back towards Scotton Hall. 'As you've seen there are a lot of tenants and properties to manage. Goods have to be bought. Every delivery needs scheduling. The wool, grain and other harvests have to be managed and stored. Our income, outgoings, costs and prices all have to be calculated.'

I sympathised for the fellow. It sounded like he was a busy man.

'Perhaps he could do with an assistant,' said Jack, keeping his eyes on the road. 'Especially a lad who's had good schooling and can read and write and count. Would you be interested?'

My heart leapt. I hardly knew what to say, but I didn't hesitate for another moment. 'Aye,' I said, 'I would.'

'I'm not sure you'll need all that Latin though,' said Jack. 'Although that may come in useful at other times, which is why I must ask you a question. Which Church do you support? Speak the truth, for God sees through all lies.'

We'd been riding on the wagon for several hours but this was the first inkling I had Jack might be a religious man, or that this was an important issue in these parts. He looked at me now, and I returned his gaze as steadily as I could in the circumstances.

'I was raised by my father to be with the Church of England,' I replied. 'He wanted me to follow him into the legal profession but the events of recent weeks have made this impossible. I've been expelled from school. I've attended Catholic Mass with my mother. The service had a powerful impression on me but I remain confused. The only thing I know for certain is that the Queen and her laws are wrong when they punish good honest folk like Mistress Clitherow. But whether I can commit myself fully to the Catholic Church or not, I don't know yet. So much has happened, I need time to clear my head.'

'You speak well,' said Jack. 'And I'll give you the time and space you need to make up your mind properly. But once you do, if you decide to return to the Queen's Church you'll not be allowed to stay under my roof, nor take my shilling.'

'I understand,' I replied. 'Thank you for your candour.'

'Don't worry, lad,' he said with a laugh. 'I don't think it'll 'appen. Once you've been to a few Masses in Scotton, you won't want to go back to the other church. And in any case, before long Mary Queen of Scots will be on the throne and none of us will 'ave to, ever again.'

With this, he applied the brake and brought the wagon to a standstill. Scotton Hall was still some way off in the distance. The sun was shining, probably as high up in the sky as it got so early in the year, so the time must have been around noon. I expected Jack would want to get back home for his dinner soon.

'This is the Bainbridge place,' he said, pointing to the building next to us. 'My step grandmother's son Dionysus lives here with his wife. The old man gave him the cottage before he died, so it's not one of mine anymore. Dionysus is a merchant. He buys and sells grain and other such things.'

We looked at the house. It was set to a single storey and larger than most we'd passed. The wooden panels were well maintained, as was the chimney, from which more wood smoke weaved into the air. A large stock of good-sized logs was stacked up neatly outside, ready to feed the fire within. These were stored in a covered area with its own lean-to roof just outside the door.

In the kitchen garden winter cabbages were visible, although most of the area had been newly manured for spring, summer and autumn growing. At the far side of the cottage was a large boarded barn and a small stable, big enough for three or four horses.

'See over there,' said Jack, pointing to a row of terraced dwellings a little way off. 'Those are more of my cottages. The nearest one to us is the home of one of my tenants, who shares his name with me but we're not kin unless it was from a long time back. Having said that, I think

William Pulleyn does have some distant relatives over in York, including a schoolmaster if I'm not mistaken.'

My heart jumped again. Jack gave me a knowing look, and I wondered how much he knew.

'I've got some other jobs to finish off now, which would best be done alone,' he said. 'Would you mind walking back to the 'all from 'ere on your own?'

'Not at all,' I replied. I clambered down to the ground.

William Pulleyn's tenant cottage was just a few hundred yards down the side-track from Dionysus Bainbridge's house. It was part of a small group of adjoining buildings. A thin strip of cultivated land ran from the back of each. As I got closer, I could see there was also a fenced area with hen coops behind most of the houses. Small groups of birds pecked and scratched at the soil, their orange and black feathers sparkling in the sunshine.

The door of the nearest hen house opened. Maria crouched out and stood tall. I can remember the moment as if it was yesterday. Seeing me, she bent down, removed three or four eggs from her apron and carefully placed them onto the grass. Pushing one of the hens backwards with her foot, she opened and closed the gate, stepped out from the side of the garden and walked towards me. I wanted to shout and scream and run to her but I didn't. I kept on walking slowly towards her, as she walked to me.

Her clothing looked different from the apparel she'd worn in York. That had been simple but clean and somehow elegant. Her hair here was covered in the same way but the things she wore were much more rustic. Although I knew she lived in the countryside, I was surprised to discover she was a relatively poor farmer's daughter. I wasn't sure what I'd been expecting but it hadn't been this.

We reached each other about twenty yards from the house.

'You came,' she said.

'You knew I would.'

'I hoped, but I couldn't be sure.'

'What happens now?'

'You've discovered where I live but you should leave and return tomorrow afternoon. My father won't be working in the fields then and I'm certain he'll be home. It's the Sabbath. I'm alone here now and it would be improper for us to be seen together like this without company.'

'What about your mother?'

'She's no longer with us, nor are my sisters. One is dead and the other married off. It's just my father and me now. It's not an easy life and Pa struggles without Ma. In some ways he's like you. He has a temper on him. If he saw us together like this, I don't know what he'd do. He didn't wish for me to return from York. He knew I'd be well fed there.'

'What should I say to him?'

'That's for you to decide,' she replied. 'When I came home, he told me he'd like to see me wed to the surviving son of one of his friends. They have more land than us and their own cottage. The lad will inherit it. Father thinks it's the best future a young woman like me can expect in a place like Scotton.'

'But what do you want?'

'You know what I want but now you've witnessed my humble background you must decide what you wish for. I'm not ashamed of who I am or where I come from, but if seeing me in this place makes you change your mind, nobody will blame you. Apart from me.'

I heard the challenge in Maria's voice, and saw the fire burning in her eyes, as brightly as when I'd discovered she could read and write.

I looked around quickly. The wagon was gone and there was no-one else about. I stepped forward and kissed her. She didn't resist. I closed my eyes and realised how much I loved her. She held me tightly. I couldn't have been happier. After a few moments of bliss with her body touching mine, she pulled herself gently away from me, as she had the last time, and we each took a pace back.

'Thank God,' she said, crossing herself. Again, I saw the rosary beads in her hands. 'I was so frightened you wouldn't come, or come too late, or worst of all see me for what I am and no longer wish to be with me. I'd have hated you for that.'

'Maria,' I said, 'apart from my family, you are everything to me. I love you with all my heart.'

Some men and women say first love is like this. Emotional. Irrational. I don't know. The love I felt for Maria is the only true love I've ever felt, so I have nothing to judge it by. It appeared to be crazy. We hardly knew each other but I was certain she was the only woman in the world for me. Fate had brought us together. Surely, we were part of God's plan. He had a purpose for us and one day we'd know what it was. I knew I couldn't be with another. I'd marry Maria, and after that God forbid anything should happen to her. If it did, I didn't know what I'd do.

There were tears in her eyes, as we tenderly held hands. My body tingled with a nervous energy, as it always did at the touch of her fingers. We looked at each other. I knew I could make her happy and she me.

'I'll return on the morrow,' I said.

'I look forward to it,' she replied.

I walked away. She may have carried on looking at me but I couldn't be sure. I'd promised myself never to look back.

I withdrew towards the Bainbridge residence. There was a dip in the road and my line of vision was lower than it had been on the carriage. The tenant houses, including Maria's, were no longer visible. I noticed the barn door next to Dionysus's house was open. A man stood in the entrance. He must have been about Mother's age. It was difficult to see who or what was behind him.

The fellow waved a cheery hello when he saw me. I nodded in reply and continued on my way. My mind was set on Maria and what I must do next. There were two, perhaps three, immediate actions I had to address before encountering Maria's father. Up until that point I'd given it little thought, but as I walked down the hill it dawned on me I must obtain Mother's support for my marriage.

The next thing would be to secure paid work and an income. From what Jack had indicated, things appeared hopeful on that front. To become his steward's assistant, I'd need to convert to the Catholic Church but I already considered it most likely I'd move in that direction. With Maria also of the old faith my conversion appeared the right thing to do, for so many reasons.

Only the memory of my father still held me back. I was sure he'd have wanted me to be happy but never down the years had I felt such terrible guilt when I thought of him.

I think of him now. What pain it would have caused him to see what I planned to do beneath Parliament. I have to grit my teeth to suppress a scream. My broken body can't take much more. They say everyone talks in the end. Or they die. Or both. I pray for death. But these devils are too skilled. They won't let it come. They control my agony with the turn of a screw.

I think next of Robert Catesby. He was a man of true vision. And of Thomas Percy, Jack Wright and my old friend Kit. If I can hold out a little longer, they'll reach the Midlands. Once there, they'll connect up with Sir Everard Digby and his group. There are plans to kidnap the King's daughter Princess Elizabeth. Together they'll have enough men to start an uprising. Others will follow. Our Spanish friends will intervene. Once again England will become a Catholic nation.

Perhaps my arrest was another step in the Lord's masterplan? Jesus wouldn't wish for the slaughter of innocents in Parliament, particularly as some of them would have been Catholics. Perhaps the uprising will succeed in any case. Perhaps He wishes me to endure my torture for just a little longer. To do so, I must regain control of my mind. I must leave this place. Once again, I must return to the past.

# 20

Approaching the grounds of Scotton Hall a call came up from behind me. It was Mother. I turned around, surprised but pleased to see her. Holding her skirts up from the mud, she walked rapidly along the track towards me. Perhaps we could talk out here, I thought, rather than in the hall within the earshot of others. She increased her pace and quickly caught up with me.

'Guy,' she said, a little breathlessly. 'I'm glad we've bumped into each other. There is something important I have to speak to you about.'

'I too,' I replied. 'The most wonderful thing has happened. I've met Maria and she wishes for me to meet her father.'

'Oh.' Mother said. I thought she looked disappointed.

'What's wrong?' I asked. 'I know we've only met a few times but I love her with all my heart. We're both old enough to marry and I'll be sixteen next month. Jack Pulleyn seems to think I may be able to assist his steward, so there's work for me here too. Mother, I thank you so much for bringing me to Scotton. Look around you. This is paradise.'

We scanned the area we were standing in. There were woods and hedges and spring flowers on the verge. The first newly born lambs were dancing in the fields to our left. Bird song filled the air. Even the horse dung on the track was easy to spot and avoid. I breathed in the atmosphere. It was fresh and lacked the wood smoke of hundreds of fires burning in the city. We weren't hemmed in and there was space to live.

'I understand,' she said softly. 'I was young and in love myself once. With your father.' She paused for a moment. 'The whole world seemed so exciting back then. I felt so alive, in ways I didn't think possible. Every time I saw him, I felt such a surge of excitement rush through my stomach. When we went to York the city seemed such a magical place and so exhilarating compared to the quiet of the countryside around here. I think we all like to go somewhere different. It depends on what you're used to.'

'So you don't object?'

'No, Guy,' she replied. 'I don't object but I think you need to slow down a little, and plan things out before you jump straight into marriage. Make sure you have a job, work out where the two of you will live, that sort of thing. State your intentions to Maria's father by all means but do so properly and don't rush Maria into things before you're both ready. This should be a special time for her. And remember if you go to the church in haste, people will only gossip and think you've put her in the family way.'

'Mother! We haven't even…'

'I know, I know,' she said, holding up her hands. 'But that's what people will think. Would you wish to bring suspicion and shame onto Maria and her family?'

'Of course not,' I replied.

My head went into a spin. A few moments ago, everything had appeared so simple but, as always, Mother was right. Certain things had to be arranged and sorted out. I hadn't even thought of where we might live. Widow Pulleyn and Jack may not take too kindly to me bringing one of their tenant's daughters to live under their roof. And at that moment I didn't even know if the rest of the family would remain in Scotton.

By the time we reached the hall, scores of thoughts bounced around inside my head. Mother opened the door. She went inside but I didn't. I found a sunny spot in a corner out of the wind and leaned against the wall in a place not overlooked by the windows, where nobody could see me. I needed to think. I'd still see Maria's father the next day but what would I say?

It was late in the afternoon when the visitor came. I'd planned to walk past Maria's house once more in the hope of catching a glimpse of her in the distance. As I fixed on my boots at the front of the hall, I watched the man ride up the track. His mount was short and scruffy, more like a pony than a horse. The rider wore the same sort of woollen breeches and coat as Jack's men but there was something familiar about the round cut of his hair and the way he held himself.

Ignoring me, he dismounted and tapped on the main door. Shifting one of the servants aside, Jack, himself, answered.

'I wasn't expecting to see you before tomorrow, Father,' he said.

'How can we help you? Come inside.'

So, the man was a Catholic priest. Whoever he was and whatever he wanted; I was sure it had nothing to do with me. I set off down the track. For the dozenth time I began to rehearse the speech I planned to make on the morrow. The words resounded awkwardly inside my head. I'd hardly made fifty yards when my sister Anne called for me to return. I turned towards her. She looked distraught.

I hurried back and we went inside. A small group of people were sat around the table with their backs facing the fireplace in the great hall. As well as Jack and Katherine, I could see the Father, Widow Frances and Mother. Anne took her place alongside her.

'Please Father, tell the boy what you have just told us,' said Jack quietly. 'From what Widow Fawkes tells me, he's been supporting the good lady's cause in her hour of need.'

The priest looked at me dubiously but spoke all the same. 'I've received word from York that under pressure from the Council of the North, Judge Clench has reduced Mistress Clitherow's stay of punishment to just one week. If it can't be proven she has a child in her belly within that time, he's authorised the Council to make up their own mind about whether or not they should proceed with the good lady's execution.'

'This is outrageous,' I complained. 'When did this happen?'

'Yesterday,' he replied. 'The Council sent a deputation to the judge's lodgings. We have a man on the inside who works there. He heard everything. Word is being sent around Yorkshire to see what can be done. Judge Clench stood firm at first, but they kept on haranguing him until he relented. The Assizes will soon be over. It appears he doesn't want the good lady's blood on his hands when he leaves the city, but he's more than willing to hand the responsibility over to others.'

'Do you think Mistress Vavasour's message will get through in time?' asked Mother.

'I have no idea,' I admitted. 'How many days does it take for a rider to travel to London?'

I looked at Jack but he shrugged his shoulders. He was right. How should he know?

Shortly afterwards the Father left us. He'd return the next day to hold a private Mass inside Scotton Hall for the family, their neighbours, friends and servants but I wouldn't be there.

Anne was in tears. She was sad for Mistress Clitherow but her hopes of seeing Henry would all but disappear if his mother was executed. I tried to console her but failed. It wasn't easy. In the end, the Widow

Margaret was called for. She led Anne to another room where they carried out mundane tasks to divert her mind.

My mother appeared equally disturbed and took to her bed early. I spoke with Jack and it was agreed I should leave for York first thing the next morning to see what could be done to assist Father Mush, or anyone else who might be able to offer aid to Mistress Clitherow's cause. I didn't mention Pastor Wigginton. It seemed better that way.

This of course left me with a problem. I was due to see Maria's father tomorrow afternoon. With no-one else to turn to, I spoke to Katherine Pulleyn and explained the situation. She promised me solemnly she would visit Walter Pulleyn in my stead. Once there, she'd speak on my behalf and explain my intentions towards his daughter. As the lady of Scotton Hall she said she was sure William Pulleyn would listen to her. It wasn't ideal but what could I do?

Afterwards when I went to bed that night, I slept for a while but my sleep was broken by a bad dream. There were so many conflicting thoughts in my head. As I lay there awake, I heard the screech of an owl. The sound was the same in the country as it was in the city. I wondered what creature might be suffering in its talons, as they tightened around its muscles.

I felt the sharp pain myself, my mind and body suddenly awake. More questions, as I become conscious of the present. Each hour it becomes harder to steer my mind back to the past. But I must. I must go back there.

I stepped out of the bed, stood by the little window and peered outside. The moon was elsewhere but the sky was full of stars. The more I looked, the more I saw. The grass twinkled and glistened with frost. I thought of Maria. Perhaps I should visit her in the night. I reached for my day clothes but dropped them. The idea was ridiculous. It wouldn't end well. I climbed back into bed, pulled up the covers and waited for morning.

## Sunday March 20th, 1586

Jack assigned me the same driver who'd brought us over from York. But his orders this time were only to take me as far as the toll bridge at Cattal. It was the Sabbath and unfair for the fellow to spend another two days on the road. After that, I'd be on my own. I was confident I knew the way but it would be a long walk. Mother gave me the large rusting iron key for our door and hugged me. Although Anne still had tears on her cheeks, she hugged me too. Lizzie was asleep in bed.

As I left the main room Jack Pulleyn embraced me warmly and wished me luck. I suspected Mother had passed on more about my adventures in the last few weeks than I'd realised. When I was about to leave his house, he told me the assistant steward's job was mine, if I wanted it. And I was not to worry about '*the other thing*' as between his wife and himself it would be sorted. I hoped he was right.

The last one to wave me off was Frances Pulleyn. She came to me after I'd climbed onto the back of the cart. I was expecting warm words but didn't get them. The widow looked at me harshly.

'You selfish young man,' she said, in a scolding voice. 'Have you no care for your mother's happiness? You should listen to her when she attempts to confide in you. The world revolves around more than just you, you know. Now be off with you! Go and do what men do, but when you come back, ensure you sit down with your mother and ask her what needs to be done to make her happy. And when she tells you, you must listen and take action. Only then, will I allow you to swan off down the road and take up house with my tenant's daughter. Do you understand me?'

I nodded, but in reality I had little clue what she was on about. I put it down to her age and focused on my troubles ahead. The one saving grace I could see was we were travelling in the opposite direction to Maria's homestead, so I wouldn't have to look forlornly at her house. I worried how she'd take my non-arrival and the visit of Katherine Pulleyn.


It was a cold morning. At times I felt chilled to the bone strapped to the back of that old wagon. The slope down the hill into Knaresborough proved trickier than coming up the other way. Several times the wheels skidded on the ice across the track and the driver swore at the horses as he struggled to maintain control over them. It wasn't much better going up the other side, although at least the ruts in the road gave some grip to the vehicle.

The driver spent much of the time looking up to the sky. After dawn, the starry frostiness was replaced by a cover of thickening cloud. The stratus seemed subtly different to normal. The overcast sky was grey, almost translucent, and I had to pull up the collar of my shirt to keep my neck warm.

When we reached Cattal we said our goodbyes. The driver spoke to the toll-booth agent. He persuaded his friend to let me cross without paying the pedestrian fee. As I was about to leave him, Jack's man shook my hand warmly.

'Look out for Mistress Clitherow,' he said. 'I have family over in York and they say she's always been kind to them. She teaches their little ones to read and write and gives alms to the poor, even the foreigners. Most of all, she's from our Church.'

He crossed himself and gazed at the heavens.

'I fear we're in for bad weather. Those clouds say snow to me but I don't know when it will start. Take my advice, lad. Make haste, don't tarry. And if the weather does close in on you, don't be afraid to ask for shelter. You'll not be doing anybody any favours if you're found frozen to death in a snow drift.'

With these encouraging words behind me, I set off rather unsteadily along the planks of the wooden bridge. Peering down into the freezing waters of the Nidd, I was thankful no traffic came from the opposite direction. It would have been easy to become unbalanced and fall in. Despite one or two slips on the icy surface I crossed the bridge safely and reached the York side.

Once across I hurried down the narrow lane. Shortly afterwards the wind began to pick up. I reached a fork in the road and wondered what the Romans would have thought of it. I imagined a legion of them marching right behind me all the way to York. When I took the junction towards Tockwith the first few flakes of snow began to strike at my cheeks. They came from the direction of the East Riding and scratched at my face like sharpened grains of sand.

A mile later I passed the first few homes and then the coaching inn at Tockwith. I tried to peer inside the building but couldn't see anybody about. Beyond the cow sheds at the spot where I'd looked towards my home city a few days before, I couldn't see any more than a dozen yards from my face. The weather was closing in. The Minster was no longer visible.

By the time I'd come down off Marston Moor I could hardly see the tracks in the lane in front of me. After the last night's frost, the snow was sticking easily, and there was two inches or more already around my boots. If the wind wasn't gale force it was strong. The whiteness in the air was mesmerising.

Snow makes such a dull noise as the flakes flutter to earth. I looked up at the sky but my eyes couldn't penetrate more than a few feet. After that my vision became confused by the myriad of grey dots descending around me. I opened my mouth and felt the cold nothingness melt on my tongue.

The near silence was eerie. I realised I hadn't seen a soul since Cattal. Sunday was the Sabbath. People weren't out working and the weather was keeping them indoors, but at times I felt I was the only person left alive on this Earth.

The floating flakes were no longer small. In fact, they were unusually large. It was as if pieces of wool had been caught in a hedge, combined together and tossed up into the air. Now as they drifted back down to the ground, I was glad of my cloak and most of all the thick woollen hat Jack Pulleyn had given me to keep my ears warm. Without this my hair would have already been soaked through, or possibly frozen into a block of ice.

By the time I reached the western edge of Rufforth I was dragging my feet through at least a foot of the icy white powder. I knew much of the area was cut into long thin strips for cultivation but it was impossible to see any of them now, or tell one from another. All the land here, whether owned, rented or common was covered in the same pale white snowy blanket.

I was thankful for the boundaries along the lane where it was coppiced with hazel, hawthorn and brambles. The hedging prevented me from losing my way or slipping down into one of the drainage ditches. My feet were wet but if my boots became soaked through it would be the death of me, and I worried I'd struggle to get out of one of the deeper ditches on my own.

Stopping for a moment, I wolfed down the smoked meat and cheese Widow Margaret had given me in the kitchen that morning. More than anything I felt thirsty. I rubbed my cold hands in the snow and put a few mouthfuls of the icy white mixture into my mouth. It quenched my thirst a little but it wasn't enough.

When I reached the first of the cottages stretching along the road from Rufforth the weather showed no signs of abating. I didn't know how long I'd been walking and there wasn't enough daylight to guess the time. Increasingly the road was heavy going.

Trickles of water began to run down my back and legs where my clothes had become saturated. I was worried if I stopped to rest, I'd freeze and not be able to get up again. I was thankful when for the first time in a few hours I noticed signs of human life. My nose twitched red at the aromas of smoke and cooking. I didn't care if it was vegetable or mutton stew, it smelt good. I considered knocking on a door and asking for hospitality but decided against it. If I was to help Mistress Clitherow I had to get to York as soon as possible.

After passing a dozen more cottages I thought of the warmth inside but left Rufforth and its hidden people behind. I now faced the loneliest part of the journey. I'd discounted help and comfort to enter a desolate flat scrubland. The bushes and trees ignored me. Their branches wore expressionless faces of snow and ice.

The few animals I did see were twice their normal size and a different colour. Everywhere I looked and everything I looked at was white. I stood still for a moment and listened. No birds were singing. All was silent. I was alone.

I trudged on with the snow up to my knees. My progress became painfully slow. Once or twice I stepped into a pothole. One was so deep I sank right up to the depth of my thigh. When I hauled myself out I felt great fatigue. My feet were now soaked and very cold but I had to keep going.

The fields around me appeared impassable, the road little better. I was even more tired than I had been before. I wanted to stop, lie down for a while. I was sure it would be alright if I halted. Perhaps I could sleep for just a few minutes.

I was about to stumble to my knees when I heard an urgent bleating. It came from a row of sheep folds away to the left. Whatever animal was the source of the sound, it was obviously in trouble. Perhaps one of the ewes was caught in a snow drift. I knew I should leave, but I couldn't. Some poor creature was struggling.

I followed the sound and pushed myself through the snow to a dry-stone wall. Peering over the top, I saw a shepherd. His coat was white with snow. The man crouched over a whining sheep. In the next few moments I watched as together they brought a new life into the world. I'd never seen anything like it.

First there was a flurry of blood. Then out came the head, followed by two legs. Or was it the other way around? It happened so quickly. A body and more legs followed, until the tiny animal flopped to the ground.

The shepherd lifted the baby lamb and rubbed its body with straw. After that, the bloody creature took its first breath and uttered a noise, a tiny bleat. Hearing the sound, the mother lifted herself onto her feet. The man scooped the new-born infant between his hands and placed it onto the ground beneath its mother's teats. With the head pointed in the right direction, the lamb knew what to do and began to suck.

The shepherd stood upright and shook the snow off his back. The detritus around his feet had turned the ground from white to red. He clapped his hands and I saw they were blue. It was then he saw me. I must have looked trustworthy, for the alarm on his face turned into a smile. He raised his thumb. I smiled back and nodded.

'She was 'aving sum trouble but they'll both be reet now,' he said.

I left them and made my way back to the road.

At first, I felt it was wishful thinking. I focused my eyes and sharpened my mind. Had the snow begun to ease? Were the clouds a little less dense? If I imagined it hard enough, could I see a hint of blue in the sky? The hamlet of Acomb became visible in the distance. I made my way there and carried on, down the long hill into York.

# 21

By the hour I reached our house in Stonegate, it was already dark. I stabbed the iron key into the lock and stumbled inside. I was too tired to light the fire. After a few minutes of searching the kitchen, I found some bread and cheese and ate it, washed down with two jugs of small beer.

When I'd done my ablutions, I climbed up the steps, took off my things and found a night shirt to wear. Still shivering but with some presence of mind, I picked up my wet clothes, took them downstairs and placed them on a rack near the fire to dry the next day.

After that I ascended the ladder and took myself to bed. How I loved it. It was the best and safest place in the world. Within a second of my head hitting the pillow, I fell fast asleep.

### Monday March 21st, 1586

I overslept the next morning. At least I would have, if I'd set myself a time to get up. For the first few hours of daylight I slipped in and out of consciousness. Finally, when I heard the Minster clock chime for eleven bells I departed the world of dreams. At least it wasn't midday. I looked outside. To my surprise there wasn't any snow. It had been raining heavily and water ran down everything. I sneezed.

Despite several attempts, for a while I failed to light the fire. Mother usually dealt with these things. I hoped Maria was more competent than I was. If we had to rely solely on my abilities to address domestic chores we'd be lost. I tried again. This time the flames did take hold and with the kindling burning I placed a number of logs on top. A chill ran down my back and I sneezed again.

After an hour I felt the real first flush of warmth run through my body. The larger logs spat a few sparks onto the hearth. Steam rose from the clothes on the rack. I raided the larder and was pleased to find vegetables. Using our sharpest knife, I sliced and diced onions, turnip and another vegetable I didn't even know the name of. I placed them into a pot and partly filled it with water. Lifting it up, I settled the pot onto the stove to be heated by the fire.

It took some time but eventually the water boiled. When the contents were sufficiently softened, I ladled them into a bowl. The stew tasted awful. Despite a brief search I couldn't find the salt or any seasoning but the food warmed me through. When I finished eating, I placed the pot and my bowl onto the floor, pushed them both to the side of the hearth with my foot and suppressed a cough.

By this time, I'd banked the fire up quite high and it wouldn't have been safe to leave it. I didn't want to anyway. I stayed there watching the flames flare up and down with sweat on my temple. I could only speculate what may have occurred in Scotton yesterday and what might happen in York over the next few days. My mind played out various scenarios. I was sometimes the hero but more often than not the villain. My throat felt hoarse and my nose was streaming. I couldn't help anybody in this condition. Once the logs had burned down, I went upstairs and crept back into bed.

## Tuesday March 22nd, 1586

The next morning, I was surprised by just how well I felt. My throat was a little bit sore but I'd stopped sneezing and my back wasn't aching. The power of two good nights sleep and hot food. Downstairs my outside clothes were warm and dry. I put them on and ventured out, taking a few pennies in my pocket. It had stopped raining, but there were puddles everywhere and the cobbles were damp and slippery.

After my travels through the countryside, York appeared busier than I remembered. There were people everywhere. I bought myself a cooked meat pie and some apple juice and consumed them quickly when I returned home. I realised I had no idea where Pastor Wigginton lived and my only knowledge of Father Mush's whereabouts was limited to the place we'd met near Peasholme Green, so I decided to start there.

Before I left the house, I began to formulate a plan to break Mistress Clitherow out of prison. I understood this was an action of last resort but if we could find sufficient bold men to attempt it, the dead of night would be the best time to try. Assuming the good lady's execution was planned for Friday or Saturday, we only had three or four nights left. I damned the fact I'd lost a day yesterday but it couldn't be helped.

I locked the door and began to walk down Stonegate, when I heard a call for assistance from one of the ginnels. This one led off in the direction of Grope Lane from alongside the front of the White Bear Inn. I couldn't see anyone, so I stopped and shouted, asking what was wrong.

A man hailed back saying he'd fallen in the alleyway and hurt himself. He claimed he was infirm and needed a hand to get to his feet. He was probably just drunk, I thought. I was in a hurry but remembering the lamb, I felt I couldn't ignore his plea for charity. If the wrong people found him, he'd be robbed for sure, so I ventured to see what had befallen the fellow.

When I rounded the corner, I was no longer visible from Stonegate but I could see the man, laid out flat on his back halfway across the snicket. Other from that, he appeared well enough. When he saw me, he smiled and reached out his hand. I walked towards him. The poor creature was shabbily dressed, and I realised he spoke with a foreigner's accent. He must have been another immigrant but no matter where he came from, he needed my help. As I reached down and pulled the fellow up to his feet, I thought of myself as the Good Samaritan, right up until the point when he punched me in the stomach.

Winded for a second, I stepped away from him. The beggar's trying to rob me, I thought. But I was young and strong, and I'd been taught well enough at school how to fight like a gentleman. I squared up to the fellow. He'd caught me unawares but if he tried to strike me down again, God willing I'd parry his blows and return the compliment with twice the force.

'Be you Fawkes?'

I turned around. A second man was now standing behind me. And he'd brought a mate. His accent was similar to the miscreant I'd helped from the floor but I couldn't place it. The newcomers edged slightly apart from each other. They began moving towards me. The ginnel was narrow and their bodies blocked my way. The alternative escape route was to dash towards Grope Lane but that way was impeded by the fellow who'd punched me.

'Are you deaf? Be you Fawkes?'

'Aye,' I said. 'Who wants to know?'

My mind was racing. Probably my best chance was to rush past the single man and make a break for it. I checked my original attacker. Now fully standing, he was a rough looking man, and I could see he was the biggest of all three of them.

'One of your friends from school wants to send you a message,' said the second ruffian.

The three of them came at me at once. I punched and kicked but they were too many and too strong. In just a few moments two of them had me gripped by the shoulders, and the first man began hitting me. I grimaced and squirmed to avoid his blows but one caught me savagely above the eye. After that I struck my head back violently, as hard as I could. I felt the crunch more than I heard it. I was pretty certain I'd broken one of the men's noses.

There was some hissing and swearing. One of the fellows released his grip on me. Twisting hard I shook off the other. My body spun around, until all three of them were stood on the Stonegate side. If I made for Grope Lane now, they'd probably catch me but I had a chance. I was about to run for it, when the man with the bloodied face un-sheaved a knife. It wasn't fancy but big and sharp enough to tear my insides out. My stomach contracted. I felt alone and afraid.

'What's all this noise?'

It was my attackers' turn to whirl around to see who was behind them. A gentleman with a fancy hat had stepped out of the side door of the Bear Inn. He looked quite the party goer. I couldn't see his eyes but expected he must be drunk. The distraction was probably my best chance to get away but if I took off, there was a chance they'd kill him there and then.

'Who the shard are you?' asked the ruffian holding the knife, blood dripping from his face.

'A gentleman swordsman,' replied the fellow in an East Riding accent.

He swished his cloak to one side to make his scabbard visible.

'Shard off, lad, or I'll stick you as well as this ginger runt. I mean it, man. All three of us have got blades.'

'I recognise your accent,' said the newcomer. 'I dare say you're from over the Pennines? If I were to ask the Corporation to check out the records of registered paupers from those parts, would you show up? If so, they'd have you working somewhere like St Anthony's Hall today. So, you're probably vagabonds who haven't even registered. If that's the case, if the Corporation catches you, they'll have you doing hard labour in no time in one of the correction houses. Or they'll send you back home. How do you fancy that?'

'This is your last chance you little sh…'

The knife flew from the man's hand and landed in a puddle with a noisy splash. I'd hardly seen the gentleman move but in less than a second he'd stepped forward, unleashed his blade and disarmed the bloodied man with a flick of his wrist. It was incredible. I'd only seen speed like that from one swordsman before.

I pressed my back to the wall, as all three of them high-tailed it past me. They knew they'd met their match. My rescuer took off his hat and stepped towards me.

'Jack Wright!' I exclaimed. 'The Lord be praised. What are you doing here in York?'

'There's a good woman in peril who needs my help. And now, I find schoolboys being beaten up in the street by scoundrels. This city has gone to the dogs since I left it.'

He secured his weapon and reached his hand towards me. I shook it warmly.

'But why aren't you in St Peter's learning Latin with my brother and the other little oiks, Master Fawkes? And who were those fellows who attacked you?'

'It's a long story,' I said. 'I've been expelled from school for hitting Thomas Cheke. Do you remember him?'

'Yes, nasty lump of horse shit, just like his old man.'

'Those ruffians were paid by Cheke or perhaps his father to attack me. I don't know how far they would have gone if you hadn't come when you did.'

'Let's say you've had a lucky escape. When a man pulls a knife in a city like York, he usually means to use it. I take it it was you who made the mess of the fellow's nose?'

I nodded.

'Good lad,' said Jack, as he mock punched my shoulder. 'What else have you been up to?' He looked up and down the ginnel. 'Have you seen sense yet and moved to the old faith?'

I nodded. He smiled.

'Before I share anything else with you,' I said. 'I must you ask one question. Who is the good woman you referred to?'

'Mistress Margaret Clitherow, of course,' said Jack. 'I've come to rescue the Pearl of York.'

# 22

Once Jack had finished in the alley what he'd come out to do, we went inside together. He led me through the tap room to a quiet table in the corner, out of earshot of the other patrons. I watched him carefully detach the scabbard from his belt and place it, with no little tenderness, onto the bench next to us, as if it was a family heirloom or a valuable antique. Once he was satisfied it wouldn't roll off, he called a serving woman to the table and ordered food and ale for two. After that we talked.

I discovered Jack had only recently arrived in York. His first priority had been to find suitable stabling for his horse. He then checked himself into the White Bear, where his father stayed when the family had business in the city. There were now several hours to kill before a scheduled conference in the evening with a small number of men who'd travelled to York with the same purpose as he.

'You can accompany me,' he said. 'We're meeting in the upstairs room in the Black Swan at Peasholme Green.'

'But that's a well-known haunt for the Queen's men,' I replied.

Jack laughed. 'What better place to meet then? Who would think to look for us there? But don't worry we'll take precautions. We'll not be arrested. Do you want to come?'

I nodded eagerly. For the next few minutes I informed Jack of my role as Father Mush's eyes and ears in the courtroom. He appeared suitably impressed. Kit's brother was only a few years older than us but his body language and words were so much more self assured and mature. He said he was keen to have Kit alongside him in the days ahead and planned to collect his younger brother from school that afternoon. I asked how he'd be able to do this.

'I'm going to tell Headmaster Pulleyn we have an urgent family need and must travel to Hull. Our uncle is dying. It's a common enough occurrence to make it plausible.'

'Do you think it'll work?'

'Of course. I visited the same uncle myself several times when I was at St Peter's.'

A few hours later I was delighted to be reunited with my best friend. I'd abandoned any idea of linking up with Father Mush and Pastor Wigginton. Perhaps they'd be at the meeting. Perhaps not. It didn't matter now. I'd found men of real action. For the first time since I'd heard of Judge Clench's climbdown I felt confident we'd free Mistress Clitherow from jail.

Kit seemed equally pleased to see me, although he winced a little when he saw the state of my face. The area around my eye was already swollen and sore to the touch. When I told him the vagabond's message about the source of the attack, Kit cursed Thomas Cheke and swore vengeance. I told him I'd get my own back on our enemy in time but he shouldn't do anything about it, at least for now. The last thing I wanted was for Kit to be expelled. One of us had to complete our education.

'How are things more generally at school?' I asked.

Although I'd been busy, I realised I missed the place, particularly spending time with my friends.

'It's hardly the same without you,' said Kit. 'Rob is alright, but there's no fight in him, and I think we may need that soon.'

'How so?'

'There's been a shadow over St Peter's since you left. Word has it Cheke senior pressed for Headmaster Pulleyn to be arrested, but the Corporation and Ecclesiastical Court have refused. With Archbishop Sandys on his side, I think he's safe from investigation for now but the atmosphere in the school is like poison. Obviously, some of the boys know I'm a Catholic. They say you must be too. The only thing stopping Craven and the others from having a go at me in revenge for Cheke's beating is the threat of expulsion. To be honest, I'm surprised you haven't been arrested.'

'The Sheriff's men are busy enough with the Assizes and Mistress Clitherow to worry about small fry like me,' I said, although Kit's words worried me.

'In any case,' he said, his face brightening up. 'Perhaps with what Jack's planning, I'll never have to go back to school again. We'll save the Pearl and become fugitives, living off the land.'

It was a romantic idea, if not a realistic one, but either way it wasn't for me. I wanted only to remain anonymous and for the deed to be done, so I could quickly escape back to Scotton.

'One other thing,' said Kit. 'The girl's gone. You know, the one you like, the old man's cousin.'

'Oh,' I said, trying not to give anything away. I didn't lie to Kit but felt uneasy for not sharing the truth with him. Maria's whereabouts were my secret. I'd share the information with nobody, not even my best friend.

In the hours which followed we drank a great deal of ale, played cards in the inn and waited impatiently for the time to come to set off to the meeting. During the quieter moments I thought of Maria. We needed a place to live. I wanted to develop more practical traits so I could look after her. Most of all, I wanted us to be together as husband and wife. First, I'd need to convince her father that I was a better bet than his friend's son. I wished again I knew how Katherine Pulleyn had got on.

Eventually it was time to leave. I felt an unconquerable pride as we marched through Petergate. We had Jack in the middle, and Kit and I on either side flanking him. As we strode manfully through York's city streets, Jack's confidence was contagious. I knew my arrogance must be partially down to the ale, but Mistress Clitherow had been correct. Why should Catholics have to skulk in the shadows? I felt twelve feet tall. Good men working together in the name of a righteous cause is a most wondrous thing to behold.

It was a small room and the eight young men packed it full. There was a ninth downstairs. The pock-faced fellow remained in the bar and acted as look-out. At the first sign of trouble he was to knock loudly on the ceiling with his walking stick. Two potential escape routes had been agreed, and half the men nominated to each.

No names were used during the meeting but Jack had whispered to me before the start, the one who'd do most of the talking was Thomas Percy of Beverley. He was the oldest fellow in the room, with a smart looking beard and very fine clothing, but I doubted if even he was thirty.

'There's no chance word will reach York from London in time,' he said. 'Pinning the Queen down isn't easy, and the time needed to travel both ways is too long. We'll be lucky to get something back in a fortnight.'

The faces in the room looked gloomily down.

'No, if Mistress Clitherow is to be saved this must be a northern operation.' Percy continued. 'I think we have two choices. I've sent word to my cousin, the Earl of Northumberland, to seek his personal intervention. If he travels to York and speaks to the Council, they'll have no choice but to agree a delay.'

'What if your message doesn't reach him in time?' asked Jack. 'I know he travels around a lot.'

'In that case we must act ourselves,' replied Percy. 'This is the second alternative course of action. Word from Ouse bridge is that the good lady's execution will be held on Friday morning. If I receive no message from my cousin before Thursday evening, we'll go in overnight and force her release.'

'But the prison is well guarded and the walls are strong.' The objection came from one of the attendees I didn't recognise.

'Nonsense!' exclaimed Percy. 'A small force of determined men can easily get in there. The guards are ill paid and clearly open to bribery. They'll stand aside or pay with their lives.'

'Wouldn't it be better to attack when they come out of the Ouse Bridge prison on Friday morning?' asked another.

'Certainly not,' replied Percy firmly. He seemed to be a man who knew his own mind. 'It's likely they'll be expecting trouble on Friday. As well as the Sheriff and the Corporation men, they may have extra guards from the Council of the North. No, if we're to successfully break the good lady out, the only time to do it will be overnight.'

'What happens then?' I asked, unable to help myself. Jack had instructed Kit and I not to say a word, but I think the ale got the better of me.

'Never mind that, lad. We'll have fast horses waiting and we'll spirit her away to a house in the Wolds.'

'But after that?'

'What do you mean?'

'Where will Mistress Clitherow live? What will happen to her family? What if...' I found myself involuntarily repeating the same arguments Pastor Wigginton had used against me.

'Too many questions! What if, what if, what if...' Percy rolled his eyes at me. 'Let's worry about the Pearl's future once we've secured her present. By the way, can you ride a horse, lad?'

'Aye,' I said.

Percy stared at me; scepticism writ large across his face. 'Is that so? Tell me, when and where did you last ride?'

'Last Saturday morning in Scotton,' I replied boldly.

'Scotton, you say? Who do you know there?'

'I was staying with Jack Pulleyn, the master of Scotton Hall.'

Percy laughed. 'The scoundrel's grandson. I'll be damned. He's a good horseman though.'

As suddenly as my interrogation had begun, it ended. Percy's countenance adopted a thoughtful look. His grey eyes scanned the faces of the other men in the room. After a moment, he said, 'So then, lads, which of you can I count on if things turn sour, and we have to storm the jail?'

Every man raised his hand, without hesitation, Kit and I included.

'Good men,' said Percy. 'You'll all be in the attack party. Except for you.' He looked me in the eye once more. 'You're sure you're good with horses, boy?'

I nodded.

'Then I want you to accompany Poxy Joe. You'll hold the steeds and wait for us outside the city walls. I'm not sure he'll be able to control them on his own. I assume the rest of you can ride as well as this red-haired lad?'

The others nodded.

'Right then, that's enough for now. We need to keep these meetings short and sober.' I felt he glanced at me again. 'We're to meet in this same room, at the same time tomorrow evening. Remember, when we sat down tonight, we all swore an oath of secrecy. Nobody else must know of this plan. We're conspirators now. From here on in, we must stick together through thick and thin. If anyone finds out or catches us they'll call us traitors, and we'll be hanged at the Knavesmire. We wouldn't want that, would we?'

No, I thought. But this time I managed to keep my counsel.

### Wednesday March 23rd, 1586

I spent the next morning to-ing and fro-ing between our house on Stonegate and the White Bear. We shared a fine dinner in the inn just after noon, and I could feel my strength returning. I'd gone home after the Black Swan meeting but my friends had stayed up drinking. Jack and Kit now looked jaded. They headed up to their room and returned to bed.

I'm not sure if it was from guilt or boredom but in the afternoon I decided to do as much useful work around the house and garden as I could. Once I'd cleaned a few pots, there was little to do inside, so I collected seven or eight larger logs from around the yard and chopped them down to firewood size. When I finished, I leant on the handle and admired my handiwork. The pile I'd stacked was as neat as anything I'd seen in the countryside.

I wondered what else to do. Mother seemed to have sorted most things out before we'd left for Scotton. But when I checked the freshwater barrel, I discovered it was only a quarter full. Given this, my final task was to carry bucket after bucket of clean water from the well down the way. I poured the contents of each pail into the cask, replaced the lid and started again by journeying back down the street until finally it wasn't possible to get any more liquid inside. It would probably turn your stomach, but it was fine for cooking, washing and cleaning.

By then my muscles ached, but in a good way, from hard work. As beads of sweat dripped from my forehead, a few trickled down my back and I wondered if it was time to wake my friends. A familiar head popped around the side of the house. It belonged to Pastor Wigginton.

'Hello, young Guy,' he said. 'I'd heard you were back in York. What in God's name have you been doing? Your face looks as red as your hair.'

'Carrying water and cutting wood,' I replied, pointing to the log stack. He didn't look as impressed as I'd hoped.

'What do you know about the good lady?' he asked.

'Only what the gossips in the street say,' I said warily. 'Is it true she'll be put to death in two days time?'

'Aye, it is,' he replied. 'Perhaps we should talk inside, and I can tell you what I know?'

Once within the house I invited him to sit at the table but he kept his coat on. There wasn't a fire and I suppose he may have been cold.

'We thought we'd succeeded in persuading Judge Clench to place all proceedings on hold for at least four weeks. This would have given sufficient time for the jury of matrons to confirm Mistress Clitherow has a babe in her belly. And it would have been almost inconceivable Mistress Vavasour's despatch wouldn't have got through to the Queen and back in that time.'

'I hear the Council pressed him?'

'Aye, they did. One of our mutual friend's friends works there and witnessed everything. Several Council members visited the judge at his lodgings, accompanied by Justice Rodes. The group kept going on and on at Judge Clench, demanding he waive the stay but he steadfastly refused.'

'What changed his mind?'

'The Council's non-legal Secretary, Henry Cheke, took the old man to one side. We don't know exactly what was said because their words were spoken in whispers. Whatever it was, a bribe, a threat or something else, it made Judge Clench mightily angry. He began shouting and his face turned to thunder, but after that he backed down.'

The parson's own face darkened a little, and he affected a voice similar to the one I'd heard in the courtroom. '*You must keep the woman out of harm's way for another week. After that I'll give authority to the Council of the North to do whatever you see fit. Whether you proceed with the court's sentence, or defer it, the responsibility for Mistress Clitherow's fate will now lie in your hands. And your hands only. Any future punishments will have nothing to do with my Assizes court.*'

Another man washing his hands of the good lady, I thought, picturing Henry Maye.

'Can we not change his mind? Make Clench see he risks the Queen's displeasure?'

'We could try but we'd have to find him first. The Assizes has moved on. Even if we did speak to the man, I think he'd simply turn us away and say Mistress Clitherow's fate is no longer his responsibility. Whatever happens to the good lady now is down to the Council. If Judge Clench was once inclined to show her mercy, he's abandoned the idea.'

'Will she still not repent? Or change her mind and make a plea?'

'No, I've tried. Believe me, I've tried. I've visited Mistress Clitherow in her cell almost every day for the past week. She shares it with a married couple, as Puritan as they come, but even they've given up attempting to convert her from the old religion. The husband ignores her completely, and I fear the wife's fallen under her spell. I wouldn't be surprised if she converts the other way around and becomes a Catholic, herself, before the week is out.'

Parson Wigginton sighed. He looked tired. I believed him fully when he said he'd done all he could do to save Mistress Clitherow.

'In truth, I have failed,' he said with some resignation. 'But everyone else has too. Archbishop Sandys has sent churchman after churchman into that jail to tease or cajole her. But in the end, one by one, they have all turned tail and returned to the Bishop's Palace to shake their heads at his stony face. Even Lord Mayor Maye has visited his stepdaughter on more than one occasion. The first time he begged her to apostatise, for the memory of her late mother, although he's changed his tune since. Now he simply rages at her, claiming she's plotted suicide all along.'

'How does Mistress Clitherow react to all this?'

'In the same manner she deals with everything. She smiles and gives us that look which says she knows she's right. She believes she's part of God's great plan and is doing His will. She prays a lot and raises thanks to the Good Lord for wishing her to die in such a horrible fashion in His holy name. Bloody Catholics and their martyrs…' The parson shook his head.

'The only thing she's worried about is the manner in which the sentence will be carried out. The court order states she should receive her punishment naked, and she's aware she'll be seen by men who aren't her husband. She wept when she realised this and has spent much of her time since sewing a long shawl which she hopes the Sheriff will permit her to wear on Friday morning to cover her modesty.' He shook his head again. 'The whole thing is madness.'

'Is there nothing we can do to protect her?'

'No, I think not, other than… an armed rescue perhaps.' He looked at me then, his eyes attempting to read mine.

I met his gaze. My own eyes stared back, as I adopted the same neutral look Jack Wright had given me at least a dozen times in the last twenty-four hours, when he was holding a deuce or an ace in his hand.

'What happened to your eye?' he asked after a while.

'I was thrown off a horse in Scotton,' I lied.

The pastor studied me, looking disappointed. I liked and trusted the man but I was sworn to secrecy.

# 23

In the early evening I returned to the White Bear, joining Kit and Jack at our now familiar table. Jack ordered ale but I didn't drink so much this time. We talked quietly and played cards, betting little wooden sticks rather than money. A few times I saw Jack furtively glance towards another table, where a stranger sat alone supping his ale even more slowly than I was.

'Don't look at him,' whispered Jack under his breath, as he carefully placed a playing card face up in the centre of the table. 'I think he's a watcher. Whether he works for the Council, the Corporation or someone else hardly matters, he mustn't know where we're going this evening.'

'What shall we do?' asked Kit excitedly.

'Make a fool out of him,' replied Jack coldly. 'If we attack him, or if he knows we've shaken him off deliberately, he'll report us for sure. We need to make him feel so inept he won't want to say anything. Whatever I ask you to do now, do as I say, and we'll meet up in less than an hour's time outside St Saviour's. Once we're there, if there's any sign we're still being followed, we'll come back here and turn in for the night.'

Jack slapped the rest of his cards onto the table. 'I'm bored!' he declared, in an unexpectedly loud voice.

Kit and I put our own cards down too. The game was obviously over. Jack gathered up the cards and the wooden sticks, before tucking them all inside a tin box. After wrapping a piece of string around it to keep it shut, he placed the box inside his coat.

'Let's go and get some real action,' he said. 'Kit, how would you like to break your duck?'

'What do you mean?' asked Kit. He turned his head and winked at me.

'You know, the sort of stuff that happens in Grope Lane,' replied Jack, pretending to talk quietly. 'It's time brother you became a man.'

'What about me?' I asked.

'I'm only paying for my brother to have a woman. You'll have to pay your own way, lad,' he said. 'It's past your bedtime anyway. I think you should leave now.'

'Well, if that's the way you want it,' I said, playing my part. 'I shall.'

I scraped my chair noisily, stood up, picked up my drink and quaffed the final inch of my ale. Once I'd finished, I slammed the empty mug back down onto the table and left.

When I was outside the inn, I looked up and down the street. Nobody appeared to be paying me any attention. I passed my house and cantered up Stonegate towards Davygate. It wasn't a sensible direction from which to walk to St Saviour's but it would give ample opportunity to spot if anyone was following me. Even though it was dark, there were still a few people about. After my attack in the ginnel I intended to stay on the main streets. This wouldn't make it easier to throw off any potential pursuers but it was a price worth paying to remain safe. The memory of the bloodied man's knife flashed through my mind.

I reached the meeting point at the church, well before the others. Even then I had plenty of time to walk one way and then the other, to listen for footsteps and to watch out for shadows. I was fairly certain no-one was pursuing me but I still felt inside the lining of my coat. The sharp stones I'd placed there earlier were still there, next to my sling. Although they'd be of little use at close quarters, I felt somehow reassured to know I had some protection against the Philistines around me.

Kit arrived next. He was on his own. When he saw me, he began to grin. 'I've never been inside a stew before,' he said. 'And on a school night as well. What do you think Headmaster Pulleyn would say?'

I looked wide-eyed at him.

'Don't worry, I wasn't in there for long. Jack seemed to know the layout of the place very well, including where both the doors were. As soon as we went inside one, he shooed me straight out through the other, with instructions to come here.'

'Where's Jack now?'

'I don't know. I had to hurry off and leave him there. He told me he'd wait until the coast was clear, but I wouldn't be surprised if he was up to something else in the meantime. You know Jack!'

Kit smiled and winked at me, but I remembered the sad looking face of the woman in the alley and wondered if she worked in the place. I hated to think Jack might be with her. Thankfully he wasn't.

'That'll teach the dolt,' smiled Kit's brother a moment later, as he approached our spot in the shadows outside St Saviour's Church. 'I wonder what he'll say to his masters? I swear to you, the man couldn't arrange a cock-up in a whorehouse. I think he'll just say he watched us all night, we had a few jars, the ginger one left us, and Kit and I turned in for the evening.'

'Why was he following us in the first place?' I asked.

'It's me they're after,' said Jack. 'Everyone knows Kit and I come from a recusant family. Since I left school, I've become a little more active, shall we say, in my support for the true Church. I'm sorry if you've been seen with us, Guy, but hopefully the watcher will have no idea who you are. Let's go to the Swan now. We'll be there in five minutes.'

The main bar of the Black Swan Inn was dimly lit and largely empty. Poxy Joe sat on a wooden stool in his sentry position. His head turned a little too quickly and none too subtly towards us when we arrived. For a second his eyes scanned our shadows nervously, until he recognised Jack's hat. Ignoring him, as Jack had instructed, we walked to the narrow winding staircase at the far end of the bar.

Within the meeting room, Thomas Percy was also in position. His imposing body filled the space at the head of the table. Two others sat near him. Neither man had spoken during the first meeting and I got the feeling, along with Joe, they were part of his entourage. After a few moments the other two fellows arrived and the meeting commenced.

Percy outlined the plan. Assuming no word came from his cousin, the main group would meet alongside the docks on Skeldergate at midnight tomorrow evening, whilst Joe and I would exit the city earlier in the day, before the gates were locked up for the night. This resulted in a sensible question. How was the main party going to leave the city? Percy responded by saying they'd bribe or shoot their way out. The answer resulted in a few nervous looks around the room, as everyone realised this wasn't a game. It was real, and real people would get hurt. Some may be killed.

I had to admit I was impressed by Percy's grip of logistics. Joe and I would bring the horses and wait in the darkness in one of the orchards within sight of Lounlith postern, a people-only entry point on the south-western edge of the city. Joe would be given a timepiece, so we'd know exactly when the main party would be coming towards us.

Percy said he'd checked the place personally and there were never more than one or two guards on patrol. At night sometimes there was just a lock and chain to break. If there were no guards, Joe would use a pair of metal cutters and break the chain. If there were guards, the main party would attempt to use money or firearms to get past them. As a last resort gunpowder would be used to blow the gate wide open. I asked if I could do this but Percy said I should stick to my job and look after the horses.

I was worried about this task. I wondered if Jack or Kit realised I had so little equine experience. Leading the steeds along couldn't be that difficult, I thought. And once I was on one, I'd just have to wait and see how it went. There was no way I was going to stand down.

A cache of swords, knives, matchlocks and powder had been assembled. These would be distributed around the main party when they met up. Additional weapons would be stored with the horses to replace any lost during the raid and subsequent escape, and for Joe and I to use if necessary.

A temporary safe house was waiting in a village on the eastern side of the city. We'd have to cross the River Ouse on horseback to reach it. Percy's thinking was that if we escaped to the west, the authorities would think it unlikely we'd double back on ourselves. Once the initial search was over, the group would disperse, and Percy and his retainers would transport Mistress Clitherow to a secret cottage in the Wolds. For safety's sake most of us didn't know the location of either the safe house or the cottage.

He began to outline his plan to gain entry to the prison when the talk was disturbed by two sharp knocks on the floor. My heart jumped into my throat. We were about to make a run for it, when there was a single knock, the signal for all clear. Nobody believed it but Percy told us to stay where we were. He placed a pair of dice onto the table and scattered some pennies around it. We each grabbed a few coins and created a small pile for ourselves.

There was a knock on the door.

'Come in,' said Percy.

The door opened.

Two men entered the room. I recognised them instantly. The first was Father Mush. He was followed by Pastor Wigginton. One of Percy's men stepped behind them and closed the door. Everyone else stared at these representatives of two different religions.

'Hello, Father,' said Percy carefully, addressing the Catholic priest. 'Do you fancy a game of chance?'

They obviously knew each other.

'Gambling is the Devil's work,' uttered Wigginton.

'Shush man,' said Father Mush. 'We have more important business here.'

'How can we help you, Father?' asked Percy.

'I recognise this man,' said one of the men staring directly at Pastor Wigginton. 'You're the Protestant preacher who spoke during Mistress Clitherow's trial.'

'You keep strange company, Father,' said Percy suspiciously. 'I ask again, how can we help you?'

'You're planning to rescue the Pearl, aren't you?' said Father Mush slowly. 'Don't deny it, Thomas. The Lord sees everything.'

'I don't know what you mean. We're just a few Yorkshire lads who've got together to sip ale and play dice.'

'I see no ale.'

'That's Joe's fault. The chap with the walking stick downstairs. It's his round. He's very slow. He's had the pox you know. He's never been quite the same since.'

'I forbid it,' said Father Mush angrily, raising his voice.

'I too,' added the parson but everyone ignored him.

The challenge of wills here was clearly between Thomas Percy and Father Mush alone. Everyone knew it. The two men looked at each other with hardening faces. Their eyes narrowed. If the Father hadn't been a holy man, it might have come to blows.

'There's no other way,' Percy said deliberately. 'You tried to get a message to the Queen. I've attempted to contact my cousin. But we're out of time. In thirty-six hours, they'll place a sharp stone beneath her back, hoist a door over her body and crush her slowly to death. And for what? Not for harbouring a priest. Not even for being a Catholic. Not for anything else, other than refusing to make a plea in a trumped-up trial where they'll force her own children to testify against her. By God, man, I won't have it!'

He slammed his fist down loudly onto the table, causing the dice to fly up and the nearest stacks of pennies to fall over and roll away.

'You use the Lord's name in vain.'

'No, I use it in anger. As any right-thinking Catholic man would do. This is horrific. If we let them do it to this woman, what will follow? Will it be our children next? No! We must put an end to this outrage. Here and now, in York.'

'But the lady wishes to be a martyr.'

'Haven't you seen enough of those already? Richard Kirkham, William Lacey, James Thompson, Hugh Taylor, Marmaduke Bowes. How many more do you want, Father? I say, No!'

Father Mush glared at him. As he struggled to think of what to say, his Protestant colleague intervened.

'I'm no Catholic,' said Pastor Wigginton. 'But I abhor killing of men and woman in the name of religion. Whether it's Catholics murdered in the name of Elizabeth or Protestants burned for the good of Queen Mary, it's all wrong. And for every willing martyr, there's a dozen innocent souls behind them, with no wish to die. Yes, I intervened in the courtroom. I asked the judge to use God's law and not the Queen's but he wouldn't listen. But unlike the rest of you, I've spent hours in Mistress Clitherow's cell. I've implored her to convert from her religion, or make a plea, but I failed. And then I was delighted when we thought she was pregnant. The actions of the Assizes and the Corporation and the Council are an abomination, but you must ask yourself one thing. What does the good lady really want?'

'What do you mean?' asked Jack.

'More than anything else now, she wishes to die.'

'Because he's created a bloody martyr out of her,' said Percy, pointing his finger at Father Mush.

'Aye, partly due to that, but for other reasons too,' said the parson. 'She won't convert because she's true to your church. She won't make a plea because she knows if she does it will bring danger to others. They'll find a way of implicating her husband. They'll torture her children, or the Flemish boy, to get more information. She won't give the evidence which would save her, for to argue the priestly things were found in a neighbour's house would mean others would be arrested and treated badly.'

Nobody spoke for a moment. The parson took a breath, before continuing on with his sermon.

'If you strive to set her free and you do get away, what then? They'll arrest and punish a hundred others. Some of them, and some of you, will likely be killed. Some of those guarding her will certainly be. And on whose slender shoulders and conscience will all this death and destruction fall? After all this happens, every second of every day will become an agony for her.'

For half a second Thomas Percy caught my eye.

'So, I ask you to stand down,' continued the parson. 'Not for the benefit of the Queen nor the Council nor the Corporation but for this good woman I've come to admire, for her fortitude and for the importance she places on the lives of others. I didn't create the title for her, but if York is an oyster, Margaret Clitherow truly is the pearl within. You may shed a tear for her on Friday, as will I, but let her go.'

As the contents of the speech sank in around the room, not a single one of us doubted the passion and wisdom of the man's words.

'You speak eloquently,' said Percy after a few moments. 'I heed what you say.' Everyone else in the room remained quiet, until Percy spoke again. 'And on this basis, I withdraw my men and myself from this action. We'll leave York tomorrow. I won't remain here to witness what they plan to do. But I promise you this, if the ill treatment of God-fearing Catholics continues, in time we shall rise up and strike our enemies down with the mightiest of blows.'

With these words, my view of Thomas Percy changed. After the previous meeting I'd considered him an egotist and a bully. Now I saw was a man of compassion and reason, who listened to others and could have sympathy for their views. Most of all, his talk of rising up in the future made a lasting impression on me. If there was to be a plot to strike a blow against our enemies, I wanted to be part of it.

'I'm standing down too,' said Jack. 'And I take my brother and his friend with me. The notion was a grand one. We set out to support the finest of causes but we can't carry on if we risk doing more harm than good to the one we seek to protect. After hearing the parson's words, I believe we have no choice but to desist. God bless the good lady's soul.'

Jack crossed himself, as did most of the others. A few mumbled a prayer or two for Mistress Clitherow. As the meeting broke up a general gloom descended over us all.

# 24

**Thursday March 24<sup>th</sup>, 1586**

Talk of Mistress Clitherow's execution dominated York. People discussed the matter in their homes, on the street, in workshops and in merchants' premises. The hostility felt towards the good lady immediately following her sentencing had mellowed. In particular, the news of her suspected pregnancy had brought sympathy, quickly followed by outrage when the plans for her execution were reinstated.

Whilst most people still couldn't understand her obstinacy, this didn't prevent them from questioning how the Council could sanction such an action against a woman possibly with child. Even many of those set against her, thought the whole thing was wrong. Under God's law the little one was innocent. Upstanding citizens, including several aldermen, privately denounced the Lord Mayor and Corporation for their failure to intervene and prevent this atrocity.

Although there were no signs of widespread civil disturbance, it was clear people were angry. Rotten eggs had been thrown at the doors of the Common Hall where the Assizes were held. Two apprentices bared their arses at the Lord Mayor as he left his house one morning. They would have been punished, but the lads quickly pulled up their breeches and ran off before anybody could recognise or catch them. By the afternoon the Sheriff's men were making armed patrols through the streets, and the Corporation ordered extra guards to be stationed on either side of Ouse Bridge. Nobody was taking any chances.

For my own part, the excitement of playing a leading role in the good lady's rescue had been quickly replaced by feelings of melancholy, hopelessness and now increasingly loneliness.

Jack Wright shook my hand. He embraced me warmly, as he prepared to leave the White Bear to take Kit back to school. It appeared their uncle had made a miraculous recovery. But who could say when he may become ill again?

As Jack collected his bags, Kit and I spoke. 'Leave Cheke alone,' I urged. 'It's important for you to finish your schooling.'

'And let him get away with all the things he has said and done to us?'

'No,' I replied, 'he won't get away with them. One day soon, I'll have my revenge. But you must promise me not to get into trouble. It would be bad for you and for your family. These are dangerous times.'

'I know,' said Kit, shaking his head wearily. 'I shall try, but I shan't promise. I won't make you a vow I might not be able keep. If he oversteps the mark, I reserve the right to strike him down, just as you did.'

With this, we shook hands, and I fought with my eyes not to well up. I didn't know when, if ever, I'd see my best friend again. We'd been inseparable for almost a decade.

There are tears in my eyes now, for today both my friends are in mortal danger. But I'm glad we have spent these past few months together. And that I've got to know Thomas Percy well and the others too, even if we've become separated again, perhaps for the last time.

Back in York, Jack hauled Kit onto the back of his horse and we waved our farewells. I watched the mighty animal pick its way through the passers-by as it walked along Stonegate, until eventually they reached and turned the corner near to the Minster and I could no longer see them.

Without my friends and family, York became like most places in the world, cold and lonely. In one day Mistress Clitherow would be dead, and I'd return to the haven of Scotton. There was nothing left for me here, only misery.

I couldn't bear the thought of being at home on my own in Stonegate. Every room seemed so empty without the background noise of Mother working, Anne chatting or Lizzie humming out a tune. So instead I wandered the streets, not thinking but still knowing where I had to go. Every gossip and conversation I passed on Parliament Street was focused on the fate of Mistress Clitherow. There were armed patrols everywhere, but of course they ignored me, for I no longer marched proudly in the centre of the street. I skulked in the shadows, in the periphery.

When I reached the Ouse Bridge, I encountered four imposing figures bearing halberds and wearing Corporation livery. The quartet was spread out evenly across the roadway. They stared fiercely through grilled helmets at anyone who might step onto the crossing but they didn't physically stop us. Any man brave enough to walk across that day simply had to squeeze past them, as I did, weaving my way past their padded shoulders.

Beyond the guards, around the prison, were more armed men, and further on on the far side of the bridge, another four. I kept on walking, the stones still in my pocket, not knowing what I'd do. When I reached the civic cross, the prison was on my left. The windows were narrow and uncovered, no more than arrow slits. With wooden shutters around them, there was no glass to be broken. Additional armed men stood by the door.

I hadn't seen Mistress Clitherow since the second day of the Assizes. I closed my eyes and imagined her in her small cell inside, with its damp stone walls, hardly any light and a shared bucket for a privy. In her hands she held a blunt needle. Her fingers were red from sewing. The Puritan's wife sat alongside her, rocking back and forth, gripping the good lady's newly constructed shawl. Both prayed in unison for their salvation.

'Hey, what are you doing here?'

I opened my eyes. I'd wandered too close to the prison. The words came from Henry Cheke. In my reverie I hadn't seen him emerge from the doorway, accompanied by the Lord Mayor and Sheriff Fawcett.

'I recognise your description from my son. Lanky and ginger and now with a bruised face. You must be Fawkes. Sheriff, this is the lad who was expelled from St Peter's for attacking my boy. I want him arrested.'

'On what charge?' asked the Sheriff. 'It looks like he's already been punished.' My face was still a mess from the attack behind the White Bear.

'I'll think of something,' said Cheke.

'No, you won't,' replied the Mayor sharply. 'That's not how things work around here. The Corporation works by the rule of law. I've had enough! We can't always keep dancing to the Council's tune. Now be off with you, lad, before I change my mind.'

I turned around and walked away as quickly as I could, heading back across the river towards the centre of the city. When I reached the four soldiers, I braced myself for the call, which must surely come at any moment to arrest me, but I was wrong. It never came.

I stepped off the bridge, passed by St Michael's Church, turned into Spurriergate and broke into a run. Even then most people continued to ignore me, nobody caring why I might be in such a hurry. I didn't stop until I reached our front door in Stonegate. Only then did I catch my breath and steal a glance behind me but other than a few groups of gossiping men and women there was nobody there. I turned the rusty iron key and fell inside.

Despite my fright, I didn't stay at home for long. The emptiness of the house haunted me, as if the absence of my family meant something awful had happened to them. I headed off to Peasholme Green. Where else could I go? The grass behind the Black Swan was as wet and muddy as always when I crossed it. I weaved my way past the tenements and through the poor streets until I reached the house where I'd met Father Mush. This time the door didn't open as I approached.

I knocked and waited. Nobody came. I tried again. Eventually the door nudged a little but the woman who answered acted as if she couldn't speak English. In any case, I could hardly tell her I was looking for a Catholic priest. After a minute or two of miscommunication and attempting to look past her skirts, she closed the door and I left.

I'd given up all hope of finding the Father when a second door opened across the way. A small child beckoned for me to come over to him. By the time I reached the spot where he'd been, the boy had disappeared but the door remained ajar. I stepped inside. I felt myself being pulled into the room by a strong long arm. The door closed.

'What do you want?' asked the Father from the shadows. 'I thought you no longer wished to be associated with me.'

Even in the dim light I could see he was exhausted, as if he hadn't slept for a week. Yes, I was angry with him but who else could I turn to? I felt lost.

'I'm not quite sure,' I said. 'I just don't want to be alone. My family has gone away and I can no longer see my friends at school. I feel like a fugitive.'

'It's not an easy life for sure,' said the priest, relenting a little. 'Sit down. I've got some news to share with you. It comes from York Castle.'

'Has the good lady been moved? I thought she was on the Ouse Bridge?'

'No, the Pearl's still there, alright,' said Father Mush. 'But I've received an update today about my colleague Father Ingleby.'

I remembered the shouting I'd heard that night after we left The Shambles.

'How is he?' I asked.

'Not good, but he's alive. One of the aldermen has broken ranks with the Corporation. He's disgusted with his colleagues for doing the bidding of the Council. He told a friend of mine Sheriff Fawcett has been holding Father Ingleby secretly at the Castle prison.'

'Why secretly?'

'So they could illegally torture him. They've been trying to make the Father confess he's stayed in The Shambles under the protection of Mistress Clitherow and has had earthly relations with her. They wish to humiliate the good lady and remove the kindness the city's people now feel towards her.'

'Oh.' I couldn't think of what else to say.

'The blackguard Henry Cheke was also involved. But they've failed. Father Ingleby has remained silent, apart from his screams. Once they've done with Mistress Clitherow, I expect they'll try him and send him to the Knavesmire.'

'This is terrible,' I said. 'I am sorry.' I realised the two priests must be friends. If somebody had done this to Kit or Rob, I couldn't imagine how I'd feel, or what I'd try to do to stop it.

'What's done is done,' said the Father. 'We can't change that now, nor what will happen on the morrow. But there's one last thing we can do for the Pearl. I was planning to carry out this job myself but, just as you told me, it's dangerous for me to be seen walking the streets. Perhaps this specific task would be better served by another.'

I looked at him. 'What is it?' I said.

'When the last drop of life has been crushed out of Mistress Clitherow, her soul will ascend to heaven but her body will remain here on earth. We must find her remains and ensure they're given a decent Catholic burial. It's what the good lady and the Good Lord would want.'

'How can I help with this?'

'Three days of suffering was mentioned in court but that was the old way. These days so much weight is placed upon the prisoner it's rare for any poor soul to remain alive for more than a quarter of an hour. It's not merciful but it's something at least.'

It was still horrific. The blood ran from my face. And what if there really was a baby inside her?

The priest spoke again. 'Afterwards, they'll attempt to squirrel her body away and place it somewhere in an unmarked grave. We can't let this happen. I need you to be my eyes and ears on the streets of York one last time. When they take the Pearl's body from the Ouse Bridge, I want you to follow them, and find out where they take her. Then later, when the time is right, we'll re-inter her into a secret holy place. Will you do this?'

'Aye,' I said. 'But what about Pastor Wigginton?'

'He can no longer be part of our plans. The rationale for my temporary truce with the man has come to an end. The parson won't betray us, but from now on we can no longer trust or confide in him. After all, he's a Protestant heretic, just like the rest of them.'

The Father shared with me what he knew about the plans for the morrow. With Thomas Percy, Jack, Kit and the others gone, and Father Mush unable to move freely, the best hope of saving the good lady's body rested on my shoulders. It wasn't the rescue plan I'd envisaged for Mistress Clitherow, but it was all we had left.

# 25

**Friday March 25th, 1586**

I woke early the next morning in Stonegate feeling as bold as brass. I'd borrowed a sword from Jack Wright and was ready to take on the Council, the Corporation and anyone else who dared to threaten the Pearl of York. Today was the day I'd become a man.

I grit my teeth. The pain begins to tear me apart. My self-deceit makes me feel better but it can do me no good. God sees everything. These reconstructed recollections are more than half-truths. They're lies. There was no sword and I've never been so frightened or full of despair. Even here in my torture chamber, with no hope, I'm not afraid to die. When death comes, I'll embrace it. As one of God's soldiers, I'll enter paradise and be with Maria again.

The truth is that morning I felt terrified, for myself and for Mistress Clitherow. The sound of my heart beating deafened everything, and my mind filled with dread. Despite the comfort of Uncle Thomas's bed, I didn't sleep at all but lay awake listening for the sounds of boots made by men in the street come to arrest me. By the time the bells rang for five, I pushed away the bed covers and began to dress. My hands were shaking.

I didn't think I'd be able to break my fast but I'd promised Father Mush I'd eat a bowl of porridge, sweetened with honey. It would give me sustenance during the morning, he said, and keep my hunger at bay during the long day ahead. Each spoonful required an effort to swallow but somehow I managed to force and keep it down.

When I left the house, it was dark, and the streets were empty. A thick mist had risen up again from the city's rivers, making it almost impossible to see anything more than a few feet ahead. Although I could find my way well enough, I knew every inch of the road, my heart was on edge. Every time I heard a rat in the gutter or a cat on a roof, I thought it was the Sheriff's men come to take me or the vagabonds returning to finish their attack.

By the time I approached Ouse Bridge, my legs were trembling like syllabub jelly. At any moment I thought they'd collapse in a heap beneath me. I was now in the Devil's lair and had to be doubly careful. But with only one bridge over the River Ouse in York, unless I could find a friendly boatman, this was the only way I could get to the place Father Mush had told me about.

Squinting my eyes, I tried to tell if the bridge remained open and what might be in front of me, but I couldn't make out anything. I placed one hand onto the damp stone wall above the river and wondered what I was doing there. I should be in Scotton with Mother, Anne, Lizzie, Maria and Jack. But I wasn't. I edged forward and saw an orange glow, surrounded by swirling murkiness. Soon there were clearer cut lines of metal surrounding the illumination. A long staff reached up from one side of the bridge. In the dim light, I realised the glow came from a lamp.

Staring almost blindly upwards, I walked directly into the body of a guard. Colliding with the man's shoulder, I bounced back off him. The fellow swung around, as surprised as I was. With an involuntary action he released his halberd. The axe-head dropped sharply downwards, slicing through the fog towards my face. I prayed to God.

The heavens heard me. The blade failed to strike. At the last moment the man grabbed at his weapon and caused it to fall harmlessly to the ground. It landed a few inches from my foot. As the sharp iron struck the cobbles it created a short-lived spark of light.

'You stupid dolt!' the man shouted. 'I could have killed you. What are you doing? Where are you going?'

'To work,' I lied. 'I'm an apprentice at the bonded warehouse on Skeldergate.'

'Then be off with you, boy,' he said, 'And for God's sake whistle a hymn or something, so the other sentries know you're approaching and don't try to slice you in two, as I nearly did. You were almost done for then, and what's worse, I would have lost a day's pay for the trouble you would have caused.'

At least that's what I think he said. I had a problem concentrating. An instant ago, I thought I'd die.

'Go on, then,' he said. 'Carry on.' As he picked up his halberd, he called out more loudly. 'Man coming through. There's a lad crossing the bridge. Seems harmless enough. Let him pass.'

Heeding the fellow's advice, I began to hum a tune but all I could thing of on the spur of the moment was *'Hark, hark!'*. I think it had been playing along in the back of my mind ever since the immigrants had attacked me in the ginnel.

*'Hark, hark! the dogs do bark,'* I sang softly but loudly enough for a man in front of me to hear. *'Beggars are coming to town. Some in rags, some in jags, And some in velvet gowns.'*

I repeated the line several times until l reached a second set of guards. These were stationed around the prison building. I couldn't see the men clearly but their faces appeared as fatigued as I felt. They spied me cautiously but with little interest, and I passed them by.

The hairs on the back of my neck stood up as I walked past the prison. There were more lamps here and it was brighter than at the edge of the bridge. I stopped chanting the rhyme for a few moments, and imagined Mistress Clitherow inside, now on her knees paying homage to God. Beneath my breath, I prayed to Him to save her. Knowing it unlikely my first request would be satisfied, I added a second, asking the Good Lord to approve Mistress Clitherow's wish, so she could wear her shawl to mask her nakedness when the time came.

And then I was past the jail and approaching another set of guards standing outside the toll booth building. I began chanting the words of *'Hark, hark!'* once more. One of the soldiers glanced sympathetically at me, as if I was a simpleton. Beyond him, I strode past the toll booth and reached the far end of the bridge. Here, a fourth and final set of sentries protected the southern perimeter. Descending the incline, I sloped off the bridge, and emerged back into the darkness.

I couldn't see anything but closed my eyes anyway. I took a deep breath and breathed out slowly until my chest was empty. I shook my head and tried to clear my thoughts. It didn't work, but I had sense enough to thank the Lord Jesus Christ and Parson Wigginton for preventing Thomas Percy and the others from raiding the prison. I don't know which side would have prevailed but it would have been a bloodbath. Brave men would have died, and I suspected we may not have got the good lady away. I imagined myself standing alongside Poxy Joe and the horses, listening to the fighting and gunfire from our position near the Lounlith postern.

The visibility was no better when I opened my eyes. If anything, the fog seemed thicker. I didn't know the streets as well on this side of the river, so I held out my hand, creeping over to the left until my fingernails scraped at the walls of a house. Holding my fingers against an uneven line of stone, wood and plaster panel, I continued on until the turning to Skeldgergate. From here the wharves and warehouses jutted out over the river.

Father Mush had taken a risk by stationing me inside one of these buildings. If the good lady's body was carried over to the far side of the Ouse, or ferried downriver, we'd lose sight of her forever. But to his credit, he was confident her remains wouldn't be transported through the crowds in the city. The waterway remained an option but what else could we do? We didn't have a boat. And even if we had one, if we followed on the river we were bound to be spotted and arrested.

When I reached the second warehouse, I ran my hands along the walls in search of barred windows. Ignoring the first two openings and a door, I carried on until the third. Five strong iron palings were imbedded into each frame to prevent men from gaining entry and stealing the valuable goods inside.

It would have been almost impossible for anyone but an infant to squeeze through the bars, but I'd been told the middle piece of iron was removable. I felt the stones behind it with my fingers. They were jammed together, firmly holding the paling into place. I moved one piece of stone to the left and slid another to the right. After a few seconds a gap was created. I felt again and the iron bar was loose but it wouldn't come out easily. It took me several minutes of pushing, prodding and pulling before I heard a definitive click. With a final scrape, I managed to free the bar, but immediately I lost my grip on it. The metal bar slipped through my fingers and dropped to the ground with a loud metallic clang on the far side of the wall.

For an instant, I stood stock still. The Father had told me the Merchant Adventurers employed night watchmen, and I'd need to be careful, to get in quickly and quietly. I listened. I was scared they'd have dogs but nothing stirred. When I was fully certain no-one had heard me, I climbed onto the sill and squeezed myself through the gap, pushing by legs and body into the double-sized space between the bars. It was difficult work and I took a patch of skin off my wrist but after a few awkward moments I pushed myself through.

I clambered down on the other side, spread out my hands and began to feel along the floor. Dropping to all fours, I felt something cold touch my knee. I lifted the metal bar, slid it back into position and replaced the stones to where they'd been. Even though I tugged hard on it, the bar remained firmly in place. It wouldn't shift. I was inside.

I ventured through the darkened room, guiding myself past the rows of boxes and crates. The smell was strong but if I'm honest I had no idea what was stored in there. In the far corner I found a ladder and climbed up, as Father Mush had instructed. Twelve rungs later I emerged onto a second storey, equally full of wooden containers.

I made my way along a wall to a pair of double doors. This was where the imported goods would be hoisted up from the river, so I knew I must be waterside. Someone had fashioned a spy hole in the left-hand shutter and I carefully peeped through it. The early morning was still dark outside but there was an orange glow, which must have come from the bridge. I sat and waited.

When dawn came, the sky was still grey. Eventually the mist lifted a little. I watched on as the guards were relieved by twice as many men. The new shift appeared more alert than their predecessors but even from a distance I felt their faces had taken on a haunted look.

Within an hour the bridge was so crowded it was difficult to cross it. Extra soldiers arrived, this time wearing the colours of the Council of the North. Orders were issued. The troops formed a double cordon on either side of the crossing and began removing the ordinary citizens from the bridge. Most were pressed back onto Ousegate, where hundreds of others jostled behind them. Half the good people of York seemed to out there. An even bigger throng filled the streets beyond.

As the church clocks struck eight, the day was lightening. Sheriff Fawcett and a few other dignitaries arrived, making their way onto the bridge with the help of a dozen halberdiers who threatened the crowds around them. It pleased me to see how roughly the men were treated, pushed and barracked as they went. For once, their responses were muted. They had to be careful. Serious trouble could break out at any moment.

When they reached the prison, Fawcett and a few of his men were permitted entry. The remainder were ordered to join the cordon. If something happened and there was a panic, if the crowd surged forward, there could be mayhem and slaughter. I had no doubt dozens of men and women, both Protestant and Catholic, could be injured or killed, either by the crush or by the weapons pointing toward their faces.

After a few minutes the prison door opened. The Sheriff reappeared, followed by a group of soldiers. The men marched in formation, creating a square. In the centre walked Mistress Clitherow. It was the first time I'd seen her since the trial. She appeared to be frailer. Her goodness shone out over all those around her. She looked like a butterfly which had landed on a pile of shit. Whilst the men's apparel was mostly brown and grey, the good lady wore the simplest white shawl and matching coif scarf on her head. She must have been sorely cold, but at the same time perhaps her mind and body were numbed by other things.

Father Mush had thought the execution would take place inside the prison but he couldn't be sure. The priest was worried the Sheriff might move Mistress Clitherow to a different location, perhaps York Castle or the Knavesmire. Now I wondered which way they would go.

Leaving the bridge, at least on the York side towards the castle, would be almost impossible. Fawcett turned the party back towards the wharves of Skeldergate. The crowd was smaller on this side, and the double line of halberdiers easily pushed them back. I readied myself to make haste. It looked like they were about to venture off towards the Knavesmire. But the group halted at the toll booth building on the southern side of the crossing. From my viewpoint the party was now relatively close to me.

There were shouts and screams from the crowd and cries of torment but suddenly a hush came over them, as if orchestrated from the heavens. The wind must have blown my way because I heard the good lady speak. 'Good Master Sheriff, let me give alms to the poor before we go any further. My time is short.'

Fawcett seemed uncertain but after a moment he allowed Mistress Clitherow to walk back across the bridge towards the silent crowd massed on the city centre side of the crossing. My mother's friend's hands were bound but when she reached the line of soldiers, she somehow managed to use her fingers to open a bag of coins. The contents dropped out, one by one, onto the floor. As she retired, the troops followed her lead and took a few paces back, exposing the money. Nobody in the crowd moved.

'Shame on the Sheriff and the Corporation!' shouted one man.

The atmosphere began to turn nasty. There were jeers and hollering. I looked at the good lady. Was that a tear in her eye? Behind her, there was a sudden uproar. I glanced back. At the same moment the throng surged forward. Halberds were lowered and metal struck into flesh. The results were quick, bloody and decisive.

A woman screamed and several men appeared to be injured. The people at the front pushed their bodies back in an attempt to retreat, whilst others, immigrants and locals alike, crawled at their feet. What was happening? What were they doing? When the crowd pulled back, I could see. Mistress Clitherow's coins were all gone. They were desperate times.

The crowd jostled and stared with hostility at the soldiers.

Recognising family friends and neighbours amongst them, I prayed to God nothing worse would happen. After a few tense moments both sides pulled back a yard or two, until there was clear space and daylight between the two ranks. A small number of bleeding men and women were lifted up and passed back over the heads of others along Low Ousegate towards the rear of the crowd.

An ominous silence washed over the hordes of angry citizens on both sides of the bridge. A startled gull flew past me above the warehouse, squawked and emptied its waste into the river. For the first time that morning I heard the whistle of the wind above the sound of the water, but it was soon drowned out by the military noise of marching boots, as the Sheriff and his men escorted Mistress Clitherow back past the prison. Her bare feet made no sound at all.

When they reached the toll booth building, I realised Fawcett and his prisoner would now be invisible to anyone on the Low Ousegate side of the bridge. Perhaps that's why they chose this place to do their dirty work. He ordered one of his men to open the toll booth door. The good woman, a junior sheriff and four guards accompanied him as he walked inside. A Protestant parson joined them and the door was closed. There were no windows in the booth on my side of the bridge. From then on I watched on blindly, like everyone else, as events unfolded within.

The crowd waited expectantly, without being able to see, hear or really understand what was going on. After a few short minutes the toll booth's door was flung open. It was too soon. Surely the crushing couldn't have happened yet? Two of the guards quick-stepped outside, conversed with two others and the four of them all made their way quickly through the cordon towards my side of the bridge.

The shock hit me. The men were headed towards the docks of Skeldergate where I was hidden. Soon their passage was masked by the houses and workshops but I knew the soldiers were coming my way. There was little I could do. Should I run or wait? But if they were coming for me, it was already too late to escape, unless I jumped into the river. I braced myself, and hoped I'd put up a decent fight. I listened for their entry into the warehouse and watched the ladder intently. They'd have to come that way to get me.

But nobody came. Two minutes later I saw the uniforms again. The four guards shoved their way back through the crush onto the Micklegate side of the bridge. As they approached it, the line of halberdiers opened up and let them through. The men's hands were full. Both original guards dragged two men behind them and the others hauled another a man and woman each.

I looked at the captives more closely and, to my surprise, saw they were beggars. Some used the docks as a hiding place from Corporation patrols during the day and the night. But what would the soldiers want with them?

The guards pushed all eight beggars through the door into the toll booth. More than a thousand people must have been stood on the sides of the bridge. They waited as whispers circulated. Like me, many made a silent prayer and hoped a miracle might happen.

It wasn't to be.

I recalled Judge's Clench's words in the courtroom. '*You will be returned from whence you came. Once there, in the lowest part of the prison or another suitable building, you will be stripped naked and laid upon the ground. Your hands and feet will be tied to posts and a sharp stone placed beneath your back. As much weight will be laid upon your body as it can bear. You will be pressed to death, slowly, until additional weights will be placed upon you and your life will be brought to an end.*'

I couldn't see anything, but in my mind I witnessed Mistress Clitherow's execution. I saw them place the sharp stone on the ground. I watched her lie down. I witnessed her hands and feet being tied to posts. I saw them place a large flat piece of wood over her body. I thought of her baby as finally I watched them pile heavy crushing weights upon her.

I've never forgotten that first terrible scream. The guards raised their halberds ready for action. The sound of the good lady's agony was almost unbearable but the crowd didn't shift an inch. One of the soldiers was sick, as was I. I threw my guts over the shutters in front of me, spreading vomit all over the place.

There was a longer shriek. It was almost inhuman. Mistress Clitherow must have been experiencing unbearable pain. Her back and ribs must have been breaking. I'd witnessed executions at the Knavesmire and seen death in battle later but never had I heard death screams of a woman like this.

I found it too much to bear. I covered my eyes and tried to push the picture of the good lady's suffering from my head but it wouldn't go away. My mind filled with the most awful visions of Mistress Clitherow's body breaking and bleeding. And then I saw the baby, screaming in pain. Soon I was sick again and again, until at last there wasn't a single oat left in my stomach. All that remained was the taste of bile.

My head throbbed and the screaming continued. I peeped through the shutters. Tens, maybe hundreds of people were crying, including some of the soldiers. I wondered how the others could even hold their halberds, and not rush into the toll booth to put a stop to this madness.

When the screaming ceased, I wiped my brow and chin with my sleeve. How could anyone inflict such terrible torment on another person? I prayed to God He'd find a special place in heaven for Mistress Clitherow, and the Devil would reserve the worst place in hell for all those who'd done this to her. I began to think of the day ahead. At least it was finished.

But it wasn't. The third curdling wail was shorter and sharper and the most terrible yet, a completely un-joyous cry of unspeakable pain. One of the Corporation soldiers dropped his halberd at this. He broke ranks, rushed to the parapet and tried to climb over the wall, as if to jump into the river. But two men in Council livery followed and pulled him down. I think he must have been arrested but I didn't see him after that.

The fourth cry was the longest and the last, Mistress Clitherow's final death throe. I prayed to God for it to be over but the screaming continued. No matter how much I tried to cover my ears, I could hear it. On quiet windless nights, I hear it still.

After a time, God knows how long, the tone of the noise changed. The cry became throatier and more muted, until eventually it stopped altogether, although for a time I could still hear the strange wailing, if only in my mind.

Minutes passed.

The crowd stood stock still, shocked and in total silence.

The door of the toll booth opened, and finally I knew the Pearl of York must be dead.

The junior Sheriff stepped outside into the cold air, his head in his hands. He stumbled, fell to the ground and began crying like a baby. The beggars came next, every one of them weeping. At the time I thought their tears must be for Mistress Clitherow but later I thought some of the teardrops shed must be for themselves, when they realised they'd been cursed until the end of their days and beyond.

The truth rarely remains hidden for long. Stories began to spread through the city of the intrigue and horror which had taken place within the toll booth. In a premeditated action, every guard had steadfastly refused Sheriff Fawcett's order to place the heavy weights upon Mistress Clitherow's prone body. It was one last desperate chance to save the good lady's life.

Lord though, please don't forgive any of these men for the possibility was forsaken. When threatened with imprisonment or torture, the soldiers shamelessly searched for homeless vagabonds and forced them to do the devil's work instead.

And so the morning passed. The vile crushing of Mistress Clitherow was carried out by eight vagrants in fear for their lives. I closed my eyes, and when I reopened them, I'm not ashamed to say, tears ran down my cheeks. Later on, when I was totally certain it was all over, I said a long prayer for the good lady in Latin.

I swore I would never again have a charitable word to say about the Protestant Church, nor anyone who supported it. It and they were my mortal enemy, forever. Most of all, I felt a burning hatred rise up inside me against all those who'd corrupted this once holy Catholic country. The archbishops, the mayors, the sheriffs and judges, the Members of Parliament, the heretical Queen Elizabeth of England and all her bastard cousins.

# 26

For a little while time stood still. Citizens and officials stumbled around in a state of disbelief. Surely this was a dream they could wake themselves up from? With the increasing realisation it wasn't, they wondered at what they'd done. My own mind went blank. The King of Spain could have ridden a horse naked across the bridge and I wouldn't have seen him.

The sense of smell is a powerful thing. The slightest whiff of bile takes me back to that day. When the stench of my sick became too much to bear, I crawled across to the other shutter. As I did so, the world began to move again. An anonymous official handed each beggar a few coins and they were permitted to leave the bridge. One of them, a woman, tossed her ill-gotten gains angrily over the side. The pennies hung in the air for a moment, above the side of the bridge, before descending down into the dark flood waters below.

I lost sight of the group as they made their way through the sullen crowds towards Skeldergate, presumably thankful the good people around them had no idea of the evil deed they'd been forced to do. I don't know what happened to them after that. Most beggars don't live long anyway, especially during the colder months.

It was a good hour later when Sheriff Fawcett, his underlings and the priest emerged from the toll booth. At least one of the men seemed visibly upset but I had no sympathy. I'd have happily ripped out his heart in the same manner they slaughtered the innocent priests on the Knavesmire. If I felt fear and despair before, like the contents of my stomach, this was gone. Rage welled up inside me.

Eventually the crowd began to disperse, although some were obviously reluctant to leave the place. Many women in particular milled around for hours without speaking a word. The most sullen of atmospheres spread across the city.

But nothing lasts forever. Two corporation officials arrived and requested the road be reopened. After a suitable timeframe the cordons of soldiers retreated. People, animals and vehicles were allowed back onto the bridge, whilst heavily armed guards remained in their stations in front of the prison and toll booth.

If the Council of the North had positioned watchers where I was, they would have identified a multitude of ardent followers of the old faith during the day. Prayers and signs were discretely made by many a passer-by towards the toll booth where the good lady's body lay broken. Others gripped rosary beads in their hands as a secret mark of respect for her but none of this changed anything. Mistress Clitherow was dead. No longer a mother but a martyr, to be celebrated for her cause. I thought of Father Mush and scowled.

My biggest surprise came late in the day, during the twilight of dusk, by which time the bridge was much quieter. No crossing tolls had been levied in the afternoon and there'd been some passing traffic, though markedly less than on a usual Friday and by now mostly everyone had returned home, many to eat fish.

I first noticed the boy because of his gait. He walked slowly and awkwardly towards the prison from the Ousegate side of the bridge. When he approached the civic cross, I could see there was something incongruous about him. The lad looked nervous and unaccustomed to wearing such a fine suit of clothes.

Upon reaching the toll booth, the boy sank to his knees and prayed. He was close enough now for me to recognise his face. It was the foreign lad Johann. Tears streamed down his cheeks. I could hear his sobbing, and whining voice apologise and beg for the good lady's forgiveness. I'm sure he received it. Mistress Clitherow would have considered the lad as much a victim as she was.

After a few seconds of this, one of the Corporation guards took an interest in Johann and began shouting at him. Another grabbed the boy by the shoulder and hauled him to his feet. Hearing his foreign accent, the man told him to 'Sod off!' back to where he came from. Johann staggered across the bridge, assisted by a heavy boot in the back from one of the men. I never saw him again.

The Flemish butcher's boy's repentance did him no good. A week later Johann's body was found floating in the Foss. His throat had been cut, whether by a Catholic in a futile act of vengeance or by a Protestant to prevent him from speaking about his treatment, it mattered little. The boy was dead, another victim in this religious war against us.

Eventually darkness came. Lamps were lit on either side of the bridge. Another was raised over the prison and a fourth by the toll booth. Afterwards, apart from the hourly bells, the evening turned to silence. I think it was just after ten when the guards were replaced. The night shift paced up and down for a while but after a few moments of chatting, the men no longer spoke to each other. Each found a resting place to lean on in as comfortable a position as possible, until the scene became quiet and still. It appeared Sheriff Fawcett had postponed moving the body until the next day but even with a mighty thirst, I continued to watch for any sign of movement.

I heard footsteps quickly approaching our house in Stonegate through the darkness. Realising Henry Cheke's men were there to arrest me, my body jolted. I sat upright. After a few moments of panic, I realised where I was. I'd fallen asleep.

I looked out through the crack in the shutter towards the bridge. I could hear one, maybe two men crossing the roadway beneath but I couldn't see anything. The lamps had been extinguished. There was no moon or stars. I knew the bridge was there but I was blind to what was happening upon it.

What was that noise? I listened. The pattern became steadier. A wagon and horses were approaching from across the cobbles. Instinctively I knew it was time to move. I crawled to the corner and felt for the ladder. I pushed my legs into the opening and gripped the rungs with my feet. I climbed down past the goods imported from the Baltic. Feeling my way, I edged around the ground floor wall, until I finally found the window I'd come in by. I removed the loose bar and squeezed myself through it.

Once outside I didn't bother to replace the paling but ran along Skeldergate. I could hear the cart again. It was coming back from the bridge. Someone was driving it up towards the road into Micklegate. If they whipped the horses, I wouldn't be able to keep up with the pace but at least they were on my side of the crossing.

I took a risk and dashed up Fetter Lane. There was no light here at all. I couldn't see anything under my feet. Whatever was there, I went straight through it as if it wasn't. I heard the scurrying of vermin but ignored it. Running as swiftly as I could, I hared up the incline, thinking of my mission.

The route was further than the alternative but it seemed less likely I'd be seen this way. My best hope of regaining ground on the wagon would be if there was a hold-up at Micklegate Bar, waiting for the gates to be re-opened. Like the other routes through the walls, these would be locked and guarded at night. I hoped the Council and Corporation hadn't arranged to keep the bar open.

By the time I rounded the corner and entered Micklegate the carriage had passed. There was an absence of sound and movement in the darkness. Not being in the best condition, I placed my hands onto my knees and attempted to summon breath. The side of my stomach hurt. I tried to listen above my panting, and for the briefest of moments I thought I could hear horses's hooves and wheels further up the hill. And then the sound was gone.

My mouth was dry and my body ached from lack of food and exertion, but I galloped up the paving towards the brow of the hill. This was my last chance to catch them. When I reached the part of the road where it flattened out, the cart was still there. Discussions were taking place beneath two bright lamps as to whether the wagon should be permitted to transit.

The men driving the cart weren't wearing Council or Corporation livery but civilian clothing like my own. One of the sergeants of the watch laughed at them. The gates began to open. The two men accompanying the cart climbed back onto their seats at the front of the vehicle. I dived onto the rear and managed to grab hold of a rail just in time to stop myself from being launched back off it.

The guards on the gate looked at me quizzically. I made a thumbs up. One raised his fingers back at me. The others were counting out money. I suspected they didn't care who or what was on the cart, nor who was controlling it. Neither did they know if it was accompanied by two or three men.

Of course, the fellows driving the carriage knew full well there was only the pair of them. As soon as we passed through the gate, I ducked my body down low to avoid being seen if they looked back. I knew I would be silhouetted by the lamplight from the bar.

The wagon's trailer was covered with a layer of hard yellow straw. It scratched at my face and hands as I pushed myself beneath it. I edged towards the centre of the carriage and caressed something cold. I retracted my hand and gasped in horror, knowing I'd just touched part of Mistress Clitherow's murdered body. The good lady must have been lying in state beside me. I prayed to God she was still wearing her shawl.

I wanted to jump off and run away, but I couldn't. I had to remain. I found a position next to the side-rails of the wagon and moved myself further away from the body. I stayed there as long as I could but often when we hit a bump in the road, Mistress Clitherow's cadaver would roll over and one of her feet would touch me, until I gently pressed her lifeless corpse back onto the central planks of the wagon.

The cart turned a corner, and after a while we began to climb a hill. We both slipped backwards towards the rear bars of the trailer, until the wooden rails prevented our bodies, one alive and one dead, from falling onto the road. Looking through the straw I picked out the glow of a candle here and there but I couldn't make out which way we'd gone. Even if I'd known, I had no way of getting a message to Father Mush to inform him of the route.

Eventually I plucked up enough courage to place my head into the air and took a good look around. The driver was staring forwards intently with his reins in his hands. His mate sat next to him holding a lamp, which he angled forward. Not much light fell to the ground but just enough it seemed for the driver to keep his horses on the right track.

The journey proceeded slowly. I lay down and wondered what to do next. I wasn't afraid to fight the men. In some ways I wanted to. But I worried about what would happen if I wasn't successful. Yes, I could be injured or arrested but more importantly if they escaped, we'd lose all track of the good lady's body. I decided to wait and see what would happen.

Despite the irregular bumps in the road, the lull of the cartwheels became quite hypnotic. I felt fatigued and fell asleep for a second time. My mind and body were exhausted.

I have no idea how long I slumbered. The wagon must have turned a sharp corner, for my head struck the side rail. It wasn't a hard blow but the shock brought me back to my senses.

Almost everything was in darkness. The dim light emitted by the coachman's lamp picked out hedgerows and field edges but no houses. We must have left York and journeyed into the countryside.

To keep my mind alert, I concentrated my thoughts on Maria and our future life together. Time passed, perhaps an hour, perhaps less. The men at the front of the wagon whispered something for the first time in a while. The carriage slowed and stopped. I felt a weight shifting, as one of the men left the vehicle. Had we reached our destination? Was this the burial point?

Everything was quiet. It was early, too early even for the dawn chorus. A spray of liquid hit the ground next to the wheel.

'Too much sharding ale earlier on,' said a voice from the front of the wagon.

'The ale's fine,' replied the fellow who'd alighted. 'God's to blame for making my bladder too small to hold the stuff. And now the seal's broken, I'll need to go every hour. Just you wait and see.'

'I'd rather not. And I'd be careful if I was you. You don't want the Archbishop's man at the farm hearing that sort of talk. They'll have you arrested for blasphemy.'

'I'd like to see 'em try. I'm done now anyway. How long do you think it will take us to get to Tockwith?'

The planks in front of me strained to the side for a moment.

'In the daytime, half an hour. But at this speed God only knows. Gee up!'

The trailer jerked itself forward. If Tockwith was our destination, it seemed there wasn't far to go. And from what I could make out, there'd be at least one man waiting for the carriage there. I decided to jump off the wagon at the next opportunity and follow on foot for the rest of the journey. At the rate we were travelling I didn't think they could lose me, and I preferred the shroud of darkness to a moment longer lying alongside the mistress's corpse.

We began to make a slow ascent. If this was the track I'd followed previously, we were probably moving along the edge of Marston Moor. I shifted my body warily and wearily towards the back of the trailer, being careful to stick closely to the side of the wagon. Moving slowly, I sat up and looked forwards towards the two men at the front. Both continued to stare intently at the dim light on the road ahead.

I dropped myself quietly down onto the ground, worried they'd feel my movement, as I had theirs. Luckily my leap coincided with the thousandth jolt of the trip. If they noticed my departure, they gave no sign of it. I remained crouched on all fours on the road for half a minute until my immediate surroundings became enveloped in darkness. At that stage I stood tall, brushed some of the straw from my clothing and began walking towards the faint glow of the lamp ahead of me.

## Saturday March 26th, 1586

When we reached Tockwith, the wagon halted alongside the coaching inn. The driver applied his brake and clambered down to the ground. He loosened the harness which had been holding the horses and patted their flanks. The other man placed his lamp onto the vehicle's seat and alighted. He stretched his back straight and muttered a few words under his breath to his companion. A moment later the wooden panelled door of the inn was pushed open, and I recognised the fellow who emerged as the same man who'd helped Jack Pulleyn's driver feed his horses only a week before.

The coachman held aloft his own lamp. I could see from my vantage point he was dressed in his day clothes, as if late night visitors were a common occurrence, or expected that night. There was a quick exchange of words, and the fellow ushered the driver and his mate across the threshold into his establishment. A shaking glow of light emerged from inside the door as a candle or maybe an extra lamp was being lit.

I edged myself forward until I was a little closer to the walls of the inn. Continuing to conceal my body in the shadows, I peered through a pair of leaded windows. A plump woman was showing the driver and his mate to their table at the centre of a deserted dining room. Moments later, she handed the men flagons of ale, before ladling steaming hot broth into bowls already laid out in front of them.

Keeping one eye on the coachman, I crept slowly back from the carriage to the far side of the inn. The fellow went about his work busily. Once he'd completed unharnessing and feeding the horses, he leant back against a stone wall next to the vehicle and yawned. I'd expected him to at least take a peep at the gruesome cargo on the trailer but he didn't. Either the fellow didn't know what was on there, or he knew full well what it was. Perhaps he didn't care.

I shifted slowly away from him until the lamp on the wagon was out of my sight. When I reached a small row of cottages, I began to look for something to eat but more than anything I wanted to quench my thirst. In the darkness I discovered an animal's drinking trough but even in my troubled state, it smelt too badly for me to imbibe from it.

Fearing I wouldn't find anything, I remembered my first visit to the village. I was sure there'd been a cow barn. I made my way across the lane towards where I thought it might be. As I did so, my nose twitched in the darkness. Despite the gloom, it was hard not to notice the strong smell of cow dung. I knew I'd found the right place. Tracing my way around the side of the byre, I stepped into something on the ground and almost stumbled. Thankfully I didn't make a noise.

Bending down, I felt around the rim of a hollow vessel. It must have been about the height of my knee. I rocked it back and forth with my hands but there was no sound. It was empty. After that I reached around the ground with my fingers, until after a few moments I came across a second container. When I shook this one, there was the tell-tale noise of sloshing liquid. Not much, perhaps only a pint or so, but when I sniffed at the contents my heart lifted. It was definitely milk. I assumed these containers were regarded as empty churns returned for washing and refilling in the morning.

With no little effort, I lifted the heavy churn and poured the liquid into my mouth. It wasn't off and the milk tasted good. Once I'd downed all I could manage, I licked the froth from my lips and set the urn back onto the floor. Milk ran down my chin. I mopped it dry with my sleeve and wished I hadn't. The sniff of yesterday's bile took me back to the awful events. My heart filled with grief.

My misery and the night silence were abruptly broken by the sound of a chain being dragged across the yard. When the chain jerked and it could move no more, a dog began to growl. Although I couldn't see anything, I felt the animal staring at me, straining on its leash. Fearing it would loosen itself or begin barking, I slipped away.

The noise ceased but I was certain the hound was stalking me. I stopped and waited to be attacked. I can remember the fear clearly. I've always been frightened of dogs. Father once told me I was attacked by a mastiff near our house in Petergate when I was an infant. I can't remember it.

Hearing no more sounds from the hound, I stealthily returned to the area next to the coaching inn. Relief ran through my veins. There were no dogs here and the coachman hadn't moved. I took a spot in the shadows on the far side of the road from the wagon and waited.

Some time later the two men emerged. Money exchanged hands but I couldn't see how much. The coachman nodded his thanks and reset the horses. The tired looking driver and his mate climbed on board and the wagon set off. The coachman shook his head and wandered over to the inn. The large woman who I supposed was his wife waited at the door, candle in one hand, her purse in the other. He dropped the coins into it and they went inside. The lights were extinguished, and I assume the couple went to bed.

I proceeded after the carriage. The small glow of movement in the distance told me they were headed on the road towards Cattal. Surely, we weren't going to Scotton, I thought.

I was right. Within a mile or two the driver had slowed the carriage down and the two men began conversing, although their words didn't carry as far as me. The horses' speed had reduced to almost nothing at all. From my place some way back along the road, I could see the driver and the other man turn their lamp towards the right-hand side of the road. They were obviously looking for something.

Apart from the glow of the lamplight everything else remained enveloped in darkness but there was no longer silence. The first birds were waking. One by one they began to sing their morning songs.

The men continued to scan the gloom on that side of the road and my gaze followed. After a few moments I fancied I saw a light. Before long the fellows on the wagon saw it too. I looked again. There was definitely a candle on a shelf or in a window across the fields to the right.

'Here's the track, I can see it,' hailed an excited voice from the wagon.

The horses pulled off the road. I counted twenty paces and crouched myself down. For the next few yards I caressed the ground with my hands until I made out a pair of ruts, concluding this must be where the farm lane joined the road. There was a narrow track here, with hedging on one side and a drainage ditch on the other.

A blackbird chirped loudly from a bush, almost directly into my ear. I took a few steps along the muddy ruts and stopped myself. The cart had slowed ahead of me and now came to halt, alongside the candlelight. There were movements between the candle and lamp, and the sound of at least three men's voices. I knew they were talking but couldn't glean what was being said.

There was no sign of the sun on the horizon and no stars or moon in the sky, but the day was becoming lighter. Believing my task would be best served by remaining hidden, I began to look for a more private vantage point. Once the sun was up, the track would be exposed. I pushed my way around the hedging until I reached a denser thicket of trees. Despite the lack of summer canopy these were packed closely together, and I guessed if I lay low enough on the ground it would be a good spot to hide.

The men must have entered the cottage because for some time nothing stirred. The next thing I heard was a door opening. I saw a light from inside illuminate four men as they passed through a doorway. They no longer needed the lamp. One of the fellows went behind the cottage and I fancied I saw something flash between his legs. To my horror I realised it was a dog.

The creature galloped straight towards me. I tried to bury myself further under the leaves but within seconds the hound entered the woods. I heard rustling and sniffing, and within moments it was upon me.

I closed my eyes in terror. But when I opened them, the animal licked my face. The dog was a collie. I could hear its tail wagging. They were diligent farm workers and good guard dogs but this one was spoilt. It sniffed at my coat. I reached into the lining and found an old piece of dried meat. The dog chewed it eagerly but it must have gone bad, for the collie coughed it out. Sensing I had no more food, the beast lost all interest in me and raced back to the house.

With the dog gone, my gaze returned to the men. They began to unload the cart. The good lady's body was wrapped inside an old linen sheet. Only the bare feet which had touched me earlier poked out from beneath. The two fellows who'd brought her here carried Mistress Clitherow's cadaver to the far side of the cottage, accompanied by the two other men. One was a farmer by the look of him and the other a Protestant parson.

The farmer pointed away from the house. I couldn't blame him. I wouldn't want a grave outside my front door. They must have already prepared a place in the ground because they lifted the body between them and carried it over to a patch of disturbed earth and manure.

Once they reached the right spot, they lowered the corpse, still in its cover, into a hole until it could no longer be seen. The parson said a few words over the unmarked grave. After this, the others began shovelling animal dung into the hole. When it was full, they created a large mound above and around it. Mistress Clitherow's body was gone. Or so I thought.

When the men returned to the carriage, the priest and the farmer went over and talked to them. There was no hilarity or laughter. All four appeared to be affected by what had gone on. The driver's mate began forking the now superfluous straw off the back of the trailer, until suddenly he stopped and let out a shriek.

The dog began barking. The others rushed over. The man sank to his knees. He was still on the trailer. Slowly he lifted something into the air. They all looked upset. I focused my eyes. At first, I couldn't see what was troubling them. And then I saw it. The man was holding a human hand.

I couldn't imagine how it could have been sliced off the good lady's body by the force of the weights placed upon her but there it was. I shuddered and looked at myself but I couldn't see any traces of blood. It must have lain on the carriage beneath her body. The priest ordered some instructions. The farmer dug a new hole in the corner of the dung heap. The driver's mate placed the hand into this and the two men quickly covered it with more manure.

Not long afterwards the carriage trundled past me. Three men were sat upon it. The parson was leaving too. Once they were gone, the farmer fed his dog. I thanked God the creature hadn't found the hand

and run off with it. After that, man and dog walked off together across the fields, to do some job or other. I picked myself up, looked at my clothes, covered in mud, straw and leaves and set off towards Scotton.

# 27

**Thursday June 23<sup>rd</sup>, 1586**

During the next few months I was too busy learning a trade and creating a home from the house rented to me by Jack Pulleyn to consider the changes I was going through. The treatment meted out to Mistress Clitherow, before and after her death, had had a mighty impact on me, and every Sunday I attended Mass. Each day I found myself becoming increasingly devoted to the true religion and more repulsed by false Protestantism and all those who practiced it.

I only regretted my father hadn't had the opportunity to understand the lies which underpinned the Church he'd supported for so long and had so fervently believed in. If he had, I'm sure he'd have rejected it, as I did now. On the other hand, I was pleased beyond words by how much solace Mother had gained from her own re-conversion. Each day she became more like her old self, confident and content with life again. We didn't talk much, but I could see the unofficial Sunday services and country air in Scotton worked wonders for her.

More often than not, the weekly Mass would be held in the great room at the centre of Scotton Hall. The congregation included the Pulleyns' immediate family and friends, neighbours and wider relatives. Amongst them was Dionysus Bainbridge, although I never saw his wife. Widow Frances told me the poor woman didn't have long left in this world. A priest visited her frequently and was ready to administer the last rites when the time was ready.

Married life suited me. I loved Maria with a passion. Everyone remarked how devoted we were to each other. Of course, we had blazing rows occasionally. I discovered I wasn't the only one with a fiery temper, but to me, wedded life was bliss. After a few weeks I couldn't imagine being without Maria. I knew one day we'd have a son, and name him Thomas after my uncle. Looking back, I can hardly comprehend how a man can be so happy. But I was.

If my new life consisted of hard work, religion and marriage, there were still a few threads to be tied up in the old. I'd travelled back to York twice already. This would be my third and final visit.

The first time, I'd informed Father Mush of Mistress Clitherow's body's whereabouts. I'd heard since he'd led a successful rescue mission to recover her remains. These were now buried in a hidden place, the location of which even I wasn't told. Father Mush insisted the fewer people who knew the better, and I believed him. I heard it said the good lady's body parts hadn't decomposed at all before her reinternment at the secret Catholic site. All apart from her hand. This had been returned to York to be looked after by Mistress Clitherow's friends, until a suitable place of safety could be found for it.

My second trip to the city was at the beginning of June. The weather was much warmer by then. Mother and I spent time sorting through our house in Stonegate, so we could rent it out. When I was twenty-one, my father's properties would become mine. Only then could I decide what to do with my longer-term future. In the meantime, I was happy with life in Scotton. For a time, us Catholics appeared to be able to live there un-harassed by the Protestant authorities. I guessed they had enough on their hands dealing with recusants, hidden priests and the like in the larger towns and cities like York.

After his months of torture, Father Ingleby was finally brought to trial. He pleaded guilty to the heinous crime of being a Catholic priest in England. On the first Friday in June this brave man was transported to the Knavesmire where, after a short ceremony, he was hung, drawn and quartered. Another death. Another martyr for our cause.

Even though we were in York at the time, neither Mother nor I had the stomach to go along to witness this. Those who did reported Father Ingleby died as bravely as he'd lived. But there was something else. As the Father climbed the gallows he was taunted by members of the Council of the North. The barracking delegation was led by none other than Henry Cheke. From that day on, I hated the father as much as the son.

I hadn't forgotten about Thomas Cheke. I'd sworn revenge for his role in my expulsion from St Peter's and the beating I'd received from the vagabonds he'd paid to set upon me. In fact, I'd already devised a plan to exact this. The key would be to find a time when he was outside the school grounds. For this, I enlisted Kit's help, and he gladly contributed to my scheme.

And so, a few weeks later I found myself crouched down in a small space in the early morning, hidden in a corridor within the walls of the King's Manor. I'd received a message from Kit a week earlier that Thomas Cheke would be visiting the building during the previous evening. Apparently, he'd spent much of the last few weeks boasting how his father had promised he could spend the night with a serving girl. I waited nearby and watched on as Cheke entered the gates of the complex. Security wasn't tight and I simply followed him inside. I kept my distance and he suspected nothing.

My plan had been to storm into the bed chamber immediately after he went in there, beat him up and make my escape. Few people were aware I lived in Scotton, and those who did know, such as Headmaster Pulleyn and Kit Wright, wouldn't give me away. In any case, I doubted Thomas Cheke would even report the attack. To be beaten up by a boy like me beneath his social status was unfortunate. For it to happen a second time would make him look a fool.

Unfortunately, I'd underestimated how busy the corridors would be that evening. Meetings were underway between the Council, Corporation and representatives of Parliament to address the issues brought about by uncontrolled immigration. Ironically this meant an influx of dignitaries into York, and many of the rooms in the Manor were being used to host them.

I watched Thomas Cheke swagger up the stairs. How I despised him. Once he was out of sight, I bounded up the steps two at a time and caught a glimpse of his back as he pulled a door closed. I knew which room he was in.

But after that, there were people everywhere. Thankfully they left me alone but I knew a noisy commotion in one of the bedrooms would warrant attention of a type I'd no wish to receive. I retreated to the ground floor. After a quick search, I located a quiet corridor on the south side of the building. One of the doors off it led to an old storeroom. From the dust and cobwebs the place had obviously been unused for some time. I cleared a space in a darkened corner and hid there until morning.

Thursday was a school day. Even if Cheke was allowed to stay overnight, he'd need to return to St Peter's by seven. With this in my mind I crept back up the stairs, positioned myself beneath a table in the far corner and hoped nobody would see me. I waited.

It wasn't long before the door he'd walked through the evening before opened. But then came my surprise. The fellow in front of me fiddling with his tunic wasn't Thomas Cheke. It was his father. I couldn't fathom it. Had they been in the room together? I decided to wait for Henry Cheke to leave, so I could challenge his son alone.

But I was given no choice. My hiding place wasn't as good as I believed it to be. Henry Cheke could see me.

'Who's there?' he demanded. 'Stand up man. Cease lurking in the shadows.'

I crawled out from my hiding place and stood up. Any moment now, I thought, he'd call for the guards.

'What are you doing here, boy? Are you looking for my son?'

To my surprise and presumably due to the shadows, he didn't recognise me. He must have thought I was one of Thomas's friends.

'I don't know what he's promised you but there's nothing we're going to share outside the family in here.' Cheke laughed. 'I sent Tom back to St Peter's last night after he'd had a go on her. It can't be far off seven bells now. You'd better run off and join him, or you'll get the birch.'

I stepped carefully towards the stairs. It was disappointing but I knew I had to take this opportunity to escape. As I did so, my red hair must have become more visible in the light.

'By God! It's you, Fawkes!' exclaimed Cheke. 'You've got a sharding nerve coming here, you little swine. Tom told me you've turned into a Catholic. Don't you know the King's Manor is no place for your sort? I'll have you arrested. We'll send you to the gallows and scoop out your insides in the same fashion we did with the idiot priest Ingleby. And if you won't make a plea, I'll crush the life out of you and make you scream like that slut of a butcher's wife.'

After all that had happened, the horrible man's comments against Father Ingleby and Mistress Clitherow were too much for me. I stepped forward and threw a punch at him. I wasn't a bad size for my age but Cheke was better fed and more solidly built. He absorbed my blow easily.

After a second of indecision, I saw Henry Cheke make up his mind. He wasn't going to call for the guards. He was going to teach me a lesson, one I'd never forget. And he neither. He hit me hard on the chin. I staggered back a pace. His fist struck me again. I shook my head. An evil smile crossed his features. He knew he had me beaten and licked his lips. What an unexpected pleasure this would be to pummel his son's Catholic assailant unconscious, possibly even to death. He knew he could get away with it.

Before I could dodge him, he landed a third blow. How could Members of Parliament fight this well, I wondered? Another punch. A pain in my shoulder. The next one caught my eye. The cut above it had healed but now it re-opened. Blood spurted out. He raised his nose and smelled victory.

Cheke charged at me. I stepped aside. His body swung out over the stairs. For a moment he teetered there. With a tilt, he managed to face me. He held out his hand. I could have grabbed it. I could have saved him. I didn't. He started to speak. I butted his face. I kicked his knee. I pushed his chest hard with the flat of my hands. He lost his balance and fell.

Fractions became seconds. I counted. He descended. His head struck the stone steps. Blood splashed out. There was surprisingly little noise. Finally, he landed. His body stopped moving. He lay at the bottom, his neck stuck out at an awkward angle. I tiptoed downstairs and touched him. I expected he'd grab me but the man didn't move. His eyes were staring. He was dead.

Only then did I consider what might happen next. The guards would be coming. They'd arrest me. I'd be beaten and tried for murder. Possibly treason. Prison. Execution. Death. No more Maria. For a second though, I thought it was worth it.

I saw a movement at the top of the stairs. A shadow danced across the cold stone at the pinnacle of the steps. I looked up. A female figure floated above us. She gazed down, scanning the scene, from the top of the stairwell. I held my breath. The light was poor. Was this some sort of an angel? Or perhaps a ghost? Mistress Clitherow's ghost?

The entity descended towards me. Her hair was loose and uncovered. She was beautiful. A shawl was wrapped around her shoulders. White linen. I wasn't sure whether to run or to scream. It was unreal. I might be in a dream. It was hard to move. My legs became leaden. Yes, it must be a dream.

Light entered the building from along the corridor. The early sun was rising. When the figure reached the final steps, I saw she was no apparition. The girl was as human as I was. But younger, perhaps a little older than my sister Anne.

When she stared into Cheke's face there was no love there. Only hatred. Dark memories. And then silent rejoicing.

'I'm glad he's dead,' she whispered. 'But you should go now. I'll return to the bed chamber and pretend I'm sleeping. The day servants will come this way soon. They'll find his body. With no-one else around, it will be clear to all he tripped and fell of his own accord. Such a tragic accident. No-one will care. Nobody liked him.'

'Thank you,' I said.

'Thank you,' she replied.
And we each went our own way.

# 28

**Thursday November 7th, 1605**

Henry Cheke's life was the first I ever took. For a time, I was determined it would be the last. I never told my friends or family, not even Maria, about the events of that morning. Of course, I had to inform Father Beckwith during my next Confession, but he instructed me not to worry. The priest said it was obvious I was contrite. With a few words and a blessing, he absolved me completely of the sin of murder. After that, he advised me never to speak of the matter again.

Heeding the Father's advice, I placed Henry Cheke into an area of my mind and kept him there. I didn't discover if Thomas mourned his father, for I exchanged life in York for wedded bliss in Scotton. I never saw him again but heard talk he was knighted by the Scottish king. What a match they make for each other.

Following that morning I was determined to become a good man. I wanted to live a long and quiet life. I tried to devote myself to hard work, God, and most of all my family. Perhaps in the end I loved them too much. Does the Lord become jealous?

For three long glorious years I learned much, working day and often night for Jack Pulleyn's steward. Both men believed I had a talent which deserved to be nurtured beyond Scotton. With the legal profession no longer an option, Jack made contact with Viscount Montague and I became part of a large Catholic retinue in Sussex. I had to spend time away from Maria and baby Thomas, but we agreed it was the best thing to do. Once I'd established myself in the role, my family would follow.

Whilst I was working in the south, the pursuivants came a-calling to Scotton. Searching for priests, they turned many a good family out of their home. Nobody, not even Jack Pulleyn, could stop them. Vile men ransacked our cottage and, whilst I'm not certain of exact events, I heard rumour enough to break my heart.

Maria was badly affected. She refused to return to our broken house. And when the plague visited Scotton in the weeks which followed, it struck down the kind family who'd taken her in. When I returned home a month later, Maria and Thomas were buried six feet underground. My body felt empty and my mind filled with rage. It's never gone away.

With nothing left in England, I said farewell to my tearful mother, Anne and Lizzie. Once I could access Father's properties, I sold them and moved abroad. They say some people join the army to forget. I enlisted for the Spanish cause in the Low Countries to kill Protestants. I had a death wish, but it wasn't suicide. That's a sin without absolution.

In the decade which followed many men suffered a similar fate as Henry Cheke. Some I killed with my bare hands, but most died without me ever having to see their faces. They cowered within buildings which I brought tumbling down with my gunpowder like the walls of Jericho, every last one of them a Protestant. After what their kind had done to Mistress Clitherow, Father Ingleby, Maria, Thomas and many others, there could be no compassion. They deserved to die.

It takes an educated man to make up the right mixtures and calculations for munitions. I quickly earned the trust and respect of my colleagues in the army, if never their affection. More than once I heard myself described as a man of few words and even fewer friends. That was fine by me. It was the way I wanted it to be. If you let people into your life, eventually they will leave you and, when they do, the void their departure makes creates an illness in your soul. It's an affliction I've suffered for fifteen years.

But soon I'll find peace, and be with Maria and Thomas again, in paradise.

I can't say I wasn't pleased to join forces once more with my old friends Kit and Jack Wright. They may be older now but they're still good men. They know I'm reliable and utterly devoted to the faith. Add to this my knowledge of explosives and it's no wonder our friend and leader, Robert Catesby, sent Thomas Wintour to Madrid to find me. I didn't take much persuading. The bastard of a Scottish King's a Protestant, a heretic and a liar. As such, there can be no doubt. He has to die.

My friends smuggled me back into England, and I took up residence in a rented house in Westminster, working under cover as a servant for guess who? Thomas Percy! He's still an enigma. One moment full of bluster, the next sensitivity. It was he, of course, who gave me the time piece, so I could set the fuse. But it was I, not he, who ensured the powder wasn't spoiled and was ready to use.

How I wish they hadn't caught me. How many more Protestant heretics could I have killed?

So far, I've only divulged the name of my alias. Since my return to England I've not been Guy, not even Guido (that's a story in itself) Fawkes but John Johnson, a hard-working serving man from Netherdale. Often when we were married and alone, Maria would call me by her secret name, particularly in her happiest moments. How I miss her.

I hear footsteps. The devils return. By my own judgement, I've been in this chamber for two days, perhaps three. I've cried and grimaced through the pain. 'Tis strange to think I was once a schoolboy but these memories of the past have helped me endure and seen me through. God knows I've been true to Him. If I've done bad things and plotted others, the Almighty understands my reasons why.

I've remained silent for longer than most men could, but it doesn't matter what I tell my torturers now. Catesby and the others will have reached Warwickshire. Digby and his band will have kidnapped the princess. Once the uprising begins, it will spread across the Midlands, Yorkshire and Wales. Vengeance will be ours. Finally, the holy war will sweep towards London. The Spanish will come, with their ships and their army. Within a few weeks, England will be a mighty Catholic country all over again. I may not be alive to see it but my life's work will be done.

My thoughts return to the beginning of my journey and Mistress Margaret Clitherow. She refused to submit to their heresy and they killed her for it. Along with Maria, she was my inspiration. We fought the same fight. When the door opens, I'll make my confession. I know what I'll say. I've fought for a foreign power. I've attempted to kill the King. I wanted to blow up his Parliament. He'd have deserved what he got. And when they ask me why I did it, I'll tell them. It was for a girl and the Pearl of York, not treason and plot.

## THE END

# Author's Notes on Fact and Fiction

Guy Fawkes and Margaret Clitherow are arguably the best-known male and female citizens born in York in the North of England during the Tudor period. Although their deaths were twenty years apart, both were executed by the state for their devotion to the Catholic cause.

Yet the pair hailed from loving Protestant families. Today we'd describe them as middle class. Guy was born in either High Petergate or Stonegate. He went to a private school. His father and grandfather worked for the Ecclesiastical Court of the Church of England. Before getting married and moving to The Shambles, Margaret lived in Davygate. Her natural father had been a successful businessman, an alderman and a Sheriff.

The city of York had gone through turbulent times. Following decades of decline, during Elizabeth's reign the population and local economy began to recover, although death through disease and religious persecution were still prevalent. Margaret's father died from illness when she was fourteen, Guy's when he was only eight. We can only guess what impact these and other events may have had on their lives. Nobody knows the exact reasons why they converted to Catholicism.

In March 1586 when Margaret was executed, she was in her early thirties. She'd become a Catholic a dozen years before, under the influence of a group of local women, including Dorothy Vavasour and Anne Tesh. All three spent spells in prison for non-attendance of the official church service. Unfortunately, Dorothy Vavasour didn't outlive her friend by long. She died in prison in York in 1587. The story Guy hears of Anne Tesh's execution being reduced to life imprisonment is true.

The details included in the book about Margaret's husband, John the butcher, her dead mother Jane and stepfather Henry Maye have been described as accurately as possible, with a little artistic licence added here and there to fill in the gaps. After Margaret's execution, the long-suffering John Clitherow was released from prison. When eventually he re-married, his bride was a Protestant.

Margaret sent their son Henry away to a seminary college in France, although Henry's friendship with Anne Fawkes as described in the book is fictional. Despite attempts to convert her, Margaret's daughter

Anne Clitherow remained a Catholic until the end of her days. After being imprisoned and running away several times, she finally escaped, left the country and entered a convent.

Henry Maye was inaugurated as Lord Mayor of York in February 1586. It is believed he was the main driving force behind his stepdaughter's arrest. We can only guess at his motives, and whether he and Sheriff Fawcett really believed Margaret would disavow her religion. The story of Margaret's dousing in the Ouse on the way to York Castle is taken from a historical account.

Much of the evidence against Margaret was based upon the testimony of a young immigrant boy, as described, although the name, back story and fate created for Johann in the book are purely fictional. Henry Maye's speech denouncing Catholics and immigrants is also a concoction, but you never know. The Council of the North and York Corporation were often in competition with each other during Elizabeth's time. Both organisations were known to have a direct influence on Margaret's case. Judges Clench and Rodes were the presiding officers during the hearing.

When describing Margaret's arrest, her appearance at the Assizes and later execution the story has leaned heavily on a specific account from the time. As with any historical record, whether the details should be fully believed is subject to conjecture. Interestingly, the account in question was written by one Father John Mush.

It includes a detailed description of the debate in the courtroom. Of course, the Father couldn't have been there in person, unless he was a master of disguise. To prevent his arrest, Father Mush would have needed someone else to be present to act as his eyes and ears. Assigning this task to Guy Fawkes is one of the major fictional devices used in the book. Although much of Pastor Wigginton's role in the story is fabricated, he really did visit Margaret in her cell and encourage her to abandon her beliefs. According to Father Mush, the parson also made a passionate intervention in the courtroom on Margaret's behalf during the arraignment.

Without direct input from the woman herself, the real reasons behind Margaret's refusal to enter a plea aren't easy to confirm. In my view the reasons given in the book are as credible as any, but there's no evidence Father Mush attempted to turn Margaret into a martyr. To complete her sad tale, there really were claims she was pregnant. When tests proved inconclusive, Judge Clench delayed the execution but afterwards, under pressure from the Council, allowed the horrific sentence to proceed.

According to Father Mush's account, the guards refused the Sheriff's orders to place the heavy weights onto Margaret's prone body. Instead they brought eight beggars into the toll booth and forced them to do it. Afterwards her body was taken away and buried in secret. Father Mush claimed it was found six weeks later beneath a dung heap, with no decomposition having taken place. Margaret's body was transported to a secret Catholic burial ground and hasn't been found since. A relic claiming to be her right hand is currently in a display case in the Bar Convent in York.

Following the execution, Queen Elizabeth wrote a letter to the people of York saying Margaret shouldn't have been executed, because she was a woman, and the action wasn't carried out under her authority. By then, of course, it was too late. In October 1970, Pope Paul VI declared Margaret a saint as one of Forty Martyrs of England and Wales.

In March 1586 Guy Fawkes would have been an impressionable youth of almost sixteen. He would have been well aware of Margaret Clitherow's case and the barbaric punishment meted out to her. This could well have affected him. Something certainly triggered Guy to move away from his father's Protestant beliefs. Most probably there were many Catholic influences on him at the time, at home, in school and quite possibly in the dark streets of York.

Before she married Guy's father Edward, it is believed his mother Edith was a Catholic. After Edward's death, she remained a widow for almost a decade, a very long time in those days. When eventually she remarried in 1587, her new husband was Dionysus Bainbridge. His own first wife had recently passed away. Dionysus was the son of Frances and stepson of Walter Pulleyn of Scotton Hall, now a Grade II listed building. The Pulleyn and Bainbridge families were most definitely Catholic. In the years which followed the Fawkes family moving to Scotton, both Guy's sisters Anne and Elizabeth married local Catholic men.

One of York's many claims to fame about Guy is that he went to St Peter's School, one of the oldest in the world. Unfortunately, no educational records exist from the time. We don't know when he started, or when he left. Or if he was expelled… The school wasn't sited at its current location in Bootham but based near the horse fair, where the Union Terrace Car Park is today. Perhaps one day there'll be an archaeological dig there. Who knows what they may find beneath!

We do know Headmaster John Pulleyn was a secret Catholic, as were Guy's fellow pupils and future Gunpowder Plotters Jack and Kit

Wright. Robert Middleton also attended the school. He later went on to become a Catholic priest and was executed for his troubles in 1601.

Thomas Cheke was another Peterite old boy but his actions and animosity towards Guy in the story are fictional, as far we know. Thomas was knighted by King James and went on to become a Member of Parliament like his father. Unlike Guy, Thomas Cheke lived on to the ripe old age of 89.

Coming full circle, Thomas's father Henry Cheke was associated with the Council of the North. He also played a role in Margaret's case, with Father Mush reporting Cheke senior intervened in the courtroom by driving the claims Catholic priests lodged with *"comely and beautiful young women"* like Margaret *"to satisfy their lusts"*.

Henry Cheke's death on 23rd June in 1586 remains a mystery. Only hours before, he was heard cruelly mocking the recently executed priest Father Francis Ingleby. Cheke's body was found at the bottom of a flight of stone steps in the King's Manor with a broken neck. There were no witnesses, and no reports of a red headed youth seen leaving the area.

What happened to Guy Fawkes, Jack and Kit Wright, Thomas Percy and others two decades later in 1605 is well documented. But I can't end without mentioning Maria and baby Thomas. Although evidence is very limited, some historians believe Guy met and married a young woman called Maria Pulleyn from Scotton, and they had a baby son called Thomas. If this is true, mother and child must have sadly died in the years which followed the story, perhaps from plague or another disease.

When he was twenty-one, Guy cashed in his inheritance and left England to fight for the Catholic Spanish cause in the Low Countries. More than a decade later he returned to take part in the Gunpowder Plot, under the pseudonym of John Johnson. The rest, as they say, is history.

I hope you've enjoyed the story and others will too. Please tell your friends and book clubs! Tony has also written ***Remember, Remember the 6th of November*** and ***7th November 1617***. The profits from his books have raised a significant amount for good causes. It's especially useful for self-published works to receive reviews on Amazon and Goodreads to spread the word. The author and good causes supported by the profits from this book will be grateful if you can spare a few moments to post a review. Thank you.

Printed in Great Britain
by Amazon

82271307R00140